Miss Chance

By the same author

Rogue Lion Safaris
Hong Kong Belongers

SIMON BARNES
Miss Chance

HarperCollins*Publishers*

HarperCollins*Publishers*
77–85 Fulham Palace Road,
Hammersmith, London W6 8JB

www.fireandwater.com

Published by HarperCollins*Publishers* 2000
1 3 5 7 9 8 6 4 2

A catalogue record for this book
is available from the British Library

ISBN 0 00 225779 3

An extract from 'along the brittle treacherous bright streets' is
reprinted from *Complete Poems 1904–1962* by E.E. Cummings, edited
by George J. Firmage, by permission of W.W. Norton *&* Company.
Copyright © 1991 by the Trustees for the E.E. Cummings Trust and
George James Firmage.

An extract from 'The Waste Land' is reprinted from *Collected Poems
1909–62* by T.S. Eliot by permission of Faber and Faber Ltd.

This novel is entirely a work of fiction.
The names, characters and incidents portrayed in it
are the work of the author's imagination.
Any resemblance to actual persons, living or dead,
events or localities is entirely coincidental.

Typeset in Sabon by Palimpsest Book Production Limited,
Polmont, Stirlingshire

Printed and bound in Great Britain by
Caledonian International Book Manufacturing Ltd, Glasgow

For CLW, whom I courted on horseback,
and also for Dolly Dolores VII
(who may feel inclined to sue)

PART ONE

Schooling

1

You can't control the people you love. The phrase had invaded Mark's head like a parasite. It squirmed and wriggled around for, it seemed, most of the night. You can't control the choice, and having involuntarily chosen, you can't control the person either. Neither sleeping, nor quite waking, it seemed important – no, essential to the processes of life – to encapsulate the dual notion in a perfectly honed epigram. Final line to a winsome poem, perhaps. Or first line of a Morgan short story. Though love wasn't really her subject, was it?

Or was it? But nobody ever did quite understand her stories, she said; and he was the only one that ever understood her jokes. Until now, presumably.

Days were easier, of course, and evenings really not too bad. There are, of course, disadvantages to being left by your wife, but it is a great opportunity to look up old friends. Mark had done a lot of work on that phrase as well.

'Callum?'

'Oh God, you. Need me to talk you out of suicide again?'

'It's either a beer with you or the gas oven.'

Banter. Make light. A jest. Guess at the horrors, if you wish; but Mark preferred banter. He had made this resolution, he liked to think, to protect the world from boredom: who wanted to hear about his banal predicament? But it protected him too. Not thinking. Forget the night, and its wakefulness and its vain pursuit of perfect epigrams. And anyway, it was in the Morgan tradition, was it not? She had left him, not in a storm of tears or temper, but with a jest. Rather a loving jest. But then she would, wouldn't she?

Callum told him that Naz was on late turn and he was in sole control of their boy, and so he would not be available for drink and solace until ten. Which was far too long. And left Mark flicking through the address book once again: a name, a number, an inspiration.

He had passed her before. And kept going. Now he looked again. Well, he reasoned. Why the hell not? True, he had not seen her since that night when they had concealed the objet d'art – but these were not normal times. A state of emergency had been declared: this would be a serious escalation. So escalate. His hand made a series of minute advances and retreats over the telephone.

Melody. No one is called Melody, his mother used to say.

'Mel?'

'Good God.'

He remembered her voice too, every nuance. Somehow, he had not expected to. 'I'd love to. But I can't. I can make Saturday lunch, though, if you don't mind coming out to Radlett.'

'No one lives in Radlett.' His mother's son.

'My horse does.'

'Fancy you still having horses. It must be ten years at least since I last sat on a horse.'

'One horse. Though I have another I'm supposed to be exercising right now, a nasty stroppy bugger of the kind you used to adore.'

'How lovely to hear your voice talking about horses again. People don't change, do they?' He heard with mild surprise the affection in his voice, and thought again of their last meeting, and its horror.

'So why don't you come and hack him out tomorrow morning, and then we'll have lunch?'

Mel. There had been a time when tumbling in the hay had been no metaphor. But horses . . . Mark had no wish ever to sit on a horse again, but anything was better than solitude. Sure. Great. I'll be there.

The house was too big. A few days ago, it had felt like half his; now he knew it was all hers. Her Islamic draperies, her gods and goddesses, dancing Shiva, the knotting of the banister, the one remaining maze. Morgan was present in every way but one: a conjuring trick quite typical of her. Not fair. And damn it, what should he wear?

'It's funny,' Callum said, a fair bit later that same Friday, when such subjects as life and the departure of wives had been fully discussed.

'No it isn't,' Mark said.

'How I used to envy you two. The perfect couple. I used to think: why can't Naz and I be like that?'

'You're all right, you two?' Mark was alarmed. Other people's problems were the last thing he required. Besides, he needed their stability. He needed someone to envy too.

'Oh, we are. But we've had our problems. Like everybody. When she spent all her time at the centre.' A centre for Muslim runaway females, Mark knew. 'And I wished we had the perfect balance you two seemed to have.'

Perfect balance: the terrible unexplained absences, which she would still more terribly explain, were he to ask. And then an involuntary memory: the night she brought him hot and sour soup. Tenderness in a Styrofoam container; her famous spy's mac, buttoned especially high, arousing more than his suspicions . . .

'Look, Mark, I've been thinking. You know what you need to do?'

'Tell me.'

'I've got this theory. Most of us make a terrible balls of our adolescence. Very few people ever get a second chance. But you can have your adolescence all over again, and this time, you can do it right.'

Mark was charmed by this. 'All right. What do I do?'

'Get a motorbike. Get laid. The order doesn't matter. You must just do both as soon as possible. Like you used to do with those bloody horses you used to tell me about. Fall off, get back in the saddle again as soon as possible. I've got a present for you.'

Mark had been wondering about the roll of paper Callum had brought to the pub. He unrolled it, as requested. A poster; no, two posters. The first, Brigitte Bardot wearing nothing but a few flowers, blooms that emphasised rather than concealed what lay beneath. The second showed Marianne Faithfull in

5

Girl on a Motorcycle. She wore a leather jacket unzipped to the navel.

'Put 'em on the wall when you get home. Make you feel adolescent.'

'Not precisely my adolescence.'

'This is *classic* adolescence. Think how much Morgan would hate them.' Especially the tits. Mark saw, with startling vividness, Morgan's burlesque breast-cupping: she had done this no more than a handful of times, but always making him laugh at moments when you'd have thought laughter impossible. 'You're the only one that ever understood my jokes.'

'What you want is one of those hot little trail-bikes . . .'

Later that night, Mark used Morgan's dressmaking pins to attach Brigitte and Marianne to the Islamic textiles that hung from the walls. They looked like a pathetic and utterly unconvincing act of defiance. Which was why he liked them.

Morgan. A woman you don't meet every day; nice double entendre. Nothing in their life had been banal until that moment. She had even used a banal phrase to explain it all when, clad in an Edwardian walking-jacket with lion's-head buttons and a fur trim, she had paused for a moment with the door ajar. Leaving him, after ten years in which they had seemed to live a life somewhat out of the common run, in this hopelessly banal predicament.

'But I didn't enjoy it,' she said, more than once, by way of self-justification. 'I kept wishing it was you.'

Though that had been years ago, when such matters were discussed.

Which reminded him. He had better read *Othello* over the weekend. Get his thoughts ready for Monday morning. Goats and monkeys!

And he still hadn't decided what to wear. His riding clothes were presumably still at The Mate's, with all the rest of the horsey gear. If she hadn't thrown them away, of course. So they might as well be in China. He felt uncomfortable with the idea of riding in ordinary clothes. Almost as if riding were an ordinary thing. Had Morgan ever seen him in jodhpurs? But he would have remembered the stinging jest. Ten years; more, a dozen. But presumably you could ride in cowboy boots. After all, cowboys did.

So he was dressed in what were more or less his normal working clothes when he set off for Radlett the following morning. Black jeans, black cowboy boots, the oldest pair from his collection. Morgan had bought them for him on one of her trips to New York. The heels sloping back just a fraction, the toes rather noticeable chisels. The kids called him Clint, which was gratifying of them. Especially when you think what they called him at the old place.

If you pass the Wagon and Horses you've gone too far, she'd said. We can't have that, can we? he'd replied, weakly flirtatious. So he did a 180 in the pub car park and headed back towards town. This time he found it: an unmade track leading away between a row of fifties houses, behind a large concrete stand, apparently for the dispatching of lorries. Not terribly country. There was a cleared area, where a few cars were parked, and beyond it, a five-barred gate. Mark parked, locked, opened.

It was an act that called into being a pair of large, pale Labradors. 'Along this particular road the moon,' Mark said to them kindly, offering to each wet Labrador nose a hand, 'if you'll notice follows us like a big yellow dog. You don't believe? look back.' Morgan, reading those words to him. The Fifth Avenue bookshop or store. The dogs, apparently much soothed by E. E. Cummings, parted, allowing his advance. Mark passed through the gate. And passed in a single sniff to that other country, the place where they do things differently, in which a cup of tea can produce a dozen volumes, the good past.

Horses: the sweet scent of their dung. The companions of his youth, the stamping, silent auditors of his first love. The wild flights across country, the terror at the start of big competitions, like rather bad peritonitis, the power, the leaping and turning. The solitude, the companionship. The early morning rides that were also hay-room trysts. The collection of rosettes, of kisses.

How do you expect to pass your A levels when you spend all your time at that stable? When we moved to the country it was not with the intention that you become a bumpkin. Besides, nobody is called Melody. She is, I grant you, a sweet child. Or would be if she could talk of anything but horses.

The Mate was wrong. Naturally, they had talked of everything from the menstrual cycle to the movement of the stars.

It is odd, the way that even when awash with memories, the details of the face you once loved best in all the world come as a surprise. That slightly crooked and more than slightly intoxicating smile from thin unsensual lips. 'Mark!'

He kissed the lips, as an old lover should, though lightly. He then hugged, as an old friend should, doing the job properly, chest to chest. And was hugged back: 'You look wonderful.'

'So do you. Troubles suit you.'

'I always liked you best in riding clothes.'

Holding him at arm's length, she raised an eyebrow at that last remark: single, strong, black, ironical. He had not forgotten that, at any rate, nor the storms the challenging, teasing eyebrow could precipitate. The last storm, the objet d'art. Best not think about that. But no empty compliment: she looked more than wonderful – fit, honed, wind-battered. Jodhpurs do, after all, tend to emphasise rather than conceal. Mark remembered his surprise when first caressing a body that lacked stomach muscles of cast iron. 'And I'm glad you got rid of that perm.'

'It has been a long time, hasn't it?' They both knew precisely how long, but they were not going to speak of that, were they? 'Come and meet Ed. Presuming Ed for short.'

Ed was very big and very black, without a trace of white on him anywhere. He was standing, tied up, tacked up, beside a burly dark bay, but Mark knew his manners and ignored the second animal, complimenting Ed before doing another thing. A slim, crooked stripe on the nose of the bay.

'This is Gus. You'll like him. He's a sod. Just like old Trevor.'

'Trevor was not a sod. You just couldn't ride him.'

'What about that time he decked you at Aston?'

'That was my fault. He even tried to jump it. It was his gameness that was the problem.'

She shook her head. 'Ungenuine sod. Are you riding like that?'

'Can you find me a hat?'

She returned a few minutes later with an ancient and, it turned out, slightly too large velvet riding hat. 'Stop wheedling and get on.'

'Just introducing myself. They're not machines, you know.'

Mel, mounted, was already looking down at him. A correct riding position is also something that tends to emphasise rather than conceal the woman beneath the not overly loose red sweater. Mark looked at her in a confusion of delight.

He undid the head collar without looking to see how it undid, ran down the stirrup irons. Reins in left hand, hand on the pommel. Left foot in left iron: his body doing all these things apparently without reference to himself. Lowered himself with agile softness into the saddle. The horse shifted into a walk, but Mark did not correct him; merely soothed with his right hand.

They passed through the gate, which Mel opened adroitly for him. Mark swung his left foot forward almost to Gus's nose, and tightened the girth a hole. Unthinking, essential movement: like turning on the light when you get home, or listening to the answerphone.

2

Mark's body remembered everything as he lay diagonally across the acreage of the bed, possessed by an overmastering physical content. 'The size of the bed is primarily an option for comparative solitude,' Morgan said, 'rather than one for gymnastic exhibitions.'

He felt the beginnings of an ache in the small of his back, and what he hoped was the conclusion of one at the top of his thighs. But that was no matter. Absurdly, he sketched the closing of his hands, leaving a gap for the reins between third and fourth fingers.

He had returned home to find the red light morsing from the answerphone, and reached out a hand to call its ghosts into being. Mark, why do you never remember to switch on the answerphone? Is it done deliberately to upset me, or is that aspect of it just good luck? Remember, I've read Freud too, you know. But it was not, of course, her; it never was. Just three messages for her; news of her departure had yet to spread. Had she collected the messages already, dialling in from whatever place she now occupied? What if she called now? The fourth message was for him: Callum. Come and share a takeaway with me and Naz – that is, of course, if you're not out getting laid.

Which was good, especially as even Sunday was now under control, no longer the yawning void that Sunday traditionally presents to the newly abandoned. He had an appointment with a woman of startling good looks and slightly more startling force of character. He had to meet her in Radlett, where else?

Mark carried two pints of beer to their table in the Wagon and Horses. She still, it seemed, drank pints. 'Here's to you, Mel. And thanks. It was great to sit on a horse again.'

'He went well for you. But then you've always liked sods.'

'He's not really a sod.'

'You always say that. He's normally a complete bastard to Theresa, out on a hack.'

'I didn't give him anything to fight.' This was true. And without anxious hands tugging at his mouth, the horse found himself fighting a ghost and grew tired of his own temper. He was easy. And Mark felt that quiet, savage sense of penetration: infiltrating the strange land that lies between two species of mammal. The border-country; the land of his youth.

The pub was nicer than Mark had expected, peopled mainly, it seemed, with regulars, a few in riding clothes. There was an early autumn fire, and the food was as pub food should be. They sat with second drinks before them: 'To speak only physically,' Mark said, 'it seems that every need bar one has been taken care of.'

Mel smiled in honour of this, and then added a grain of malice to the smile. She leant back in the chair and called to an adjacent table: 'How's that brilliant mare of yours, Kath?'

The next best thing in the world to talking about yourself is talking about your horse. She had Kath's attention at once. And Mark's. Blue-black hair in a crop that was somehow softened at the edges; tough face with eyes made huge with eyeliner. Navy-blue eyes, more or less, Mark decided, and a navy-blue jumper that had clearly been applied with a spraygun. Muscular body that looked hard, but was no doubt soft enough in places. Who was it that said after an abortive tryst, I have touched the hottest and the coldest parts of a woman?

Mark was taken aback by this lubricious thought, but still managed to elbow his way into the conversation. 'How wonderful to have a brilliant mare. What does she do?' James Joyce, that was it. No need to read Joyce till spring.

Kath looked at him accusingly. 'What she did was jump. What she does now is hang about eating her head off.'

11

'Got a leg?'

'Christ, I wish it was something simple like a bowed fucking tendon.' Harsh London vowels, with oddly softened consonants. 'She's gone in the brain, that's the problem. Gone sour on me. I've been too soft on the old trollop. Let her get away with too much.'

A tourist who sits at a pavement café in Paris with his ears open slowly finds his schoolboy French returning. After the second drink he is inclined to venture a subjunctive. 'What's she done?'

'Affiliated, last two years, few red ribbons. I don't want to have the old bitch shot, but what else can I do? She'd make someone a lovely hack, except she'd probably kill them.'

'Vicious?'

'Nah. Pussycat. Just fucking mad.'

'She sounds sweet,' Mark said. He had intended nothing more than facetiousness, weakly flirtatious. But Kath turned and looked at him properly for the first time, bright with eyelinered challenge. 'You can have her if you want. I'd take a grand for her.'

'Is this your usual line of sales talk?'

'I mean, can you *ride*?' Meaning rather more than can you sit on the top and steer.

'It's been known.'

Kath leant back in her chair and aimed sweatered breasts at him. 'Do you want to try her out?'

Morgan was the past mistress of all out-cooling games. Years ago, Mark had shown her a disgusting playground trick, in which he had looked and sounded as if he were scraping together the broken ends of the bone in the nose. 'If you ever do that again,' she said, laughing, disgusted, 'I will leave you. I will take it as a signal that you simply don't want me around any more, and I shall pick up my bags and leave.' Perhaps a thousand times since, Mark had seized his nose with both hands. 'Try me,' she always said. 'Go on. Try me.' And Mark never did. Being quite certain she would leave. The jest demanded it.

'I'd love to try her,' Mark said.

12

They agreed: Sunday morning at eleven. And then Kath turned back to the friends at her own table. Mel raised an eyebrow at Mark. 'Well?'

'Seems rather a sod.'

3

Mark loved his Jeep, but he had always been embarrassed by it. It was not the right vehicle for driving between Islington and Herne Hill. He would not have chosen it himself; Venetia had bought it for him, in a particularly wild fit of generosity, a few birthdays back. But now it had real mud round the wheel arches. There's glory for you, as Morgan would say.

A couple of miles beyond the Wagon and Horses, Mark entered an almost Venetia-like maze of narrow lanes. Kath's instructions were precise: past the metal barn, left at the lone brick house, right at the crossroads. And all within the annular M25. It did not seem physically possible; there was surely no room for these fields. They were a trick, or a piece of magic: through the looking-glass, down the rabbit-hole. The journey had something of the not-quite-rightness, the slightly-sick-making sense of disorientation that people found in Morgan's stories. That Mark found in Morgan herself: though he would never have admitted to that. Against his will, he thought briefly of Morgan's last party: the one to celebrate the Herne Hill job, and her publication of *Alice*.

And then, as promised, the yard. Mark swung in, and parked the appropriate Jeep beside a consonant four-berth horse lorry. At the gate, two Jack Russells welcomed him noisily from four feet off the ground, Jack Russells being unaffected by gravity.

'Shut the fuck up,' greeted Kath.

'Hello,' Mark agreed.

'Made your will?'

'I've left everything to you. I thought that right.'

She laughed. She was dressed as yesterday, the blue-black sleeves

14

rolled a little short of the elbow. The revealed arms were full of sinewy strength. 'Come and meet the old trollop.'

Accurate reconstruction of significant first meetings is always difficult; perhaps even undesirable. Over the years they acquire a carapace of mythology. Mark always claimed that his first sight of Mel was of her jodhpured buttocks: love, he stated, at first sight. Perhaps it was as he said; but if not, the false memory was the true one. He remembered Morgan's clothes, the dead zebra, her air of secret amusement, at a joke that had never, it seemed, quite palled. Until last week, of course. Or their first meeting when actual words were exchanged. The lumberjack shirt. I'm a monster too. You must learn that.

'I didn't fancy you at all. I found you rather odious.'

'I adored you from the first.'

'Precisely why I found you odious.'

He remembered something of that first encounter with Trev, the horse of his youth. It was not the first sight of the big blaze face that he recalled, but the moment he patted the neck and felt the extraordinary hardness of muscle. 'A lot of horse,' he had muttered. Knowing from the single touch that the horse had been schooled and damn well schooled, too. And the horse had lowered his head just a fraction, a pink fleshmark just below the blaze, and then lifted his head with a jerk and a biff, smiting Mark lightly below the sternum and knocking a little breath from his lungs. 'Boisterous sod, aren't you?' Feeling a hint of challenge, of male-to-male empathy in the touch.

Trevor had swaggered from his box, looking ready to take on the world. But Kath led Mark to a horse that seemed to have no presence whatsoever. She was looking over the half-door of a nice roomy box: bay head, white star, preposterously large ears. She looked meek and kind: a soft touch. 'Hello, trollop,' Kath said, slapping the bright neck a few times before entering the box, bridle over her shoulder, saddle on her stripped forearm.

Mark stood diffidently at the door, watching Kath tack up with neat, precise movements. 'She's tiny.'

'She's jumped five foot, it's nothing to her. She may be 15-one, but look at the arse on her.'

15

'She needs the pelham?'

'Can't always hold her in that.'

She led the mare out into the daylight: autumn sun made the bright bay coat gleam like a conker. Mark had always liked his horses dark and burly and tough but something about this meek-looking animal seemed to slip beneath his guard. Not his type: dangerous and intoxicating thought.

New departure; same old route to disaster. 'Take her for a little run around the field,' Kath said. 'Get the feel of her.'

Mark put on his re-borrowed velvet riding hat. In his jeans and his cowboy boots and his riding school hat, he felt a complete phoney. He felt Kath judging him; the mare had not yet begun judging him. That would come in a few minutes.

He took the reins from Kath, just above the rings of the martingale, in his left hand. And with his right, reached out to touch her.

He had expected to make his hard hello-Trev slap, his boys-together greeting to his boisterous champion. But his hand refused to do anything of the kind. Instead he stroked, nibbled the neatly pulled mane with his fingers. The mare looked at him for a while. Then, very lightly, she touched his shoulder with her nose. Mark was absurdly moved. 'Hello, angel,' he said. Too soft for Kath to hear.

4

In the beginning, it was Mark that had been the star, not Morgan. It was he they pointed at in the students' union, not she. That day, the day when he first set eyes on her, he was absolutely at the peak of his powers; his perihelion, as he later put it. And he dressed like the star he was. Everyone wore black in those days: but Mark wore over his black jeans and sloppy black polo-neck a green cardigan with leather buttons. It looked like something a middle-aged man would play golf in. His father had worn it to play golf in. Mark's posthumous adoption of it was part mockery, part tribute, part self-mockery, part elaborate reverse dandyism. He had also just bought his first ever pair of cowboy boots: a dramatic move away from the Doc Martens required by convention. The cardigan, the boots: as a star, he could dare such things. He could do nothing wrong.

Undergraduates write poems: it is a condition of the age. But Mark was *a poet*. 'You know,' as a stage announcer had once said: 'like T. S. Eliot and Wordsworth.' In his second year he produced what he called, with becoming modesty, a slimy volume. The university poetry magazine, *Penyeach*, had done the publishing, and it was sixteen pages long and all the poems were by him, there's glory for you. It was named for a knot he had learnt in the Cubs: *A Round Turn and Two Half Hitches*.

His poems made people laugh. Boy meets girl and hands her a garland of ironies. He wrote of the tangles and knots in sexual negotiation, caught undergraduate angst neatly enough: neatly enough, at any rate, for angst-ridden undergraduates to recognise themselves.

He would have died rather than admit it, but it was not his words

17

that hit home, but the delivery. He was good at audiences: he liked it; he rose, quite literally to the occasion, standing taller than was his custom, eyes scanning the audience, sharing an intimate secret with – oh, several hundred on big days. It was nothing to him, tall and confident in bearing, his voice full of pretended perplexity, rising at the end of sentence as if to question even his full stops. He was preparing a second volume of similar sliminess to be published the following term, called *Running Bowline*, for the line in 'What Shall We Do with the Drunken Sailor?' It was about the hideous embarrassment to which youth is prone. The best poem was unabashedly autobiographical: 'The Night of Serial Buttock-Fondling'.

He was often asked to read a poem or two in the interval, when a decent band came to play. The sound of laughter coming towards him from many hundred voices was wonderful, and Mark, despite the attacks of rather bad peritonitis that gripped him before these big readings, adored it above all things. Occasionally, *Penyeach* would organise a reading for a smaller and theoretically more discerning audience, and he would watch the other poets do their nervous stuff, would laugh when appropriate or nod wisely, and offer fulsome congratulations, there being no side to him. And then read his own poetry. Last: always last.

There was always a reading in Freshers' Week, naturally. By the beginning of the final year, his place of honour was assured. He strolled in as a piece of easy routine, a man comfortable with his own pre-eminence. Nothing was ever the same afterwards. And he didn't even meet her: he didn't dare. Or as he put it to himself at the time, not his type.

It was the usual sort of crowd: nervous, sneering, reluctantly admiring would-be poets, a lot of black clothes and Doc Martens. 'And now to close the evening, Mark Brown will read us something.'

Mark, slightly nervous till that moment, took the floor like a great and well-beloved actor making an entrance, his extreme modesty of bearing somehow emphasising his incalculably lofty status. He shoved a handful of hair away from his eyes and pulled out a slimy volume, not without looking in the wrong pocket first, to an affectionate titter from those that knew him. The book had been folded in half and crammed into the back pocket of his jeans, what a way to treat a sacred object. He went straight into the poem: no preliminary remarks, not even a title. And led them into a web of mistrust and deceit, the poet no less a liar than his mistress. The poem ended 'come lie with me and be my love', nice double entendre, but Mark read it thus: 'Come lie?/ with/ me?/ and be/ my/ love???' The unasked questions hung in the air as he surveyed his audience in the brief silence that followed. Then the comprehending smiles: and the applause.

Mark read one more poem, the one he had written after he had learnt that T. S. Eliot found the fireworks of the peace ceremony more disturbing than the bombs of the enemy: a contradiction that converted neatly enough into student love. Standing tall and confident, eyes scanning around his audience as was his invariable custom. All were to be included: he spoke to all.

And bang.

Bomb; or firework. It is extraordinary how many trains of thought you can keep running at the same time without derailment. Mark thought this even at the time, while he continued to read. Also thinking about a poem he might write, recalling a childhood incident in which he had walked into a glass door. Also feeling the same shock he had endured on that occasion, as if the air itself had turned solid and knocked him silly. Also wondering if what he felt was a strong sense of attraction or a strong sense of distaste.

And all without missing a beat in the reading of his poem, save that he was now reading to an audience of one. He did not dare look away, save for an occasional glance down at his got-by-heart poem. Had he tried to regain his normal audience-scanning insouciance, he would have been lost. And every time he looked up from his page, she was there. He read to her, every word to her, and she listened, her head a trifle on one side, each hand clasping an elbow. She looked quite insufferable: and he could not look away.

A little triumph of self-mastery: he reached the end without disaster. He thanked her modestly, accepted her applause, though she seemed to be clapping in a special ironical way that made no actual sound. At last he was able to sit down, to face a different direction, while the *Penyeach* editor made his speech about all contributions being welcome.

'Well done, my love,' Christine said from her place at his side. 'I've always liked the fireworks one. Never heard you read it better.' And she gave him a small kiss on the cheek.

Fireworks of peace. 'I need a drink.' Christine at once reached into her bag and produced, with a Mona Lisa smile of triumph, a can of beer. 'Adorable woman.' Mark kissed, opened, drank. Then, the speech being spoken, he got up to do the sort of chatting that is required on these occasions, there being no side to him. Eventually the gathering thinned out, and Callum said it was time to go home.

The three of them walked back to the flat together. 'Been talking to the weirdest woman,' Callum said.

'You mean the one in the black and white coat?' Christine asked. 'Where do you think she got it from? It looked *genuine*.'

'She said you were winsome, Mark.'

'I bet she says that to all the girls,' Mark said sourly.

'Did she like the poetry?' Christine asked.

'Said you were E. E. Cummings with capital letters, Mark. Is that a compliment?'

'I'll have to think about it.'

'But was it genuine? I hope you asked.'

'Not in so many words. I asked her where she got it. Said she picked it up secondhand.'

'That means it's genuine,' Christine said. 'What a nerve. I could no more do that than fly. I mean, going to a poetry reading, a fresher – a *fresher* – wearing a zebra-skin coat. You've got to admire that, in a way. I mean, a *dead zebra*.'

5

The armchair was deep and leather and comfortable, but she had acquired a taste for ritzy surroundings. The fire had been lit, though it was rather early in the season, and reasonably warm. But it was that sort of hotel.

Mark had not sought the meeting, but was delighted when it was suggested – no, insisted upon. 'Er,' he told the waiter confidently. But she would pay, snatching up the bill purposefully when she had done so, to tuck into her slim not slimy black wallet, another trophy for her expenses, entertaining British snowboarding champion or the latest naked actress. Or something.

'Bloody Mary,' he said. 'Please. Spicy.' Her favourite drink, as it happened. And there she was, too, walking in, gazing about shiftily, spotting him. He stood to kiss her, nicely, on each cheek. 'Bec. Good to see you.'

'Good to see you, little brother. Spicy,' she said to the waiter. 'Bloody Mary, please.'

She sat. Then shook hair away from her face and smiled, both uncharacteristic moves. The hair was long, fair, undyed, worn in two long halves that normally allowed only a pale strip of face to be seen. 'I've known women who hide behind their hair like fawns in the undergrowth,' Morgan said. 'Your sister lurks behind her hair like an ocelot in ambush.'

It always amused Mark, to hear how many people were genuinely afraid of Bec, or Rebecca as everybody else in the world called her. Not that he found such fear incomprehensible: there were at least a thousand occasions in their shared past when she had beaten him up. He was just delighted to learn about subsequent victims. 'Why do you think,' he had once asked

21

Morgan, 'she didn't go in for women's glossy magazines? Why men's?'

'Mountaineers don't look for the easiest way up a mountain,' Morgan had said. 'They shin up the North Face.'

'And how are things at *Edge*?'

The packet of tipped Gauloises already on the table, the brief clack, the gold bonfire of the Zippo. 'Good,' she said, hissing smoke. 'Preliminary figures for August are the best yet.'

'Why was that?'

Her hair had fallen in front of her face, and from its depths she gave him her pitying look. 'Should have seen the babe I put on the cover.' She shook her head, not in negation, but to offer him a little more face, softened with concern. 'But look, Markie, what's this all about? Oh, thank you.'

She took her drink, sipped, as Mark told his brief banal story that led to his long-term banal predicament. She gave him uncritical sympathy. 'But no nervous breakdown yet? No suicidal despair? Isn't that what you're supposed to do?'

'Oh God, Bec, don't think I haven't thought about it. But mostly I've managed to keep too busy.'

'Game plan is to get suicidal as soon as you can find a window?'

'Nice double entendre, Bec. But listen, talking about being busy. I wondered if you knew. I mean, you did all the packing up that time, when I was away for the autumn term.' He meant, but did not say, after their father's death. 'And I just wondered if you threw away my riding stuff. Or not.'

'Your *riding* stuff? Good God, is this another fashion statement?' She had always been unkind about cowboy boots.

'Perhaps. If so, I think I may have got hold of the ultimate fashion accessory. I think I might have bought a horse.'

At this she laughed, really laughed, almost a giggle, an unusual thing altogether these days. 'You mad little bastard.'

'That's roughly what everyone else has said.'

Bec said: 'He ruined his life with that horse and that silly girl. It's not my fault he didn't get to Oxford. It's all the fault of that silly girl and that fucking horse.'

Mark grinned, a little warily. The words still brought a flash of pain. 'She got the adjectives the wrong way round,' he said.

'Cabin-trunk,' Bec said. 'I remember distinctly. Loads and loads of stuff. Massive cat's cradle of leather. Clothes.'

'Boots?'

'You and your boots. Yes, boots on silly sort of false legs. Either in the trunk, or alongside. Up in the attic. No chance that The Mate will have lugged it out. Even if she were to call on all her super-powers. Weighs a ton.'

'Still less Ashton.'

'That would be a bit grossly physical for him, wouldn't it? You still going up there and talking to the little shit?'

'Well, I do go up there every now and then. To see The Mate. As you know. And that does rather involve seeing Ashton.'

She wagged her head, bringing more hair forward to narrow the Gothic arch through which she looked out at the world. 'I don't know how you can do it. I can't bear even the thought of sharing the same postcode. Even for half an hour.' She shook her head again, reducing the width of the strip of face to about two inches. Eyes very fine, very troubled. It was only about the hundredth time they had had this conversation. In family life, language is not a medium for the exchange of information.

'Have you seen The Mate of late?' Mark asked.

'Took her to lunch last week. The usual fifty-five mentions of Ashton. Jesus, she *knows* what it does to me.'

'She can't help herself. Like biting on a bad tooth. She only mentions him to me about once every meeting. But always that once.'

'But you go home, and he's actually there. And you sit at the same table as him, watch him pouring the wine in Dad's place, and you manage to hold down your supper.'

'I know, Bec. It's not a betrayal of you. I just wasn't there.'

'I know you've always felt bad about that.'

'Oh, Bec. Coming back from my jaunt. Swaggering up the drive with my tales of the conquest of Europe. It was the worst, the worst thing ever.' Not a medium for the exchange of information.

She smiled a sudden wreath of smoke. 'Worse than the night of serial buttock-fondling?'

'You and your memory. But I know it was much worse for you being there. But you must understand that my going back is still some way of trying to . . . I don't know . . .'

'I know there was never any actual adultery, and so they thought that made it all right. As if the only available sin was fucking. He darkened the last years of Dad's life –'

'Bec –'

'And the hour of his death. She brought Ashton in –'

'I know –'

'– to give him the comforts of the Church. She brought his chief tormentor in life to torment him on his deathbed.'

'Bec.'

'Two more, please. Spicy. I know,' she said, turning back to Mark, 'that you think I'm unbalanced on the subject.'

'No one is balanced on the subject of death. Your own, anybody's. Except Lao Tzu, perhaps.'

'No!' A cry of pain. 'Ashton is to do with bloody life, God rot him. How to fuck up various people's lives, while all the time smiling and making jokes and doing favours and being obliging and urbane and amusing.'

'I understand . . .'

'But you weren't there. You didn't watch him worm himself into the family, while I was at home doing my sentence on the *Hertford Mirror*. I saw it all happen, before my eyes, in slow motion. Saw Dad become a sad old bastard, in slow motion before me.'

'Bec.'

'Fathers and daughters, I know, I've read Freud too, you know.' A line of Morgan's, that, originally. It became a line of Mark's, now a line of Bec's. 'Did I ever tell you what I nearly gave The Mate for Christmas last year? I found a complete Freud in a secondhand bookstore, and I bought the lot. Bloody expensive they were, too. Still got them at home. I chickened out.'

'Would she have got the joke?'

'Too obvious. That was the problem. We had an argument on precisely that subject. She simply couldn't accept the idea of unconscious motivation.'

'You *talked* about it?'

24

'I think we were talking about you. And I said that everyone seeks in marriage to replicate the relationship with the parent of the opposite sex. But she sat on it at once. At once. Schupid nonsense,' the last two words being another impersonation, 'so perhaps she could see the dangerous ground on the far side of the hill. With her X-ray vision.'

'Thank you. Spiritual infidelity.' The first to the waiter.

'You always did need a good sub, didn't you? Infidelity. We'll have no redundant adjectives when I'm editing. You know how fond he was of the Victorians? Palgrave?'

'I know –' This was the bit he couldn't bear. It always made him cry, every time Bec told him. He always tried to stop the conversation at this point. Always failed.

'And I used to read to him when he was in hospital.'

'I know, Bec –'

'And every time he asked me to read "Cynara". And every time I read it, his eyes filled up with tears. It was torture for him; it was the only comfort he could look for. That I could give him. That any one could give him.'

She shook her hair over her face and ignited a Gauloise. Mark wiped the corner of each eye with a discreet knuckle. Both drank.

'I'm sorry, Markie. You're the only one I can talk about it with.'

'Rob –'

'Never knew Dad. Hardly knows The Mate. He's tremendously understanding, but he doesn't understand. And never met Ashton, of course. So bitching about him doesn't have the same kind of resonance.' She smiled a little at this last frivolity.

'All well with Rob? With you and Rob and so forth?'

'I hope so. I don't know what I'd do without him. We both lead such busy lives, you know. But it's always good when we bump into each other. He cheers me up.'

'Making millions?'

'Doing all right.'

'Tell me, Bec – do you understand what he does?'

'You know, it's funny you should ask that. It's been very much on my mind of late. He came back from a really good day, and

25

there I was, home, and so he told me all about it. And you know, I didn't have a clue what he was talking about. No unconscious motivation. I really tried. And he's explained it all so many times that I daren't ask him again.'

'It's stocks,' Mark said with great authority. 'He goes out to work and spends all day broking the bloody things. Like a fishmonger.'

'Who mongs fish. Thanks for your help, little brother. You seem quite chipper, for a man with a broken heart. Are you putting your life back together?'

'I'm trying, Bec. But I'm joining up the wrong bits.'

'Interesting. Got laid yet?'

'How macho you are, Bec. How very wise they were to give you the job at *Edge*. No. But I think I might be in love.'

6

Mark made two long and graceless hops. What to do now? Take his left foot out of the iron? Scramble on board any old how? Ask Kath to hold her head, an offer already refused? The mare was seriously silly, and she made him look seriously schupid. Out of his depth.

With the third hop, Mark found he had enough leg beneath him to make a spring, and without considering the matter, sprang. It was not that he did anything seriously bloody comic, like leaping clean over the horse's back, but his leap was out of all proportion to the animal beneath. Trev had been all but two hands higher, after all. But he caught his balance, caught it rather neatly, in fact. Touching her neck lightly with his right hand to get his bearings, lowering himself into the saddle with the softness of a butterfly alighting. Rather a passionate butterfly. As someone had said about something. Slipped his foot into the second iron. 'God, you ride long.'

Kath, smiling to herself, perhaps at the mare's restlessness, perhaps at the implied compliment, said, 'Shall I hold her head while you adjust the leathers?'

But the mare seemed to have stopped spinning round and round, and now she wanted to walk. Walk terribly fast, with neck-stretching, head-nodding strides. Mark swung his left cowboy boot forward to tighten the girth. Damn it, it was him, that passionate butterfly. Which poem? But perhaps he had borrowed it from somewhere. Up two holes on the left; up two holes on the right.

'Hello, angel,' Mark said softly, as he took up a contact. That is to say, he moved the reins so that the bit moved in her mouth. That

27

is to say, he reached out to touch her. The touch of a passionate butterfly.

Yes, it was part of the unpublished Morgan-gone sequence, the last poem he ever wrote. Unfinished: well, she came back, didn't she? That time. The mare was eager to trot and Mark agreed that she might, and she responded to the thought alone. And decided to take control. She moved with huge jerky strides like a horse in a trotting race, leaning on the bit, seeking to extract his arms from their sockets. Mark checked again. At this, she cantered, quite the opposite of what he had intended. Another mild check: this time she started to hop like a rocking horse, making every second stride without putting her forefeet on the ground. Checked again, she tried to canter on the spot. This was not lack of schooling. This was craziness. It was seriously alarming.

But the odd thing was that Mark was not seriously alarmed. To his surprise, he heard himself laughing out loud. For she meant no harm; he knew this with absolute certainty. No malice. Just a little madness, nothing more. It is the tendency of the novice or frightened rider to yank at the horse's mouth in times of trouble, but all Mark's youth had come back to him: not to his mind, but to his hands. And his hands forgave, not blaming; and softened. And his legs squeezed her forward and suddenly, she was moving with power and purpose, and it was beautiful and she knew it as well as he did. Suddenly he was not sitting on a horse, but riding. Riding round the big green field with his borrowed hat slipping towards his nose and the chisel toes of his cowboy boots poking foolishly out of the irons. Riding.

Without further discussion, he asked for a canter, but she understood him all wrong, confused and mad again, and flung her head up. Mark, standing in the stirrups, had a perfect view of the white star on her forehead. Then a whack on the chest: he discovered that he had moved his head a few inches to one side. He had missed, by a hair, a broken nose.

'All right all right,' he told the mare without resentment. 'Let's be sensible horses, yes?'

And she found a bigger pace for him, a huge rolling canter, and he rode high and forward and balanced, and as he rode his hands made a thousand adjustments and counter-adjustments, more or less of their own volition. The mare asked tiny questions with every stride, and every one needed answering: the flow and counter-flow of information and opinion. Language.

'Put her at a jump or two if you like.'

'We like,' Mark said.

He looked at the car-tyre jump with purpose and looking was enough. Beneath him, an angel spread her wings.

7

She suggested that he make a night of it. Do his sorting 'after Marce'. So on Saturday evening he drove the Jeep into Hertford-shire. He had told his mother that he would be coming alone, because she did not care for impromptu arrangements. 'Oh,' she said. It was one of her more devastating monosyllables.

The Jeep carried him as if on rails on his own crosscountry route to Codicote: huge march of the railway viaduct across the Mimran valley just visible against the darkening sky. He remembered the Christmas walk to the A1, his mother's tears.

He found that he had pulled in at the White Horse. He parked neatly, wondering if this was procrastination or a crass need for a drink. Not that he would go short at The Mate's, but that was not the point. Or perhaps it was a tribute to his father, to that last drink, the time they had talked about teaching. Cultural transmission, Mark. The most important job in the world.

The pub had been gutted and refurbished at least once since he and Mel had drunk their illegal teenage drinks. Hands held, halves of lager, The Game, the sudden gulping retreat back to the stable-yard, deserted now, the scented, pricking double bed of hay. Tip: always bring a horse blanket if you intend to make love in a hay-barn. Did she laugh and laugh with her doctor husband? Did she play The Game? Or was she quite different: a different person, a different time?

Would you like me to laugh and laugh? Shall I be a silly giggly girlie for you? Morgan, I prefer your silliness the way it is. And that night when she had read for him a poem, seizing the book from the pile beside the bed:

after all white horses are in bed

Love without punctuation.

But love is not really about bed. To believe so is to sentimentalise. The avowals, the grappling, the giggling, or for that matter the poetry: these are only marriage when marriage is gone. You remember the beginning, the end. You can't reconstruct the bit in the middle. The bit that mattered.

Telephone her? But he had no number to call. Write to her, via her forwarding address? Suggest a civilised meal, a grown-up discussion? And always returning home to the morsing answerphone, the shoal of messages for her diligently transcribed. These days he never forgot to switch on the answerphone. If she collected her own messages from afar – it was impossible that she did not – why did he never catch her? Why were there no phone-crashing retreats from his voice? His finger reaching out to press the button, the messages from her friends, her admirers, her editors. Waiting always for her voice: never hearing it. They knew something was up, these callers: well, I knew it wouldn't last. Not really up to her standards, was he? Mark's darkest secret the one he had somehow managed to keep secret even from himself: that he agreed. The daily robot valediction: end of final message.

Sitting in a pub snivelling into your pint, sentimental bastard. This would never do. Would his saddle fit the little mare? That was the only question that mattered. And besides, it was time for Drinks Before, as his mother always termed that ceremony.

He parked outside the house that was more like a vicarage than the vicarage, as his father had said when they moved in a decade and a half back. 'Darling.' A kiss accepted on each cheek. 'Come in and pour me a nice drink, it's time for Drinks Before.'

It was a peculiarity of hers never to pour her own drinks 'except in extremis, darling.' So Mark poured her a generous gin and generously helped himself to whisky. She would say, 'Well, "cheers".' Relishing the vulgarity, the inverted commas.

He carried the tinkling glass to where she sat in her high wing-backed chair, the table beside her towered and castellated with books. He placed a mat on the nearest book and then the glass.

'Well, "cheers".' She sipped, and then added another ritual phrase: 'I can *feel* it doing me good.' She smiled a trifle winsomely as she said this. Her hair was apparently freshly crenellated into new grey ramparts. 'Did I understand you aright?' she asked. 'On the telephone?'

'In what particular?' As always, Mark found himself echoing his mother's eccentricities of diction.

'*Horses*, darling.'

'Oh, horses, yes.'

'You know, when your father and I moved to the country, it was not with the intention that you became a *bumpkin*.' Not the first time she had said this. 'That silly girl, and that fucking horse.'

He did not make the joke about the adjectives. 'I saw Mel the other day.'

'No one is called Melody. And she still has horses?'

'So do I. I've just bought one.'

'Oh, *darling*.'

'That's why I want my riding gear.'

And he looked up, to be struck by a sudden knifing glance: The Mate's X-ray vision. He and Bec had a shared fantasy, to which their father had been privy, that their mother possessed super-powers. 'And Morgan does not approve? Hence her absence on this visit?'

'Morgan doesn't know anything about it. She is not around. She has taken leave of absence.' What an extraordinary way to put it.

'Oh.' The monosyllable hard, condemning.

'Yes.'

'Oh, darling.' And the descent into tears. 'Oh, darling, oh dear.'

Then the doorbell. The tears, though copious, seemed to shoot back into their ducts by an act of will.

8

Mark looked down from his eminence of 15 hands and one inch and admired the sweatered bosom below. Bosomina, he remembered, and especially Sexuella. 'All right if I give her a spin in the school?'

A reasonable request. Why the slight hesitation? 'Sure. Shall I take her head?'

'Don't bother. I expect I'll manage.'

They walked across the yard to the outdoor school, the flat sand-floored oblong, nicely fenced, the dressage letters around the sides: KEH on one side, FBM on the other, letters arranged as they are in every school in the world. A pile of showjumping poles and jump-stands to one side, a decent-sized fence set up in the middle of the sand. Bloody hell, if that was her idea of a practice fence she was serious all right.

Kath strode ahead to open the gate, and he squeezed the mare forward. But oddly, she didn't respond. As if there were a loose connection in her wiring. Instead, she stopped dead. Mark patted affectionately. 'We're not going to do anything difficult, miss,' he said. 'Don't worry. Let's go.' And this time kicked.

A terrible thing happened. She did not go forward, as he asked. She went up. What non-riders call rearing. Horsey people, not in the main ones for euphemism, usually call it a stand, or standing up. Rearing is too naked an expression, too terrible an event.

Some horses rear in uncontrollable terror, a rare one might even do so in malice. But she rose almost in calm. She stood to her full height with controlled grace, and having risen, stayed there, perfectly balanced. Body perfectly vertical. Mark felt his left leather slip from the saddle; he remained in place with pressure of his knees

33

and one hand on her chest. If he lost balance himself, he would pull the mare over backwards, on top of him: potentially lethal, that, especially on concrete. He stayed still, so did she. After holding the position for, it seemed, several weeks, as slowly, as gracefully as before, she lowered her front hooves to the ground.

Mark, riven with terror and dismay, found himself patting the mare's conker-brown neck. Patting? Shouldn't he be beating? He had, after all, a borrowed stick in his hand. But he soothed, soothing himself, perhaps, more than the mare.

'Can you put the leather back for me?'

'Sure.' Avoiding his eye.

The leather reattached, he walked the mare in a circle outside the school, patting, talking. Edging always that little closer to the gate, canny horseman he. And then, easily, unemphatically, turning her to the gate. It really should have worked.

And she was up again, that eerily poised balance, half an inch from disaster.

He tried again, perhaps half a dozen times – and the same, every time. Every time.

Kath took charge. 'Right. I'll take her head. You use your stick. We'll get her in and the little trollop won't go up this time.'

Always with shame Mark remembered going along with this plan. Only once, but once still counts as betrayal. One attempt, three crisp whacks. He didn't enjoy it, but you don't have to enjoy it for it to count as betrayal. And she got away from Kath, and stood again: high, serene, proud. And riven with terror. Like her rider.

Then beautifully, almost soundlessly, she lowered her hooves to the concrete. Instantly, Mark put his right hand on the pommel and flicked his right leg to dismount athletically, landing neatly on his toes, more or less chest to chest with Kath, looking straight into her navy-blue eyes.

'Had enough?' Contempt in her voice.

But love was moving hard within him. 'I'm going to buy this little mare from you. And I'm going to get her right.'

'A good beating will sort her out, don't you worry.'

'Let's put her away and discuss the matter, if that's OK with you.'

Mugs of instant coffee in the tack-room, smell of leather and neat's-foot oil. Kath had changed her note of challenge to one of dismay. 'Look, I can't sell her. I've got a reputation to look after. I never thought she'd be that bad.'

'My risk.'

'Look, how about a long loan, with an option –'

'I couldn't do it if she wasn't mine. I have to be committed.'

'But it's crazy.'

'I know.'

'Tell you what, I'll buy her back if –'

'No get-out clause. Or it wouldn't work.' It was a long time since Mark had heard himself sound so sure about anything. Uncannily clear in his mind, he made arrangements, wrote a cheque for £500, post-dated so he could get some money into the account. A sinewy handshake, not lingering, on the deal. A very level stare.

He walked back to her box, alone. He had no treats, no extra strong mints, no carrots. He was not yet a horseman. He placed a hand on the mare's bright bay neck. After a moment, she touched him with her nose, holding her head against him. Touching him.

Kath saw him back to the Jeep. 'I hope it works out.'

'Thanks. Oh, what's her name, by the way? I suppose I ought to know.'

She laughed sharply. 'Miss Chance.'

'Ha.'

'Last fucking chance, more like.'

'No,' Mark said. 'Second chance. We all need one of those.'

She looked down to where he sat in the driving seat, door still open. She had one elbow on the door, standing nicely balanced on one hip. A sudden rather gentle smile. 'Have you always been crazy?'

He smiled in return, and said farewell. It was a couple of miles down the road before he remembered what he should have replied. A line from a book somewhere, or perhaps a cowboy film. No, a book, one Morgan had been keen on. I guess I ain't never been put to the test before.

9

She looked at him admiringly. 'You really are a bloody fool, aren't you?'

'I know what I'm doing.'

'It's because you fancy her. Admit it.'

'Not the point.'

'Just want to impress her as the master horse-tamer. Well, I should warn you that she lives with Jim the fat farrier, and she's tamed a few million horses herself. If you'd asked me, I'd have told you that. And I could have told you a fair bit more about that mare of hers. Of yours, I mean.'

Mark had driven from Kath's to make arrangements about keeping Miss Chance at the yard where Mel kept Presuming Ed. He discussed it with the yard's owner, Jan, and then went to watch Mel and Ed complete a schooling session. As she finished, he hastened to tell her the news.

'I already know a fair bit about that mare of mine.'

'Good boy. Stand still.' She looked back at Mark. 'I mean, that was a nice little jumping mare, but she *spoilt* it. She jumped it in a puissance event, and I think she won – cleared damn near five feet, that I do know. But the mare was overfaced, she's only seven, it was too much for her. She got frightened silly.'

'It happens.'

'And Kath, well, she can ride all right, don't get me wrong. But I know how she treats a reluctant jumper.'

'I'm sure you're right.'

'Let's put you in your box, shall we? Oh, you want a mint, do you? Well, here we are. She beats the crap out of them, that's what she does. What she has done is to terrify the life out of a

horse, and then beat it up for being frightened. So the horse has –
well, had a nervous breakdown, basically. You'd think she'd know
better, but oh no. Typical showjumping type, no patience. Wants
results, wants them quick. And so she smiled sweetly at you and
persuaded you to part with a load of money for damaged goods.'
She was putting a light rug onto her horse, turned away from
Mark, busying herself with the straps.

'I couldn't help myself, Mel.'

'You should know better. I know you're in a vulnerable state
right now, but you can't go forking out five hundred quid every
time you fall for a pair of blue eyes.'

'Brown eyes.'

'God, he doesn't even know what she looks like. Blue eyes,
almost invariably a touch of blue eyeliner.'

'No, Mel. Brown. One on each side of her head. Ears also brown,
very large, pointed.'

'You stand there for a bit and cool off and then I'll turn you
out, all right?' She closed and bolted the stable door behind her
and neatly flipped the bottom latch with her neatly booted foot.
'Are you seriously telling me that it's the mare you fancy?'

'Something about her.'

'Damaged goods, Mark.'

'I know.'

She put her head a little to one side and raised an eyebrow above
one of her own blue, not navy, eyes, though not in invitation to
the delights of the hay-barn. 'Have you become a sucker for lame
ducks in your old age?'

'It's the spark in her –'

'It's the damage that's the attraction. Isn't that right?'

'Stop trying child psychology on me.' A standard marital riposte
of Morgan's, as it happened.

Mel was smiling to herself in a thoughtful sort of way. Then she
turned to him. 'I always thought you wanted the part of lame duck
for yourself.'

'Me?' Mark was outraged. Morgan had, more than once, said
much the same thing.

She grabbed his arm suddenly, impulsively, in a fashion that took him back through a dozen years, to a period when they had both been unsure of themselves, but each quite certain of the other. 'I think you're mad, but never mind. I'll help you all I can. Because you're going to need all the help you can get.'

10

'Port, Canon?'

'Thank you, Doctor.'

Ashton took from her a decanter and poured himself a decent slug, then gave the decanter an interrogative waggle. 'Port, Mark?'

'Thanks.' It's like heavenly cough mixture, his mother had said once, and having said it once, said it often. He helped himself, and then poured a top-up for his mother, as she preferred.

The port ceremony was much beloved by his mother, who adored ceremony in all things. It used to irritate Mark profoundly. There had been a time – shortly after his Mel and Trevor period; shortly before what he must now think of, since it was concluded, as his Morgan period – when he used to smoke roll-ups as the port was passed. Reforming your parents is never easy, or for that matter possible. But at the time it had seemed important to try.

No longer. The port did not irritate him beyond speech, and he could listen to the facetious intimacies of the couple sharing the table with him without wishing to slaughter either of them, unlike poor Bec. Without smelling the whiff of betrayal in every smile.

His mother for the most part liked evasiveness in conversation, but there was a time and place for stronger conversational meat. That was at the dining table, at what she usually called the Cheese Stage, but was really, of course, the Port Stage. The cheese stood before them more or less untasted, though Ashton was boldly eating with his fingers a slim strip of feety Stilton. The Mate supped slowly. She had no palate for wine, and bought whatever Ashton told her, but she knew a little about port. 'I have applied my mind,' she said, a favourite concept of hers. Mark had not applied his mind and knew nothing about port, save that it was prime hangover material, and when he stayed the night he always drank two or three glasses too many.

'The bishop's letter,' she said, 'was about the marrying of divorced persons.'

The remark was addressed to Mark, so he replied. 'I am sure you've told the bishop that divorced people are married, whether they like it or not.' The bishop was an old enemy, a liberal and progressive type, prone to all the religious gimmickry The Mate most despised. He was, Ashton had assured Mark, rather afraid of her, with her doctorate in theology and her letters to periodicals and her books.

Ashton pushed his chair away from the table and leant back, a man at his ease, hands clasped behind his head. An absurd figure, perhaps: clad in cassock, no modern trouser-clad clergyman; about his waist a purple sash some four inches wide, the ends of which hung almost to his knee when standing. That made his outfit the more absurd, because standing, Ashton was an inch or two over five feet, or a good six inches shorter than Mark's mother. His absolute ease of manner in all circumstances was a considerable weapon: he was a man quite without dwarvine crankiness.

'I had a couple come in today,' he said, or rather 'tud-*AIR*', for he spoke in an extraordinary bray, with etiolated Oxford vowels and a mannered stress on unexpected words. He could have been a figure of fun, a humorous clergyman from a farce, running from bedroom to bedroom with – well, no, not his trousers down, obviously, but with his cassock round his waist, perhaps. And yet it was his self-certainty that carried the day. It was a thing narrowly achieved, but it made him a formidable rather than a ridiculous person.

'Indeed?' His mother's tutorial voice, she always the teacher rather than the taught.

'Both divorced. I think I might marry them.'

She raised her eyebrows, both of them, skyward. 'Pray continue.'

'I know you believe, as an Anglo-Catholic –' or rather *kyath*-lick – 'that marriage is a sacrament –' *syack*-rament – 'and therefore incapable of reversal. As you may know, Mark, I have occasionally

40

married divorced persons when there seem to be grounds for what the Romans call lack of due discretion. When, for example, a woman is bullied into marriage, absurdly young, generally *preg*nant –' distasteful condition, that, no Roman relish of the full quiver – 'and incapable of fully understanding the vows she made.'

'Dubious and dangerous,' said Mark's mother.

'Marriage?' Mark asked. 'Or its annulment?'

Mark had shifted onto dangerous ground, and his mother might have taken him further. But Ashton was not about to relinquish his story, nor she to interrupt him. 'I have never married a doubly divorced couple. I was rather struck by what the man said to me. He said, my fiancée was the innocent party –'

'Insofar as there is such a thing, Canon.'

'I think I can accept that there is, Doctor, in a rough and ready fashion. She should not be penalised for her innocence, he said.'

'That was quite well argued,' Mark's mother allowed.

'And then he said, I was the guilty party in my own first marriage. I made a terrible mess of things. I can promise you two things. One, I will make more mistakes. But two, I will never make that particular mistake again.'

'The boy is not altogether a fool.'

'Hardly a boy, more or less your age, Mark. And I thought: can there be such a thing as a sanctified second go? Can one make a case for the blessedness of the second chance?'

'St Peter had three chances,' said Mark's mother. 'Look where that got him.'

'The papal throne,' Ashton said. 'And you will recall that he also had a second chance for martyrdom. He muffed the first one. But then he turned round and went back.'

'Are you comparing martyrdom and marriage? I have always fancied St Sebastian as a kind of role model . . .' Mark earned a moment of laughter for this.

'Marriage is not about having a bloody good try,' Mark's mother pronounced. 'Modern marriages fail because each party enters into a contract with a built-in get-out clause. It is the opposite of Macbeth: getting out is easier than going on. Divorce is not a rescue package for a failed marriage. It is the acceptability of divorce that actualises failure. Darling, another smidgen of that heavenly cough mixture.'

Mark poured for his mother, passed to Ashton who poured, passed back to Mark. Bloody affected nonsense, she came from the lower-middle classes of Manchester. He poured himself another sticky helping, that really must be the last.

'So you would not marry divorced persons?' Mark asked his mother. 'Under any circumstances?'

'I didn't say that. I speak about the complete failure of those whose duty it is to comment on the matter to comprehend even a little of the subject.' She spoke as one with a right to speak. Mark thought suddenly and distressingly of 'Cynara'. 'Nobody, but *nobody* has ever told the truth about marriage. If you read modern newspapers, you would think that marriage was a life-long tumbling in the hay.' Always bring a horse blanket. 'The older myth, little better, is that marriage is a meeting of true minds, the thing that happens when you meet the one perfectly suited other person. Rubbish. Marriage is a mystic state, certainly, but not in the way we are taught. It is my belief that *any* two people can make a marriage work. All it requires is the joint and total will of both parties. Nothing more. Nothing less.'

'That's mystical?' Mark asked.

'Certainly. It is a violent assertion of the will. The mystery is that two people will exactly the same thing. That is why marriage is the most terrible and devastating of all the sacraments, not excluding the last.'

'Who was it said,' Ashton asked, 'that he preferred funerals to weddings, because marriage was so depressingly permanent?'

Mark's mother pursed her lips in secret pleasure at this: what his father had always called her pussy-face. 'Good,' she said. 'Very.' And Ashton received a smile of deep appreciation, deep affection.

> But I was desolate and sick of an old passion,
>> Yea, all the time, because the dance was long:
>> I have been faithful to thee, Cynara! in my fashion.

The inevitable dole of tears: a single one, unwiped, his upper, non-pillow-facing eye. So Bec always said, anyway. He wasn't there.

11

'Are you the animal man?' She turned beseeching brown eyes on him.

Mark smiled hugely, straight into her uncannily wide red mouth. It was impossible not to. 'It's my most famous quality.'

'Oh dear, you're *not* the animal man, are you?'

'*An* animal man.'

'I mean the man from the Animal Rights Association or whatever it's called. They promised someone would come, and I do want to join because I *love* animals.'

'But not animal men?'

'That's why I'm a vegetarian, you see. But I hate fish. So I eat them *all* the time.'

Mark's eyes kept slipping from her lovely eyes and her lovely mouth to her lovely jumper. Or rather, her lovely jumpered bosom, its colour a pale kitten, kitten-soft and positively demanding to be caressed. Mark would have sold his soul, had Mephistopheles been available and bargain-hunting, for half a minute's double-handed fondle. 'Poor fish. Are you quite heartless?'

'Oh yes. I'm a *monster*, and *utterly* without feeling.' She looked meltingly at him. 'Who are you,' she asked, 'if you're not the animal man?'

'I'm the poetry man.' Her face did not light up. He pulled a copy of *Penyeach* from his shoulder bag. 'See, admire, buy. There's a poem by me in it.'

'What's it about?'

'Sex,' Mark said promptly.

'Then I wouldn't like it. I only like poems about animals, you see.'

44

'But not poems about fish?'

'Oh heavens, do people write poems about the filthy things? I shall never look at poetry again, in case I find one about fish. But you see, I'm not really a poetry person. Though I rather think my floor-sharer is.'

'Which one?' Half a dozen bedrooms led off the communal sitting area in which they talked.

'Knock there,' she said, indicating a door. Then she lowered her voice to an almost voiceless whisper. 'If you dare.'

Mark, daring, knocked. There was no call of welcome. But after a moment, slightly too long a moment, the door opened. And she was looking at him with a look of assessment. After a fraction, she widened her eyes at him. For just a second, or perhaps rather less, there was an increased area of white around the iris, a little as if she were a startled horse. But she was not really startled at all. She was, as it were, ironically startled. All Mark's sense of bantering ease fell from him. She seemed to possess to a very high degree a talent for unease.

'The poet,' she stated rather than asked.

'The winsome poet.'

At this something slightly odd happened. She gave a sharp two-syllable laugh. If Mark had not already decided that nothing could be more remote from this person's experience as nervousness or giggling, he might well have called it a nervous giggle. It was perhaps a turning point in their relationship, and Mark failed to recognise it. It is possible that everything would have been different had he done so. 'Oh dear, I did say that, didn't I?'

'So I believe.'

'Were you terribly hurt?'

'There are adjectives I would have preferred.'

Concern crossed her face. 'Oh dear. I am sorry. Have you ever found that when you meet people for the first time you find yourself quite by accident saying exactly what you are thinking?'

'Is that supposed to make me feel better?'

'No, it isn't. I was expressing interest in the phenomenon.'

'That's all right then. But look, I am here to sell you the latest phenomenal issue of *Penyeach*.'

45

'I bought one at the poetry reading. To read your poem.'

'See, you can be nice, can't you?'

'No, I can't. I just wanted to read it.'

'And having read it and loved it you went on to buy my book.'

'I did, actually.'

'A person of wealth and taste. Did you find it winsome?'

'I did, actually.'

Afterwards, they were to argue about what happened next. Mark said that her offer of a cup of tea was obviously an expression of interest in him, and intended to be understood as such. She maintained it was no more than good manners. My floor-sharer, she said, offered refreshment to the animal man, when he arrived. Visitors got tea: sexual feeling had nothing to do with the matter.

She made tea in the shared kitchen. Mark watched her trickle a palmful of green pebbles into the scalded pot. He watched her accomplish this small domestic task, wondering at her. The skirt was longer than was fashionable, and, since not black, startlingly unusual. But it would have been unusual, not to say startling, in any age. It comprised seven or eight horizontal layers of tartan, which ought to have clashed appallingly. She wore a tartan lumber-jack's shirt, mostly red. The get-up really should have dominated her, but it failed utterly.

It is the custom for students to go around in some sort of near-fancy dress. Mark's own outfit, which included a soft tweed fishing hat and a Norfolk jacket with many pockets and odd patches of leather, was of that school, though the fact that it was part of his father's legacy almost legitimised it. Its intention was broadly ironical: not the case with the baffling, and eye-baffling crisscrosses before him.

'Come to my room,' she said.

Again, Mark took this – not exactly as a come-on, but certainly as a signal of mild intimacy. He had not been fobbed off with a seat in the communal area, after all. But she later insisted that the invitation was purely a matter of logistical convenience. The cups were in her room, you see.

No, really, she was not beautiful. Nose too big. Eyes that

indeterminate colour they call hazel, but which is really bits of everything. It can be anything you like. Cheekbones pronounced, but not classically high and mysterious and Slavic. In some way broad, and rather Eskimo-like. Hair dark, remarkably thick, cut to her shoulders.

She certainly wasn't sexy. Mouth too thin, expression too forbidding, no tits. As she sat on the floor, Mark saw that she was wearing tartan tights.

Mark felt an *interest* in her. He admitted that to himself at once, but understood quite clearly that this was not a sexual interest. He sat on the floor and admired her room. It was not like every other student room in the world, with its posters tacked to the wall with blue putty. The minute space, more cubicle than room, was filled with a collection of Hindu pictures and objects. Not the ancient and deep art fashionable a decade and more ago, instead she had chosen loud, Mickey Mouse pictures of fat-cheeked dancing maidens and electric-blue Krishnas. There was a large statue of the elephant-headed Ganesh, and a multi-brachiate dancing Shiva. Pumpkin-breasted girls wore appalling simpers on the scarlet slashes of their mouths. The hearty vulgarity of this collection made the room more than a trifle sinister.

Behind the tiny bed stood a collection of snowstorms. Mark reached out, took one, shook it. Snow fell on plastic Venice, a gondola slid an inch beneath its plastic hemisphere. 'They're horrible, aren't they?' she said.

'Yes.'

On a hook behind the door the dead zebra hung from a coat-hanger. She poured tea: pale green. Milk or sugar not so much as suggested. 'It's gunpowder tea. I hope you like it.'

'So do I. Do you?'

The sudden not-quite-giggle, as if she had been found out. 'I had to have it, you see. For the name.'

'Talking of names, I'm Mark.'

'Oh good. I'm Morgan.'

Mark smiled.

'And if you're working up a joke, I've heard it.'

47

'No, no – I mean, you've got a Celtic mother? Or father?'

'Celt-loving. Mother. You mean for once I don't have to explain that I wasn't named after the car I was conceived in –'

'No.'

'– or the sisterhood-is-powerful woman or the –'

'Morgan le Fay. Fata Morgana. Wise woman. Mirage.'

A pause, a rather cool look from not beseeching, not brown eyes. 'How well read you are.'

'I may not have been to Oxford, but I have been educated, in my fashion. Is the ambiguity deliberate?'

'Usually. Which one?'

'Morgan. Wise woman? Or mirage?'

'I try to be both.'

Mark wondered if there was a winsome poem he could work up around this ambiguity. They talked, sipped tea. When you are talking to someone you have just met for the first time, you drink your tea before it has cooled and you scald your tongue. They talked about the university, and the course she was doing, and the hall of residence she was living in.

'I call them Sexuella and Bosomina. They're both medical students. They sit out together in the communal area and giggle for hours about things like black men's penises.' A slight hint of distaste, that reminded Mark of Ashton. 'I mean, I lived with a black guy in California, and I know.'

She seemed at the same time much younger than he, as was right for a first-year student, he in his final year. And yet much older, richer in experience. As if she had had the sort of experiences that actually matter. There was something about her quite foreign to studentkind: a worldliness.

She was reading philosophy. Philosophy was futile, Mark told her helpfully. Literature was the thing. Philosophy attempted to systematise the universe and could only be measured by its degree of failure, whereas literature, based as it is on genuine truth, is, you see, when it comes to the put-to –

'Oh, I know, I know,' she said. 'But there's no point in *studying* it, is there? And of course philosophy is futile. That's why I love it so.' She was in love with Descartes.

'But it's not *true*,' Mark explained, with all the authority of a third-year student.

'Of course it isn't. But such bliss, if it was.'

'He says that reason is all there is to life. By that line of thinking, a cat, a dog, a horse, a new-born baby, a brain-damaged child –'

'All so lovely.'

'You can't think that. He says animals are just clocks, automata. No thought, therefore no existence. Therefore no –'

'He's sweet, isn't he, my René?'

'He's a *monster*.'

'I know, I know. But I'm a monster too. You must learn that.'

12

Mark did not go to Mass or Marce, but instead went to the attic for communion with his past. He found the trunk that Bec had packed for him a decade back, brought it down, not without effort, and opened it. At once a hogo of neglect.

But after a moment, bravely he plunged. And really not too bad, really not too bad after all. A vulture's nest of leather, certainly, but damp and mouldy rather than dry and cracking. A rescue was possible. Saddle soap and gallons of neat's-foot oil, that was all that was required.

Clanking bits, various snaffles he had tried, the kimblewick he had used for cross-country after the bugger had buggered off with him. And there the saddle, bundled in anyhow, but the tree not apparently broken, and stirrup leathers and irons and all. If it did not fit the mare, he would at least sell it and buy another.

And there the boots, a generous parental gift, kept in shape by the pair of wooden trees, looking no more than rusty. Soft leather, the brief laces at the ankle. And jods, yes, a couple of pairs of fawn jods, coarse-looking and unfashionable compared to the neat and stylish haunch-huggers worn by Mel and Kath, but serviceable enough. And there his white competition jods. Not that there would be competition.

He took off his trousers there and then and pulled on a pair of musty jods. Elasticised material clamped his calves and thighs in a loving embrace. Could you have a Proustian squeeze? He did up the waist: they fitted. He felt dashing and purposeful, as of old. And there was his huge Barbour, very mouldy and in need of rewaxing. But it would still keep him dry, of course it would. And there the showjumping jacket, filthy, but rescuable. Lungeing cavesson: he was going to need that. No rugs. A disappointment. He would need rugs: but still, this was treasure enough.

And there at the bottom his priceless collection of rosettes: faded, blue and yellow: a few of them red. The red one from Potton: Lord, but they had flown that day. Galloping through the finish, teeth in the mane, spectators scattering, and he patting and patting the hard, sweaty neck; Trevor, like his owner, half-crazed with delight at his own daring.

And his jockey's skullcap, too, beneath a rusty black silk. He tried it on, did up the leather strap beneath his chin.

And goodness, there was the flat cap he used to wear around horses: green cord, well faded. He tried that on, too; it felt damp to his fingers. Birthday present from Mel, his eighteenth. In the mirror he saw a figure from another world. A figure that knew nothing of the poet, nothing of the Cartesian Morgan. More than the skullcap, the flat cap made him look like a horseman. He could see himself, lungeing the little mare, in his rewaxed Barbour, the ancient cap over his eyes.

He removed the hat, and lobbed it back into the trunk. Everything else followed. Then an idea struck him. He went into the garage and started poking about near the back. It was an area that had scarcely been touched since his father died. For a while it looked hopeless. But then he spotted a filthy piece of tarpaulin. Standing on boxes and leaning over bundles of newspapers, he seized it. And it was, it really was his or Trevor's New Zealand rug. It would need re-proofing. But it would do, if it fitted. And there, wrapped up inside, was Trevor's night rug, and even a string vest or sweat-rug. Aladdin's cave, that's what it was.

He carried everything out to the Jeep, and smiled – almost a pussy-face – at the way the Jeep looked right when full of horsey kit. And so he poked about the kitchen in a fine good temper, looking for food. He decided to make a coq au vin; the ingredients were all there, perhaps by design. It was a dish she always liked him to cook.

She arrived, the house now reeking of wine. 'Oh, you heavenly infant,' she said. 'I know I ought to prefer you to come to Marce, but it is truly wonderful to come home to your cooking. I shall surely go to hell for thinking such a thing.'

'Do you think,' Mark asked, 'it's time for Drinks Before?'

It was over the port, Mark taking a mere half-glass, since he had to drive, that his mother at last brought up the subject that had been oppressing them both all weekend. 'This business with Morgan,' she said. 'Is it irrevocable?'

Mark had been quietly terrified of this moment. He feared the weight of her disapproval: of his fecklessness, of his helplessness. Once again ruining his life in a moment of folly. No Oxford, no proper job, now no wife. 'I think it might be.'

'Oh dear. Oh *dear*. And are you – er – committed elsewhere?'

He decided not to make a joke about Miss Chance. 'No. Not my line, really.'

'Oh, what a pit-pit. What a pit-pit.' Mark had heard her use the expression to cover eventualities from a disappointing birthday present to the outbreak of nuclear war. 'I am *very* sorry to hear it. But, Mark, listen to me. I have known parents express dismay when their children have problems with their spouses. I remember when Madeleine took sides and blamed Anthony for the break-up with his girlfriend. As a result, she didn't see Anthony for two years. Or perhaps he turned up, grudgingly, at Christmas. But he married Anne, as you know, and everything worked out for him. And Madeleine accepted the situation and there was a reconciliation. And a scar too, no doubt, and certainly a long and painful gap. I don't intend to have a long and painful gap. So please understand this. I know you think me a judgmental person, and with justice. But there will be no judging from me in this matter. I value you more than I value my own capacity for judging.'

Mark laughed, touched, and said: 'In this one instance?'

'In this one instance.'

13

For once, Mark was able to park right outside, so that was a bonus. He lugged the trunk, step by step, up to the front door, and then with a brief back-snapping exertion carried it into the hall. The rugs? Too stinky. He would leave them in the car till he had bought the re-proofing stuff. He fetched the bag of bachelor shopping, the heat-up meals, the beer; also a treat he had planned for himself, beancurd, oyster mushrooms, fresh chillies of the terrifying little green wrinkled kind. He knew what to eat, but not how to fill up the evening.

She had been.

At first nothing more than a twitchiness. Mark felt like James Bond finding that the hair he had stuck to the wardrobe door was no longer there. There had been an invasion, he was sure of it before he found any hard evidence. Then things became clearer. There was a coat missing from the hall, the one that billowed about when she wore it, as she almost always did, unbuttoned. And the Burberry was gone too, her famous spy's mac.

Would there be a note? His heart stopped for a second as he considered for the first time the fantastic possibility that she was still there. He wanted that very much, and wished with all his heart to avoid it. And of course she had gone. And anyway, he would have noticed her car in the street, the famous Flying Toad Citroën DS. No, she had come and she had gone. Taking, no doubt, papers from her study and books from her shelves and clothes from her wardrobe. And some treasures, of course. Had she taken her less portable treasures? The snowstorm collection? Dancing Shiva? That would be an irrevocable step. But come. That had already been taken, had it not?

He walked into the sitting room: the great Islamic drapes were still there. And then a double take: his own, or Callum's addition to the décor had gone. Marianne Faithfull and Brigitte Bardot were no longer pinned to the gorgeous fabric. How childish: she had torn them up in a fit of post-feminist fury. No she hadn't: there they were on the long, long sofa, rolled loosely together. And something pinned to the drape behind the sofa, where Marianne had, hand on zip, so recently pouted.

Mark went to inspect it. It was a snapshot he had taken himself. It showed a naked woman. She was looking at the camera with an expression of frank irritation. The woman was Morgan.

He laughed out loud. He laughed in sheer delight at the beauty of the move. The picture was years old. He and Morgan had once spent some weeks in Greece and, in a deserted cove, Morgan had removed her clothes to swim and bask. She was caught half sitting, half lying, drying in the sun after her swim when Mark, driven by twin irresistibles, lust and the love of a jest, had sneaked up on her with the camera. She had divined his intention a fraction before he had pressed the shutter, hence the irritation.

But she liked it, when they examined the pictures in post-holiday nostalgia. 'I like the way that clothes or their lack is a matter of supreme indifference to me. All that concerns me is my urgent need to give you a bollocking.' And she had pinned the picture to her notice board in her study, along with odd postcards, notes to herself, various trouvailles. She received visitors in the study, and some of them remarked on the picture. 'It's very revealing, isn't it?' she always said. 'It reveals my temper.'

But it didn't, not really, because the incident had ended as such incidents must, when people take off their clothes in the sun. The picture was revealing all right, and it revealed a great deal more than temper or tits. Perhaps, Mark thought, it revealed their marriage.

'But it's not an erotic picture at all,' she said. 'I am unaware of my nakedness.'

'Precisely what makes it erotic.'

'Besides, I've got no tits.'

'It was you that lectured me on the power of understatement.'

'I did not lecture you on the power of no statement at all.'

'Nor would it be relevant to do so, in this case.'

'Lordy, Mr Brown, you say the sweetest things to a girl.'

And so on. Mark looked around the burgled flat, seeking a note. There was none. Just the picture, then. What was its meaning? For surely it had a meaning. 'Why do people always ask me this?' Morgan said. 'If it had a meaning, I would hardly waste my time with it, now would I?' It could not have been the work of a moment to find it. It had served its turn on the notice board, and must have been fairly deeply buried. She had gone to some trouble to make this meaningful statement, if statement it was, if meaning it had.

Did it mean that he was to forget her? Or did it mean that she knew who dominated his heart and mind, and that it was neither Brigitte nor Marianne? Was she in some way offended, to the point of jealousy (remember Sexuella) by the garlanded and zippered pin-ups? Was she competing with them? Saying that her own naked irritation was a more potent matter than anyone else's seductiveness? And perhaps she was right.

Perhaps that was the meaning. Lust, and the love of a jest.

What does it mean, Morgan? I loved *Alice* but what does it *mean*? I loved *Arachne* but what does it *mean*? And she would reply to them all only with an expression, the one he called your bloody little sphinxy smirk.

'Listen to this one, Morgan.' He was brandishing the newspaper from which he had extracted a gem. 'This bloke, mean, miser, hoarder, larder full of tins for when the bomb drops. But his crusty old heart is touched by a local convent's appeal for food for the starving orphans. So he gives away a box of tins. Realises a week or so later that he has given away his *dummy* tins. In which he kept a fortune in cash, jewels, gold coins . . .'

And Morgan had snapped into wonder at this, head on one side, cogs of her brain visibly turning. 'Yes. Yes. Yes.'

'But it gets better; there's a pay-off. One of the nuns is last seen heading for the airport in plain clothes and a taxi . . .'

She shook her head decisively. 'No. Leave the nun out. She spoils it.'

'But surely that's the cream of the jest?'

'No. She spoils it. Keep your nun to yourself.'

The story had made it to her first volume, the one called *Alice*, without the flying nun. Neither quite moral nor quite cruel nor quite funny. 'It's futile without the pay-off.'

Same expression as the one in the naked photograph. 'I know.'

'The meaning is that there is no meaning?'

'Stories don't have meanings. They have shapes. Your story had a good shape, till you brought in the flying nun.'

Do pictures have meanings, when pinned to Islamic drapes? Every picture tells a story. But what was its shape?

The kitchen was pleasingly bare, free from all clutter. He took a Sabatier from the knife-block and tested it gently with his thumbnail. Like a bloody razor. He gave it a quick caress with the steel and then scalpelled mushrooms and bean curd and chilli for hot and sour soup. Not too hot, she would say. Or too sour. Well, this soup was going to be a belter.

14

'Perdition catch my soul But I do love thee!' Mark said, 'and when I love thee not, Chaos is come again. Does that answer your question?'

'No,' she said. 'Because chaos comes anyway. Even though he never stops loving her.'

'But that's wrong. He couldn't love her right at the very end. Because he kills her, right?'

'Right, Jim,' said Mark, rightly, scanning his audience, all to be included. 'Any thoughts on that one? Jane?'

'He *says* he still loves her. Says that he – what is it? – that he just overdid it.'

'One who loved not wisely but too well, exactly.'

Jim, slouching in his chair at the back, long hair falling over his face in a manner that reminded Mark of his sister, said: 'Is Desdemona really faithful, Mr Brown?'

'Everybody says so. The Moor included, at the end.'

'But I mean, in that scene with Cassio, she's obviously flirting with him, isn't she? I mean she really likes him. She says so.'

'Is liking someone infidelity, then?'

Jim seemed to have been looking hard at the back of Jane's neck as he spoke. So perhaps there was a hidden agenda; after all, there generally is. Jim was the official propounder of the view that Shakespeare was overrated; well, every half-decent group needs one of those. Mark was not sitting at the desk provided, nor was he standing up and walking about. He was sitting among his audience, on one of the spare desks, foot on one of the spare chairs. His right ankle was on his left knee, revealing a great deal of dusty black boot. Clint indeed.

'Do you get the impression that Desdemona's a really sexy lady, Mr Brown?' This was Ralph, the official Lawrentian; every half-decent group, etc. He had a strange helmet of black curls and a wonderfully dramatic pair of sideburns, no doubt the envy of the rest of the males. Inevitably there were a few giggles at this piece of daring, but Ralph intended a serious question beneath the showing-off, and Mark took it as such.

'You clearly do, Ralph. Tell us more.'

'Well, Cassio obviously fancies her. And Othello is crazy about her. Nice double entendre, Mr Brown.' Mark laughed hearing one of his own tricks of speech amiably turned back on him.

'Maybe Iago too,' Jane murmured, from somewhere near his right boot.

'Very intriguing point,' Mark said.

'So maybe Othello has some kind of real ground for his suspicion, Mr Brown.' This again from Jim.

'Is being an attractive person a form of betrayal, then?' Mark asked.

'It is if you are trying to cause trouble,' said Susan, who signed her essays 'Soo'. 'I mean, if she wanted to upset Othello by flirting with Cassio, then she was betraying him, wasn't she?'

A boy, dressed in pointedly conservative style, Roger or Richard somebody, said: 'But did Shakespeare really intend us to worry about all this, Mr Brown?'

'Ah, the intention problem,' said Mark. On his knee, as always, there was a clipboard, that might have held notes on *Othello* but in fact held the names and notes for the recognition of the members of this new class. 'It's a very important point, er, Roger, and one we'll come back to next week, when we do an unseen poem. But in the meantime, hold your horses.' Susan or Soo murmured something to Jane beside her, and both giggled softly. Perhaps something to do with horses and cowboy boots. 'In the meantime, I want you all to think about sex.' This naturally got a laugh. A smooth and serious boy drew breath for a question. 'And if you're asking if sex is relevant for the exam, Sandeep, then I'm disappointed in you.'

Sandeep was well able to deal with a sally of this kind, as Mark had observed in previous classes. 'I mean only to ask, Mr Brown, if the examiners will be shocked by such matters.'

'As I've told you before, Sandeep, examination technique is something that will be discussed fully and at length in the last week of term. Worry about it then. For the next few weeks, I want you to worry about the play.' A bell rang sharply. 'There, doesn't time fly when you're talking about sex? Some thoughts, please, on paper. We've been talking about betrayal: right, tell me more. Take any one character in the play, and follow the theme of betrayal. Who, if anyone, does he or she betray? By whom, if anyone, is he or she betrayed? Let yourselves go. It's a big subject, after all.'

By rights, Mark should have written up his notes for the day before he left. That had always been his usual practice. But she was waiting for him. And besides, he wanted to catch the light. Soon the hour would go back and evenings would become a wilderness of gloom. Rushing from school to the stable-yard, he was returning to his youth with a vengeance. He scribbled a few things to remember, notes for his notes, on his clipboard, and then hurried to collect his bag, and its usual ton of books. For he had to drive to Radlett.

For he had to drive to Radlett to work his horse. The yellow dogs leapt and curvetted at his entrance: 'Don't bark,' Mark told them. 'I live here now.'

Jan lived in a small lair with the tack-room behind her, where she smoked cigarettes and talked energetically to the telephone. She was doing exactly that when Mark arrived. 'Nigh sauce,' she was saying. She had the telephone tucked under her chin like a violin and was cleaning tack with both hands. She waved to him with a sponge full of saddle soap. 'Bloody great big thing, nice bit of bone, up to your weight, easy. Nice paces, nice manners, and he'll carry you all day. No world beater but he's a nigh sauce.' She pointed at the kettle and then at Mark and herself. So Mark obediently made tea, though he was itching to get at the line of boxes. Jan, still selling hard, eventually put the phone down. Mark rewarded her with sugared tea.

'Well,' she said. 'She's 'ere.'

'Settled in all right?'

'No trouble. Kath brought her over this morning, nigh sauce, happy with everything, bless her.' Jan had a straggle of dark curls, jumble-sale clothes and more than a touch of gypsy. She ran the livery yard and bought and sold horses. Kath laughed in his face when he had told her that he was planning to keep the mare at Jan's, and told him that Jan would 'have you for breakfast'. 'I turned her out after lunch 'cause she got restless in her box, and she got on fine, seemed to take a shine to Ed, bless him.'

'No dramas, then?'

'Course not.' And she wouldn't tell me if there were. All yard managers treat owners like amiable idiots, which in a sense is fair enough. They also treat all horses as if they were their own. 'Brought 'em all in just before five and fed 'em.'

'She ate up?'

'Every scrap. Nothing worried her. She's a nigh sauce and she'll not give you no grief.' It is axiomatic that all yard managers know more about the horses in their care than do their owners. Jan explained about livery bills and their payment, the times when the yard could be visited, where the light switches were, the system for leaving messages and where the keys were hidden when she was away buying and selling or, as she occasionally did, sleeping or eating in her own home. All of which was essential information, but Mark wanted to see his horse. My horse.

Jan showed him the tack-room, and the place she had cleared for him, with a rack for saddle and for bridle and room on the floor for his trunk. She even helped him shift this item into its place, which was beyond the call of duty. 'Right then. You'd better ride your rauce.'

'I'll just lunge her today.'

'You get on her. She won't give no trouble.'

'We'll see.' A stock dismissive of his mother's. Mark opened the trunk and removed the things he wanted. Including his green cord cap. He put it on his head. Horseman. He walked along to the boxes: a dozen heads, peering over their half-doors around three sides of a square. A strange joy seized him: the essential contradiction of it all. The mixture of cosy domesticity with deep wildness. That was the contradiction in this pleasant evening sight:

the contradiction in everything to do with humans and horses. You seek wildness without wildness; you seek to tame without taming. And that last, that was precisely the problem that lay before him with this daft, lovely and troubled animal.

A head, bay, with a white star. He entered her box, talking soft greeting nonsense. A horse likes to hear the mood, read the intentions of the animals all around, equine, human, carnivorous. A horse always likes to know where every one is, and hates above all to be sneaked up on. The constant talking of horsey gibberish is a request: may I have permission to enter the border-country?

Mark slipped over her head a leather head collar that bore on a brass plate the name Trev. A gift, ancient but unforgotten, from Mel. It fitted well enough, on the topmost hole. He attached a lead rope by its clip and asked her to walk from her box. He tied her to a ring set in the wall, or rather, a loop of baling twine threaded through the ring. His fingers tied the quick release knot.

The mare accepted all this without fuss, even with kindness. The bouncing assertiveness of her madcap canter round Kath's field, the terrifying vertical stand – these seemed matters connected with another horse, another being entirely.

Mark picked out her hooves with a hoof-pick and she lifted each foot in turn with easy courtesy. Then he brushed her vigorously with a body-brush, knocking the dust and scurf from the brush with a metal currycomb. Each movement took him deeper into the past. Trevor's obstreperous behaviour before a show: he knew, all right, always read the excitement in the air. But the mare was kind and accepting, though she fidgeted uncomfortably when he brushed too hard. 'Sorry, darling,' he said softly. He had never called anybody darling. Nor angel, for that matter.

He removed her head collar, certain she would not take advantage of him. Put on Trev's lungeing cavesson. Not to bother with surcingle and side-reins and stuff. Just attach the lunge-line to the ring on the nose, and grab the lunge-whip.

A crisis was approaching. The trick was to pretend that it wasn't, because horses read human body language better than humans read horses'. Annoyingly, perhaps disastrously, he felt his pulse quicken. Pretend it wasn't. 'Come, miss.'

She saw the school ahead of her and stopped dead, as if she had walked into a wall. She had never seen it before. It was not the school where Kath had worked her, where Kath had tried to reform her with a series of beatings, where even Mark had hit her three times. But it was still a school, and she knew it. It was a Bad Place.

She stood a full inch taller, looking at the sand, every part of her expressing her not-quite terror. Damn it, Mark thought, I forgot my gloves. And hard hat, but I won't need that, will I?

'Come on, miss. Walk forward.' Give her a bloody good belt and she'll walk forward all right. A statue, staring forward at the bland sand, the abode of dragons. Mark let her stare for a while, mane-nibbling with his fingers, talking soft horsey gibberish. All right then. We'll walk forward now, shall we?

Three paces, and another dead halt. Mark tried again, patting, talking. Plenty of time. Hope to God no one sees, they'll think I'm the softest bloody touch that ever sat on a horse. Give us your lunge-whip, old son, and we'll get her through.

'Walk on, please, miss.' And suddenly she was through the gate, and wild with excitement or terror at her own daring, and was dancing, threatening the safety of his toes. 'Ah, the madcap,' he said, much made up by this success, oblivious of the flying hooves. 'I remember the madcap. Run about, then.'

And he was lungeing his horse in a circle, bracing himself against the wildness of her flight, taking a half-turn of line behind his back to stop the horse from water-skiing him across the school, and she ran her craziness to its end and at last started to work, and Mark kept her to it with little gestures of the long lunge-whip, never touching her.

And then all over again on the other rein.

Make much of horse. His old riding teacher's instruction at the conclusion of any demanding piece of work. And Mark made much.

Back in her box, she was fêted with extra strong mints, and the smell of the minty breath of his horse was to breathe in the good past. He had reached out and touched her; his touch had been accepted. He stood for a while outside the box, leaning on the

62

half-door, she looking out, occasionally touching him with her nose. Must leave. Bloody D. H. Lawrence to read. Write up those notes. Listen to the answerphone. Please God, not another surprise visit from Morgan. Perdition, he thought, catch my soul.

15

Rather rum. One of The Mate's favourite expressions, and it seemed to cover every aspect of the situation. It had, indeed, been one of the rummer weekends of a life not untouched by rumness. And one of the rummest people he had ever met. By far the rummest he had ever kissed. What to make of it all?

It was hardly a personal triumph, for all the kissing, the being kissed back and the promise that he would kiss again. That strange night. Had he passed the test she had set him? Or had he abjectly failed? Did she know herself?

It had been a time stolen from the common run of things, that much at least was certain. But it had not been a lover's idyll, a dalliance of hearts and bodies, of tempers and reconciliations and promises and plans. She had wept, yes, but only for the pier that stretched out into the sea. Rum.

It was thirty-six hours of magic, but not magic as the term is commonly understood. It was magic of the subtle, ambivalent and sinister kind that you find in Celtic myth. 'Do you think you could learn to mildly dislike me?' she asked. 'It would make things so much easier, don't you see?'

'Perhaps. Could you learn to mildly dislike me?'

'Oh, but I already do.'

'That's all right then.'

'You're so pleasant, you see.'

'Only nineteen hours before I kiss you again.'

'I'm looking forward to that.'

Well, Mark thought, walking up the stairs to the flat. Now a little less than twelve hours before he kissed her once again.

He opened the door and called out Callum's name, but there

was no reply. Then he saw a note pinned to the table by a knife, a regular means of communication: I'm at Chris's. Could you come round right away? Whatever the time of night? It's not life and death, but it's important. All right?

Horror. For a moment he wondered if he wasn't going to faint. Christine. Or perhaps throw up. He had not been in the mood for reality. What had she done? What did she know? Not that there was anything to know. Or not really.

He sat down for a good while longer, being appalled. But after a while, even being appalled runs out of steam. There was nothing for it but to go and face it. The reproaches: though what had he done for which he should be reproached?

Ten minutes later, he was knocking at Chris's door. Callum answered: 'Oh, thank God.'

'What's happened?'

'Go to the kitchen. I'll tell her you're here. She's been listening out. Then I'll explain.'

Callum's face, his voice were neutral, carefully so. Mark went and stood about feebly in the kitchen. He wondered if there was beer in the fridge: she might have bought one for him. But it would not do, to look for it.

Callum came in. 'It's all right,' he said. He sat down at the kitchen table. Mark sat also. 'Thing is, she can't speak. Physiological thing. I mean, it's not her fault, she's not putting it on. Had the doctor round. It's some kind of locking-up. It'll unlock in a day or so. Happens sometimes to people in shock.'

'What's happened, Cal?' Mark's own voice was not at its clearest.

'She saw you going to the station.'

'How?' Perhaps that syllable was a complete giveaway, but if so, Callum gave no sign of understanding it. Anyway, giving what away?

'We've been having quite a chat. She writes things down. New term resolution, remember? She was going to work every Saturday.'

'Oh Christ, at the Cottle Reading Room.' Which was near the railway station.

'She was having a coffee break.'

'Oh God, at the Voyagers.' Which overlooked the station entrance.

'And she saw you and –'

'But look, Christ, what is she on about? All I did was catch a train, and anyway nothing happened –'

'She saw you with a girl. And she knew at once that you were in love with her. By the way you were walking.'

'Jesus, that's ridiculous, I mean I was –'

'Tell me about it sometime. But maybe you should see Chris now. And tell her what you want to tell her.'

'Oh God.'

Mark went and knocked at her door. He then realised that waiting for a reply was foolish, so he called, 'It's me' through the wood and then walked in. She lay on her mattress on the floor, a double mattress purchased primarily as an arena for gymnastics. Though that was not its function now. She lay under the covers, face on the pillow half-hidden by a straggle of fair hair. Body present, mind apparently absent, kidnapped by aliens. 'Pretty child,' his mother had said.

Chris sat up in bed, shifting the covers back. Not naked. Quite well wrapped up, in fact. Mark had been intending to embrace her, to kiss her face, but he did not do so, for reasons that eluded him. With odd, dormouse-like movements she rootled about for a notebook and pencil and wrote a word for him. Sorry.

'Oh, look, Chris, Jesus, it's me that's sorry, all my fault, I didn't mean to cause you any distress, it was hopeless of me, I'm such a bloody fool, but look, honestly, nothing happened, you've got it all wrong.'

I love you.

Oh God. 'I'd never do anything to hurt you, it was stupid of me, inconsiderate, I just went to the seaside, you see –'

Are you sleeping with her yet?

'Christ, no, not a thought of it, not an option, I mean we did spend the night there, but, you know, no hanky-panky. I mean nothing at all, no kissing and cuddling or anything. Just talking. I mean, she's weird. I don't even like her very much.'

You're in love with her.

Mark explained at considerable length and with some warmth that this was not the case, and never could be. She wrote down one of his own favourite rejoinders, one he had used to tease her, laughing, a thousand times and more. She wrote, the lady doth protest too much. 'Oh Christ, think what you like, Chris, but I know what I feel, and I know what happened, and I tell you, nothing's changed so far as you and I are concerned. Not if that's what you want.' Mark had been ready to sweep her up into his arms at the conclusion of this avowal, but somehow it didn't seem the moment. She was writing on her notebook once again. This time only very brief and rather brusque movements of the pencil. She then lay her head on the pillow to indicate that the interview was over. Mark rambled on disconnectedly for a while, but she did not respond. He tried laying his hand on her shoulder, even leant over to kiss her face, but she was hard, rigid, locked solid. So after a while of sitting in silence, in case she should wish to speak or at least to make some sign, he got up and left. He said as he went: 'I'll be back tomorrow. All right?'

In the notebook she had inserted, after the second word of the second line she had written for him, two further characters. ∠D.

'You all right, Mark?'

Mark was standing in the kitchen with his hands clasped around the back of his neck. 'Sure.'

'What have you been up to?'

Mark turned and smiled brightly. 'I rather think I've been fucking up my life, actually.'

'But what did you do?'

'I mean my life as well, of course. What's the plan?'

'Julie's away for the weekend, coming back tomorrow morning.' This was Chris's flatmate. 'So I'll hang on here for the night. Keep an eye.'

'You're a good man, Cal.'

'Sure.'

'What about that Asian girl you were going to ask out?'

'Ach. Nothing came of that. What do you expect? Just as well, really. Imagine the ructions that would cause.'

'Cal, I need to go and think things through for a bit.'

'Suppose you do. Don't waste too much time feeling guilty.'

'Believe me, I've far more worrying things on my mind than bloody guilt.'

Callum smiled. 'See you.'

He had been interested in her, he would certainly go that far. The level of interest at which you walk into cafés as if keeping an appointment, eyes scanning the tables as you try to look as if you can't quite remember whether she said the Café des Amis, or Mister Crumbs or Tudge's. Nodding to acquaintances, not stopping. Passing to the next café, same careful air of preoccupation, damn it, she must be late, that sort of thing. On one occasion he found Sexuella (or was it Bosomina?) and a large bun, both looking almost esculent. 'Are you looking for Morgan?'

'Oh, hello –' what the hell was her real name? – 'Clare, no not at all, just passing by . . .'

'Because you've just missed her.' Damn and blast it all to hell. Melting eyes: 'I know you're not the animal man now, but can you cook?'

'What? Oh, I'm rather good, actually.'

'Because Morgan has to find a man who can cook by Wednesday. It will be her turn to cook the communal meal. She said she can't cook, so we told her to find a man. Can you cook fish?'

'Do you like kedgeree?'

Her eyes expanded hugely, vast egg-white rims around the almost equine brown. 'I adore kedgeree. It's my favourite, favourite thing.'

'I have to go.'

'I look forward to my kedgeree. Do you have a message for Morgan?'

Mark smiled, a smooth quip rising to his lips. And failing to emerge. His lips havered. It was an absolutely horrible moment. He felt colour rising up the back of his neck, a rising tide of blood in his face. Come lie with me and be my love, he had thought. And almost said. Winsomely.

It was Saturday morning that he actually saw her. Wearing a suit, a longish skirt and a longish jacket made from some huge floral material of the kind used for covering chairs in country hotels. About the neck was a fox-fur stole, a head, complete with ears and eyes, biting the white-tipped brush. 'Don't panic,' he called in greeting. 'Hold still and I'll throttle the brute before he pierces a vital organ.'

'Good morning, little poet,' she said. 'Is that the best you can do?'

He had not gone out of his way at all, not really. Walking to visit a friend, taking the more southerly route, which just happened to pass the end of the drive that led to her hall of residence. But he quite often walked that way, quite often visited that friend. He could hardly stop doing so for fear of what he might think of himself. Now could he?

'Where are you off to, on so fine a morning?' It was a fine morning, too, filled with that certain brightness you find sometimes in late October, when the turning of the seasons seems to be suspended for a day.

'I'm going to the seaside.'

'No one goes to the seaside.'

'Precisely why I am going. I shall walk along the beach and not talk to any one. Especially not to students. And I can't stand here talking, because my train leaves in twenty minutes.'

'May I carry your bag to the station?'

'It isn't heavy.'

'Good. Because that's not why I asked.'

'Lordy, you say the sweetest things to a girl.'

'I practise at nights.'

'How very pleasant you are. Sign of a weak character, I expect.'

'You're a bit nasty, aren't you?'

'Oh no. I'm actually quite a lot nasty. But look here, Mark dearest –' Mark's heart lifted at the sound of his name, remembered as if by a miracle, and the albeit ironical endearment – 'I would be flattered and delighted if you were to carry my bag to the station.'

Somewhere along the way, it was decided that Mark should accompany her to the seaside. She was naturally to claim that he had intemperately imposed himself on her solitude, he that she had made him gushingly, insistently welcome. He had sufficient money for his ticket. On arrival, he extracted next week's cash from a cash machine. And so they walked to the seafront and promenaded. 'All my life,' she said, as if this period covered incalculable aeons of time, 'I have wanted one of these.' They walked along reading the name of the chalets: Seahorses, Valium, Happy Days, The Manor Hut. One or two more ambitious: Thalassa, Roaring Boys. And one called Summer's Lease. They liked that one especially.

At the end of the chalets, they walked down to the sea and back towards town along the shingle beach, a little chilled in their townee garments, the Norfolk jacket, the hothouse flowers, as the seawind flicked whitecaps towards them. 'I'd love to live here,' she said. 'But only in winter.'

'You like the sadness?'

'I think summer is much sadder. In winter, people don't expect to enjoy themselves. They do in summer, and it's people being disappointed that I can't stand. Things promise so well, you see. And it's the saddest thing in the world. But in the winter, at the seaside, there's no hope. I take a lot of comfort in that. You can feel safe.'

They retreated inland, into the town, past the boating lake, empty of all traces of navigation, the shuttered tea-kiosk, the row of dumb cannons that guarded the primly elegant houses. She was enraptured by a place called the Sailors' Reading Room, and by its boisterous, big-breasted wooden mermaid: Bosomina with a fish's tail, she suggested, and they giggled. They walked on to the pier, the disappointed bridge that stretched out into the heaving greyness. The sun had gone in now. Naturally everything was closed, wooden shutters covering every manner of entry. But it was brightly painted and cheerful, a suitable emblem of a prosperous little town.

But it was here that she inexplicably wept. A few small tears. So Mark took her in his arms, uncomprehending, and she cried a little longer in comfort, and he kissed her face, not understanding, not understanding at all.

'The pier,' she said. 'The seaside. It's so sad.'

'Why? Don't cry.'

'It all starts to well. I ought never to have come. I should have known that this would happen.'

So Mark kissed her again, and this time located her mouth, and, surprised at his daring, tongued her softly, without urgency. She seemed unsurprised, accepting, participating.

They broke away and surveyed each other across the un-disappointed bridge of their four arms. 'I specifically didn't want this to happen.'

'Then you shouldn't have asked me to join you.'

'I don't recall doing so. But that was very pleasant.'

'Wasn't it? Shall we do it again?'

'Oh yes. Certainly.' She took one arm from his waist and looked at her watch. 'In twenty-four hours.'

'Not before?'

'Certainly not. I hate to be rushed. At one fifteen on Sunday afternoon. You may kiss me then, if you still wish to.'

'I'll have to see how I feel.'

'You do that.'

Mark was half affronted, half delighted at this suggestion. He did not know whether she was failing to take with due seriousness the business of kissing, or whether, on the contrary, she was taking it with very great seriousness indeed.

They lunched on coffee and sandwiches served with much garnish outside a brave café that flaunted its piney tables in the reappearing autumn sun. Afterwards, they walked further, out of the little town, towards the little harbour. A pair of heavy horses grazed in a field, great thick-necked creatures with body-builders' bodies. They approached Mark, hoping for titbits but he had no mints about his person. Instead he gave them torn-up handfuls of grass. 'Drayhorses,' he said. 'I bet they deliver beer for the brewery we passed.'

Morgan remained on the pavement, not advancing to meet the animals. 'I quite like the idea of them,' she said. 'I'm not sure that I care for the reality.'

'Is that something to do with Plato?'

71

'Certainly. I quite like the idea of you too.' They walked on to the harbour and looked at boats. They found a bench, which was, she said 'conveniently low, like the Dodgson poem'. And so they talked and talked, as people must in such circumstances. And the light began to fade, so they walked back into town. Mark suggested a drink, and she insisted on the Lord Nelson, 'so handy for the Sailors' Reading Room'.

After a while, Morgan decided she would like to eat there too, so they had fish and chips. A little silence followed their meal, Mark unsure of what should be the next move, unsure even if there should be one. He felt in complete submission to the passing whims of fate.

'I have a raving ambition,' she said after a while.

'Tell me.'

'I want to drink coffee in the lounge of that hotel. The pretty one I liked.'

Mark looked at his garments, which were essentially, despite his father's Norfolk jacket, the clothes of studentkind. Then at her clothes, and her style that came from a world that no one, not even the doorman at the Swan Hotel, could aspire to. But her statement also held something of a dare. She had a sudden relish of challenge, of the meeting between play and serious matters.

'Let's give it a go, then,' Mark said, not to be outdared.

She did it very prettily, with great self-certainty, like an aunt taking a favoured nephew out for a treat. The chairs were deep and full and flowered. 'We're only here to see if your suit matches the chairs.'

Around them, couples, all between twenty and forty years older than they, sipped coffee or drank what The Mate would have called drinkie-sort-of-drinks and conversed in lowered voices. There was no music. The place was comfortable and expensive without being at all grand. It all felt right, a fitting end to the day.

'I think I'm in love,' she said.

A dare, a challenge. Mark felt a treacherous stab of delight at this foolish remark, but he already knew a good deal about her jokes, her ironies. 'Oh-ah?'

She looked at him for a moment, assessing. 'You really did that rather well. But tell me, are you in love also?'

'You're in love with the hotel. With the seaside. With the pier.'

'I'm in love with the day.'

'Then so am I. We seized it all right, didn't we? A shame days have to end.' She looked at her watch. 'How long till I kiss you again?'

'Er – thirteen hours and fifteen minutes. But in fact, it was the question of the last train that was oppressing me. It is leaving even as we speak.'

No matter, Mark said. They could hitch, they would get back eventually. Morgan wondered about getting a taxi all the way, which to Mark sounded like the private funding of a moon launch. But then she looked at him with sudden great certainty; behind which there was something else as well. Perhaps doubt. Perhaps fear. Perhaps even hope, who knows? 'Mark dearest, you are to be trusted, aren't you?'

And then she walked up to the reception desk and booked a room for the night. The audacity of such a move was simply staggering. Students didn't do things like that. They didn't even think about doing things like that. She spun them a yarn about a car that had broken down, to explain their lack of luggage. They didn't, she said, impossibly worldly, need to believe her. Step this way, Mr Francis, and Mark managed to avoid looking over his shoulder, because he was now Mr Francis, husband of Mrs Francis.

'I have a credit card, Mark,' she explained patiently, after they had been shown to their room. 'I'm frightfully rich, you know.'

The room was delightful and flowered and quite four-postered. Morgan asked Mark to make her a cup of tea from the kettle in the corner. She then retreated to the bathroom and returned washed, stripped of make-up, clad in a long white silken garment that she might or might not have been wearing beneath her gorgeous suit. She looked for once a little young. She settled into the bed and Mark asked if she wanted a biscuit with her tea. She took one with thanks, and started to read a book: Borges, *A Universal History of Infamy*. Mark had neither book nor idea of how to comport himself. He looked at her from a chair. Bare arms, faint outline of the upper body beneath the white silk, dark hair freshly brushed on bare shoulders, young, bare face. After a while, feeling his gaze, she raised her eyes. 'I'm tremendously happy,' she said. 'Really quite terrifically happy.'

Mark took the Gideon's Bible from its drawer beside the bed, and turned to the Song of Songs. Stay me with flagons, comfort me with apples: for I am sick of love. His left hand is under my head, and his right hand doth embrace me . . . By night on my bed I sought him whom my soul loveth . . . Thou art all fair, my love; there is no spot in thee.

'Do you think we might sleep?'

The rose of Sharon, and the lily of the valleys. Mark went to the bathroom, washed, returned naked, loins wrapped in a towel. The light was extinguished, she was lying, as if asleep, facing the edge of the bed. Well, what did you expect? Letting his towel fall to the floor, he slipped into bed, leant across, placed a hand on her exposed shoulder, and placed a single kiss on the few exposed square inches of her bare cheek. 'Good night, Morgan.'

'Ng.'

She seemed to sleep at once.

Mark was awoken by her morning withdrawal from the sheets. 'Hello. You don't have to sneak about, you know.'

She turned to him. 'I was just thinking how much like a rodent you look.'

'Come and talk to me.'

Rather gingerly and rather to his surprise, she did. Lay on the bed, his left hand under her head, his right hand embracing, he beneath, she above the covers. He was alarmingly aware of the naked body beneath the silk; he was too wise or too fearful to explore its possibilities. If she wanted her wishes to be defied, to be ravished, then she had chosen the wrong companion. Certainly, he liked the idea of it, this violent assertion of the will, nice double entendre. He liked the idea, but did not seek the reality. Instead he sought complicity; conspiracy. And he conspired with her to lie quiet and chaste. He regarded the morning sun of another bright autumn day as it pierced the small gap between curtains that were

74

flowered like her lovely suit, and he thought that perhaps she would one day lie with him and be his love. Unsuited.

They breakfasted in great good humour and at some length in the stately dining room. Eventually they promenaded anew. 'I think I shall spend my life in one of these chalets.'

'Which one? Roaring Boys?'

'Oh no. Summer's Lease. Without a doubt.'

She needed to work; she had to produce 2,000 words on her heavenly René by the following afternoon, but still they dallied, for there was still much to discuss. At quarter past one, as they strolled again by the harbour, Mark embraced her kindly, and was embraced back in the same fashion. Softly, undemandingly kissed.

They might have left then, but she discovered that meals were served in the chandlery, and she had to explore its possibilities. The place sold kettles and string and fresh vegetables to counteract scurvy; also bacon sandwiches and tea. 'Do you think we might kiss again at a reduced interval?' Mark asked.

'Oh yes.'

'Halve it? Twelve hours?'

'A bit fast, that.'

'Nice double entendre.'

'Indeed. Eighteen?'

'Excellent.'

The light was failing as the train pulled out of the station. They sat facing each other. 'Happy,' she said. And crossed the small chasm to sit beside him. Allowing unsurprised his arm to pass behind her shoulders.

16

'Don't you think he's a real horse, Mr Brown?'

'Well, I do have a problem there. The poor thing is so busy being the life-force, so busy being a potent symbol –'

'Walking phallus, Mr Brown.'

'Thanks for that, Jim. I'll bow to your expertise on the subject.' Laughter, rather cheap laughter.

'But what Lawrence is getting at, Mr Brown –'

Jane interrupted Ralph's defence of his hero. 'Are you all *right*, Mr Brown?'

'Eh?'

'You've worn the same shirt three days running. You've changed your jeans, but they're just another dirty pair.'

'Sorry if my standards are slipping. It's knowing you lot for half a term. Just look what happens.'

'I mean, is everything all right at home, Mr Brown?'

Jane sounded as if she really wanted to know. He had never thought of himself as the sort of teacher that seduces his sixth form. Not physically, anyway. 'You're very observant, Jane. Fact is, the washing machine's broken down and I'm too thick to mend it.'

A teacher who calls himself thick will always get the cheapest of cheap laughs; with this rather bright class he won a cheap titter. It was distraction enough to ride out the moment, but Jane's eyes asked him, oh yeah?, with hard, world-weary compassion. Well, some of these children knew more about marital stress than he did, after all.

Because Jane was right, he really was a little too close to the edge for his absolute ease and comfort. He had not planned this lesson on *St Mawr*; he had arranged to give himself an easy morning by

76

showing the class a chunk of the video of the Olivier *Othello*. This always got some interesting reactions, not to mention cheap laughs. Rolling eyes, so vieux jeu. But that morning, he had gone to the English department common room, and the resources room that led from it, and had found the video gone. 'How can people be so *fucking* inconsiderate?'

A voice from the common room. 'What's up?'

Shame: he had thought himself alone. But rage was still stronger than shame. Stepping back into the common room, he asked: 'What's the point of having a fucking resources book if people ignore it and fucking help themselves?'

Mark's voice seemed to have no difficulty in reaching those notes above the stave normally attained only by coloratura sopranos. He found himself under the compassionate and rather too intelligent brown eyes of one of his nicer colleagues, his deputy, no less. 'Are you all right, Mark?'

'Sorry, Annette. Bit stressed this morning.'

'Something wrong?'

'One or two things not absolutely ideal.'

'Work? Or life?'

'Work is great, apart from the phantom video-nicker.'

The return to light banter indicated that he had found some kind of control. She put her head on one side, really rather fine eyes, lightly outlined, beneath a short, soft flop of dark hair. 'Too much of cliché, this sort of thing,' she said. Touched his arm. 'But all the same, if you were to buy me a drink sometime, I expect I'd drink it.'

Mark was very touched by this. He understood the messages within messages. 'Thanks, Annette.'

'If we teachers don't look after each other, who will?' She left for her own class. Mark spent three minutes thinking hard about St Mawr, the big stallion, and his influence over all those other D. H. Lawrence characters. More importantly, skimming through the text to make sure he had the names right. Always the names, scribbled onto the clipboard: Lou, yes, and Mrs Witt. Rico, Phoenix, Lewis. And he had gone to his class and taught as best he could. Not realising that he was giving himself away.

And he was deeply wounded in his pride, in the dark secret heart of his pride, as Lawrence might have put it. He had fancied that he was coping really rather well, what with horses and friends and so on. But what with Jane and Olivier and Annette, he seemed to be making it clear that he was hardly coping at all. It was something that came as a shock to him: he had cherished the illusion of control. Too much of cliché, that sort of thing.

He was running a bit short of the life-force himself, not to mention the walking phallus principle. But at least he had a horse, and not a symbolic one either. And there was a pay phone in the staff-room, if he could get there early enough in the lunch break to grab it. He could leave a message.

But in fact, he caught her between patients.

'Mark, are you all right?'

'I'm wonderful. Look, Mel, will you be at the yard tonight? Because if you are, I wonder if you could give me a hand.'

'Is this the big one?'

'Damn right.'

'I wouldn't miss that for the world. If you're tacked up at half-seven I'll be there and ready to sell tickets.'

'You're an angel.'

The long schoolday reached its end, as all days must, even long schooldays in the lives of slightly deranged schoolteachers who are too close to the edge for their absolute ease and comfort. Mark wrote up his notes for an hour, and then drove to Radlett. The clocks had gone back, and for the first time that year he needed to switch on his lights as he drove out of school. He parked, walked through the gate, exchanged greetings with the big yellow dogs. Walked into Jan's lair and took off his trousers.

''Allo,' Jan said, arriving. 'You pleased to see me, or is it really the big one?'

'I'm always pleased to see you,' Mark said. 'But it's the big one all right.' Pulling on another pair of trousers now: tight grip of elasticised fabric around his calves. Proustian grip.

'Been long enough, ain't it?'

'It's been exactly the right amount of time,' Mark said. 'I've timed it to perfection.' He eased his feet into the tall black boots.

78

They slipped on easily, but when he tied the ankle-laces, he felt their tautness against his legs. Prepared.

Lunge her from the bit. First. That was the thing. Bridle, then, knot the reins over the withers. Saddle, lunge-line, no, use two lunge-lines today. That would do it. That would do it all right.

The little mare watched him approach, her head over the half-door. Was she pleased to see him? Disappointed? Quite indifferent? Dogs always give themselves away, and to any one who will have them. A horse never does. And what is true of horses is doubly true of mares.

He thought of Trev, his old gelding, no walking phallus. Tough and strong and decent and just the slightest bit of a sod. She was no sod, this mare. Whatever she was, she was not that. Submitting to his grooming with good grace, he knocking off the mud from the field, time to get her clipped out and rugged up. Brushed her down: but gently, not too vigorously, she did not like that. She accepted the bridle, which held not the pelham used by Kath, but one of Trev's old snaffles, a much kinder bit, and she had lunged happily enough in it. And happy enough under a saddle too, another bridge crossed. He had nowhere else to go now. Except forward, of course.

'You won't actually kill me today, will you, darling?' he asked her.

'Good God. I know those boots. Any one would think you were going to ride a horse, or something.'

'Mel.' Odd to meet the love of your boyhood when wearing the clothes of your boyhood. In those very boots, in those very jods, shoved down impatiently to his knees – but hush. Enough of that. Kissed though lightly her mouth – well, how else should they greet? 'Come, darling.'

And he led the conker-brown mare from her box, and she walked with him unhesitatingly to the school. Mel switched on the lights, and watched as he fastened the lunge-lines, one to each ring of the snaffle, the far line passing along her body and under her tail. He did not trouble with a whip: the mare had no need of one, and besides, he had enough to do with the two reins, for all that his hands were relearning their long-unpractised tasks of horsemanship.

And she trotted her circles willingly, rather showily, in truth. He brought her to walk, halt and back again with a touch on the lines, and then worked her in the opposite direction, changing the rein, rather clumsily, and repeated.

'She's listening.'

'Yes.'

'Nice paces. Gets off the ground a bit.'

'Doesn't she?'

Mel watched a few minutes longer. Then: 'I haven't actually got all night, you know.'

'Nor has she. You're right. Let's go.'

He halted the mare, and Mel came to take her, removing the lunge-lines, unknotting the reins, speaking kindly. Mark walked to the corner of the school and swapped his green cord cap for his jockey's skullcap, rusty black silk worn slightly high in front, the peak turned up. Very dashing, that.

The mare was walking happily enough with Mel. They turned and approached him, the mare moving with that huge elastic extended stride that was so disconcerting in her.

Mark went up to them both without fuss. Quietly patted. The most normal thing in the world. Only the most absolutely and totally momentous event in the history of the world, that's all. But don't tell her that. Let her think it's nothing special. It means nothing: only everything.

Mel held her head. Mark put his left foot into the iron and in a single clean movement, mounted. Alighted: a passionate butterfly. Squeezed with his legs: go forward, go forward, please go forward, please don't go up.

Mel first leading, then dropping her hold and walking alongside and then letting the mare walk away from her. And almost without her realising, she and Mark were on their own. Away, together, free. 'All right, darling. Just us, now.' He walked a circle, changed the rein, walked another.

Forward into halt, as his riding teacher had always said, or rather bellowed. Make much of horse. And Mark made very much indeed, and slipped his feet from the irons and leapt lightly to the ground.

'You,' he said, 'are an angel. You are a beautiful girl.'

'And me?'

'Oh yes, you too, quite definitely. Thanks, Mel.'

'Now it all begins.'

She had not stood up, she had not reared. She had, in short, trusted. Having been trusted. And this was not nothing. It was certainly more than enough for now.

Mel watched him as he untacked, fed extra strong mints. She was wearing black jods that looked like faded jeans; they showed her every bone and muscle. Hair black, tied behind her neck. Eyebrows black, unironical. 'Good start.'

'It's that all right.'

'What's the plan, Mark? What are you aiming her at?'

'Whatever she wants. It will make itself clear, I'm sure.'

'I mean, are you going to compete her? You're not just going to mess about?'

'I can't say, Mel. How can I? It's up to her, isn't it? Competing may just bring all her troubles back again. If she just wants to be a merry old hack, that would be good enough. Wouldn't it, darling? Just charge about the countryside and not give a fuck for anyone. I don't mind that.'

Mel laughed. 'You've changed such a lot. You used to be so impatient with Trev. Always the next event, the next plan, the next goal. So ambitious.'

'Trev was that kind of horse. Driving and impatient himself. It's the horse that makes you the kind of horseman you are.'

'I don't think that's true. You're so tolerant of failings, now. I mean this mare, she's pretty hopeless in her way, aren't you, dear? But you really don't mind. If you can turn her from something hopeless into something you can just about live with, you'll be satisfied, won't you?'

'Oh yes.'

'Remember when you used to tell me about all your plans for life? How you were going to be a famous poet and a champion rider? Now you're a schoolteacher who has deliberately chosen a hopeless little horse. Retreat from perfectionism, is that it?' The eyebrow was ironical again.

'How can I have been seeking perfection? I wanted to marry you, didn't I?'

She laughed out loud at that. 'You nasty bastard. Anyway, you never said so.'

'Didn't I? Perhaps I should have done.'

'Wouldn't have done you any good. I was seeking perfection myself in those days. Still am.'

'And Ed is going to be a dressage champion?'

Eyes flashed briefly. 'Going to be bloody good.'

Walking affectionately close, but not touching, back towards the tack-room. A cup of instant coffee, Mark thought. Good. But then home, damn it, home damn it, home.

17

A pile of books hit the table and then, only slightly more gently, a cappuccino. 'But what,' said the intruder, 'is beauty?'

Morgan's face, candlelit. 'Last time I saw you, you proved to me that you didn't exist,' Mark said. 'I was more than happy with that.' It was an acquaintance of his, a person normally known as Philosophy Dick, disturbing the calm of the Café des Amis.

'But I want to know about beauty,' he said, pushing his face forward. Lean, bearded, convinced he possessed that queer thing, genius.

'If you mean will I furnish you a definition of beauty, then I find you meaningless. If you mean "what is beautiful?", then if you don't know, I can't tell you.'

Dick placed his chin on his hand and gazed at Mark for a while. Then he looked briefly through the pile of books that Mark had brought to the table himself. Then he drank some of his coffee. 'You were wrong about art,' he said eventually.

'What did I say?'

'I can't remember. I made a point of forgetting. I mean, you were wrong in thinking that art had any importance.'

'You have proof of this, of course.'

'Naturally. You know that book you told me to get? *The Penguin Book of English Verse*? Well, I got it. Read it last night, actually.'

'You did what?' Only 400-odd pages of solid poetry from Thomas Wyatt to Dylan Thomas.

'Read it in a sitting. Quite interesting, really, isn't it? Dropped some speed. Went through it quite carefully. I thought it had quite a lot of interesting stuff in it. But I could see that you're wrong. I mean, it's all rather a lot of fuss about not very much, isn't it?'

'Much of the world shares your opinion. Rather vulgar point of view, really.' Mark was cautiously pleased with that. 15-love.

Dick was a person with a quite outstanding gift for table football. That was the key to the way his mind, to use the term loosely, operated. 'I've taken a vow of celibacy,' he said.

'Oh good. Many would offer you every encouragement, and most of them female.' 30-love.

'Trouble is, I've already broken it.'

'Callow boasting.'

'I'm really cut up about it, actually.'

'Anybody I know? Perhaps I ought to go and commiserate with her.'

'Shouldn't think so. First-year Philosophy student.'

'You disgusting cradle snatcher.'

'She frightened the piss out of me, actually.'

'Very frightening things altogether, these women.'

'I mean, she wore a coat made out of dead zebras. And that was too much, you know what I mean?'

'Christ. Jesus.'

'That's what I thought.' He took a final swallow of coffee. 'Look, I must love you and leave you.' Dick always said this. 'I think I'll go to bed now.' He gathered his books together and left Mark alone with his horror.

Until that moment he had fancied himself – no, until that moment he had really been a man in the midst of an idyll. The two or three weeks that had passed since his trip to the seaside had left him entranced, enchanted, bewitched. He was lover and, in some mystifying fashion, beloved.

The eighteen-hour kiss had come at 7.15 on Monday morning, and to claim it, Mark had risen earlier than he had ever risen in the history of the world. He found her awake, clad, made-up, composed, discomposing. They kissed, drank coffee, talked, fell into a half-doze, fully clad, in each other's arms, on her slender hall-of-residence would-be-chastity-enforcing bed.

It was agreed that a twelve-hour kiss must follow. He arrived at her room at 7.15 in the evening to claim it. It was given and received in calm. She had work to do that night. No, supper was a bad idea. But a six-hour kiss? 'There seems,' she said, 'to be no escape.'

And so, at 1.15 in the morning, he crept up the stair of her hall of residence, tiptoed into the darkened communal area, past the doors leading off, doors that presumably contained, and presumably separately, Sexuella and Bosomina in blameless slumbers. The animal man came slinking through the night to claim his prey. How would he find her? Fully clad, resisting, protesting? Naked, in hitherto unrevealed lasciviousness?

He did not knock, but eased the door softly open. She slept, a single fat candle guttering at her side, face gentle in the flame's soft light, sinister Rembrandt chiaroscuro in the hollows of her face. Warm light on warm shoulder above the sheet.

Eyes opening unsurprised. A smile, very faint, very deep. 'You come,' she said, 'most carefully upon your hour.'

'It is now struck twelve. Get thee to bed.'

'For this relief much thanks,' she said. A moment's pause. 'I'll not say the next line.'

'No,' he agreed.

'All the same, a fine time to pay social calls.'

'Methinks the lady doth protest too much.'

He was sitting beside her on the bed, just above the crook of her knees, looking at her softened face beneath him. For answer she sat up, allowing the sheet to fall from her. She was, she was. He claimed his kiss.

'Thank you,' she said. Afterwards. Afterwards: the best word, Mark thought, in the dictionary, and sleepily pondered a winsome poem. 'That really was the perfect seduction,' she said. 'I adored every second.'

'I endeavour to give satisfaction.'

'I'm talking about seduction, not cockcraft. Stop preening yourself.'

'I know perfectly well what you are talking about. I always do. That's why I'm here, isn't it?'

'Perhaps you do. Perhaps it is.' She thought about this for a while. 'All the same, I think I prefer to be sphinx-like. I like to keep people worried.'

'Have no fears on that score. You keep me worried all right.'

'Do I, Mark? I'm so glad. Do I mean that? I wonder. What really worries you? Are you worried that I am trifling with you? Or are you worried that I'm going to insist on marrying you?'

'Both,' Mark said. Mark's reply was merely glib. That his remark was essentially the truth was still hidden from him.

Later, quite a good bit later, she said: 'You don't mind my tits being too small?'

'Too small for what?'

'You know.'

'Morgan, I adore every cubic inch of you.'

'Do you really?'

'Can you ignore the evidence?'

'Even when presented in cliché form?'

They did not ignore the evidence.

And so it began, and so it continued. In slow motion, and not without pauses. A lunch here, a walk there, and, sometimes, a night. The obsessions of love were played in a minor key: it suited the subject, after all. It was an idyllic love affair, and it was her kind of idyll. Mark was quite unaware of the fact that he was playing entirely to her rules. It was as if they had become his rules, as if it was his kind of idyll.

Until now. Mark pondered his options, as he sat before his empty coffee cup. A jealous scene? But he knew the answer to that one already. I gave you no promises, Little Worthless. She occasionally called him that fond name, because of her current obsession with Kipling's stories for children.

Leave her for good, then? Nice double entendre, anyway. A very good idea. But it struck a note of pure terror. Mark preferred words like reluctance, or disinclination: but the mot juste was terror. No, he told himself: leaving her was not quite within the realms of possibility. To be struck dumb? That was the right sort of idea. Then she'd be sorry. To kill Philosophy Dick, then put his own head in the gas oven? That was the best idea yet. That would have the right sort of impact.

86

'You still here?'

It was his potential murder victim. 'I thought you'd gone to bed.'

'Just wondering if the zebra chick was in here.'

'I thought you'd sworn off her.'

'I just bumped into another philosopher. Not as profound a thinker as me, of course.'

He waited for a moment, inviting comment. Mark quoted from *The Second Jungle Book*.

> 'In August was the Jackal born;
> The Rains fell in September;
> "Now such a fearful flood as this,"
> Says he, "I can't remember."'

Philosophy Dick ignored him. 'And I told him about my vow of celibacy and the zebra chick.'

'Yes.'

'Well, I lead a very sheltered life, you know. It turns out that the zebra chick has been sleeping with my ethics tutor all term.'

Mark found that he was unable to speak. Game, set, and match.

And championship. 'So I want to see her. I want to know what he's like in bed.'

18

She had brought him to despair. The principle problem was hiding the evidence. He had it in his left hand; the thing to do was to sneak it into a rubbish bag and get home before anybody noticed. The fact of the matter was that he had staked his entire ability to deal with life on this one frail and impossible thing, and she had let him down. And still the nagging, unadmitted thought: it was he that had done the letting down.

All sense of balance had gone, nice double entendre. Why had he done this thing? Why had it begun? Why had he fooled himself? How could he ever have thought he was good enough? She had brought him close to a howling storm of tears, closer than any of the other events of the past few unpleasant weeks.

Perhaps it would be better next time. But he had thought this for a week and more, and each time it was worse. He was making it worse. He was making her worse. Now look at the ridiculous state of you.

But nobody about, was there? Thank God for that, anyway. He shoved the door open and there was Mel taking her clothes off. Damn it, damn, it, damn it. 'Hi, Mel.'

'Hello.' She placed her skirt on the chairback, carefully, sat and pulled on her jods, the faded black denim-type jods. Stood, zipped. 'How's madam?'

Mark stood before her, saddle over left forearm, bridle hanging from his left shoulder, hard hat shoved onto the back of his head. Evidence concealed behind his thigh. 'Bit of a problem.'

Her head, bowed over her black boot, looked up at him, concern, unironical, in her eyes. 'Lame?'

'Worse than that.'

'She's not standing up again?'

'It's worse than that too, in a way. She's gone off me. In a big way. Gone sour.'

She pulled on her second boot, stood. Unbuttoned her dark shirt, turned from him as she removed it, hung it on a hanger. Black bra. How slim she still was. How hard her stomach no doubt still was. Red T-shirt, over her head. She turned back to him. 'Tell me.'

Black sweatshirt again; red fleece over that. Grooming kit in her right hand, bridle over left shoulder, saddle over left forearm. Turned, examined him carefully, as he stood chastened before her. 'Was that your new schooling whip.'

'It was.'

She laughed, though mostly kindly. 'Oh, poor old Mark. Remember with Trev that time? When you hurled your whip into the field? Never did find it, did you?'

'It was either that or beating the crap out of a horse. And neither of them actually deserved it.' Embarrassed, he took the broken whip from behind his thigh and shoved it into the paper sack for rubbish that leant against the wall. He had snapped it into four pieces with two sharp, hard movements.

'Expensive in whips.'

'The other way can be expensive in horses.'

'You didn't hit her?'

'She didn't do anything wrong. It's me. I can't ride her.' He had sat in the saddle, tears of frustration pricking at his eyes. And had suddenly dropped the reins and lifted the long, slender whip and carefully, almost pedantically destroyed it. 'Mel, I don't think I can ride any more. I think I've lost it. Lost the feeling, lost the touch. I just can't get it right. I can't *think* right.'

They walked together to the boxes and Mel, silent, placed the saddle on the top of Ed's door and suspended the bridle from its cantle. 'Hello there, my handsome lad. Out you come. Here's your head collar. Let's get your rug off. What's she doing?'

'Resisting. I mean, really resisting. Resisting everything. Sticking her nose up in the air. Blocking me off with her mouth, on both sides. Obedient – I mean, she goes where I ask her to, makes her transitions. But always as if she had a couple of dead rats hanging from her martingale.'

'What a big stone. Good boy. How long have you been riding her in the school?'

'A couple of weeks, when she was going sweetly. Then all this week, it's gone wrong.' He felt the hint of tears again at this avowal, a shake in his voice that never quite manifested itself.

Mel brushed away at her horse, sleek, black, recently clipped. Absorbed in him. Cleaned her brush with the metal currycomb, then began grooming on the far side from Mark. All in silence, as if she had forgotten he was there. Then she spoke. 'She needs to get out.'

'Christ, I daren't risk that yet, Mel. She'll stand up, I know she will. As soon as she gets worried, she'll be up.'

'So what if she does? You'll cope. Look, I'll come with you. Saturday morning. Come for a nice hack with me and Ed. She needs a bit of fun, your girl. She's supposed to be a good fun horse and you're not giving her any. You're not letting her be herself. She needs to muck about, she needs a bit of play.' She fitted the bridle, the saddle, led Ed out.

'You mean love is not enough?'

She laughed at this, as she was supposed to. 'Love is only the starting point. Leg me up.' She used often to demand this small service back in the days of Trev and the hay-barn: a tease, a token of intimacy. She turned to her horse, bent a slim left leg at the knee. Mark took ankle and knee, and, as if she weighed nothing, she flew to the back of her horse, alighting like a passionate butterfly. And rode away.

19

They had no secrets. 'Are you still involved with her? Or not?'

'Mel, I wish I knew. I mean, obviously I'm involved. But I don't know what kind of involvement.'

'You mean you're involved but you don't know if she is?'

'Oh, she's involved all right, in her way. But I have no idea whether or not we are . . .'

'We're what?'

'It's a mot juste situation.'

'Don't know if you're going out together? Don't know if you're still sleeping together? Don't know if you're having an ongoing relationship?'

'Well, I suppose we might go out again. And I suppose we might stay in, too. We certainly relate to each other, in a strange sort of way, that's the problem. I mean it's not a one-sided thing, not exactly, anyway. We can't help but have a relationship. So it can't help but ongo.'

'But not as a relationship with a capital R?'

'And when it comes to sleeping together, perhaps we will do that again. I mean, she does rather tend to sleep with people. Even me.'

'But not on an exclusive basis? Or even semi-exclusive?'

'I'm sorry, she says. I didn't really mean to sleep with him. I was rather cross about it. I'd much rather sleep with you.'

There was a pause in honour of this. Mark stared at the ceiling. Then Mel said: 'But aren't you fearfully jealous? I remember that dreadful row we had after I snogged that –'

'Oh God, that prat, public school hunting type –'

'Piers, his name was. Quite a dish, as I recall.'

'No taste, you.'

'Precisely what every one had been telling me for the previous year.'

Mark lightly punched her soft shoulder to punish her for this tease. 'But no, I only really felt appallingly jealous once, and then not for terribly long. I don't want to go out and kill her, or them; I don't go about racked by doubt, obsessed by the thought of them writhing about together.'

'But you've given it a lot of thought, all the same.'

'True. But I don't deeply mind, in some ways. I just wish it didn't happen. Not because I can't bear her to be with someone else, but because I want her to be with me. I want her to want to be with me.'

'You haven't tried chasing other women and getting your revenge?'

'I haven't really had time to think of anybody else.' He laughed suddenly at this really rather terrible impertinence. 'If you see what I mean.'

'I see what you mean all right, you bastard. But you're not going to go and see her over the holidays?'

'I don't suppose so. She was staying on for a few extra days to do some work, and I assume that entails sleeping with her unethical ethics tutor. And then she was going to London. I don't know what that entails. Or who.'

'Perhaps she'll call you. If nothing better turns up under the Christmas tree.'

'Perhaps she will.'

'And you'd go running?'

'Oh yes.'

She touched his face with her fingertips, really rather tenderly. 'Mark, has it struck you that you are playing your hand really rather badly? That you are making it quite appallingly obvious that you love her a great deal more than she loves you?'

'I know, I know. I know what it looks like. But it would be totally wrong of me to play it any other way. It's what she really wants. Or needs, even. Because I sometimes get the dizzying feeling that – well, how shall I put it? That I am the real love of her life.'

This was a lie. It was the first time Mark had ever formulated the thought in words. Even as he spoke them, he thought he was indulging in a more than usually dangerous form of self-deception. 'I sometimes think that we are somehow stuck together. And all that sleeping with other people is merely a pathetic attempt to escape her inevitable destiny.'

Mel turned round, propped herself on one elbow, and looked down at him smiling, one eyebrow slightly curled. 'You know something? You're hopeless. Completely and utterly hopeless. She's clearly impossible, you're completely impossible, the whole thing's impossible.'

'Oh, I know that.'

'And stop looking sad or I'll beat you up.'

An ancient threat, one usually followed by action. 'I'd like to see you try,' he said, as their tradition demanded.

'Oh yeah?'

'Yeah.'

She leapt at him with fists flying, and he seized her as she punched, and for long and splendid moments they struggled gloriously. 'Jesus, is that your parents' car?'

'Christ.'

They dressed with desperate haste, flying and fumbling fingers, sudden terror giving way to shared and giggling delight. A door opened below them. They pulled the covers of her small bed together. A brief flying kiss, tongues and all and they were brother and sister again. 'Mum?'

20

She was nowhere to be seen, of course. Mark closed the door with more emphasis than was strictly necessary and dumped his bag beside the knotted banister, where it fell with a heavy thump of great art. He most especially did not wish to be alone.

'Mark?'

So he went upstairs to find her. He was not, in fact, greatly mollified.

She kindly laid her book aside when he entered – *The Magician's Nephew*, always a favourite when at a lowish ebb – and smiled kindly enough. He lowered the lid of the lavatory seat and sat on it.

'Why so late?'

'Told you. Staff meeting.'

'And have you eaten?'

'No.'

She examined him thoughtfully. 'Why so curt and clipped and generally out of sorts with the world and your wife?'

Mark put his elbows on his knees and his hands under his ears and observed her for a while, not without appreciation.

'A bad day? A bad meeting? Problems with Prince Myshkin?' This last being the headmaster.

Mark had not intended to tell her: it went too deep, and besides, she wouldn't understand. But the words blurted themselves out, beyond his control. And as they began to do so, he knew she'd laugh. 'I got ketchup-bombed.'

She laughed. 'Oh Mark, I'm so sorry.'

Well of course, she wouldn't understand, how could she? Shouldn't have brought it up. 'Never mind. Forget it.' He got up.

94

'Are your clothes ruined? Good job you don't wear five-hundred-pound suits to work.' She was consumed with quiet merriment.

'It wasn't a direct hit. Glancing blow. Bit of splashback.'

'Could have been worse, then.'

'No it couldn't have been bloody well worse.' Mark had seized the door handle.

'Oh Mark. Do tell.' She still made no move towards him, lying back at ease but her face softened and Mark felt his own mood soften. 'Why is it so dreadful, Mark?'

He looked down at her for a moment, and then sat down again. 'Morgan, you won't understand. It's a teacher thing, you see. But – well, I was one of the few that hadn't been bombed, and I fancied it was because I am one of the better teachers around. Both liked and respected by the kids, you see? Unlike the other idiots. I'm not the sort they would consider dropping a ketchup bomb on. And – well, the little bastards did it, and I'm just the same as all the other poor sods. The poor sods I'd been slightly despising ever since the bombing began. And I feel so bloody dreadful, Morgan, I feel so bloody dreadful.'

She got to her feet, and stepped over to him, kissed him lightly on the lips, and turned to take a towel. 'Wash the stains of ketchup from your body while I find something to wash the stains of ketchup from your soul,' she said. And was gone.

Mark obediently removed his clothes and stepped into the bath, adding hot water. Almost at once he heard the front door slam. Now what? Now where was she off to?

He read up to where Polly disappears without so much as a puff of smoke, and then he got out and dried himself and put on a dressing gown. And there was the front door opening, and there was Morgan with a pair of bags, wearing her famous spy's mac, buttoned up to the neck.

'I have a thing for thee,' she said.

'Will I like it?'

'Hot and sour soup from the Chinese takeaway. Cold beer.'

Mark was touched to the bottom of his soul.

She decanted the soup from the Styrofoam container into a bowl for him while he poured beer into a glass. Both were excellent and took up his attention. It was only when he had all but finished that he thought to ask her why she was still wearing her famous spy's mac.

'I was in a hurry.'

And he began to guess and to laugh.

21

Joybells rang out over Hertfordshire. 'Happy Christmas to a trio of Browns.'

'Happy Christmas, Ashton,' Mark said. 'Poky little sermon, that.'

'*Flatt*erer. You say that to *all* the girls.'

'I thought it dangerously close to Pelagianism myself,' said The Mate. 'But it is the season in which we must allow you to be a man of goodwill. So happy Christmas, Canon.'

'Happy Christmas, Doctor.'

They did not kiss, or shake hands. Barely smiled. It was a moment of quite startling intimacy. Bec did not speak. She had not sung the hymns, nor joined in the responses.

They walked the short distance from the church to the house that was more like a vicarage than the vicarage. Light frost was already visible on the windows of the cars parked outside the church, the midnight air unforgiving.

'Troublesomes?' Mark asked as they removed their coats in the hall.

'Darling, that would be heavenly.'

Mark went to the kitchen, switched on the kettle and took three glasses. Added to each honey, a modest amount; lemon juice, ditto; whisky immodest, unditto. In each a spoon, to prevent the cracking of the glass. Poured hot water, and stirred each with a vigorous clank, a percussion trio. It was a ceremony his father had once performed, though as a quartet, on just such high days and holy days: the Easter Vigil, the First Marce of Christmas. A family drink: Troublesome Whisky.

They toasted each other, Happy Christmas, and all drank. Then Bec raised her glass again: 'To Dad,' she said.

'Oh darling, absent friends, absent friends.' Mark's mother raised her glass and then lowered it without drinking, her eyes pricking with tears. Mark, within range, stretched from his chair to pat her hand. She smiled at him and said: 'How he used to complain about making the Troublesomes.'

'Waste of time,' Mark said, a fair approximation of his father's voice. 'Waste of good whisky. Ridiculous drink.'

'But he always drank it,' Bec said.

'Always made it for me. Always complained. Always in the same words.' His mother drank, a good slug this time. She smiled at her son, her daughter. 'I can feel it doing me good.'

The previous Christmas had been full of tears and grief and reopened wounds. But now there was at least a sense of routine, or ritual, to their loss.

The Mate went to bed after finishing her drink. Mark and Bec sat up over one more, a nontroublesome whisky. It was the first time they had been able to speak alone since Mark had returned. Bec was still living with her mother. She spoke of her work on the local paper, and its pleasures, her promotion to chief reporter, a surprise and against precedent, because she was still a junior, her affair with the news editor. She was now doing a good deal of work for the national papers as a sideline, one that sometimes earned her more than her salary. She was busy, fulfilled, happy: and grieving still.

'You must get out of this house,' Mark told her. 'Why don't you move in with what's his name – Pete?'

'Nah. He's awfully sweet. But it's not the right thing to do. It's not going to last for ever. He's a small-timer. At heart he's a Provo.'

Mark knew that she meant a person from the provincial press. 'So you'll have to go to London.'

'My indentures aren't up for another three months. Then there's the question of getting a job.'

'A smart girl like you doesn't need a job. You just need an address in London. Work'll come.'

'You mean freelance?'

'I suppose I do. Why not?'

'Because it's bloody frightening, that's why not. I haven't dared think about it. Not out loud. But, Markie, I do believe you're right. I bet I could do it. I bet I could – you little problem-solver, you.' She sipped whisky, looking pleased, and Mark was deeply pleased at pleasing her. 'But what about your brilliant career, Markie? When's the next book of poetry? What's the next big step?'

'I think I've done poetry, Bec. I haven't written a poem all term. But – promise not to laugh? I'm thinking quite hard about teaching.'

She did not laugh. Instead, she looked amazed. 'I thought I was the one who couldn't handle grief.'

'Dad would be pleased, I know.'

'I think he had higher hopes for you.'

'Only when The Mate was listening. He had to toe the party line, then. Had to go along with the idea that teaching was a second-best sort of thing. That teaching was like being a Provo. An admission that you had a second-class mind. But once or twice –' once only, Mark knew, but the occasion was an immense one, and he didn't think he could tell it without tears. It had been one of those rare pivotal moments: a point at which his life had swung effortlessly in an altogether unexpected direction. He had only just begun to realise it, over the past fortnight. It had happened in the White Horse, the man-to-man pints before he set off on his conquest of Europe, and the talk all of the future. And his father had, quite uncharacteristically, talked of vocation, and belief, '– once or twice, he talked to me about teaching, and how he believed that teachers were – well, important. He didn't put it in those terms, because he wasn't the sort to, and anyway, it would have been a declaration of hostility to The Mate. But he was telling me what he believed. Telling me he never lost his faith.' And there were tears, of course, but just a couple.

'And you feel the same thing?' Bec asked this almost tenderly.

'I think I might get to feel it. I think I ought to give it a try.'

'Just to spite The Mate?'

'Do you think it will upset her? She must have given up hope. She can't really still see me as an international lawyer with a double first from Oxford.'

'People don't, you know. Give up hope. Not if they are given to hoping.'

'Perhaps I should prepare for trouble.'

'Always.' She had not yet taken to vigorous smoking, but she already wore her hair in its narrow Gothic arch. She shook this for a moment, to reveal a little more of her face than was normally permitted, and laughed. Kindly, but laughed.

She gave him some records he wanted; his mother gave him a cashmere sweater he did not: V-necked, infinitely soft, pale yellow, generously made, reaching his thighs. It was a jumper for the person she wished him to become. He gave her a facsimile edition of the *Strand Magazine* printing of the Sherlock Holmes stories, Sherlock Holmes being one of his mother's few literary self-indulgences. 'I adore to go slumming as a middle-brow,' she would say, in these moments of relaxation. She said this when she opened her present, as Mark knew she would. For Bec he had found a hardback edition of *Scoop*. Both gifts had gone down rather well.

They breakfasted very late – the term brunch was not permitted – on devilled kidneys and the drink his father used to call Fuck's Bizz. 'Jamie, must you really behave so nouveau?' 'Mais je suis bien nouveau, my love.' 'Then you should attempt to conceal the fact.' Mark cooked the kidneys. He also cooked the Christmas dinner, which they had for dinner, The Mate being punctilious about such terms. I prefer to dine, she always said, at dinner-time. Besides, Ashton was unable to come at lunch-time, having parochial duties until the evening.

So Mark cooked turkey and chestnut stuffing, though he drew the line at bloody sprouts. Ashton was generous in his praise, as well he might be. The claret they drank tasted like stewed pennies, as if Ashton had gone to considerable trouble to achieve the impossible and find an alcoholic drink that Mark could not drink. If so, he failed, but it was a close-run thing. After pudding (Bec did a salad of tropical fruit) they settled to the Cheese

100

Stage which was really the Port Stage and drank heavenly cough mixture.

'Are you happy, Doctor, with your children all around you?'

'I am, Canon. Busy people, but they give me this week, do you not, my darlings?'

'Oh yes,' Mark said recklessly. And passed the port.

On Boxing Day, they went for a walk in the afternoon. They always did. They took the loop through the wood that took them to the dead-straight way along the disused railway embankment. Two or three times, they were passed by horses, Mark running an absent-minded appraising eye over the beasts and their riders. He thought of Mel, on her own long ride on this traditionally horsey day.

'I'm so glad you got rid of that horse,' his mother said.

'Just the day when I get a pang for old Trev. Mel says he's still going a treat for his new owner. The woman we sold him to.'

'Horses, darling. So mindless.'

'Horses have minds all right. Just a different sort.'

'Well, then. Escapism. Escape from real life.'

'Horses are real all right. Horses are life.'

But she smiled at this conceit, knowing that Mark spoke idly; with nothing more than agreeable nostalgia. 'Schupid nonsense,' she said. 'I'm still glad you gave them up.'

'Ah, it was great. I'll never go back to it. But it was great at the time, and I wouldn't want to change any of that.'

The Mate was a tireless walker, and they covered a good deal of ground. They did not get back till the winter light was almost gone. Bec made tea (his mother insisted on Earl Grey, which Mark, disliking, drank without comment) and ate toast with the dripping Mark had saved from the turkey: great chunks of black jelly and a good twist of sea salt.

'So nice,' his mother said, 'to be all together.'

'He's a silly old sod,' his sister said. 'But it's good to have him back for a while.'

The telephone rang out, very unexpectedly. But perhaps it was Ashton: Mark's mother plucked up the phone that lay within reach of her favourite winged chair. She spoke briefly, and then held the receiver at arm's length, as if it were a dead rat. 'It appears,' she said, not covering the mouthpiece, 'to be for you.'

Mark was rather taken aback. Callum? 'Who is it?'

'I have absolutely no idea,' The Mate enunciated clearly. 'A female person.'

Oh God. 'I'll take it in the hall.'

Mark returned to his family a few moments later. 'I'm terribly sorry, everyone,' he said. 'But I have to go to London.'

'Oh darling.' His mother's eyes filled with tears. 'Darling, surely not now?'

'Markie,' said Bec. 'Must you?'

'Sorry. Sorry, everyone. But yes. I really must.'

'Must it be today, darling? Can't we have Boxing Day together? There'll not be a train, you know. Oh, Mark, do stay.'

'Sorry. No, I know, I'll hitch. Look, I'm really sorry about this. But I have to go.'

'But, Mark –'

'He's going, Mother. Don't bother arguing. Look at him. The poor boy's in love.'

'Oh, Mark, are you really? What a pit-pit.'

'Perhaps she's nice and you'll like her,' Bec suggested.

Mark laughed, surprising himself. 'She's not really terribly nice, no.'

He threw things into a bag – records, new jumper, clothes, toothbrush. Kissed the two women – Bec whispered 'Good luck, Markie' – and set off at an extended, elasticised walk towards the roundabout, where he could hitch a lift along the A1. He might even be there within the hour. What had he done to his family? Oh dear. What a hideous ghastly mess he had made of things. What a pit-pit. He was filled with shame, remorse, hope. Shame, modest; remorse, ditto. Hope immodest, unditto.

22

'Thank God you're awake.'

Mark laid aside *Lord of the Flies*. 'What's up?'

'It's the devil. Oh God, it's the devil.' And she laughed in that special way she laughed when greatly moved.

'What happened?'

'He flies away in a helicopter with the blonde.'

'That's all right, then. I had every confidence in him.'

'And the priest is left hanging by his neck from the mast.'

'The priest who is the devil?'

'And he says something like, well, we got away with it, then. And she smiles at him, and oh, Mark –'

Mark, laughing himself now, asked what happened.

'She smiles. Sort of like this.' And she smiled at him winsomely, and the smile broadened millimetre by millimetre, gradually showing more and more teeth, and broadened and broadened and widened and widened, and Mark felt a prickle at the back of his neck, and his shoulders twitched in a half-shiver.

'My God, you are a terrifying woman.'

'I'm a terrified woman. And she says' – and her voice went low and guttural and sinister – 'No, not you. You're mine!'

'Yes?'

'And he looks back and it's not the blonde at all, it's the devil-priest who's beside him in the helicopter –'

'Oh God, and they cut back to the ship and it's not the priest hanging from the mast –'

'It's the blonde and, oh God, it was such a terrible movie, and it's got me terrified out of my mind.'

'Come here and be comforted.'

And she turned and smiled at him and the smile broadened millimetre by millimetre, gradually showing more and more teeth, and broadened and broadened and widened and widened and Mark had to look away while she laughed and laughed in her fear and took comfort in his terrified arms.

23

'Then you put the fabric softener in here, and close the drawer – do you really need to write this down?'

'I need certainties. Close the drawer, OK?'

'Then twirl the dial. Don't mess about, for your jeans and shirts and jocks and socks just put it on to programme three.'

'Programme three.'

'Pull the knob out and off it goes.'

'That's it?'

'That's it. Life really is that simple.'

'Morgan made it sound so complicated. Washing, I mean.'

'I know what you mean all right.'

She wouldn't trust him with her silks and her appliqués and her embroiderings. 'What about the drier?' Wouldn't trust him.

'Don't bother, you'll only shrink everything. Just hang 'em high. It's not as if you're short of space here. You do know how to iron?'

'There's no limit to my talents. You want a beer?'

'Of course I want a bloody beer, what do you think I'm here for, to help out a mate or something?' He took the can, snapped it open and sat down, placing his feet on the kitchen table. 'So now your kids will stop complaining that you're a tramp going through a midlife crisis.'

'Well, it'll do us all good if I make that fact less obvious.' Jim's speech for the prosecution, when they turned to *St Mawr* again: 'But it's pathetic, Mr Brown, these people falling in love with horses as an escape from real life. All that stuff about how perfect the horse is, it gets on your nerves, doesn't it? I mean, horses are not really that good, are they?'

And Jane saying, almost, murmuring: 'But the story's not about how good horses are, is it? It's about how bad relationships are.' And Mark had felt that terrible, wonderful, dangerous emotion: teacher's elation; that moment of that's-what-I'm-in-this-bloody-profession-for. He knew how to enjoy this, every teacher does. But he also knew how to guard against it; perhaps every good teacher does. Mark knew that he hadn't given her this insight himself. He hadn't made her sharp and clever and sometimes even wise, any more than he had made her pretty. All he did was to show her that it mattered. Being there. It was good enough just being there, sometimes. And poor Jim quite crestfallen. Jim, it is a very hard road you have to travel, if you have fallen for a woman that much better than you. 'Thanks, Cal.' Mark opening his own beer.

'Marianne looks a bit sultry in the kitchen,' Callum said, observing where Mark had rehung his gifts. Morgan, pebble-breasted, at least by comparison, irritated, shortly to submit to (or was it solicit?) his embraces, remained neatly pinned to the warp and woof of Islam.

'But it's not about how good pin-ups are,' Mark said.

'No. So how is the rest of the programme going? I still think that for out-and-out unabashed sublimation, there's nothing to beat a motorbike. A horse is nothing compared to that; it's the nearest you ever get to feeling like God.'

'Horses aren't a substitute for sex,' Mark said. 'They're a substitute for a relationship.'

Callum looked at him for a while. 'That doesn't sound like much fun.'

'Correction. It *is* a relationship.'

'As in uncritical love?'

'You're thinking of dogs. You want criticism, you get a crazy mare.'

'But in this relationship, you have the whip hand, right? Nice double entendre, Mark. And talking of nice double entendres, how about getting back into the saddle?'

'I thought I told you I'd been riding her for three weeks now.'

'I mean getting back into the saddle after a nasty fall.'

'I haven't fallen off.'

'Christ, I was right, the man's mad. I'm not talking about horses. I thought you were supposed to be the poet around here, but no, just another literal-minded –'

'Oh, women. Don't bother my head none about women.'

Which was a lie, of course. He considered the sexual possibilities of each and every woman he had dealings with – without intending any serious action, of course, almost as an academic exercise, but as something that added a certain zing to the day. Seeking not so much naked intimacies as the sudden crackle of static that cuts across a conversation. He would not have admitted as much to anyone, not even to Callum, but he had a mental league table of women, one based on an inflated and altogether unrealistic view of their or his possibilities. It was refreshing, he thought, to think of every single woman in sexual terms. Perhaps some men did this all the time, regardless of their domestic situation. It was an idea that obscurely distressed him.

He speculated on a chance meeting with Kath, at the Wagon and Horses. The significant looks over the beer, the car park embrace, the repairing to – well, too cold for tumbling in the hay, but that was the general idea. Jan showed no particular desire to have him for breakfast, or even for dinner at dinner-time. The promised drink with his deputy, Annette, had taken place, and they had talked long and earnestly of marriage and teaching and then marriage again. And she had gone home to her husband whom she loved. The crackle of static in the air.

'I keep waiting,' Callum said, 'for you to tell me that you've taken up with your old girlfriend again.'

Mark smiled involuntarily at the thought. Last Saturday morning, the heady pursuit, the chase and capture, the plunging bodies. 'Mel?' he said. The joy. 'Married and all that.'

'I'm not asking you to marry her.'

He remembered the last time they had shared a bed, rather than the last time they had made love. She was in a nasty bedsitter at the time, her husband, Tom, abandoned. She was in love, though not with Tom, or Mark. She had taken the bedsitter in order to make herself available to a sensitive troubled man who worked in the same clinic, an osteopath, and apparently a gifted one. 'A

107

healer, Mark, no other term will do. He makes me ashamed of my machines, and of the whole business of physiotherapy.' But he had a wife and four children, and was, she said, racked with guilt, a rack being one of the few machines Mel did not operate as part of physiotherapeutic routine. Oh, he was beautiful and gentle and kind, he loved her so much and he felt terrible about it. And she loved him and she felt terrible too. Nevertheless it was the best thing she had ever done in her life. She was sad but glad; did he understand that?

Mark understood all right. But he let her explain anyway, and it being around three in the morning by the time they had reached the end of her great love and his exquisite guilt, they had turned to the bed together and slept, as chastely as he had once slept at the seaside.

Morgan was away, of course, in New York. And throughout her month-long absence (visiting her mother, of course, but whom else did she visit? She would tell him, if he asked, but not unless. And he would never ask), he had spent much of his time with Mel, and a fair bit more with Tom. Go-betweening.

'You can't imagine,' Tom said, 'what it does to you. To think of the person you love. Embraced, you know. Bouncing about. But it's not that I can't bear the thought of them, er, making love. I can't bear to think of them laughing. Laughing with no clothes on, do you see what I mean? You understand the distinction I am making?'

'But I hate to hurt him,' Mel said. 'Just as *he* hates to hurt *his* family. It isn't as if there was any pleasure in it. Only love.' Sad, smug, utterly in love. A gone girl, as Morgan was to say.

'I tumbled a nurse the other day,' Tom said. Which was his right, really: after all, he was a doctor. 'It was absolutely brilliant.'

'I only want everyone to be happy,' said Mel. 'But I think all four people are doomed in their different ways, to unhappiness.'

'All eight,' Mark said, brutally: and made her eyes a little damp.

Coded enquiries were increasingly put to him during the go-betweening month. Who was cracking up? Who was in a position of strength? Did he mention me? Does she still think of me?

'Thing is, Mark, I'd sooner be unhappy with Mel than happy with anyone else.'

'But, Mark, why can't he say things like that to my face?'

'It's enough that he feels them.'

'You think I've been a stupid cow all along, don't you?'

'Yes.'

'Call her now, Tom. This is the moment.'

'Are you sure?'

'Yes.'

And Tom had done so. And before long, he and Mel had set up house together again, the guilt-laden bone-cracking father of four and the brilliant bouncing nurse abandoned. And Mark too.

Perhaps he reminded them of their sundering, rather than of their reunion. Perhaps they always meant to call him. But they never did, and they had ceased to meet. There had only been one meeting since that time, just the one, on that dreadful occasion of Morgan's Last Party. Until, after his own sundering, Mark had called Mel.

And there was no question of attempting yet another seduction of her, still less of succeeding. He was too much a part of her marriage to consider disrupting it. She was a living, much-embraced proof that marriage could work, even when garnished with betrayal. Or at least continue.

'Well,' he told Callum, 'the thing's not on.'

'I bet there's someone you've got your eye on all the same.'

Theresa. Sad, funny. Owner of Gus the Sod. Married, it seemed, to another sod. About whom she was seriously funny. Shorter than the women he was used to, different shape, being hippy and bosomy, overdose of womankind injected into jods. Rode nicely. They had taken to tack-room gossiping. One good thing about a livery yard, you get to meet plenty of women. She had, of late, taken to touching his forearm. When they parted. When she walked past him. And when she walked away, he wanted to touch, not her forearm. Wanted to hear her laughing, not at her own stories of various sods.

'Not really,' Mark said. 'Just all of womankind, really. You know, I don't think I realised before just how sexually attractive women are.'

'You never had much difficulty in falling for them.'

'That was in my selective period. I used to think that some women were more attractive than others. Now I've realised that the entire sex is the most exciting thing that ever happened in the history of the world. I mean, everywhere you look, there's women. I feel like an adolescent in a nudist colony, when I'm in the staff-room, at the livery yard, or in the pub. Admittedly all the women have their clothes on, but that hardly seems to matter. It's outrageous enough that they exist.'

Callum laughed, and then changed the tone by asking one of those questions of piercing directness, the kind that is just about permissible in those friendships of very early manhood, those passionate relationships in which every kind of intimacy is permissible save the physical. Later friendships lack this element entirely; early friendships that persist tend to lose it. But occasionally, in times of deep trouble, they can revert. And so Callum asked: 'Were you faithful to Morgan?'

'Er . . . more or less.'

Callum laughed. 'What the hell does that mean? Either you were or you weren't.'

'Once. And by once I mean once since we got married. Nothing like – well, you know.'

'Just for self-respect?'

'Not exactly.'

'Uncritical love?'

'Sort of . . . mindless viciousness, really. It's a bad memory. You know how the sexual element becomes . . . well, less important in a long-term relationship?'

'Nope.'

'What do you mean?'

'What the fuck do you think I mean?'

Mark laughed in sudden delight: delight at what, he was not quite sure. But all the same it was delightful. 'I suppose you're going to tell me that you've never been unfaithful?'

'I haven't. Since you ask. Not since the day Naz and I got together.' He looked rather disconcerted at the disclosures he had forced on himself. 'Haven't had time.'

110

'Is this the Islamic tradition of compelling fidelity through exhaustion? Or is it because you're so gorgeous and such a ram?'

Callum laughed again, partly in delight at his own wit. 'I don't give a fuck,' he said. 'Nice double entendre, eh?'

'Doesn't quite work.'

And Callum went home to his home, abode of bliss, leaving Mark to the very worst hour of the day. His nightly preference, each night rejected, was to make strong coffee and sit up late, anything to put off the bit when you lie down in the dark and think things through.

But she had gone well tonight, had she not? Schooled merrily and willingly and rather gorgeously forward. No whip had been broken. He schooled without one; didn't need it. The joys of Saturday still filled her.

Dodge the traffic, Mel had said. Ride away at eight. And Mark allowed himself to be persuaded, because the thought of the mare and the empty roads cheered him and wiped away a good deal of his fear. Fear – yes, he admitted the word. That made it easier, did it not? For he did not know what the mare in her madness would do, should she become seriously stressed in the traffic. He was filled with a great uncertainty, but then so was the mare.

Stealing through the sleeping town, just as he had when he went to claim his 7.15 kiss. Greeting Mel, co-conspirator of the morning, tacking up, and then Ed and the mare striding out boldly together, the mare peering at everything, but surely she was entitled to. They halted at a T-junction, and it was here that the worst happened. She stood. And Mark laughed and patted her, and she put her front feet back on the floor and carried on. Laughed? Patted? But this was not the bleak and terrified reaction of a horse half mad, a horse perplexed in the extreme, a horse in the middle of some kind of nervous breakdown. This half-stand was something quite different, he was sure of it: it was more a kind of engaging daftness. He felt no fear, none at all but then why should he when there was nothing to fear? She meant to harm. Her fear and her delight were very close things, but so they should be. Horses are designed to flee and for them, fear is a kind of pride, a kind of joy. That was the worst, and it was nothing. Nothing that mattered, anyway.

She was crazy all right, but she was not mad. And Mel had led them into a network of bridle paths, and Mark was dismayed that such lovely places could exist so close to London. Through the looking-glass: and the mare, who doubtless knew these places from her time with Kath, skipped and jogged and skittered, and Mark soothed and soothed without sternnesses.

A hill stretched ahead of them, the path along the edge of a ploughed field, and it was easily wide enough to ride two abreast. Mel turned, just in time to see the mare fling her head up in craziness. But not madness, and anyway, Mark half expected it, dodging nimbly to take the blow on his chest instead of his nose. She grinned, Ed beneath her already anticipating her, already looking to run: 'Come on, then.'

And eased Ed in a big, stretchy canter, and the mare followed as if she had been fired from a bow. A horse, Mark knew, has a fairly large brain and uses nearly all of it to co-ordinate its movements. It is in movement that a horse understands itself and the world; in movement the rider briefly touches that understanding and shares it.

And Mark, standing in the irons, head low, teeth in the mane, came charging alongside, and Ed, being male or half male and proud of his right of precedence, responded, and the mare, joy-filled, responded to his response, dropping her withers into a hard, flat gallop, and suddenly Ed was left behind and the world was all before them. 'Bear right!' Mel called. 'Start to pull up when you see the tree.'

And the path swept round the edge of the field, and still the mare galloped, and then a big oak tree, and Mark now standing erect, weight back, and the mare slowly coming back to a trot, a walk, and Ed alongside now, and both horses blowing and snorting and flinging their heads about in self-delight. 'Good lad. Good lad. Of course, *you'd* sooner be doing circles in a school and breaking whips.'

'Mel, you are always right. I just didn't think she was ready.' Patting and patting.

'You just needed to trust her. Did you have any control in that snaffle?'

'Not much, no.' An unremoveable grin, not self-delight, delight in the mare. 'Control is for wimps.'

The horses were walking now, Mel holding her reins by the buckle, so they looked like the long stroke of the letter D. The little mare would not walk on a loose rein, instead kept jogging off, and Mark corrected and let the reins out again, and again, and again, endlessly patient, relaxed, amused. And it seemed that the process relaxed her, in the way that the crazy but not mad mare would always relax. He understood her ten times better than he did half an hour ago.

'Mel?'

She turned sideways in the saddle, and beneath the brim of her black riding hat curled a black eyebrow at him. 'Well?'

'Do you think I could get her jumping again?'

Mel laughed outright. 'Some people are never satisfied.'

'Mel?'

'Yes?'

'Thanks.'

'Shut up. You know what your trouble is, don't you? You've forgotten the basic principle of life.'

'I thought that was my trouble. But I'm sure you're going to remind me.'

She looked down at him, Ed being a hand and more higher than his little mare. Smiled, knowing the real, solid power of her words. 'When in doubt, kick on.'

And Mark gave a great shout of laughter, and the mare hopped and turned her ears back at this foolish noise and Mark patted her and apologised to her, laughing still. How many times had they used this expression, one to the other? In what places? In pubs. At the start of cross-country, a spell to banish rather bad peritonitis. In the hay-barn.

Kicking on. Mark roamed restlessly around the vast house, its high ceilings, the floor-to-ceiling sash windows that overlooked the Islingtonian night. The Trafalgar balcony outside, peopled or godded with Indian gods and godlings made in plaster, bright-painted: a blue Krishna, a pink and merry Ganesh. On the wall of the big room, the gods of the Great Gangetic Maze. Where was she now? Who lay beneath her spell? And when would she tell him to leave their house, her house, her mother's house, a gift, an indefinite loan? Was she even in England? She had kicked on all right. Kicked over the traces. Traces being reins, of course.

Horsey terms lie fossilised in the daily speech of the world. A list of them unwound through his mind. Long in the tooth. Put him through his paces. Headstrong. Put his back up. Get the wind up. Fed up: a horse that has eaten too much and can't be ridden. Yes, fed up to the back teeth. Horses, not humans have back teeth: there is a gap between the front teeth and the back teeth, where you put the bit, called – what was it? – the diastema.

Rattling around this huge house, filled with treasures not his own. Brigitte, though. And Marianne. The scowl of the pebble-breasted one. When in doubt, kick on. Fed up to the back teeth.

24

'Don't look at me in that lustful fashion.'

'If I can't look at you in a lustful fashion now, when can I?'

'Don't do it. It's disgusting.'

'Besides, it's not lust. It's love.'

'No wonder I am disgusted.'

'What shall I do then?'

'Tell me a joke.'

Mark laughed at the absurdity of it, laughed with great delight. And of course obeyed. 'A horse walks into a bar –'

'And the barman says, "Why the long face?"'

'No, no, no, this is a different joke. It's got more foreplay.'

'Oh good. I don't want to miss out on any treats.'

'It's a white horse, you see, and he walks into the bar and the barman says: "Good evening, sir. What can I get you?" And the horse says: "I'll have a whisky, please." And the barman says: "What kind of whisky would you like, sir?" And the horse says: "Well, what kind of whisky have you got?" And the barman says: "Well, sir, we've got Famous Grouse and we've got Bell's and we've got Teacher's, and if you like Irish whiskey we've got Jameson, and we've got a range of malts, too. And also, we've got a kind of whisky that's named after you." And the horse says: "What? Eric?"'

And she laughed and laughed, laughed as if she would never stop, laughed and her tears flowed generously over her face and some fell onto his shoulder, and still she laughed and laughed and Mark laughed in delight at her delight, delighting in pleasing her so well, and wondered if there was any kind of eroticism in life that could possibly compare with the eroticism of married life.

25

He walked from Hampstead to Islington, but that was no great matter. The driver, rather sportingly, picked him up before he even reached the A1, and talked about plays. He had just seen a Pinter play called *Betrayal* and thought it perfect.

Mark was convinced that he did not usually stop for hitchhikers, but Boxing Day travel seemed to involve them in a shared conspiracy. 'It's all told backwards, you see,' he explained, before dropping Mark outside Belsize Park tube station, even going a little out of his way to do so.

Mark walked boldly on, savouring the privilege of having London to himself, the dark streets, the occasional thrum of car tyres. Tasted also the privilege of his destination. Fear and a kind of pride filled him.

It was walking into the square that shook him. He had known that Morgan was – well, not short of a bob or two, that was the way he had expressed it. But the houses shouted that she was *rich*. That was a different matter altogether. Money hardly seemed to matter in the rough-and-tumble of student life. It was no more than an intriguing affectation, like the time when Philosophy Dick, God damn and blast his rotten soul to hell, had shaved his head.

But he saw now that he had got it wrong. In misunderstanding the nature of money, he had entirely failed to understand Morgan herself. Money was a difference between people that went deep: marrow-deep, soul-deep. It was as if she were a different species of mammal. She was amusing herself with him, nothing more. Lady Chatterley playing with the hired help. Doctor tumbling a nurse. Slumming it. A holiday romance, seducing the waiter, the return half of her ticket safe in her pocket. She would go back to reality. No, he thought, in words often quoted by his mother in all sorts of odd contexts, here is no continuing city, here is no abiding stay.

Number 33. But he would have guessed that anyway, without need of numbering. A very great deal of the upper half of the door was taken up, not with a brass knocker but with a brass or brazen Celtic knot.

She would be hard with him, unsmiling. She would be naked, running to his embrace. She would be in bed with another. Not the unethical ethics tutor: no, yet another – young, rich, one of Morgan's kind.

Mark did not ring. Absurdly, he walked around the square again. Touch of peritonitis. Observers would assume he had missed the number in the dark. Or they would ring the police and complain that an insufficiently wealthy stranger was lurking suspiciously around their square. Really, this was not love. It was more like going to do your Part Ones. The only degree worth getting is a first or a third. No one who got a first ever made that remark, she had told him.

He was approaching the brazen knot again. Another circuit? No. That would be too much. He pressed the button. Unnervingly, no sound came. Rich people even have a different kind of doorbell.

'Mark?' After a long pause (she did not want him) the wall spoke: a parody of her voice.

'Yes.' A brilliant response, that. The door uttered a sharp clack and opened of its own volition. Not quite of his own volition, Mark walked through it.

'Mark. How pleasant to see you.'

Not naked. But apparently alone. A black garment, a little like a nun's habit, but with a rich panel of embroidery, most of it pink, that reached from the neck down to what fashion experts like Mark called the tits. Though to be fair, the garment did not permit the smallest hint of what lay beneath to be observed. Arab, he guessed, Bedouin, he learnt later. The fabric was thick, apparently a little like a gymslip in texture, and reached just above her ankles; her feet were bare. There was more pink embroidery at the cuffs, which were shoved back a little to reveal her wrists. Her ankles, her feet, her wrists: perhaps that was the way of Islam: you became a connoisseur of the anatomical fringes, pulse racing at the sight of a particularly neat ankle, the softness of an indiscreetly revealed inner wrist.

Not quite smiling. She had a way of merely relaxing the inexorability of her expression, that very slight widening of the rims of her eyes, a kind of coded tenderness, and it did more for Mark's pulse than even her neatly turned ankle, her soft inner wrist.

'Thank you for coming all this way.'

He smiled at her with a degree of affection that surprised him. 'You despise me a little for coming all this way.'

Again, and a little more, she softened her face for him. 'Only a tiny bit.'

'That's nice.'

'I despise myself rather more. I really wanted to see you. I even made Mother buy some beer. Several days ago. Hoping you would come. Wasn't that far-sighted of me?'

'There's a secret area of dangerous kindness in you, you know.'

'But I rise above it more often than not. Are you not going to kiss me?'

Somehow, he had not quite dared to embrace. He wanted a moment in which he could walk around her two or three times. But all the same, at her request, he took her, rather gingerly, in his arms. Kissed, aiming for the mouth. She responded to this with an altogether unexpected violence.

A moment later, drunk with his own daring, he seized the Bedouin garment by the hem with both hands, and raised it high above his head; and hers. Gracefully, she bowed into his pull, curving easily away from him. And now quite naked; and Mark, barring a few adjustments fully clad, tumultuously celebrated his arrival into the world of knots and mazes.

Afterwards, he sat alone on the sofa, goggling at the room. Morgan brought him a beer in a heavy glass of unusual shape. Condensation misted its outer surface. For some reason, the glass, the beer, the condensation told him what it was like to be among the rich. She sat demurely beside him, leaning lightly on one arm, feet tucked up on the sofa. Not touching; watching. It

118

occurred to Mark that she really rather relished the incongruity of all this.

He sipped his beer. It was the finest drink he had ever had in his life; he suspected even then that it was the finest drink he ever would have. 'It occurs to me,' he said, 'that you really rather relish the incongruity of all this.'

'I do. Though I expect I shall dress in a moment. I wonder what would be suitable.'

'Don't bother on my account.'

'But I must do. It will give you too much pleasure if I don't.'

'I can see how that would be a bad idea – Morgan, it's awfully nice, and beer and no clothes and so on. I really am most awfully glad to be here.'

'I'm glad too. Though I don't really know why. That rather bothers me. It bothers me very much. Look, Mark, will you stop looking at me with that disgusting expression on your face?'

'No.'

'It's not the real me, like this.'

'It's the only time that I can look at you properly. You're so dazzling when you have your clothes on.'

'Why, thank you. If that's a compliment.'

'I'm not sure if it is. It's true, though. But please don't worry about it. Just sit there a bit longer. It makes me happy, you see.'

'You come to this house and notice nothing. Have you no visual taste whatsoever?'

'There is much in the house that is visually intriguing. And I am being intrigued by it.'

'I think I had better put some clothes on and then explain the house to you.'

'Intriguinger and intriguinger.' A line she borrowed later for *Alice*. Mark was always proud of his contributions, many of which she was quite unaware of. There was a part of him that even considered these contributions as the ultimate sign of her indebtedness to him; of her need.

'Somebody once told me I wore my nakedness as if it were clothes.'

'Then he had never seen you dressed.' Mark was able to say this

119

without a tremor, without a qualm: something that would have surprised him had he considered the matter. 'Tell me about that one then. For example.' He pointed to the picture that dominated the room, hanging before them, filling an entire wall, and it was a wall that took a bit of filling.

Perhaps the room also wore its nakedness as if it were clothes. Wooden floor, in blocks, very pale. Massive sofa, huge lights, glass table, no other furniture. The main picture was about ten feet by six. It was chequered, and oozed rather sick-makingly if you looked at it for too long. The maze itself wound bewilderingly along its endless chequered path. Morgan explained that it was called *The Knight's Maze*. It had a solution, of course; all her mazes had solutions. Repeated moves, forward and diagonal, sideways and diagonal, took you to journey's end. Little scraps of algebraic chess notation were to be found here and there, perhaps decoration, perhaps cryptic clues. No, they must be clues: already he had a feeling of how the maze-maker thought. The path shifted and turned in doglegs and hairpins and chevrons. Knight Mare, Mark thought, and for a moment pondered a winsome poem. But the poem had already been made, and stood before him. And Mark was pricked very deeply: better than he could have made it.

'Show me more.'

'I must wear something.'

Mark reached to his bag and threw her his v-necked cashmere. Amused, she put it on. Something about the colour, the texture, or possibly just the intimacy – but certainly, Mark had never seen her quite so beautiful.

And so the tour began. Morgan showed him knots and mazes, mazes and knots. A couple in brass, like the one on the door. Some strange ceramics, with a knot, in relief. A pair of huge glazed dishes, that made two halves of a maze. A maze made of painted drinking straws, another from twigs and branches attached to a vertical surface. There were knots in carved and polished wood, painted in tiger stripes. There were spherical knots in metal, sprayed silver and gold. There was a maze made with coloured wires, another with tiny electronic parts.

It seemed that everything that could be a maze was a maze,

everything that could be knotted was knotted. Over and under. In and out. Everything was a puzzle. Everything had a solution. Everything formed a pattern with everything else.

And all this was the world of Morgan's mother. 'Is she mad? Or does she have the clearest mind in the universe?'

'Are the two conditions incompatible?'

That silenced him for a while. They climbed the stairs: the banister was a kind of plait, a little like a rather formal jungle vine, which finished in a fine upstanding knot at the foot. The bathroom was tiled in blue and white, very simple, but the patterns traced a maze. 'Is she a dilettante? Or a monomaniac?'

'Both. As you see. Every year or so she falls in love with a new medium. But never with a new subject.'

'Does she sell them?'

Morgan led him to a room on yet another level upward: an office, a studio, a shrine. Computer – then something of a daring example of advanced thought – work bench, easel, a large number of tools of the more technical kinds. One wall was filled from floor to ceiling with framed photographs: pictures of mazes and knots, and always a woman standing in front of them, sometimes shaking hands with a man in a suit, always a different man. The woman was small, slighter than Morgan, but with the same cheekbones. Eyes very large, much larger than Morgan's, almost bulging from their sockets.

Morgan explained something of her mother's clientele, her links with architects and architecture: the porticoes and atriums with their knots and mazes. 'She takes on two, maybe three commissions a year,' Morgan said. 'Occasionally holds an exhibition for her nonarchitectural work, every couple of years. She could sell a lot more – she has lots of fans, people like her stuff. But so does she. She keeps a lot of it. As you may have noticed.'

They walked downstairs again. 'You don't draw yourself? No secret files of mazes and knots?'

'I might write them.'

The answer chilled him, dismayed him. It was the first time she had let slip this ambition. He felt unmade. The Knight Mare poem would be a futile waste of space, of ink. But not her

121

mazes, her knots. He was a dilettante, a passionate butterfly. Not she.

It was alarming, being so close to real art.

The fridge was alarming, too. It lay in the basement kitchen, double-fronted, taller than himself, and had a device that at the push of a button vomited ice. It held absolutely colossal quantities of food. Mark had never seen so much food outside a shop. The deep freeze was completely filled with meat. Nothing but meat, great thick slabs of frozen beef. The best cuts. Beef, yes. And veal.

'Mother eats nothing but meat,' she said. 'With the occasional green salad.'

Mark cooked at her request a fish pie. She liked kedgeree, the first dish he had cooked for her and her floor-sharers, but this was her favourite. There were some potatoes, of the exquisite fir-apple kind, doubtless for delicate steak-following salads. Mark mashed them brutally.

'We'll eat in my room. I can't get comfortable anywhere else.'

The room held a double bed. No pictures, but a six-foot-tall dancing Shiva. There was no hearty vulgarity about this one: it was perfect, dull gleam of silver, four arms of infinite grace. 'Mother's gift. A bribe. To take my Hindu pictures down.'

'It's one of the loveliest things I have ever seen.

She placed a pair of huge candlesticks, complex and knotted and clearly the work of the absent maze-maker, on the long low table. Lit fat church candles, one in each, and left the matchbox on the table.

There was a bottle of wine, not in the fridge. Mark opened it. Plenty of ice. They drank clanking Chardonnay from goblets that looked as if they had come from the court of King Arthur. They carried wine and fish pie up to her room.

'You only called me because you can't cook.'

'Perfectly true.'

They sat on the floor, Morgan tugging her or his cashmere jumper modestly into place: the downward tug revealing just a little more not-quite cleavage. Mark found himself talking about Christmas. He quoted his mother on the subject: 'Xmas has

122

displaced Christmas. Christmas is a twelve-day ritual that starts at midnight on December the twenty-fourth. Xmas is a six-week frenzy of anticipation that ends at the same moment. On Christmas Day, the secular folk have nothing left but their disappointment.'

'Venetia and I, we have a ritual of ordinariness,' Morgan said. 'We have outlawed Christmas. We do not say Happy Christmas. We say good morning. We don't eat turkey, we have meat and salad. We have no presents.'

'Always?'

'This is the second year we have done so. My father walked out on Christmas Eve three Christmases ago. And Mother said we would never have Christmas again.'

'Dramatic.'

'That is Venetia's way. She likes ritual too, but she makes it up as she goes along. We give each other presents at New Year's.' Mark noticed the obtrusive American S. 'That's when she gave me my Dancing Shiva. Last year.'

'An insensitive time to leave your family, Christmas.'

'He used to bring girls back to the house. We all knew it went on, but he rather insisted on making it obvious. Mother caught him in flagrante.'

'Does your brother not come home for – well, I can't say Christmas, can I?'

'Kay? We haven't seen him for a long while. Not since the last Christmas.' Mark knew that her younger brother, named for a knight in Malory, had gone out of sight. He was thought to be living in London somewhere, but had abandoned family life. Mark had not realised how total this abandonment was. He ought not to have brought him up. Her face, in the candlelight, surveying Shiva's infinite grace, told him so. Perhaps that was why he was here, why she had called him to share her unChristmas. She called: he came. That was perhaps his point.

'Why so sad?' But it was she asking him.

'Am I?'

'Your face in the candlelight. It's the sort of thing you do. You look at me when you think I'm not looking at you, and you go all sad. You go all big-eyed, like a bushbaby. Why are you being a bushbaby?'

'I'm happy, Morgan. That's all.'

She looked at him appraisingly. 'You're happy, but it's not all. You're happy to be here but you don't trust me.'

'Perhaps that's it. There seem to be – too many unanswered questions.'

'You could ask me them.'

'You like your mysteries. So do I, really. And there never seems to be a moment – I mean, I can't suddenly, over empty fish-pie plates, ask you to swear to tell me the truth, can I? I can't ask you to swear on the Bible. Ask you to swear in the name of all that's sacred. What is sacred, anyway?'

She laughed. 'A jest. A dare.'

'Then I dare you to answer some questions in absolute and perfect truth.' Even then, Mark did not speak seriously.

'All right. If you can put the questions in appropriately jesting form. And then, if I asked you a question or two, would you answer me truthfully?'

'Always.'

'A lie for starters, fair enough. But come. Suggest a jest. I won't play unless you can suggest a jest.'

Mark stretched out his hand between the candlesticks and picked up the matchbox that lay there. 'Africa,' he said. 'I don't suppose you have ever played Africa.'

She looked back at him gravely, the light flickering on her Eskimo's face. 'I lead a very sheltered life.'

'Then I will explain.' Africa is one of the legion of drinking games played with a matchbox. You place the matchbox on the very edge of the table, label-side up. Then you flip it into the air, so that it turns around in the air at least once. If it lands label-side up, you get a point. If it lands on its long edge, you get five points, and must shout: 'Madagascar!' And if it lands upright, on its short side, you get ten points. And you must shout: 'Africa!' The first player to reach twenty-one is the winner. There are no deuces.

The game's beauty comes from the declaration factor. You can continue flipping for as long as you please. If you stop of your

124

own decision, you keep the points you have scored on that turn. But here is the point of the game: if the box lands label-side *down*, then all points scored on that turn are forfeit.

They had a dry run, which Mark won. Morgan experimented with the technique of flipping. An altogether unusual silence of concentration fell upon them. Games are there to be won, after all. And they were to play for frighteningly high stakes.

No hypothetical questions. You were accountable for your answers for a period of not less than the rest of your life. Answers must be full and complete as well as factually exact. Up to two follow-up questions were permitted.

Mark felt a small biting inside his stomach, one that increased in intensity. He remembered the few minutes before a cross-country event: before the mad charge against the clock over open country and hard, unyielding fences. I am terribly sorry, Mr Starter. Most unfortunately, I have just gone down with rather bad peritonitis, and if I went, it wouldn't be fair to the horse. And all the time, the terror growing because he knew he would say no such thing.

He knew what he would ask. He dreaded what she would ask. 'Any more wine?'

He dreaded what she would reply. 'Certainly.'

They tossed the matchbox for first go, and Morgan won. And it began.

Mark had always understood Africa as a gambling game – that is to say, one in which relish of chance and an understanding of the odds gives you the edge. Morgan, it was clear from the outset, saw it as a game of manipulative skill. She sought the perfect flip, the 360 degree somersault, label to label. Mark preferred to flip higher, with several revolutions in the air, a method that gives a much greater chance of a Madagascar or an Africa. His basic strategy was to declare after three points or a Madagascar or an Africa. Morgan declared after two points, sometimes after one.

'This is a game of contrasting moods, contrasting ploys, contrasting personalities,' Mark said in a sports commentator's voice.

'It always was. Seventeen-fifteen to me.' She pushed the matchbox to him.

The matchbox soared and spun, landed solidly on its edge:

Madagascar! Now what? Declare on twenty? Or flip again? Pah. Timidity begone. When in doubt, kick on. What was worse: the question he had to ask? Or the question he would have to face? Flip. The Bryant and May label lay face up on the table before them. Now he would know. And now he knew that revealing any amount of secrets about himself would be easier than hearing a single one of hers.

'What do they mean to you?' he asked. 'Your ethics tutor? Philosophy Dick?'

'Oh!' she said. 'What is this?'

Mark considered. 'Dick boasted to me that he'd slept with you. And then said you were having an affair with your ethics tutor.'

'Richard was a terrible mistake. He did seem so pressing.'

'Richard? Oh, him. Philosophy Dick.'

'Philosophaster Dick. Very shallow man. I didn't really want to sleep with him at all. It won't happen again. Events just rather got away from me. I got trapped by his egotism. He treated me so much like a silly bimbo I felt I had to go along with the idea.'

'And the other?' Hardness of tone; gaping wounds.

'Jim. Jim Fossey, as you probably know, because he's rather famous for books and television and so forth. Alarmingly clever: genetics, game theory, that sort of thing. To tell you the truth, I was a bit overwhelmed by him. Rather crass of me. But then I got to like him a bit. Quite a bit.'

'So it carries on?'

'I don't know. He's married, two children. Being a bit on the side is not really my kind of thing. He's very sweet, and very funny.'

'So basically it will happen again?'

'I don't recall making any –'

'I ask for information. According to the rules.'

'Oh good. Then stop looking all downcast and making me feel guilty. That's not in the rules.'

'I have a second follow-up question. Do you like them more than me?'

'Richard, I don't like him at all.'

'Which is presumably why you slept with him.'

'Which presumably was. Jim – well, wickedness and glamour

aside, he's the sort of man I really rather like. Quite apart from anything else, he's so –'

Mark really could not bear this. So sexy? So good in bed? Something of the sort, for sure. With him, Bedouin-robe-less tumbles apart, she was normally restrained, ironical, quizzical, slightly withdrawn. Always something in reserve. 'That was all really rather pleasant,' she sometimes said. It's like heavenly cough mixture. Philosophy Dick, the unethical ethics tutor – perhaps they overwhelmed her. Perhaps she liked them, because with them she could take a holiday from her position of strength. In strength was her preferred reality, but these dalliances with weakness gratified some other part of her. With them, she could afford to lose, but not with him.

'I don't really want to sleep with him again. But I probably will, if you understand.'

'Oh yes.'

'Drink some wine, Little Worthless, and play Africa. Going bushbaby is against the rules.'

'Of course.'

She had the range now, with her 360 degree flip. Two flips and a declaration. Her score climbed inexorably. Mark fell behind early, tried to catch up, started flipping specifically for Africas, a ploy of desperation and one that failed. 21–5. Humiliation.

Her face, smiling in the candlelight, chin cupped in her hand. Hand, both hands, ringless. The twist of the knife. 'Who do you love best in all the world?' she asked. 'Blood family apart – I mean, who is the love of your life?'

This was not so dreadful a question as he had feared. It was much, much more dreadful than he had feared. He had dreaded – or perhaps fancied – the idea of being forced to confess his ritual Christmas Eve dalliance with Mel. He could, he thought, slip it in, as it were, to see her reaction. But the spell of honesty was on him. 'Three women,' he said. 'Or girls. The first was my boy-girl love, Mel.' He bit off her final two syllables. Absurdly, as if she might tell him that nobody was called Melody.

'How sweet of you to remember her.'

Sharp relish of Christmas Eve. 'I still see her sometimes, when

127

I go home. It was all lovely. All terribly innocent, if you call tumbling in the hay innocent. We both had horses then, remember. A little idyll.'

'You had *horses*?'

'Didn't I tell you? I had a horse, yes, another love of my life, I suppose. It meant a lot then. As did she. Long time ago, it seems.' No more than two and a half years, in sober truth: but time passes at different speeds at different periods in life.

'So how did it end?'

'You always want to know the dirty bits. Me at college, you know. Then her at college. New people, new lives. Boy-girl love is for outgrowing. But it always remembers sweet.'

'And the second?'

'Well, I was devoted to Chris, you know. More than a year, getting on for two. We were so – so terribly settled. She was easy to be with. She made it all easy. Believed in me. I liked that. Then.'

A silence fell between them. Mark felt a terrible nostalgia for the time when everything had been easy; and a contempt for the time when everything had been so easily settled.

'Does that mean I am the third?'

'No, Morgan. It doesn't. It means you are the first. You always were the first. You always will be the first.' There was a light top dressing of irony in his tone; just enough to make these words pronounceable.

'Will you love me for ever? Will you forgive me anything?'

'I already have.'

'That's nothing. I can be much worse.'

'I have never for an instant doubted that. And I meant what I said.'

'I am the love of your life, then? Really the love of your life?'

'If you wish.'

'I don't know that I do wish, but it's awfully sweet of you, all the same. Come, love of my life. Play Africa. I can see the hint of a bushbaby expression beginning on your left cheekbone. Play Africa before it starts to spread.'

She was ruthless: once more inexorable. And Mark, wounded by her kindness, wounded still more by his own revelations, found it hard to concentrate, and paid the price. He played with glum fatalism, she with live appetite. She won 21–11. 'What are you most ashamed of in your life?'

'Oh God, Morgan, no easy questions from you, are there?'

'Nor answers. Come. Give me shame.'

'Oh God.' Shame racked him anew, and he didn't have a thought for the night of serial buttock-fondling. 'Two things.' He spoke of his return from his all-conquering trip around Europe, bouncing up the drive, home-coming conquistador, home to the news of his father's death. He had not even known that his father was ill.

'Should you have telephoned home, then? Is that what you feel guilty about?'

'You asked about shame, not guilt. I have nothing to reproach myself for. There was no requirement to phone home, only to send a postcard once a week to tell them I was alive. This I did. They saw the need for youthful adventure, cutting the ties. I don't feel guilty. I feel ashamed.'

She reached across the table and took his hand, releasing it a few seconds later. This uncharacteristic gesture brought a lone tear to his eye.

'And the second?'

'You know about that.' He spoke briefly of the night Chris was struck dumb.

'I didn't know you were ashamed of your trip to the seaside. I thought you were rather proud of it.'

'That's what makes me ashamed.'

'You said it was time it all ended.'

'So I did. So it was. Perhaps the pain I caused was inevitable. But I am still ashamed.'

His turn to start. His first flip was high and handsome, almost a devil-may-care sort of flip. With an uncompromising rattle, the matchbox stood straight and tall, like a sentry. 'Africa!' He was greatly cheered.

Next turn, he had a successful triple, and the next, a Madagascar at his second flip. The lead was unassailable. She did not abandon her tactics of caution. And it was not enough. He won 21–8. Triumph.

'Have you always been unfaithful? I mean, to each of your past – past loves?'

She nodded, acknowledging a good question. 'I have never been unfaithful, Mark. That is to say, I have never gone back on a promise. I have never promised exclusivity, and therefore I have never broken faith. Perhaps there was a boy, when I was still at school, who expected me to forsake all others, and perhaps I did agree that this was a good idea, in a fit of youthful enthusiasm. Perhaps I was unfaithful to him in that sense. But I have never promised to be exclusive to any one person.'

'But it's not really as if you fall for these additional persons, is it? It's not as if you can't help yourself, that every time you're a gone girl?'

'The thing with me is that I really don't like sleeping with people at all. No, that's untrue, unkind, I like being with you.' It seemed that Morgan was telling him more than she wanted to; more than she knew. She had never been before him so vulnerable: perhaps never would again. But if there was a moment to be seized, Mark missed it, obscured as the moment was by his own far more fascinating vulnerabilities. 'But – no one is ever going to have a hold over me. Ever. Do you see?'

'I don't want to have a hold over you.'

'Yes, you do. And you know you'll never have one. That's what you want. It's what people always want.'

Mark went bushbaby for a while, staring at the candles. Morgan bullied him into another round of Africa. Her tactics were beginning to irritate him; he gave his mind to the game. It was nip and tuck: they reached 18-all. Then Mark flipped three times in a row for a clean, courageous victory. 'Morgan – I need to know this. Are you just amusing yourself with me? Just passing the time? Do you take this – alliance with any kind of seriousness at all?'

'Oh, Mark, do you think that? I just need to keep a little distance, that's all. You must understand that. It's my way. But there's a line in Stephen Potter, isn't there, always rather a favourite thing of mine, the *Gamesmanship* books. Gambits are for use, he says, and not for overuse. I think I might have overused my favourite gambit, with you.'

130

'Can you explain what you mean by that?'

'I can't really. It's too embarrassing.'

'You are bound by the rules of the game.'

'Oh dear. So I am. But – Mark – well – look, I really like you the best. That's why I asked you to come.'

'Not because your unethical ethics tutor is at home with his family and all the rest of your first eleven are off games?'

'Mark, you're the only one I could ever have played Africa with. That's far more intimate than any other game. Far more naked.'

'Perhaps. But you still wear your nakedness as if it were clothes.'

'Haven't I revealed enough? Or too much?'

'Every layer you take off reveals another layer of doubt.'

'I don't feel that, Mark.' The repeated, chiming insistence on his name. 'I've never revealed as much to anybody. It's really rather frightening.' Mark stared at the candle a little more. 'Mark, that means that you take me in your arms and hold me for a short while. That is the correct ethical treatment of a woman who says she feels a little vulnerable. You have to act strong. It doesn't matter if I see through the act. That's just part of the pleasure. All right?'

Mark did as he was told, took her, in her soft woollen shell, into his arms. After a while other ideas than truth invaded his heart.

'What are you thinking about, Little Worthless?'

'I think it must be a perfect equilateral triangle. I'd like to put a protractor on it.'

'And one day you shall do so. But I want to ask you one more question. I suggest a final round. If I lose, my question goes unanswered, which will be too bad.'

'Winner takes all?'

'Winner loses all.' Perhaps she would ask him about Christmas Eve after all. For a second he felt rather a dog. The feeling basely pleased him.

Morgan inched her way to a handsome lead. At 18–8, she flipped twice and, as ever, declared. A point from victory. Mark flipped three times, each time successfully. Now go. When in doubt kick on. The matchbox spun high, landed on its end, teetered proudly in the position of Africa – and fell. Label to table.

'You overreacher, you.'

He slid the matchbox across the table to her. She placed her hand over his as he did so. Then took the matchbox and flipped with murderous care. Bryant and May: 21. Victory. She looked at him through the candleflame, a smile, very slowly, crawling up the sides of her face.

'Mark, will you marry me?'

Mark didn't do anything comic like drop his glass or choke on a mouthful of wine. All the same, he felt rather like that time Trevor had stumbled on landing after a drop-fence, and he had performed a not-quite 360-degree flip himself, landed solidly on his back, apparently unhurt but without a breath of air in his body. Hurt and distress then filled him.

'You shouldn't tease me, Morgan.'

'I'm not teasing. That's part of the rules of the game. All questions must be serious.'

'Morgan, stop it. I know you're only trying to outcool me.'

'Not only trying. But not *only* trying. I want an answer. Truth, please. I want the truth.'

'There are no hypothetical questions allowed in this game, Morgan.'

'Nor are there. Truth, please.'

'Morgan, you will be accountable for this for the rest of your life.' Chiming insistence on her name.

'And so will you.'

'You haven't said I love you and all that kind of stuff.'

'I really like you. That's much better.'

'Do you really want to?'

'After college and so forth, yes. I do. As it were.'

Mark wanted to ask, forsaking all others? But he did not. What would she have said, had he done so? In my fashion, perhaps.

'Mark, dearest, I am waiting for an answer.'

'Morgan, dearest, you know I will do anything you ask. Thank you for asking me. Yes. I will marry you.'

'No conditions? I had a bet with myself that you would say yes, so long as I promise to be true. I have lived briefly with two men in my life. One begged me to be faithful, as you call it, as I believe he called it too. The other said I was to do

132

exactly as I wished, but I had to be completely honest and open.'

'Morgan, so long as you are true and faithful, I want you to be completely honest and open. But if you are ever untrue and unfaithful, then would you do me a favour and please lie like fuck?'

And Morgan laughed and laughed, and came round the table and folded herself into his arms, so that they both faced the same way, her back against his chest, his arms folded across the lemon-yellow cashmere, its hem about her waist. 'You see, you do understand,' she said. 'I think we'll do very well.'

26

Sorry to let you down, she said. Are you sure you can cope on your own? Oh, no problem. I feel terribly guilty, but there's nothing else I can do. I should have thought. No, really, don't worry. I'll be fine. Sorry, she said again, to let you down. You could never let me down, he said lightly, no matter what you did. And she laughed at this let-off, relieved, and promised she'd make it up to him, and he said he'd look forward to that, and they both laughed in a teasing and lubricious fashion. Which was all very well.

But he was at the end of it quite on his own, filled with trepidation as he drove the Jeep to Radlett to join a new conspiracy, the conspiracy of the dawn of Sunday, which is deeper still than the conspiracy of Saturday morning. The idea had been to conspire with Mel and Ed and the mare – he always thought of her as The Mare, never as Miss Chance, still less of the softer names he called her to her long brown face.

But he could always take her in the school for an hour. He parked, the only car there, up before Jan. Or he could ride along the deserted roads, saluting fellow conspirators, cyclists and joggers, the occasional horse, and then, when they got to the bridle path, turn round and go home. That would be wise. Treat her gently. Treat himself gently. Not to overface her, as Kath had overfaced her in the puissance event of long ago. He stepped into the yard, pleased with his wisdom, still not permitting himself to know that the true name of such wisdom is fear. Not fear of falling: fear of taking responsibility.

'Hello, angel. What's it going to be then, eh?' She touched him with her nose over the half-door, softly. The touch moved him unreasonably, and he found the decision made. This surprised him a few minutes later, but at that small nudge it seemed a matter of the smallest importance, an easy – the only – decision to make. 'All right, darling. If that's what you want. I'm terribly susceptible, you know. A soft touch, that's me. But listen, you've got to promise to do what I say, all right?' The mare butted him again; a soft touch.

This mare was two mares, but he knew that. The softest of soft touches when he stood beside her, meek, gentle, tolerant, submissive. A different person the instant his feet left the ground. So she stood, meek and quiet as he groomed her conker-coloured coat, that horseman's flick at the conclusion of each stroke of the bodybrush.

Mark fitted her bridle and her saddle, put on his hard hat, and walked her to the gate, closing it behind him. He could already feel the spring in her step. As soon as he placed his weight in the stirrup-iron, she tried to set off walking, responding grudgingly to his sharp correction. She skittered sideways out of the drive, leaving four distinct tracks. Mark straightened her with hand and leg: 'You really must do what I tell you, or we'll have to go back. All right?'

Calmed a little by his voice, by this horsey gibberish, she even managed to stand still for a couple of seconds as he turned into the main road. But there was not a car about. And after all, he could always bail out. There was a get-out clause, was there not? No horse ever minds turning for home. Home is where the herd is.

But she had to behave. She really did. He sat deep and relaxed, but it didn't fool her for a second. She read his anxiety and kept throwing in little jogging steps. His corrections were a little stronger than usual. But they had to be, didn't they? On their own, now.

He pre-empted her stand at the T-junction by spinning her dangerously through 360 degrees, but even the thought of standing went deep with her, and with him too. She was lit up, and when he asked her to trot, she bounced into huge, booming strides as if she were towing a sulky in a trotting race. Mark jabbed his corrections at her, and she threw her head back in resentment. They

135

were teetering on the edge of control, his corrections increasingly ineffective, her eagerness worryingly close to panic.

It was only the thought of despising himself (and explaining to Mel) that made him turn into the bridle path instead of turning home. And that started her mad bouncing canter, and she reacted to his latest correction with one of her flying headbutts. He remembered that first ride in Kath's field, when this move had left him amused, understanding, brave. But now he was seriously alarmed, because the situation was seriously alarming: a long way from home already. He not patting and soothing, but tugging at her mouth in necessary but futile corrections.

He stood in the irons to get a little leverage. He had to establish control, and do so now. Balance never quite right, hands never quite right. One of her wild hops tipped his balance forward disastrously. She lunged wildly at his error, to receive a sudden harsh correction as anger gave him strength. Fighting like cat and dog, they reached the top of the hill. Fighting, he despised himself. And hated her. Is there any other relationship in which you can seriously hate what you seriously love? And why was love not enough? And the real trouble was that her failure was only his failure.

She flung her head at him again, and a great wodge of flying slobber from her mouth hit him in the face. For some reason, this made him laugh out loud. And with this small, this infinitesimal moment of relaxation, she relaxed too, just the smallest fraction. Asking, rather than demanding. And Mark, being asked, found himself giving. Giving everything.

And her withers dropped about six inches and the canter was gone and in its place her low, hard, flat gallop, and Mark perched nimbly over her withers, hands giving, hands taking, balanced like herself, and like herself, exulting. Lost in the gallop, lost in the conspiracy: us two against the world.

Later, the long circuit completed, they walked back to the yard, he holding the reins by the buckle and saluting joggers and cyclists, she occasionally jogging a few steps herself and shaking her head in self-delight. Uncorrected: reins like the long stroke of the letter D. No contact. Trust. Occasionally he patted her damp neck. 'Angel,' he said, 'I rather think you won.' Exulting.

27

'Of course you're going back to her,' Callum said.

'I didn't think you'd approve.'

'Of course I don't approve. You know perfectly well I don't approve. I'm just pointing out that you're going. My approval has nothing to do with the matter.'

'I'm not altogether certain I'm going.'

'Maybe you're not, but I am. When she asks, you go. That's the way your life happens to work.'

'Do you think I'm wrong?'

'Never mind what I think. I'll tell you what I know instead. She's caused you a good deal of pain and misery and so forth, from the first moment you met her. Now she buggers off, and surprise surprise, you start coping. You even go to bed with a nice girl. For the first time since you met her, life seems to be that little bit easier. And then this happens. And you're going to go straight back to her, knowing that the only certain part of the whole deal is more pain and misery and so forth.'

'I can't fault the logic of that.'

'And as a little bonus, it will bugger up your finals. I hope you've taken that into consideration.'

'I haven't taken anything into consideration.' Mark had told his mother that he would be spending the Easter holidays at the flat he shared with Callum. Revising. Yes, of course he would come for Good Friday and Midnight Marce and so on. But go straight back. He wanted to get a half-decent degree, did he not?

Then came the knock on the door, as he was mugging up *The Waste Land* and *Ulysses* and *The Tempest*, and a brave new world of possibilities opened up before him. A man from the florists. Bearing a single rose, which was charming of him. And her. And a message, which was devastating of them both. 'Come to New York call collect –' a number beginning with 212 – 'your ever loving Morgan.' Girl leaves boy and hands him a garland of ironies.

Mark was ravished by the neatness of the manoeuvre. Telegrams were a thing of the past, and naturally, there was no telephone in a student flat. But this showed style. For half a second he wondered if Morgan had asked him to New York solely because the neatness of the manoeuvre appealed to her. Or perhaps it was those twin irresistibles: lust and the love of a jest.

The Mate would not be pleased. She approved of Morgan, but she would be deeply unhappy about this. She was already struggling with his talk of becoming a teacher, his application for a teaching qualification in a training college near the university. 'Tell me frankly,' she had said, 'is this vocation, or a complex ploy to be near your latest lady love?' She had not yet told him that nobody was called Morgan.

And Mark told her that Morgan or no Morgan, he was going to train as a teacher, so he might as well be near to her as far from her. It had not gone down well, but at least the talk of revision had silenced her. And so he had returned to his flat and his books.

'Did I tell you,' Mark asked, 'that she asked me to marry her?'

'Every time you've been pissed this past term.'

'Sorry if I'm boring you.'

'You're not, really. It's quite interesting, in a way. Repetitious, you know. Obsessive.'

'Look, Callum,' Mark said. 'How come you're so wise all of a sudden?'

'Not specially wise. You just ask easy questions.'

'And you're a fine one to talk about obsessive love.'

'I'm not obsessive.'

'Well then. Amour fou, if you like.'

'Mark, that is so ridiculous –'

Mark addressed the corner of the room. 'His family hates Pakis. His own ideas about race were somewhat confused when he left home. College changes the views of students, but not the views of parents. So he falls in love with a Paki –'

'She's not a Paki –'

'An English-born lady of Pakistani extraction –'

'She was born in Islamabad, came over here when she was five.'

'Brought up in England but manifestly brown of skin and at least nominally Muslim by religion. So she goes home alone to her family and lies, and he daren't go home to his family because he told them on the telephone and they went ballistic.'

'She said she wasn't going to lie. But it is complicated, I know.'

'So the best thing you can hope for is that you have a shattering row and break up, because if you carry on liking each other there is a lifetime of trouble ahead for both of you.'

'OK. OK. Nice bit of analysis. But there is a difference, you know. Naz and I actually like each other. As in, I try not to hurt her, and she tries not to hurt me. I mean, Naz and I trust each other. Which is kind of nice, in a relationship, isn't it?'

'I wouldn't know.'

'And we actually like being together.'

'Oh, Morgan and I like being together. That's what the bloody trouble is all about.'

'Look, Mark, I'll tell you a very useful rule in life: don't take buggers back. If you take buggers back, you recreate the same bad situation. And you're the sort of idiot to do that again and again and again. And every time, you're stupid enough to believe it's all going to be different. Well, let me tell you something. It won't. It'll be exactly the bloody same.'

'I don't know.'

'Well, you should know. People don't change. End of story. You ought to learn that. And that means that you're always going to be hopeless, and that she's always going to be – whatever she is. Untrustable. That's how your life works.'

'Callum?'

'Yes?'

'She's five hours ahead, isn't she? Or is it five hours behind?'

28

'She looks beautiful.'

'She feels beautiful.'

'And she's really enjoying herself.'

'So am I.'

'I can see that.'

'Watch.'

Mark nudged her in a single stride from walk to canter, and collected the canter so that her stride was tiny, the energy immense, all contained by the lightest possible touch of his fingers. Her head was down, nose making a right-angle to the ground, neck a hard brown quadrant. Her hocks, he knew, were gathered tight beneath her: all the power of her held in the most glorious balance.

Mark cantered her along the long side of the school, and then looked sharply over his right shoulder. The mare followed his glance by flinging herself around in the tightest circle she could manage: no more than five yards in diameter. Mark cantered on, performed a second circle, on, and a third. He then cantered across the diagonal of the school, trotting a few strides to change the leading leg, cantering off again and repeating the three little circles on the opposite rein. He finished by riding up to the spot where Mel stood and moving from canter to halt in a single stride. And made much.

'You've got her where she wants to be,' Mel said. 'That's lovely. Look – do you mind if Theresa and I set up a few jumps while you work? Or would it spoil your preparations for grand prix dressage?'

'It's hard on a team of our calibre, but you go ahead. I'm just about finished anyway. Are you going to start jumping Gus, then, Theresa?'

That excellent smile, slow and always, even at long range, alarmingly intimate, delivered from beneath slightly lowered brows. 'I thought I'd try. I've been getting into a tangle with flatwork. Mel thought he would enjoy the change.'

'You want to be careful. Strong men duck when Mel has one of her good ideas.'

Mel gave him a single-eyebrowed look over her shoulder as she and Theresa turned away to the pile of poles and jump stands. Mark walked the mare around the sandy arena, holding the reins by the buckle, letting her relax after her work, watching the women put up a pair of modest jumps. 'I hope young Ed is doing this Grand National course as well,' he said. 'Good to see it. You dressage queens are normally far too precious to –'

'Bloody fool,' Mel said amiably. 'Best exercise you can do, to get a horse moving balanced and forward. Besides, giving a horse fun is a crucial part of training, or did they never tell you that bit?'

'They never needed to. Well, I'll put the girl away now, so I can come and watch you fall off.'

'There was a time when you might have tried the jumps. But I've forgotten – the mare's supposed to have lost her bottle, isn't she? Or is it the jockey, I wonder?'

This was appalling. Someone had once said that he and Mel were not so much brother and sister as brother and brother. He wasn't going to rise to this, was he? Yet for some extraordinary reason, the mare was already cantering: a bigger canter this time, but the same power. He cantered a circle, a big one now, using the full width of the school, and then turned his gaze to the little two-foot upright. And she followed his gaze and delight expanded within her.

She leapt, easily and merrily she leapt, followed his gaze to the second jump as they rode a half-circle, and leapt again. Fought just a little for her head on the far side: looking for more.

'Don't look so smug. She did the work. Kath did the schooling.'

But I did the re-schooling, Mark thought, bursting with the pride of it. It was me that gave her the second chance, she that took it. No, not the pride. The joy of it. 'Those aren't jumps. They're cavalletti.'

Two foot six, then, Mel and Theresa raising the poles. This time she jumped properly, rounding her back, coming in off a wonderfully easy and confident stride. 'Again,' Mark said. 'If it's not too much trouble.'

'No trouble watching you overreach yourself,' Mel said. Three foot, then. Three foot is the height at which serious jumping begins.

The mare's canter was huge, booming. She ignored Mark's sudden trepidation – or perhaps there was not enough to affect her.

Mark sat deep, leg on, to encourage forward motion, hands giving and taking, taking and giving, allowing her to find the stride she knew she wanted. And he asked her – or did she decide? – to stand off the jump, and she briefly flew, gathering herself up in a smooth single stride to follow his gaze to the second jump, and that too she flew.

'Five foot?' Mel asked.

Mark grinned, making much. 'What do you think?'

'Ripe for competition.'

'She's something, this little mare.'

'You're made for each other.'

29

'Toilets!' Mark sang out the word, anagrammatising brilliantly. 'Thomas Toilets, Thomas Toilets, Thomas Toilets!' It was his pupils' nickname for one of the great writers they were studying.

He picked up the sixteen copies of *Selected Poems of*, and put them down again. He wrote in the Resources Book that he had taken sixteen copies, and the date and the class and his name. Then he picked them up again, a small weight.

'So many!' he sang.

'So many!

I had not thought death had undone

So many!'

He took the top copy from his pile and sent it spinning skyward with a flick of the wrist. He caught it with a pleasing snap. 'You, Stetson!' he sang. 'You who were with me at the – hot gates!'

He was not alone. As he came from the storeroom to the small common room, he again found his disturbingly silent-footed deputy, Annette. Mark blushed foolishly.

'So she's come back to you?'

'Oh, hello, Annette, sorry about that. Feeling a trifle silly this morning.'

'I'm right, aren't I?'

'Oh, well – no, actually.'

'Then who have you found to comfort you?' Level brown eyes upon him, well aware that kindness makes you vulnerable.

'Er – no one, actually.'

'Sorry, Mark, didn't mean to intrude, you don't have to tell me. I enquire from the friendly interest and concern of a colleague.'

'No, Annette, me that's sorry, don't mean to be rude. I mean, thank you for your concern. But the situation is just as it was.'

'Then why the merry song?'

'Well – it's hard to explain, really. It's just that, well, my horse is going really well and I'm frightfully bucked about it.'

'Your *horse*?' That *silly* girl and that *fucking* horse.

'Yes, I have a horse and I ride it –' saying it instead of her felt like a betrayal but how else to explain? '– and things have taken a turn for the better. And so I'm leaping about and singing foolish songs and so forth.'

She looked at him, head slightly on one side, and pushed a soft handful of her shortish brown hair back over her ear. A smile, almost an affectionate smile. 'Mark, has it occurred to you that you are blinding yourself to the central emotional truths of your life?'

'Oh yes.'

'That's all right then.'

Mark almost invited her for a drink after work. But he had to get to Radlett. Get some trotting poles down. Do some serious work. And Jan had promised to bring him a schedule of the local shows. Competition.

30

She stood about six foot four and moved with such grace that she might have been on wheels. Once again love exploded in Mark's heart. With a magnificent smile, triumph of the orthodontist's art, she bade him welcome to everything she was capable of offering, gliding up to his side and stopping as calmly, as easily as she had moved. Because she was on wheels, and, clearly tall enough when in contact with the base earth, was made a giantess by her roller skates. She was a statue of liberty and Mark was intoxicated by her freedoms.

'And what,' she asked, 'can I get you two to drink today?' Face lit up by the pavement air. Sidewalk; he had to call it a sidewalk. The Lincoln Centre or rather Center behind her across the breadth of Broadway. The passing and repassing of New Yorkers along the sidewalk, each an extra in the movie of Mark Brown's Great Adventure. So many, so many. All the women were desirable. Half the women and more than half the men were clearly mad. Across the road a man was juggling with a roaring chainsaw while passers-by paid at best polite attention, a few scattering quarters into an upturned homburg or stetson. You, Stetson! You who were with me at the hot gates. The city had Mark drunk: a man in love, willingly drowning in madness. Joy filled the star of the movie. Close-up: a slow smile plays about his face as he contemplates the city in its madness. Freedom.

Though come to think of it, this mad escape was more of a dash to captivity. His mother's favourite prayer: whose service is perfect freedom.

'I think,' she said, 'we might have champagne. This is something of a special occasion, after all.'

'Oh, well, yes, jolly good.'

'A bottle of champagne,' she told the goddess. 'And we'll worry about food in a while.'

Sunday morning in the park, the New Yorkers' frenzied approach to the art of relaxation, pounding joggers, whizzing cyclists, the bitter invective at the softball games. Right over the plate, this guy's a looker, he ain't gunna swing. Next time you smile at me you smile with no teeth, OK?

She glided up to them again, bearing an ice-bucket, a foil-crowned bottle. Performed the pop, to a gratifying turning of heads. My, what fun the rich folks have. The brisk warm air of spring whipped amiably around them. The brisk cool golden wine splashed into glasses. A wonderful town.

'Well,' she said, raising her glass. 'I hear you're going to marry my daughter.' Her smallness gave an impression of immense vigour, her stillness one of great physical power. Mark had no difficulty at all in imagining her whacking hell out of chunks of marble. Her eyes powerfully brown, no halfway hazel. Mark wondered if she had X-ray vision.

'Hold her hand in a firm clasp,' Morgan had briefed him. 'Look her in the eye.' Mark, not conscious of doing either, had been easily overwhelmed, but she was used to easy overwhelming. She smiled. Her lips were too red, a young girl's colour. One odd thing. She had painted herself a cute little Cupid's bow, brutally superimposing it on her own thin, emphatic mouth. She was dressed plainly but exquisitely in black; she wore on two fingers and about her neck vast pieces of gold that were Ashanti treasures, museum pieces of incalculable value and commanding beauty.

'Well.' Mark smiled foolishly. He realised he was behaving more or less exactly as Morgan had instructed him not to. Bertie Wooster, summoned to tea with Aunt Agatha. 'So she tells me.'

'So she tells you.' She looked, ever so slightly stagily, across Broadway. The juggler had set down his chainsaw and was now juggling with three cutlasses. When would he bring out the flaming torches? 'And are you inclined to believe her?' She was a woman very much at home in her own city, but she had the city on her own terms. Accent uncompromisingly English, vocabulary larded with tart Americanisms, used no doubt to tease Londoners. Consonants hit a trifle harder than was usual in England, vowels unslurred in a way that was far more American than English. She said tom-ah-to.

'I think so,' said Mark. 'On the whole.'

Mark was terrified, utterly out of his depth. In one way, he felt as if he were talking to Philosophy Dick in Tudge's; in another, as if he were taking part in an ancient rite: the passing-on of tribal wisdom.

'Are you ready for marriage?'

'Is any one ever ready for marriage?'

She likes to play hardball, Morgan had warned him. 'A good answer. But it won't do.' A million miles from The Mate's impenetrable obliquities. 'Have you thought about what marriage means?'

'About little else. Since the bombshell was dropped.'

'I had assumed it was she that did the asking.'

'If that's an accusation of cowardice, Venetia, then I concur one hundred per cent.' Mark was fractionally recovering his nerve. Recovering his manners as well, he refilled their glasses, handling the napkin in a man-of-the-worldly way that did not dump vast amounts of icy water into her lap.

'No, it's not an accusation of cowardice.' Her trick of repeating phrases gave her immense conversational power. 'To tackle Morgan is not the act of a coward. But you are not – not invasive. You are respectful. I can see you are respectful of her. Because you are respectful of me.'

'Is that good or bad?'

'It's as you are.' Now that was something The Mate might have said. 'Neither good nor bad. It's a form of kindness; it's a form of abnegation of responsibility.' This was a dizzyingly new idea to Mark and he rejected it out of hand. He wished he had eaten a large cheese and pickle sandwich before they stepped out, a pre-emptive strike against the champagne.

She returned to her contemplation of Broadway. Mark watched a black girl with straightened hair walk past. No, surely it was naturally straight, surely she had Asian features. Perhaps an Afro-Indian outcross from the Caribbean, half-exotic, wholly New

York. She was the most beautiful woman he had ever seen. No one else turned a head as she passed.

Mark, feeling Venetia's gaze on him, turned, more or less against his will. 'Mark.' You could just about taste the R in her use of his name. 'I think you love my daughter very much.'

'Is that a good thing or a bad thing?'

At this Venetia laughed outright. The pleasing recklessness of his reply was all a part of the pleasing recklessness of his flight. His flight from revision, from the maternal dreams of his academic distinction, his literal flight (just collect the ticket from the Sales Counter in Terminal Three, it's in your name) through the actual air, and most dizzying of all, the way his life, his love had taken wing the instant he had set foot on the ground of this Unreal City.

'No, I won't meet you at the airport. You'll enjoy making your own way across town. I'll be waiting in the apartment.' And she was right: giving the Central Park address to the taxi-driver, a monoglot francophone Caribbean who spent the journey alternately talking patois to the radio and making the same remark to Mark. 'Senna Puck?' Mark kept saying yes.

And eventually they found it. The fact that there was a park right in the middle of Manhattan seemed to come as a pleasant surprise to the driver. Mark paid him with real dollars that seemed like stage, or rather film properties, thrusting them through the small window in the bullet-proof screen that prevented him from shooting the driver, and stepped from his cab, his yellow cab on the eternal film set spread out all around him, the cameras lurking unseen to record the arrival sequence. A slow smile plays about his lips as he enters the apartment building.

In the lobby his presence was announced on the telephone by a uniformed man with a thick accent of Middle Europe. This was approved by an unheard voice, and Mark was shown to a lift or elevator that fired him skyward. And there Morgan.

Greeting him in the corridor, standing before him as the lift doors swept back like a theatre's curtains. Clad in slim black jeans and a glorious shirt on which soared a mightily pinioned eagle. 'Mark, you blessed man.'

'Morgan.' He was overcome with shyness: they did not know how to greet, they had established no real patterns.

'Welcome to the madness.'

'Of the city? Of your family? Of yourself?'

'I'm alone. Venetia is out till late tonight.'

It was for him to step towards her, and at last he did so, embracing, and to his only mild surprise, was embraced back. He kissed in greeting, then in seriousness, thrilled by his daring. And more daringly still, said: 'You realise the implications of that remark?'

'Perhaps we could get inside the apartment first.'

Unbuttoning the eagled shirt. 'And now like am'rous birds of prey.'

'Tear our pleasures with rough strife.' Now naked amid a new panoply of knots and mazes, floor-to-ceiling windows, and behind her the city: the green tossing ocean of the trees of Senna Puck, and beyond, the walls of glass that made up the many-towered fortress that keeps Manhattan safe from invasion.

And Mark, high in their own fortress, rejoiced, embraced and embracing. Everything would be different from now on.

She served him beer as he lay on the sofa, she drinking tom-ah-to juice. He watches her bringing his drink, her naked body briefly blotting the panoply of the city from his sight. He looks at her, a slow smile playing across his lips.

'Why am I here, Morgan?'

'Because you love me.'

'You Carrollian or Dodgsonian thing. All right, if we must play according to Carrollian or Dodgsonian rules, why did you ask me here? Why the wild extravagance of the ticket and so on? For which much thanks.'

'I wanted to see you.'

'Your New York first eleven playing away this week?'

'Mar-ark.'

Silence.

Mark was impressed at his own sudden cruelty: cruel to himself, to her. And found himself saying: 'I'm so happy, Morgan, I'm so happy I just had to spoil it. Forgive me. But otherwise, I won't be able to believe it.'

Morgan's face softened, widening her eyes that incalculable fraction. Mark felt a flash of intuition: she knew, she understood. And for once, so did he. Suddenly, and for a fleeting second, he understood everything that had gone on between them, understood why the variously terrible things had to happen. It was the only way she could deal with the still more terrible thing they shared. Philosophy Dick, he thought. Yes, even the unethical ethics tutor. She was so happy she just had to spoil it. 'I know,' she said. 'Who better?'

'Morgan –'

'But hush,' she said. 'Not another word on the subject.'

Perhaps there should have been, perhaps he should have insisted, perhaps everything would have been different had he done so. 'But you can still tell me why you asked me to come here.'

'Because I thought New York would make you smile.'

'It does.'

'And of course, Venetia –'

'Have you told her?'

'Told her what?'

'You know.'

'You can say it out loud, Little Worthless.'

Mark feeling somehow ashamed, though ashamed of what he could not tell, said: 'Have you told her that you asked me to marry you?'

'No, Mark, I did not.' Her own consonants and vowels very slightly different from the ones she used on English soil. 'I told her that we had agreed to marry.'

'And what did she say?'

'Provisional pleasure was expressed, followed by an urgent request to meet you. I said we could meet in a few weeks, when she came back to Islington. But she said she wanted to meet you now. But I want to meet him now, Morgan. While there's still time.'

The impersonation turned out to be a good one. 'She said that?'

'She says things like that, Venetia. Very ironical woman. Very clever, very clear, and not unmad, as you once observed, as you will soon discover. But not too soon. Now, hear and attend and listen, Oh Best Beloved.' She reached and picked up from the floor her spreadeagled eagled shirt. 'There's a new Vietnamese restaurant off Fifth Avenue that you wish to visit. Dress in your finest New York chic, and let us walk through the night.'

'I want to walk into a bar and ask for bourbon,' Mark said, wandering about and looking for clothes. 'It's my life's ambition.'

Venetia smiled in acknowledgement and signalled to the sleek and wheeled giantess for menus, the champagne being all but finished. 'I don't altogether figure it,' she said. 'You are, Morgan said, an established couple. And yet you are both skipping around New York as if you met yesterday. Have you not done that being-in-love business before?'

'Not really.' Never before known the certainty of her daily presence.

'Because I have never seen Morgan like this. Ever.'

'Is that good or bad?'

'Insofar as it goes,' Venetia said, laughing very little and turning into Mark's mother again for a second. 'It's a sound basis for a nice love affair, anyway. I am glad she's having fun, and with a nice man.' The frankly shared bed, the occasional morning visitation: 'Coffee and OJ, children.' 'But there is something else. Sometimes, for all the little kisses, I seem to see you as brother and sister.'

'Is that good or bad?'

'Mark,' again that touch on the R, 'it deeply disturbs me. Mostly because of poor Kay, you know. What you and Morgan have is richer and older than a student love affair, it seems to me. And it is a sound basis for a lifelong friendship, and I am very glad for her. But I am not altogether convinced it is a sound basis for marriage.' Mark recalled his visits to Chris's parents, the – excellent – shepherd's pie, the frank brown sauce on the table, the kindly provided bottles of light ale, the man-to-man pint, the solitude of the spare bedroom. The way that nothing of importance was ever mentioned.

'Thank you, Miss,' as the menus came. 'Now what shall we have, Mark? I warn you that the food is not as good as the view.'

151

Mark contemplated the endless and reckless list of dishes.

'You probably think that I asked you here to lunch to ask embarrassing questions about yourself. Some other time; it's more important that I tell you some things about Morgan. Lobster salad.'

'Good idea. Same for me, please,' said Mark cravenly.

'And mineral water. Though perhaps we'll have a serious drink afterwards.'

'Beer, please,' Mark said. 'Rolling Rock.' Knowing you had to be specific. Quite liking the beer. Perhaps he would introduce it to England and make a fortune. And it had a horse on the label, of course.

A cycle courier shot across twelve lanes of traffic, the whistle in his mouth shrilling a warning. Behind Mark, a voice said: 'You know the situation and I know the situation, and I know that you know that I'm screwing you. Right?'

A new city to him, and one Morgan knew well. His delight in the city, his delight in her: each of these things fed on the other's increase. When she wanted to visit the great bookstores, he insisted on walking forty blocks south along Fifth Avenue. 'It's a walker's city,' he said. 'Just like Venice.'

And in Strand Books, between the endless shelves of second-hand books, she had, like a character in a film, bought him a complete E. E. Cummings, because he was a better poet than the English believed. And then they had walked on into the East Village, and he had gawped at the shops and the shoppers. And then, taken with a wild whim, she had bought him a pair of cowboy boots in St Mark's Leather Store: black, chisel-toed and calligraphed with baroque stitching. 'You don't need to buy me presents. I need nothing. To be here in New York with you, I could be barefoot and happy.'

'But it gives me pleasure. You must never deny me my pleasures, however strange they seem.'

It was a mad and ecstatic time, and Mark was reminded, for all that he seldom thought of horses these days, of that mad day at Potton. They had the fastest time by a mile, he and Trev, filled with a shared recklessness that no one could compete with, the red

152

ribbon theirs. 'I see they have taken to giving prizes for insanity,' Mel had said.

The lobster salad was excellent, the Rolling Rock crisp and cool. Venetia talked of Morgan's childhood: her precocious bossiness, the row she (Morgan, not Venetia) had with a primary school teacher. Pudding? No pudding. Coffee, perhaps, and perhaps something to go with it, a cognac?

Venetia drank coffee and not altogether inappropriate Strega; Mark chose Wild Turkey on the rocks. 'I just love ordering it.'

'Do you like drinking it?'

'Enough.'

The drinks came, Mark's glass tinkling in the hand of the wheeled giantess, smiling to give them yet another chance to admire the work of her orthodontist. Not even Trev had such teeth.

'You make Morgan happy.' A sighting shot, Mark felt. Getting the range again.

'It's been a happy week. Ecstatic. As you know.'

'But I don't believe you quite understand how much Morgan needs you.'

'Needs *me?*'

'I thought not. She acts in a slightly imperious fashion, does she not?'

'It was you that said bossy.'

'And you like that?'

'I suppose I must do. Seeing as I like everything about her.'

She acknowledged that with a smile: 'Nicely said. But it's not altogether true, is it? Now hear me, Mark. You are not going to get up from this table until you understand the nature and extent of Morgan's vulnerability.'

'Her what?'

'Yes. Precisely as I thought. Morgan has been quite terribly hurt. And she is desperately frightened that it will happen again. So she doesn't let people in close.'

Well, there was Philosophy Dick, the unethical ethics tutor, the person in London whose existence she had let slip, the one who wrote plays, the person she was with on that weekend in the country, the very tall person from the adjoining building in her

153

hall of residence, the pony-tailed medic who rode a racing bicycle. Mark was prepared to bet serious money that there was someone in New York; a 'friend', a graduate of psychotherapy had been mentioned. Who was it that had the list of his wife's lovers?

'You're the only one, Mark. The only one she has ever let in close.'

Bloom, that was it. Bloody hell, he really ought to be reading Bloom's thoughts, he had an exam to sit in three weeks. Instead of thinking them.

'If that's so, Venetia, then I am pleased. Surprised. Honoured.' But he knew it, he knew it all along. He simply refused to take it on board: refused to take that responsibility.

'Because she has been damaged, you see. You know that. You just don't realise that you know. You adore her strength, you are head over heels in love with her strength. But I know that what you truly love in her is the damage.'

'Perhaps.' Mark did not have the slightest idea what she was talking about. But he continued, in the pause: 'I've never probed. It's not that I'm not curious. But probing is not allowed. I assume that some man disappointed her.' Mark, looking back on this conversation, was to be shocked every time by the appalling naiveté of this remark. His shattering failure to understand the first thing about Morgan. His own talents for knots and tangles was wholly inadequate for dealing with these vaster puzzles.

'You are quite right, Mark. A man disappointed her. I was disappointed too, and by the same man.' For a terrible, frozen minute, Mark imagined some horrendous stagy situation of shared lovers, Lord what fun these rich folks have. Then, seeing that Mark was still about a hundred miles behind the pace, Venetia had to explain, slowly and courteously.

'Her father was a bad husband. Now, Mark, you will pardon my use of the past tense here. I used to correct myself, no, he's still alive. But it's a trick of speech I can't prevent myself from using. So understand that Morgan's father is not exactly dead.'

So many. 'Is he dead for her as well as for you?'

'That is the question on which it all hangs, I guess. I don't know.' She paused, sipped Strega, contemplated Broadway. Mark's turn.

154

Oh, he was used to discussing relationships, but only with students. He felt flattered, invited into the freemasonry of the grown-ups; at the same time out of his depth, a winsome boy.

'What was his crime?' Incest? Violence? Madness? Drunkenness? All these grown-up crimes, and he unable to understand. He looked wisely at the flashing signs before him. Walk. Don't Walk.

'Mark, he was a philanderer. A man of silly copulations. He was a very silly man who liked getting silly girls to take their clothes off. And I was a fool. I thought I could change him. But I know now that nobody ever changes anybody, because nobody ever changes.'

A sip of Strega. Eyes fixing Mark like an ancient mariner. She continued: 'So I thought he would grow out of it, and he didn't. That's the other thing you learn, people don't grow out of things. So I thought family life would slow him down. Then I thought age would do the same thing. It didn't. It speeded him up. And I thought, so long as it is hidden from me. So long as it is discreet. So long as it doesn't harm the family. And with each inch of tolerance he took a mile of silliness.'

Grown-ups didn't talk like this. People's mothers didn't talk like this.

'He was always terribly nice to have around. A very charming man. He was never unkind to me, not when we were in the same room. He was always wonderful company: you can forgive so much of a man who makes you laugh. And I thought, better that than being alone, better that the children have a father. For he really did love the children, a thoughtful and creative father, always thinking up treats, taking them out on his own, buying them special presents. And of course, they loved him very much. Then he had a small surgical operation. It was to remove a tumour that turned out to be benign.'

Mark smiled involuntarily at this.

'I see you are good at ironies. I didn't miss the irony either. It was when he was coming round from the anaesthetic. I was sitting on one side of the bed, and there was a nurse attending to him, doing whatever nurses do. And he awoke, and he addressed not

155

me but the nurse. Not in his normal voice. In the voice of some parodic Lothario in a low comedy.'

Suddenly she leered at him across the small table, pulling her painted-on Cupid's bow this way and that. She told him: 'Hello, swiddy. Lez ged bedder acquainted.'

Then she was the nurse: 'Mr Francis, your wife is here.'

And then the leer again: 'My wife's an ugly ol' cow. You're byooderful.'

Mark had been lost for words for some time now. He thought it best to continue being lost for them.

In her normal voice, Venetia continued: 'It was one word that slew me, Mark, and that was *ugly*. If he had said my wife is a *horrible* old cow then I could have coped. But that *ugly* – it cut like a knife.'

Mark had to say something, and did so.

'It was not a nightmare, Mark. It was waking up from a nightmare to discover that reality was a good deal worse. And I never forgave him. I never forgave him any more of his silly copulations. And then came the day that had always been coming, when I came back to the house to find it a disorderly house. The façade of discretion quite gone. Sheets rumpled, duvet on the floor, two glasses, bottle of champagne in the bedroom, water all over the bathroom floor. Every cliché in the book. And I became very calm and I am not a calm person. And I thought: my husband is not saying *fuck me* here. He is saying *fuck you*.'

Mark gave a grim smile in honour of this.

'And that was the end. I was prepared to be generous, though, even then. I said that as long as he was kind to the children, it would be a civilised divorce. And he was out of the house by now, but he still had a key, and he still had most of his clothes in the house, and he still had his papers, his study. That was the arrangement. But I took to locking my bedroom, which had been our bedroom. I knew him, you see. He would keep his word perfectly, as a man of honour should – unless, of course there was a chance of a silly copulation. And I didn't wish to have that particular homecoming again.'

'No.'

'So it was Morgan that had the homecoming. He used her

156

room. He used her bed. And didn't even attempt to tidy it up afterwards.'

'Oh.'

'Leaving two condoms on the floor.'

'Oh.'

'I could forgive one, Morgan said to me. But I shall never forgive the second condom.'

'No.'

'Never tell her that I told you. Never forget that I told you.'

'I never will.'

'You adore Morgan.'

'Yes.'

'And you love her, I know.'

'So do I.'

'But do you cherish her?'

'As much as she'll let me.'

'She needs more cherishing than you give her. Learn to cherish her a great deal more. Make much of her. She's beautiful and brilliant and damaged. She needs your adoration and your love. But most especially, she needs your cherishing.'

'Yes.'

'Two out of three is not enough.'

'No.'

The juggler on the far side of Broadway was in the midst of what Mark hoped were his final frenzies, for surely he had left himself with nowhere to go. A cutlass, a flaming torch and the once-again-roaring chainsaw. Didn't drop one.

PART TWO

Competition

1

Fear of betrayal. That was it. That was the conclusion Mark came
to round about four o'clock in the morning. The hour that the
Gestapo traditionally paid their calls had once again found Mark
lying there and thinking things through. He was frightened all
right: he had admitted that to himself a good deal earlier, and
fancied himself something of a hero for doing so. But frightened
of what?

Partly, it was knowing that he was certainly going to go through
with it: that there was no get-out. The rather bad peritonitis, the
distant race-memory of the bowler-hatted starter calling the world
to order: thirty seconds, Mark Brown.

But this was not cross-country, this was nothing. This was not
neck-breaking territory. And then he remembered Bec, and one
of her harangues about Ashton and The Mate. People are so
literal-minded about infidelity. So all right. He would be less
literal-minded about fear.

And it was not fear of pain and injury, it was indeed fear of
betrayal. Fear that she would betray him? Perhaps that: fear
that he would once more feel betrayal's lash. That even now,
in his new, brave and altogether well-adjusted post-Morganatic
world, he would find himself once again the victim of betrayal.
No Unwilling Victims: one of Bec's most cherished beliefs, as it
happened.

Or frightened that he would betray her. They had gone so far,
and perhaps he did not know when to leave well alone. Always
wanting that little bit more, regardless of whether or not she had
it to give. Wanting to have everything on his own terms. But did
he? Surely she wanted it as much as he did. Without knowing

she wanted it. The parasitic worm of night-thoughts gnawed and wriggled in his brain.

'But if the poet is despicable then surely the poem is despicable. That has to be true, doesn't it, Mr Brown? I mean, look at Kipling.'

'Interesting point, Ralph. There's a George Orwell essay you must look at. I'll give you details at the end of the lesson. But tell me – and I don't mean to embarrass you, because it's a good point no matter what your answer is. Have you actually read much Kipling? Has anybody?' Nobody had. 'Kipling is one of those poets we all think we know without ever actually reading.' Now hear and attend and listen, O Best Beloved: Morgan's best beloved phrase from the *Just So Stories*. 'Din, Din, Gunga Din. 'Ere's to you, fuzzy-wuzzy, with your 'ayrick 'ead of 'air. That kind of thing. We all think we know "If –". Well, just for fun, let's look at this most famous poem for five minutes. And look at it, not as a specimen of imperial thought, but as a poem.'

Mark went into his book-bag, pulled out and then put back *The Penguin Book of English Verse*, Philosophy Dick, God send his rotten soul to hell if it wasn't there already. He had probably forgotten Mark; not Mark him. Remembering thee, oh Richard. Found the poem in a Kipling anthology he had recently bought for a mere pound. Read the proud rhythmic words, scanning the faces of his class as he did so. Back to the text, always back to the text: that was the lesson he was teaching. Soon he would quote Ralph the words of his hero: never trust the artist, trust the tale. But the text, the certainty shot through with self-doubt, the unexpected subtlety of thought – he could see as he scanned the faces that it reached them.

> 'If you can make one heap of all your winnings
> And risk it on one turn of pitch-and-toss . . .'

They had tittered at 'you'll be a Man, my son!' but in the end, what stayed with them was the thought of filling the unforgiving minute with sixty seconds' worth of distance run.

But how much did the lesson, did the poem help you, if you really had made one heap of all your winnings, and really were just about to risk them on one turn of pitch-and-toss? Not enough.

Yes, and that mad flight to New York, that had been just such an 'If –' moment. One heap, and he had won, had he not? Certainly something was settled for all time in that demented, exam-wrecking (What the hell's wrong with a two-two anyway? Well, Mark, if you don't know, I can't tell you) week. But now – well, count them, February now, so the work of six months to find, and even sustain a certain kind of happiness. Or content – but call it what you will, he had brought a certain bearability to daily life. And now, to risk it on one turn of pitch-and-toss.

> And lose, and start again at your beginnings
> And never breathe a word about your loss;

Wrong, Ruddy baby, all wrong. Losing was impossible to contemplate. They had to win. Not win as in win, but win as in not losing. She and him. Would she do it right when it mattered? Would he? If, if, if.

It was moral qualities that were to be tested, no matter who you were talking about. He was never in any doubt of that throughout the endless examination of wriggling night-thoughts.

Rather a fuss to make about a horse. Hasn't it occurred to you that you are blinding yourself to the central emotional truths in your life? That silly girl and that fucking horse.

❧

Horribly cold and rainy, Barbour collars over their ears, fringe of drops on the peak of his green cord cap. He and Mel raised the ramp and Mel shoved home the barred double-latch. Looked at him from beneath the brim of her wax-cotton Akubra. 'She went on all right.'

'Old pro.'

They each tied a haynet to the back of Mel's lorry. He had already put his kit in the cab. No sandwiches; he never ate on a show day. Eating was not a physical possibility; never was. Apart from the occasional extra strong mint.

'Let's kick on.'

Mark climbed into the passenger seat, and Mel took her place behind the wheel. The obedient little lorry started at the first time of asking. 'You don't have to do this, you know.'

'I know.'

'This is supposed to be fun.'

'Thanks for reminding me.'

Half an hour later, Mel was backing the lorry confidently into a spot between one immense four-horse cruiser, and a trailer pulled by a muddy four-wheel drive. Rain was still hosing from the sky, ground already tyre-churned. The usual fraught show-day atmosphere, a little muted by the weather. They checked that the horses were happy, decided to leave them in the lorry while they paid their entry fees and walked the course.

The huge corrugated barn of the indoor arena. Stairs to a small gallery: a man in a nice tweed jacket, rather like Mark's father's Norfolk jacket of blessed memory, collecting the entry money. The class with the smallest jumps was well subscribed already. It would probably last nearly two hours. Walk the course now, if you want to; first horse starts in ten minutes.

Down below, the jumps were arranged in the classical patterns: eight of them, the turns tight but not too taxing, each jump around two foot six. 'Start at jump one, then go on till you reach eight. Then stop.' Mel remembered Mark's perennial problem of getting lost on jumping courses. Mark managed a grunt of acknowledgement. 'Look, Mark, there's nothing here that she can't do.'

'I'm not worried about her jumping. I'm worried about her going in through that bloody door.'

'Right, here's the plan. You ride in for twenty minutes. Then come in here and jump. I'll be on the floor, and I'll take her head if she needs it. I'll get you both in. Once she's inside, she'll go. You jump a beautiful clear round, then me and Ed'll ride in and jump our own beautiful clear. How does that sound?'

'Good, Mel. A lot better than it felt a minute ago. All right. We'll manage it.'

'When in doubt.'

'Precisely.'

Mark tacked the mare up in the lorry, then led her off. She hopped and skittered and spun, understanding, understanding perhaps too well the smells, the many horses, the rain, the crackle of the Tannoy. Show. She knew. She knew all right. Did she remember the terror, the puissance, the beating? Or did she know that she was with Mark now, know he would never ask for too much, never give her a beating, always trust her, always cherish, always make much? Don't be sentimental.

He put his foot in the iron and off she walked as usual, as if she had just remembered an urgent appointment, but Mark made no effort to correct this bad habit, swinging his leg over her back, patting, sitting on the wet saddle. Mud on his beautifully polished boots. He smiled faintly, down at Mel. And got it back a hundredfold.

Whack. Time-traveller: a decade and more back in a single moment. The promise those old show-days held, Trev at his bounding best and Mel at hers. He smiled again, not faintly at all this time, as remembered and anticipated joys filled him. 'All right, girl,' he said. 'Foreplay.' Too softly for Mel to hear.

It was pretty horrible out there in the practice area. Wet horses, wet riders, mostly female, mostly young, mostly in dripping water-proofs. The place crackled with human and horsey tensions. The mare bounced beneath him feeling – savouring? – the scent of madness in the air. As usual, two or three riders were obsessively jumping the practice jump – people on the ground constantly put-ting it back up again – each apparently in the midst of a full-blown and utterly inappropriate jumping lesson. Others circling, trotting, cantering.

She knew it was a show as well as anyone. She knew about the need to work with your tensions, to turn your tensions into athleticism and courage. Well, mostly courage today, girl. Moral courage. Trust, trust me.

Forget the teenagers mad with fear. We're on our own in here. And Mark eased forward into a trot and dropped her onto the bit, a fine, exuberant bouncing trot, athletic, but controlled: she had

165

her balance, her control. Head down in muscular concentration. Business.

He put her through a series of basic dressage moves, changes of pace, changes of rein. No flashy little circles, just get that balance, get the muscles warm and supple. He halted, asked her to rein back, to take half a dozen backward strides. Best exercise, for showjumping. Get the hocks beneath her.

And she responded, no madcap head-throwing. Serious game. She knew.

The twenty minutes were about done. At the thought, a hand clasped viciously at his stomach. An old enemy, that hand: that terror. Deep breaths, those were the things. Don't let her know your terror. 'All right, girl. One jump in here and it's for real.'

Up into canter off the turn, no one jumping, now look at the jump. And she made a small bound but took his easy check in good part, and then at once measured her stride beautifully, and she flowed over, landing in the same flowing canter with which she had approached. Back to walk in a stride, a handful of pats.

They walked to the edge of the arena, where a headscarfed, sodden and Barboured woman guarded the doors. 'Number?'

He'd forgotten it, of course. But there was Mel, to take the mare's head while he stripped off his own Barbour, to sit there splendid in black riding jacket, white shirt, white tie, white jods. And a number tied round his waist with a piece of string. Mel read it out, the starter wrote it on her clipboard. 'Go in after her.' Nodding at another rider, young, fair hair in a hairnet, nice little chestnut about 15 hands, both strung tight as a banjo. The doors of the hangar opened, a rider came out grinning and patting. 'Good luck,' Mark said to the vanishing hairnet.

Mark walked the mare in a circle, and felt the rain gather in drops on the peak of his new and smart black silk. She threw her head, and performed a sort of Irish hardshoe tapdance across the concrete apron before the doors. Fear. Control it. *Use* it.

One turn of pitch-and-toss. And the doors opened, and the banjo pair came out looking glum. 'All right. In you go.'

Ahead the dark arena, the threatening jumps, the fraught air of competition. Mark squeezed the mare forward towards this

166

dark cave of horror. And got nothing. She stared at the vision beyond the door like a maiden aunt finding a man in the wardrobe. That spooky feeling, when all contact between you and the horse vanishes from your hands. She had gone from him: a ghost horse.

He patted, whispered to her: go on, girl, and delivered a hefty kick. And she stood.

Not high, not much, not by her standards, but she was on her back legs all right, front legs a couple of feet off the ground. Ask me again and I'll do it for real.

And Mark once again laughed at her silliness, and laughing and dropping his reins and patting her and talking nonsense almost as daft as the girl herself. 'Don't pat the bloody thing, give it a good whack, what have you got a stick for, Christmas decoration?' The starter's riding-instructor voice. And Mark felt a reaction from ancient times, when unthinking obedience to your riding instructor was part of daily life, and even involuntarily lifted his whiphand half-an-inch. But no. He was making his own mistakes in his own way, was he not? And if they failed to get in, well, he would forgive her anyway. Anything. He put his whiphand back on the loose rein. 'Get a move on if you're going,' the starter said, disgusted at the rejection of her request or order. 'Right now or you're defaulted.'

'You foolish female. This is what you've been waiting for, isn't it?' Mel, taking the reins, and the little mare, relaxing at Mark's laughter, walking through the door with Mel at her head. Finding herself inside the arena.

And another horse entirely: a smooth and beautiful canter, not frightened at all, the whole power of the horse held in a finger. Horrible or rather ugly old cow, treating us like novices. Right then, girl.

And he looked at the first jump, and he knew from that instant's glance that it was all going to be fine. Calm, businesslike, accurate, they jumped the jumps in order. Mark even asked her for a flying change across the diagonal, and amazingly it came off, hope the cow saw that, and six, and seven, and eight, and through the finish. A neat circle and they cantered straight at the doors.

167

Forward into halt in a single stride, more or less on the cow's toes. 'Angel. You angel.'

'Well done.'

'Thanks. Sorry about the kerfuffle at the start, thanks for your patience.' Non-existent though it was. And Mark made a flashy leaping dismount, and Mel was in his arms, or at least one of them, the other still holding the reins, her lips on his and both alight with the joy of it, her Akubra falling to the ground, rain on kissing faces.

'Thanks, Mel. You were great. Perfect.'

'So were you.'

'We know.'

2

She seemed to be enjoying herself, anyway. And Mark was at least drunk. He was not quite sure how that had come about. Perhaps by drinking too much, though it had been his impression that he had avoided this rather obvious trap. Still, as his mother would have said: there it is.

It was a celebration. Partly it was a house-warming. Venetia had decided to settle permanently in New York, and had passed the Islington house to Morgan – '*and* Mark, and I hope it will be a lucky place for you both' – on indefinite rent-free loan. Along with a parting gift, the Great Gangetic Maze. Morgan took charge of interior décor after Venetia had packed her favourite mazes off to the New York apartment, had hung Islamic textiles, such bliss, so dehumanising. Mark felt uncomfortable about the arrangement, but comfortable enough in the actual house. He bought a set of carbon-steel Sabatiers and set about making it a proper kitchen instead of a place for defrosting meat.

But all in all, it was a triple celebration. Mark had a proper job at last, at Herne Hill Comprehensive, so his days of supply teaching were over. And as for Morgan, her first book had been published, the collection of grimoires she called *Alice*. These seemed to them equally fine things, and they had properly rejoiced in each other's success.

But the party somehow changed all that. It was, Mark thought later, a watershed in his life. But he hardly ever did think about it, being a past master at the art of evasion. He was aware that something was settled for all time in the throes of that party, but it was not the sort of thing you could ever think about. It was not the sort of thing you could ever quite understand. And he never told anybody.

And not telling somehow made it all so many thousand times worse. The night of serial buttock-fondling: everyone had witnessed his humiliation, knew of his remorse, adored the studiously self-mocking poem. But the events of that night in Islington were far, far worse: worse even than the poems in *Running Bowline*. The medium did not exist to express the horror of Morgan's Last Party.

You're Morgan's husband, aren't you? What do you do? Oh, I'm a literary agent. Oh, I write plays. Oh, I work in a gallery in Bond Street. Oh, I am writing a thesis on Jorge Luis Borges. And yourself? I teach. 'Oh.' Oh, Mark thought again, smiling and smiling, oh, oh, oh. Oh fuck off. Morgan, how lovely, saw the review in the *Spectator*, what a triumph. Only read the first one so far, but it's wonderful, so truly horrible I wanted to die. And you're her husband, what is it like, to be married to so vile a person, and you'd never think it to look at her, would you? You must be so proud. Yes, you would.

And Morgan, sardonic, basking, and Mark living the night of serial bottle-opening, pouring, smiling, drunk. Yes, that's right, I teach. But who wanted to listen to his conquest of the class with the bad reputation, that virtuoso bit of the teacher's craft? Oh yes, as things go, it was certainly as elegantly baked – those almost esculent slices of life, the *Spectator* said – as anything Morgan had written. And she had rejoiced with him when he had told her about it, but there was no rejoicing in her now, not for him.

Mark was not exactly sulking, but he did keep wondering just how many of the men present had fucked his wife. That sort of thing that can take the edge off a party. Her effortless transition from ludic to lubricious, and from lubricious to the grey horrors of desolation. So many: he did not know lust had undone so many. Normally this was the sort of thing he managed not to think about more often than every so often. But now he could think of little else, a drunken tourist in his own country; a tipsy visitor to his own house. What was the difference between jealousy and envy?

She looked pretty esculent herself tonight, in a sort of flapper

170

dress, black and covered with tiny black beads, a frock that fell like a plumbline and flattened every small convexity of her flat figure. She is capable of moving beyond ironical understatement to a plane on which there is hardly any statement at all, nor need for one. The barest hint is all that is required to reveal the most startling sexual folly, or the sharpest horrors to which the human mind is heir to.

Mark pouring, smiling, chatting. Very proud, yes, very proud indeed. And all the while filled with thoughts of sharpest horror, thoughts of startling sexual folly. One more drink and he'd be serial buttock-fondling.

Callum and Naz turned up and that restored his nerves a little. Naz actually wanted to hear about the conquest of 5J, and he told her the tale and told it rather well. Perfectly turned hermetic passages that cast unexpected rays of darkness on ancient questions of guilt and love.

The door. Morgan too busy to open it, of course. 'Tom, hi!' He didn't think they would come; he had forgotten he had asked them. A warm handshake, full of deep shared history. And Tom's wife looking at him with that terrible challenging smile, that terrible snaking eyebrow. A somehow challenging pause before he kissed her. 'It's been an age.' What devil made him do it? Flick his tongue against her lips for the merest fragment of a second, a tease only, a tease to answer her teasing smile. She released him, laughing with incredulous delight, and he laughed with her, and nobody else knew why. The Game. The most ancient of their shared jokes, and by far the best.

'What a place, Mark.' She made a high, stagy gesture with her right hand, drawing the eye. Her left swinging low out of sight pressed for an infinitesimal fraction his crotch. Hilarity bubbled up inside him as if he were an unusually powerful artesian well. But the rules of The Game forbade not only giggling: they forbade any recognition of anything untoward.

'Come and have a drink. What will you have, Mel, champagne or champagne?' Both she and her husband turned towards the gathering. Mark's unseen index finger made a hidden caress an inch below the bone called the sacrum, reaching what was much softer and more caressable than bone.

How many times, at shows, in pubs, at parties, on trains and buses, around the stable-yard, had they played The Game of surreptitious touching? The Game was centred around a challenge: escalation. Each advance had to be met by a still greater audacity, and had always to be greeted with a mask of indifference; perhaps a commonplace remark, certainly an uninterrupted flow of conversation.

Mark poured drinks, introduced them to people, went to get the door again, greeted, smiled, poured more drinks. Lost Tom and Mel somewhere in the party but stayed in good humour, delighting in this minute incursion of The Game, of the past, into this hateful present of the party. 'Can I top you up?'

'How kind. You're Morgan's husband, aren't you? A lecturer, yes?'

Oh, fuck off. 'No. I teach, actually.'

A slim hand snaked between his thighs. 'Oh.'

'Mark, this really is the most extraordinary house.' Somehow, Mark seemed to have walked away from the I'm-in-publishing type with his floppy jacket and his owlish glasses: not really a first-eleven type, but perhaps he occasionally got a game in the reserves. The stiffs. Not the first time Mark had made this joke to himself.

'Let me show the best maze we have left, the one called the Wild Wood Maze. Come, observing the intricate plaiting and knotting of the banister rail as you do so.' They walked up stairs thronged with talkers and drinkers to the crowds on the first floor, Mark's hand chummily around her waist. They stopped at the turn of the stairs to see the vast maze at its best, Mark's hand skating upward on a rink of black silk, briefly but wonderfully to cup unfettered beauty.

She was looking far from inesculent herself, a longish flowingish skirt in black, black shirt with the third button playfully undone, an undone button that took the reader's thoughts from ludic to lubricious, cuffs rolled back halfway to the elbow, a selection of chains about her neck. Hair in a new perm of dancing curls, shining, loose, eyes ditto. Daring.

'And leading up to the second floor, we have the knotted banister

172

continuing, as you see.' Her arm now about his waist, her hand diving suddenly and invisibly inside his waistband for an electric second. Was she drunk? Or drunk with challenge, with delight, with mischief? Or was it him, drunk enough for them both?

And now climbing the very last flight, up to the attic floor, beyond the last ripples of the visitors. 'And there is the most wonderful mazy-knotty frieze right at the top of the house. Also a priceless collection of cheap plastic snowstorms.' She squeezed in alongside him on the narrow staircase, his own hand's turn for a foray beneath a waistband, and then further south. There his tallest finger turned into a pen, and he wrote her a brief love poem, mixing memory and desire. He withdrew his ink-dampened finger and opened the door for her. Turned to close it behind him. Wickedly.

'Oh, this really is the best room in the house, too good for guests. The skylights make it a tent, a tent in the sky.'

Mark turned from the door. She wore a bland sight-seer's smile, though not a shirt. This had somehow fallen to the floor at her feet. 'Do you have another objet d'art to show me?' Mark showed her. What else could he do? 'How sweet? May I hold it for a second? Oh, very nice. Where shall I put it now? Is this the right place?'

It was the right place.

Perhaps one minute and fifteen seconds later, they broke apart, alight with a glorious hilarity. He kissed, called her angel. She kissed, called him devil.

Grey horrors of desolation.

3

'I have the answer to all your problems. Take a notebook from that small cabin-trunk you have at your feet, and a pen or sharp pencil. Write down what I tell you.'

'Mark Brown. Everybody's problems solved except his own.'

'But I have solved mine.'

'I hope you're not going to tell me to buy a horse.'

'No. Just half a dozen eggs. That will do the trick all right.'

'I fail to see how. And you may call it solving your problems. I call it distraction behaviour.'

'So do I. Bloody effective it is too. I'm taking her in a three foot class next weekend, did I tell you?'

'You did, yes. Six months, isn't it? Since she left you?'

'A bit more than that.'

'And you're getting back with that long-lost lover of yours. Nobody is called Melody.'

'Not a thought of it. Miss Chance is the only female in my life.'

'They'll put that on your tombstone.' One of The Mate's favourite lines. The waiter took away the pizza plates. Rather elegant pizzas, but not expensive, this being Mark's treat. The spicy Bloody Marys, drunk elsewhere and paid for by Bec or *Edge*, had cost more.

'Two double espressos,' Mark said without consulting, a token of intimacy. 'Two sambucas.'

Bec smiled. 'Heavenly cough mixture.'

She was very distressed. Uncharacteristically diffident when she rang up, asking if they could meet. As if it were a favour, and they did not trade in favours. Diffidence cloaked in banter;

if you can bear for a whole evening to abandon that fucking horse.

And he abandoned without considering a refusal, though not entirely without regret (he had half-planned to do a little gridwork), and half guessing that there was trouble ahead. But making a wrong guess as to the cause of the trouble. It had to be the marriage thing, of course it did, but he thought it would have something to do with a love affair. People are so literal-minded about infidelity. An affair of hers, perhaps: a tryst with the British snow-boarding champion. Or Rob, frustrated by her incomprehension of his professional life, plunging deep into the nearest secretary.

But no. He had simply had enough, he said. He cited *Edge* as co-respondent. Thin strip of face, burning Gitane in the centre of the Gothic arch, untipped, always a bad sign. Clanking a new one alight with her Zippo. 'Said he didn't mind a bit of hanky-panky, but he felt like the man whose wife had only been unfaithful twice. Once with the milkman and once with the Household Cavalry.'

'I don't follow.'

'Nor did I. But he says I'm out there giving blow-jobs to every twenty-year-old male in the country. Meaning the readership of *Edge*.'

'He married a career girl. He can hardly complain when she turns into a career woman.'

'He put it rather well, actually. Marriage is not a bit on the side, you know.'

'Does he think there's a real bit on the side? And with justice, perhaps?'

'No. And no again. He said he is just fed up with being married to someone he never sees. Except for half an hour in the evening when I'm too knackered to speak, and ten minutes in the morning and I'm not a morning person. So he says, am I really a marriage person? Or just a career person?'

'What sort of advice do you want, Bec?'

'Damned if I'm giving up *Edge*. He doesn't mind the bloody money, does he?'

'Money's not the issue, is it?'

'And I don't notice him offering to stop broking stocks.'

Mark did more listening than talking, always an unusual thing for him, as they drank the Bloody Marys. 'And we agreed right at the beginning that mutual careers were the thing, so it can hardly count as a betrayal, can it? If anybody's going back on a deal, it's him.'

'But it's not about deals, is it? Nothing is about deals, especially not marriage. Marriage is about something else entirely.'

It was not until they had extinguished the small blue flames of their sambucas that Mark had a chance to start talking. 'Listen to me, Bec. You really should, I'm an expert.'

'I'm an expert on marriage, unlike my wife, who is not around to be asked.'

'My position vis-à-vis my wife is precisely what makes me an expert. I've given more thought to the matter than most. Far too late for myself, I grant you. But by no means too late for you. For you, I have that most precious of all things, a second chance. Seize it. Seize it with both hands. Because it is the most important moment of your life. Nothing less. Are you listening hard?' Mark spoke with mock solemnity, to cover the real solemnity he intended.

'All ears, little brother.'

'Good. I shall start with a question, and I want you to answer it seriously. Tell me, Bec: do you want to stay married?'

'Yes, but –'

'No qualification is permissible.'

'Did you invent the rules of this game?'

'No. Old as mankind. Womankind too. Answer me. Do you want to stay married to Rob?'

'Well . . . all right. On the whole, yes.'

She was a little taken aback by all this. Mark was many things with Bec, but never bossy. But then it was not really Bec that he was addressing. 'You love him. You always have loved him. You always will love him.'

'But I'm not going to –'

'Answer the question. Yes or no.'

'Well, more yes than no, anyway.'

'See how simple life is? Having accepted that, understand that it is time for the Grand Gesture.'

'If you think I'm resigning from –'

'Bec.' And he instructed her to take out her notebook from the smallish cabin-trunk, and made her write the following.

6 eggs
butter
flour
Gruyère
milk
pkt salad
nice spuds
bot. NZ Chardonnay

'I cook him egg and chips and it saves my marriage?'

'It said it was time for Grand Gesture. You're going to cook him a soufflé. And it will blow him away.'

'Mark.' Genuine anguish in her voice. 'You *know* I can't cook.'

'That is precisely why it will work. You can make a cheese sauce?'

'Just about, but –'

'Then you can cook a soufflé.' He talked her through it. 'And crack 'em over a large bowl, drip the whites in, then chuck the yolks into a mug . . .' Mark really did like teaching.

'And that's cooking a soufflé?'

'Everyone thinks it's the most complicated dish in the world. They reckon it's next to impossible. But you and I know that it's a piece of piss. You'll get ten million points. Salt and pepper, you won't forget salt and pepper? Freshly ground, you can do that?'

'I think so.'

'Repeat the treatment once a week, ideally on the same day. Like Friday. I'll give you a different recipe each week. Same theory: minimum trouble, maximum impact.'

'I'm not sure, Mark. I turn myself into a little woman, and –'

'Au contraire. You are turning yourself into a very big woman. Do I contradict myself? Very well, I contradict myself. I am large,

I contain multitudes. And you're telling him, I want to save my marriage. You're telling him you love him, you always have loved him, you always will love him.' Passion in his voice, though only Bec could hear.

'I'm fucked if I'm saying that.'

'You won't need to.'

'You haven't told me to wear a diaphanous gown.'

'You won't need to.'

She laughed, the first time she had properly laughed that evening. 'All right, Markie. I'll try it. Is there anything I can do to help you save your own marriage?'

'If you can do what Jesus did to Lazarus.'

Mark was really rather taken with the idea of himself as an expert on marriage. The idea sustained him as he walked to the tube at Oxford Circus – Bec, of course, took a cab to her place in Wimbledon – to take the Victoria Line to Highbury and Islington.

The number of experts who had given him advice with the mare. Best way to deal with a chronic rearer is to burst a bag of water over her head. No it's not, not unless you make sure the water is warm. That way she'll think it's her own blood, and she'll be so frightened she'll never do it again.

No. Crack an egg between her ears. No. Reverse your whip and clonk her on the poll. No. Jump off and pull her over backwards. No. Just sit in the plate and tan her hide for her. No, no, no: the only solution is correct the shortage of lead between her ears. And do it quick, before she kills you.

And he had taken nobody's advice. Brilliant horsemanship, wasn't it? Well, on the whole, it wasn't, no. Fantastic courage, then? No. What then? He must have done something right. A small amount of horsemanship, a small amount of courage. And rather a lot of – well, call it by its right name, then. We call a spade a spade, us horsey folk, y'know. No bloody euphemisms for us lot.

Love.

Bloody fool.

That jump-off, the other weekend. He wished the advice-givers could have seen that. Wish they could have seen her walk into the ring, for that matter. The way they jumped the fences at 45 degrees to the sensible, cutting corners, saving time. You can do that in showjumping. Can't do it across country, of course, with hard fences. Fastest time, but they whiffed the last, and a pole rolled agonisingly free from its shallow cup, an audible sigh from the small audience, then the death rattle. Still, as failures go, it was a pretty glorious one. Mel beat him with a double clear, taking third overall, and the two of them laughing and hugging all brother-and-sisterly, and Mark thankful again that the horrors they shared had at last been set aside.

He gave a pound to a *Big Issue* seller outside Highbury and Islington tube, without taking a *Big Issue*, and felt reasonably wonderful as a result. He walked down Upper Street, past the late-night grocery. Outside it a pair of young males, both with spiky green hair – frightfully passé or was it back in the height of fashion again? – arguing with drunken or otherwise addled near-violence and saying 'man' a lot. Was there beer in the fridge? He could do with a beer, but surely he had plenty, and past the town hall and the pub that used to reckon the price in old money, four pounds seventeen and six, sir, schupid nonsense. And then into the quiet streets, and on to the proud square in which he lived, but for how much longer? Surely she would ask him to leave soon, and then where would he go? Radlett, perhaps. Hang around the Wagon and Horses making eyes at Kath. Get murdered by the Fat Farrier.

He did not need to walk around the square twice. He approached his door in good heart. And then stopped for half a stride. There was someone on his steps, outside his front door. This was not an unprecedented event, nor, for that matter, was stepping over a huddled sleeping-bagged body when he set off to Radlett before dawn on a Sunday morning. He regretted his quid for the non-purchase of the *Big Issue*; it seemed unlikely that he would get through his own front door without paying a toll.

'Good evening,' he said neutrally. Stoned or drunk, no doubt. But the figure got to his feet without difficulty, indeed, with some grace. And smiled in the most charming way possible. 'Oh, hello.' As if he were the householder, Mark a chance caller.

Mark hesitated, uncertain whether to plough on through, or to reach for small change. He found himself pulling out his key, to look like a householder himself, and one with every right to be where he was. Not such a good plan, of course, if the visitor was a violent burglar, but the smile had filled the occasion with all kinds of social niceties.

'Oh,' said the visitor. 'Do you live here?' He had what used to be called John Lennon glasses, a head that seemed to be completely bald, perhaps shaven. He wore a leather jacket of the biking kind and below this, rather unusually, a kilt. Below that he wore a pair of cowboy boots of a beauty that rivalled even Mark's. Such clothes seemed to demand violent, assertive manners, and perhaps a very great deal of drugs or drink to back them up. Or perhaps the obsessive sexual aggression that some people adopt as a form of power. The clothes seemed rather out of step with the genuine charm he scattered about without perceptible effort.

'That's right,' Mark said, smiling despite himself. Only an instant later wondering what the admission had let him in for.

'I'm so sorry to give you trouble,' the visitor said. 'You see, I used to live here myself, and I was passing, and I thought I would drop in. But there's nobody at home. So I thought I would sit here for a moment in case anyone turned up. You wouldn't be anything to do with my sister, would you? I'll push off, now with many apologies –'

'Hang on,' Mark said. 'What is the name of your sister?'

'Curious question,' said the visitor, without offence. 'Curious name, too. Name of Morgan, believe it or not.'

An ocean of understanding flooded Mark's brain. 'Hello, Kay,' he said. 'I'm Mark. I married Morgan, but she's not here. Still, come in and have a drink.'

Mark opened the door, and Kay followed him in. Reed-thin and boneless, three or four inches taller than Mark. And something not quite right about him. Something not quite of this world. 'Beer? Wine? Whisky?'

'You know, what I'd really love is a cup of tea.'

'Fine,' said Mark, with hardly any irritation at all. 'Come into the kitchen.'

'So do you know where Venetia is?'

'She's been living in New York for, oh, six, seven years. In the apartment on Central Park.'

'And Morgan?'

'To tell the truth, I have no idea.'

'Golly. I was going to say, how unusual. But perhaps it isn't, with Morgan. When do you expect her back? Later tonight?'

'I haven't seen her for more than six months. She walked out. And simply vanished.'

'How terribly Morgan of her. Leaving you all on your ownio. So she's somewhere in London?'

'I suppose so. But I haven't a clue. I just send her mail –' he had picked up the Americanism from Morgan '– to a friend of hers. I just have the address, don't know the friend, can't pump her for information. Or him.'

'But you have the house. Not such a bad swap, I suppose.'

'It's still Venetia's. But I have permission in writing to stay on here for a bit, formal letter and so on.'

'But you haven't seen her?'

'Not since.' Stop weeping, Little Worthless. Oh, that night, that night. He had performed *Othello* and *King Lear* with bits of *Hamlet* thrown in, and nothing had affected her composure, still less her resolution. Stop weeping, Little Worthless. I'm a gone girl.

And she was. Leaving with a small overnight bag to he knew not where, he knew not whom. Then the diurnal raid in which she pinned to the drapes the grumpy, shortly-to-be-ravished reclining nude. One other visit, in which she took practically everything portable that she owned; who had helped her? And the polite, even rather affectionate letters making arrangements about the running of the house, the forwarding of the mail. And not a word about her own life.

'Does she do any kind of work?'

'Don't you know? She's rather famous. Written two collections of short stories, very successful, wonderful reviews. Something of a cult figure. I expect there'll be another coming out this autumn, it's about time. She also does a small amount of very highly paid journalism.'

181

'I always thought she'd find her own place in the world. And you? Are you a writer too?'

A rather passionate butterfly. 'I teach.'

Kay's face brightened altogether unexpectedly at this news. 'How terribly brave.' His head was covered in a very fine, almost babyish sort of bum-fluff, hinting with fine understatement at a receding hairline. He had a way of stroking his scalp with his right hand.

The tea was made. Mark took, for he had been right, a beer from the fridge, and carried both into the sitting room. Kay sat on the sofa on which his host and his sister had, so many years ago, on Mark's first entry to the house – but never mind that now. Mark gave him his tea, in a cup and saucer the size of a smallish chamber-pot, Morgan's favourite, as it happened, for deskside gulping of green tea. Kay took it with a smile of thanks, really such a charming smile, and crossed his legs in a little flounce of tartan.

'Kay, I adore the kilt.' Because you have to say something, really, though Mark hoped that the compliment would not come across too gay, merely as a man of the world unfazed by gaiety.

Kay gave a self-deprecating pout. 'Bought it in an Oxfam shop. Do all my shopping there, can't afford anything else, but dear, such treasures. And I had to possess this. I had a party to go to, and it seemed really rather the thing.'

'How was the party?'

'Well, I had just left when I decided to come here.' Slow caress of scalp. 'I tend to leave parties rather early these days, I'm such an old bore, you see.' He looked at Mark rather directly. 'You don't really seem to be the sort to be married to my sister, if you don't mind my saying so.'

Mark gave a short snort of laughter. 'She took a little longer than you, but she reached the same conclusion in the end.'

'Always such a glamour-puss, Morgan.'

'Meaning that teaching is a humdrum occupation, and that a mere teacher would never be enough for her?' But if he had never been enough, why did she take ten years or so to work that out? Because she was a gone girl. Head over heels. A passion she had

182

never known before. Who? His favourite night-time thought. No doubt a person of rare glamour, rare beauty, rare perfection. Who understood her jokes.

'I'm very fond of Morgan, but I'm not altogether sure I envy the man she married.'

'She misses you.'

'Oh, my dear. I miss her so much. But it's not really been possible, you know?'

'Till tonight.'

'Perhaps it's a blessing that there's nobody here. Just little us.'

Kay drank tea. Mark drank beer. Silence. Mark took a second sip. Was Kay waiting for the question? Mark asked it, anyway. 'So what have you been up to? This past decade or so?'

Kay gave serious thought before answering. And then he turned abruptly to self-caricature. 'Oh, I've been such a silly girl.' He gave himself a smack on a limp wrist.

'Would that have worried them? Couldn't Venetia accept that? Surely Morgan could.'

'Nothing to do with them. I'm sure they'd have been absolute troopers, the pair of them. No, it's all to do with me. Everything always is. I'm frightfully interested in me, you see.'

'Then tell me your story.'

'Well – I'll tell you some. Seeing as you're a relation.' He gave a friendly parodic simper to Mark as he said this. 'No, the fact is, dear, that being a heroin addict takes up all your precious time.'

'You're a –'

'Was a, dear, was a. Such a wonderful career option, drugs. So fulfilling. All your time is spoken for. You need never be bored. Promotion is always available. Killing hours, mind, but you must make sacrifices if you want to make it to the top in any profession, isn't that right?'

Kay liked to leave pauses for Mark to speak in, so that he could interrupt. 'But you came off –'

'Well, I had a couple of really rather frightful scares, you know. Stuff that wasn't quite what it said on the label. Lying in a coma for forty-eight hours is something that rather gives you the willies.'

'I can imagine –'

'So I became a piss-cart. Isn't that unusual? Actually, it isn't all that, but never mind. I decided to come off it – heroin, I mean – and I knew I was clever enough and strong enough to do it all by my little self, but I thought the tiniest smidgen of booze might help me through the sticky bits. Bottles and bottles and bottles, all the most filthy red wine, taste it still, yucko. All that throwing up, so tedious, only worse thing in life is sobriety. But I got so frightfully fed up with it, that taste and the throwing, that I went into it properly. Addiction therapy, that sort of thing. Funny thing, coming off the booze was ten times harder than coming off the naughty stuff. And I've been sober and unstoned and as healthy as I'm ever likely to be for two years now. And *that's* why I leave parties early, that's why I am such a great big terrible old bore.'

'So you –'

'And the really silly thing is that it was all totally obvious from about the first thirty seconds of therapy what it had all been about for the past ten years. I'd concentrated on drugs so as not to be gay. Not that I'd been altogether without adventures, you understand. It wasn't the doing I minded, but the being.'

'So coming out was all it took?'

'Not really. Just one more boring part of the whole boring tedious package, yawn, I'm a heroin addict, yawn I'm an alcoholic, yawn yawn so vieux jeu, I'm a homosexual.'

'But you're all right now?'

'Well, being gay isn't exactly a bed of roses, dear. Not for me, never really had the temperament for it. Being sober and so forth isn't a barrel of laughs. But mustn't grumble, you know? I'm frightfully busy, that's the main thing. Acquiring wisdom and so forth.'

'Do you work?'

'No, dear, thanks for the compliment and all that. More or less unemployable. Spend the evenings manning a phoneline, you know, a helpline for naughty druggies. Snap out of it, I say. Be a man. And I've been studying in the day. Rather good fun, actually. I'm an undergraduate, isn't that glamorous?'

'Reading what?'

'External degree, you know, they don't actually want me camping about the campus. French, second year now, literature, the eternal verities and all that.'

'I teach English.'

'Well, perhaps you can help me with my essay, you must have read Proust, Albertine, the sweet cheat gone and all that.'

'I'm an expert on the subject.'

'Oh, you bitter, bitter boy. But don't you agree that the Albertine business makes no sense at all as an encounter between heterosexuals? We all know in roman-à-clef terms that she's his chauffeur. So it's the world's most dishonest book: can you tell me how it can also be so good?'

'My best class, Class G is worrying with that very problem, though with other books. They can't work it out either.'

'Honesty is salvation. We chaps who have been through therapy have to believe that, you know. It's the only thing that works. What I talk about on the telephone to the naughty druggies. And there's me spending the day with the most dishonest book in literature. And it happens to be the best.'

'I have a theory about this. But it takes time. More tea?'

'I won't, dear, if it's all the same to you. I've kept you up too late. I must get home, essays to write. But I'd love to hear your theory some time.'

'Drop by. Any time.'

'Thanks, dear. You're very sweet. My sister's a fool, you know. A damn, damn fool.'

Mark acknowledged this with a smile, really rather touched. 'Any message for her?'

'None. Except my love, except my love, except my love.'

'You don't want to leave an address? A phone number?'

'You want the helpline number? So you can call it if you get hopelessly addicted?'

'I already am.'

Kay laughed, with an odd note of affection. 'I won't leave a number. But I'll pop by again some time.'

They parted. Kay gave Mark a peck on the cheek as they did so. Mark felt unreasonably touched by this, touched by the whole incident. Another Francis leaving, to he knew not where, or whom. Mark got another beer and sat about thinking about things, or not really thinking about things at all. Fretting, though.

Wonderful boots.

4

Corridors are important places in the life of a teacher. They are no-places, or rather places between places. Mark, remembering *The Magician's Nephew*, sometimes thought of corridors as The Wood between the Worlds. Corridors are places in which staff and pupils meet almost as equals, where courtesies and discourtesies take on an added significance.

In a long corridor you can sometimes sight a person one hundred feet away. At what point do you exchange greetings? Is a smile and a nod enough, or should there be a word? Should you actually stop, causing a blockage in the stream of pupils and other teachers? In a corridor, teachers are also on a stage, their passage never quite ignored, pupils always quick to fantasise a falling-out, or better, a flirtation. Or spot one.

But there is also a privacy in those corridors, one that cannot be found in the staff-rooms. They had smiled at a full hundred feet, quite involuntarily, at least on Mark's part: who had smiled first?

Once committed to the long-distance smile, it is hard to know what to do next. Start waving? Shout a greeting? Remove your eyes from contact? Mark took the clown's option, miming that he was galloping up on his horse to greet her, and she regarded him with a genuine laughing sort of smile. They closed in on each other: crisis. To stop or not to stop? 'Hi, Annette.' He stepped elaborately to one side to let her pass, a courteous mock courtesy.

But she made the same movement, a mirror of his own, as they closed in on each other. Nimbly, Mark stepped to the other side; just as nimbly she mirrored him again. Within touching distance now, and again they performed mirror-steps, final paces of the

187

corridor gavotte that brought them more or less chest to chest. Laughing.

'You've read Freud?' Mark asked. Daringly.

'And *A Sentimental Journey*.'

'You're looking well.' A kind of non-invasive compliment. Mark really meant, I have a powerful urge to kiss you.

'I was about to say the same of you.'

A brief pause, of the I'll-let-you-get-on kind. But neither, it seemed, actually wanted the other to get on. What to do? One of the troubles with teaching is that the drink-after-work suggestion, key to the upgrading of matiness in most working environments, is not a straightforward option for a teacher. It is not seemly to offer beer at four in the afternoon. But to suggest a drink at a more respectable time is still more fraught. It implies a more-conscientious-than-thou approach: I shall be working after school *in* school for an extra couple of hours – but then doesn't everybody? And anyway she had a husband and a child and such a suggestion would be quite inappropriate.

'Are you busy tonight?' she asked.

'After school?'

'Bit later, perhaps.' A schooled and amiable indifference in her voice. 'You've got that nice pizza place near you, haven't you?'

I have measured out my life in pizza forks.

Mark puzzled about the invitation for the rest of the day, its various possible permutations and implications. Two things in particular bothered him. One: I mean, well, she's *married*, isn't she? And the second, still more naïve and still more overwhelming question was this: how do grown-ups go to bed with each other? I mean, if such a thing should be in the sphere of possibility. He knew how boy-girl lovers went to bed, or more frequently, to hay-barn and hearth-rug. And he knew how students went to the narrow and only-just-possible beds in halls of residence. But he realised now that he had absolutely no experience at all of how grown-ups did it.

Not the in bed, but the going to. Presumably all that button-fumbling was out of the question, no more the glorious sudden slackening of the brassiere, unhooked with shaking boy's fingers rendered deft by lust. Well, no doubt he was worrying unnecessarily; this was of course nothing more than a friendly meeting between colleagues. But it was *interesting*, was it not, to speculate on such matters?

He had planned a slightly dashing and slightly unteacherly outfit for the evening, but in the end he didn't wear it. He never got back home. It was really rather embarrassing. Because after school he drove straight to Radlett, and found that the mare had been turned out without her New Zealand rug for the first time that year, it being a fine day, and she had rolled and rolled gloriously, and was covered in mud. She took an awful lot of grooming, and then he went right the way through the elaborate schooling sessions he had planned. After all, it was essential that he did so. Only way to prepare for Sunday: long schooling session on Friday, long hack with Mel on Saturday. And then the big one. Sunday. Cross-country. It really was absolutely and totally bloody terrifying but let's not think about it, all right?

So the schooling was important, and it went well. Rein back to canter. The mare was glorious to school when calmness was upon her: rolling from her brisk backward walk into the smooth and balanced canter of her business pace. Beautiful, angel. Now try again on the other rein. Perfect. Give me such control on Sunday, girl: or at least, the memory of it. The Big One.

He untacked the mare and put her back in her box, her breath sweet with extra strong mints. And started my-God-is-that-the-timing. For this was disgraceful. This was the psychopathology of everyday whatsit, have you read Freud? What was he putting off? But better run now. So he drove rather fast from Radlett to that nice pizza place, found a parking place after only one or two circuits, and arrived less than fifteen minutes late. Just.

But alas in jodhpurs, riding boots, horse-stinky woolly and flat cap. Not frightfully Islington.

'Annette, I'm so sorry.'

'Mark, how absurd you look –' an acerbity that reminded him of The Mate and Morgan both; how odd of her to combine both roles – 'isn't there a Clark Gable film when he staggers shirtless into a Southern ballroom?'

189

She had stood up to greet him, and Mark found that they had somehow seized each other's forearms, a lightly-sketched-out power-of-understatement sort of embrace. So he thought on the whole that he had better kiss her, and he did so, aiming for the cheek and hitting the target, rather nice, something he or they had not done before. 'You earthy Lawrentian devil, you. Stinking of the base earth from which you sprang.'

'I know, Annette, I'm so sorry, look, could you order me a beer while I sneak out and have a wash? And then I'll come back all civilised.'

'What a good plan. I hope they have baths in this restaurant, or at least showers.'

But it was all right. It really was all right. Just the slightest touch more black around the eyes than she wore during the day, most men would not have noticed, just been more drawn to those fine brown eyes. Dark, thick mop of hair, thoroughly but rather impatiently brushed. And a change of clothes: one of her usual long-striding skirts, and her usual baggy boots, normal corridor wear, but she had swapped her usual mannish shirt – Mark always fancied that she looked like the female lead in a cowboy film, the woman that runs the ranch while her man is fleeing from injustice – for a black garment, a smart version of a T-shirt. It was cut quite low, though reasonably far north of her strategic high ground. It was by no means an outrageous garment, but it was not loose. It was perfectly clear, for example, that beneath it there were, for example, breasts, two in number in fact and each a fine example of the breast-maker's art. It was a perfectly respectable garment, but you would not wear it if you were talking to seventeen-year-old boys. Not if you wanted them to look at your face.

But Mark did want to look at her face or rather, he wanted to look at her face as well. He wanted to put his elbows on the table and wrap her fingers in his and look into those rather fine brown eyes and say nice things to her and have her say nice things to him. He wanted to discuss all kinds of frightfully important things; he wanted to laugh and laugh about absolutely nothing. Jokes are more intimate than sex. Discuss. Bring me four sides by Monday.

Hands and face now smelling of soap not horses, mouth tingling with beer bubbles, doing the stuff with the eyes but not the fingers, and the voice, saying it was nice, and she agreed it was nice even though she'd never been stood up for a horse before. 'Oh, but she's such a nice horse, I'm sure you'd understand if you met her,' and they both laughed at this nugacity.

And he asked her why he had the inestimable honour of her company, and she explained that her son and her husband were visiting parents or grandparents in Wolverhampton for the week-end, and Mark thought, well, stay for the weekend, but he also thought, look, I've got a show to go to on Sunday, you know, and priorities are priorities.

So naturally they talked about teaching, just as later they were naturally to talk about love. She went into teaching because she couldn't think of anything else. She called it the Retrospective Vocation. 'Pretending to myself that I was doing it because I believed in it. But it wasn't until I was able to do it that I started believing in it *properly*. Is any one as naïve as a student on teaching practice?'

A grown-up who had never had a grown-up's love affair, perhaps. 'I remember my first,' Mark said. 'I tried to awaken the young minds with Ted Hughes. The fuckers started jumping out of the window.'

'I hope it was a high one.'

They swapped stories and the talk widened to cover the whole terrible business of professional life. They had the age-old teachers' conversation about the lack of esteem in which the profession is held. Especially by their own parents. 'It was always Angus this and Angus that. Angus is going to be a doctor and who gives a stuff about Annette?'

'It was the same for me,' Mark said. 'Except I was Angus. I think that was worse. My mother wanted me to be an international lawyer.' You failed to get into Oxford because of that silly girl and that fucking horse. Then you failed even to get a decent degree from your second-rate redbrick, because of another silly girl. Now you are taking the third-rater's option. Teaching, Mark thought, was sweet revenge for the years of bullying. And the diminishing

191

returns of bullying as horsey and girly joys overwhelmed him. And then the final betrayal.

Bec turned out to be the high-flier, taking wing from her unregarded, unesteemed job on local papers. And The Mate had rejoiced, but guardedly: that too, in a way, was betrayal.

But Mark acquired confidence, then a job, then some kind of real understanding. And he liked it. He really liked to teach. 'And that was the most unforgivable sin of all.'

'But the fact is, you get unforgiving yourself, don't you?' Annette said. She spoke of parental indifference to her early traumas in teaching, that terrible first year of crisis and self-doubt. 'I've never fallen out with them. I've never quite forgiven them.'

All professions have their intimacies, and all lack ways of expressing them openly. Teaching, with its formal meetings and rare chance encounters, is short on private moments. But intimacies are inevitable, because of the turbulent and emotional nature of daily life. 'I mean, I get pangs of nostalgia for Herne Hill. The deliberately blocked lavs, the occasional semi-riot, the ketchup bomb campaign. They used to drop the ketchup bombs from the top of the stairs, down the stairwell four floors down. You would get kids walking about like victims of atrocity –'

'So you've said. So you said almost every day in your first couple of weeks, when you were trying to impress us sixth-form college softies with your street cred. We didn't find it terribly endearing, oddly enough. Did you know I was interviewed for your job?'

'Of course I did. I seem to remember speaking a few apt consoling words to you on the subject.'

She laughed. 'What persuaded you to do it, Mark?' A faint thrill at her use of his name. 'Weren't you betraying your man-of-the-people principles? Wasn't there a faint danger of pleasing your mother?'

A bit sharp, that. 'Time to move. Needed a step. Applied for lots of jobs. Applied for this one in a batch of others, more or less for a giggle. So I could be angry when they didn't even offer me an interview, typical sixth-form college, don't know they're bloody born.'

They ate pizza, which was good, and pudding, which Mark

didn't want but he did rather want to keep the evening stretching out before them. 'And would you like coffee? And a sambuca or something?'

'If you're having one.'

'Well, I'd better not have another drink, because I didn't have a chance to abandon the car.' This was inept. This was not grown-up at all. 'I mean, it's only half a mile to my place, but you know, if I got stopped –' Inept.

'I came by tube. So why don't we get in your car and park it. Then we can walk away from your car and have a nice drink somewhere.'

'We could even have one at my place.'

She looked at him consideringly. 'What a terribly sound time-and-motion sort of idea.'

5

They were talking of jealousy now. 'But there never is a way out, is there?'

'Tell me more.'

'I mean, Othello's always going to die of jealousy, isn't he, Mr Brown?'

'Character is destiny,' Mark said. 'Traditional notion about Shakespeare. Can anyone ever escape his own character? Or her own? Though Dodgson had Alice say that she will stay down the rabbit-hole if she doesn't like who she is, and avoid her destiny that way.' Didn't mean to say that. Stuck with it now.

'Who's Dodgson, Mr Brown?'

'Who's Alice?'

'Someone tell Sandeep about Alice.' Susan or Soo did. 'And can anyone tell us about Dodgson?'

No one could. But they supplied the name of Lewis Carroll when asked, and Mark explained that they were one and the same. 'So why did he write under a false name, Mr Brown, a – a –'

'Pseudonym, yes. He taught mathematics at Oxford University, and feared that writing a child's book under his own name would be regarded as conduct unbecoming.'

'Why do you call him Dodgson and not Lewis Carroll? Isn't it rather pretentious? Deliberately confusing to your poor students?'

Mark laughed at this carefully judged impertinence. 'I used to know someone who always said Dodgson. But you're right, Jane, and I apologise.' This lesson was shooting about all over the place. Do try and get it back under control. 'All of which brings us back to the question of the author and his relationship to his own work.'

I've always loved teaching, boy. Because it's the most important

194

job in the world, that's why. Teaching is the central human experi-ence. All animals, us included, of course, we all have evolution, and it's something that takes place over millions and millions of years. But then humans invented language, and with it, cultural transmission. That changed everything. Evolution was put on fast-forward. And who is in charge of cultural transmission?

Everybody, Dad.

True enough. And first in the list are parents. But second, teachers. Your mother has never thought much of the profession of teaching, but I have always thought enough of it for us both. Never regretted becoming a teacher, not once. Though I have wanted to murder the odd pupil, I'll grant you that. And the odd colleague, and certainly the odd headmaster, before I became one myself. But I've always loved it, and thought it colossally important. Another drink? My turn, Dad. Nonsense, poor student, allow me, I insist. Where do you plan to go, then, on this jaunt?

'Do you say Blair, Mr Brown, when you're talking about George Orwell? Or whatsername for George Eliot? Or – or – isn't Anthony Burgess a pseudonym?'

'I am well rebuked. And yes, he was John Burgess Wilson, and he took the name of Anthony when he got confirmed. He said something about taking off his own head and tail and leaving the peeled prawn of himself. Which I suppose is what every novelist does.'

'*King Lear*, Mr Brown,' Sandeep said. 'Isn't there that thing the Fool says? About an egg? About losing the bit in the middle, the only bit that matters?'

'What a tremendously sound remark, Sandeep,' Mark said, and put a hand in his book-bag. 'First act, isn't it?' That Sandeep, avowedly reading for marks alone, should find himself stirred by the pursuit of literature. What a splendid little triumph. How splendid to be a teacher. Mark read out. ' "I'll give thee two crowns . . . after I have cut the egg i' th' middle and eat up the meat." Yes, that's it, absolutely spot on, Sandeep. Thou gave'st thy golden one away.' I see exactly what you mean, Dad. Another pint, then, please.

Gave my golden one away.

6

Unfaithful. I have been unfaithful to Morgan. I am being unfaithful to Morgan. Sexuella or Bosomina or in fact Clare on his shoulder in the dark, tiger-light of a tiger-flamed candle throwing highlights and shadows about her tiger-striped body. He had gone to the hall of residence and found Morgan gone. Gone altogether, decamped, utterly. A note pinned to the door, layers deep in irony, concluding: 'It's been real.'

Clare had arrived a few moments later to find him weeping without restraint. Morgan had been planning to stay on an additional night after term had ended, but now she was gone, gone without telling him. Clare, it seemed, had negotiated the same privilege. And she was there, and she gave him comfort and comfort escalated in a very satisfactory fashion.

And Mark never did for one moment think that he had been truly unfaithful to Morgan, and Morgan had never forgiven him. 'It wasn't a Dear John,' she said Americanly.

'It read like one.'

'Mark dearest, I have promised you my little all –' never quite all, Mark always thought, when she made this not uncommon opening, but perhaps all she was able to promise '– and you know I never go back on what I promise. So why the misery, why the sorrowful leaping into the open arms of Sexuella?'

As if that needed an excuse. 'I thought you'd left me,' he said feebly. 'I was heartbroken.' And he had even written a poem to prove it, which turned out to be his last poem, the unpublished unfinished Morgan-gone sequence, with its passionate butterfly and its winsome passage about the tiger-striped girl.

'I shall never leave you, Little Worthless. Get that into that thick

196

head of yours. I promised. I promise but rarely, because promises are solemn things. But hear and attend and listen, O Best Beloved. I have needs too, you know. You are not the only sensitive and vulnerable one in this relationship. Among your needs is to snivel a bit and receive comfort. Among my needs is to have my jokes understood.'

'But this went too far, Morgan.'

'Especially when they go too far.'

And Mark saw that she was right. The conversation had taken place after she had summoned him to New York with a single red rose, after they had returned in such triumph. How had the Sexuella business slipped out? Had he let it be known, casually, to show that he too could devour passing esculent strangers? Lord, that one about the female spiders in 'Arachne', the main story in the collection. It was not about female spiders, was it? It was about him devouring her. He saw that now, many years too late. Class G would have spotted it like a shot. Or had she divined it, read it in the contact of eyes between the two of them? Yes, that had been the way it was, and he had admitted the truth of it, not without pride. And she had been wounded, really wounded to the quick, and something or other between them had never been quite the same. And something awful in Mark had rather gloried in that.

'And you yourself were always faithful?'

Her soft body in tiger-shadow in the tiger-flame of the candle; tiger body full and generous and rather short on ironies. Curled as if for protection inside his faithless arm. Whisky glasses on either side of the bed that had been chosen primarily as an option for comparative solitude.

He had, it seemed, worked out how grown-ups went to bed. Opening the door for her, embracing her in the hall beside the plaited handrail in a fashion that was neither unexpected nor undesired. And she a married woman, a thought that kept coming back to shock him. And he a married man and unfaithful to Morgan. Again.

'More or less.'

She laughed and patted him affectionately. 'What kind of an

answer is that? Either you were or you weren't. Fidelity is black and white.'

And Mark saw that she was right. 'There was one sort of grapple with an old girlfriend, instantly regretted and never repeated. Drunken folly at a party.' Mark spoke lightly, man-of-the-worldly, and his lightness caused him pain. He was betraying his own betrayal by brushing it off so urbanely. It's not fuck me, it's fuck you.

A man of silly copulations. That single sin had been worse than any or all of Morgan's serial wanderings. Its memory was like a root-canal filling: all Mark's best efforts to pretend the thing had never happened failed again and again; the sharp pleasure, the unbearable weight of what he thought was guilt but what was in fact shame. She never knew about it, never would.

'So, once you were married, you have been a totally faithful husband apart from one drunken fling with an ex-girlfriend?'

'As I say.'

'I just like to be sure of these things. Tell me, did you find it difficult?'

Easiest thing in the world. But then I love her. I always have loved her. I always will love her. Rather an uncomfortable realisation that, with a lovely woman stooping to folly on his very shoulder. 'Easiest thing in the world, until I met you,' he said. And then realised that wasn't quite enough. He had to do better. 'You're beautiful and gorgeous and wonderful and altogether esculent, and I can't tell you how glad I am that you felt in the mood for a pizza this evening.' Better, much.

'Thank you for saying so. I am glad we have a taste for pizzas in common.'

'Do you eat a lot of pizza?'

She was a beat slow in picking up the implications, no Morgan. But she got there. 'You're a rogue, aren't you?' Perhaps a trifle, perhaps more than a trifle miffed.

'My pizza to go, my pizza capricciosa, my pizza with everything on it.' A winsome poem composed for a winsome new love, and she smiled with pleasure, undercutting it with no ironies.

'My sweet,' she said, 'my hot fudge cake.'

Which was all highly satisfactory. It satisfied many things. Though not curiosity. 'But how often do you feel the need to eat pizza?' The question killed the jolly atmosphere, but Mark had to know.

'Just occasionally. I'm not a wild woman, you know.'

'No, no, a domestic one, beautifully bred, perfect conformation, marvellous temperament – if you were mine I'd retire you to stud.'

'No, Mark, seriously though, thanks for that *if*, because I think it means you understand. I don't leave husbands. I have had one or two sort of unintentional slip-ups in the past, that's all. And, Mark, my love, I don't think we'd better have a sort of long-term affair you know, secret trysts and all that. Because I want to stay married and mothering and so forth. And the trouble is that you're not like the one or two sort of slip-ups in the past, you're the sort that I might just fall for in a big way, and that really would be a disaster.'

Mark was stabbed by this – the danger, the confession, the opportunity slipping away from him, the easy release he was being granted. 'And be fallen for.' Not all gallantry, either.

'See what I mean? You're a darling as well as a rogue.'

'You bring out the darling in me. But your husband –'

'He's a different matter, shut up, sacred and apart. And he's a great dad and I love him. I just get attacks of youthfulness, and have had one or two slip-ups, and once I slipped up and half fell for someone who was rather a darling and rather a rogue and that frightened me so much that I was good for ever afterwards.'

Now that was more Morgan-like. That was really rather good. 'And he knows nothing? He never goes a-wandering himself?'

Morgan, reading to him, that time in New York, taking his new book from beside the bed, her own gift from the Strand bookstore, opening at random:

> along this particular road the moon if you'll
> notice follows us like a big yellow dog. You
> don't believe? Look back.

199

Body not tiger-striped, for that had always been a bad metaphor, and besides, the book hid much of her. But face curiously
solemn.

And
there's the moon, there is something faithful and mad.

'I don't think so,' she said. 'I think I'd know.'

'And does he know about you?'

'Same answer. Now for Christ's sake shut up. I don't want to
feel bad. I want to feel wicked.'

Mark kissed the top of her forehead and started to work his way
south, a centimetre at a time, with various detours. By the time he
had gone past the true ribs to the area of the false ribs – Mel had
given him many anatomy lessons – and was proceeding fast to the
floating ribs, she was not feeling bad. But he carried on travelling
southward just the same.

Dear God, I am Philosophy Dick. I am the unethical ethics tutor.
I am the whole lot of them, the entire Bloomsday list.

> along the brittle treacherous bright streets
> of memory comes my heart,singing like
> an idiot

7

She never sobbed. But every now and then she wept. With some people sobs seem to force tears from their ducts, like a powerful subterranean disturbance. But when Morgan cried, she flowed. Sometimes tears fell with a splash some distance away, like the tears of a child. Unsobbing, weeping, she seemed to lose pints of water at a time: extraordinary, life-threatening dehydrating tears. And he quite powerless to dam their flow.

It had been the most terrible shock, when she had first cried on the pier. Tears came often enough thereafter, and always for Mark with the same shattering sense of disbelief. It was as if she turned herself into another person entirely. She accepted the news about Sexuella or Bosomina or Clare with equanimity, and naturally with irony. But hours later, when they were going to bed, he returned from a bathroom visit to find her sitting half undressed on the narrow hall-of-residence would-be chastity-enforcing bed with the silent river in spate.

At such times, she was never stiff, but never sought comfort, either. She never made a move of her own volition, but never resisted him. He could mould her body like putty, and always he did so, gently turning her into an embraceable shape. 'What is it, what is it?'

Eventually finding out. 'She's so pretty and lovely and silly, she's so silly and lovely.'

Something close to a replay on their wedding night in the Luna Hotel with its view over the Grand Canal, honeymoon that was a gift of – who else? – Venetia, and she, sitting on the ridiculous acreage of the bed, an item Mark had assumed had been chosen primarily as an arena for gymnastics, clad in a new and plain and perfect silken garment. And she would not reply to his question, what is it, what is it?, but tears dampened his shoulder so that he could feel a wet place growing and spreading in the face of this silent, copious flow, and then Mark said to her, remembering that time at the seaside, that day when he had first kissed her (a second kiss to follow twenty-four hours later, after a night in a shared but chastity-enriching bed): 'It's not a disappointed bridge, Morgan. Really it's not.'

Mark never quite understood the sort of things that moved her to tears. He was always surprised. A child trapped down a well in America: the news story obsessed her, and often, during the days of the drama she wept. For the child? The parents? The world? Mark never knew, though he always asked. She was always quite inconsolable: or at least Mark was never able to provide the consolation she wanted.

That story, 'The Child at the Bottom of the Well', was reckoned to be the best thing she had ever written, and was in her *Arachne* collection. And Mark, reading the spare account, never really understood it. Oh, he picked up the ambiguities and the ironies all right, but the author? Why had she written it? What did she want him to understand? How did she want him to respond? What did she mean?

8

'I'm sorry to let you down.'

But she just laughed at him down the telephone. Guffawed, really. A dirty great dirty guffaw, nothing less. Mark had rung the yard late and in mild panic, but he caught Jan, presumably drinking tea, in the tea-drinking place: ''Allo, she's right as rain, your little girl, sound as a pound. She'll do you proud tomorrow, don't you fret.'

'Good to hear it, Jan. Could you pass a message to Mel?'

'Bless you, darlin', she's right here, drinking tea and cussing about you. I'll pass her over.'

So Mark explained that he was unable to hack out with her and Ed that morning, because, well, he was rather tied up, and he was sorry to let her down. And so she guffawed. 'I hope she's pretty.'

'But tomorrow I'll be there.' Lowering his voice just a fraction.

'I'll tell Chancey. Unfaithful, I shall say. You're a betrayed woman, I shall say. Your man's with another girl, I shall say.'

'Give her a mint from me.'

'That's not the way to treat girls, you know. It's not mints she wants, it's you. But look, Mark, are you sure this is a wise move? She'll be ever so fresh tomorrow, and the whole idea of a long hack was to take the edge off her. It's a bloody big day for her, you know. And you. If you survive.'

'I know. I'm worried all right. I've thought about little else.' This was at least half true. 'So I was wondering, do you think you could –'

'Lunge her for you? You know I would if I could, but if you remember, the whole idea of hacking out early was because Tom

203

and I are going to lunch with some friends, and I promised and I can't let him down, can I?'

'Of course you can't. Never mind. We'll manage.'

'Tomorrow, then. Eight o'clock. That's drive away eight o'clock, right?'

'Wild horses couldn't drag me away.'

'Give her a mint from me. Or whatever it is you give her.'

So Mark, being a bachelor, had to get dressed and walk through the Islingtonian streets to the twenty-four-hour grocer's to buy fresh milk and butter and orange juice and croissants. He also bought three packets of extra strong mints. Then he made Lavazza hot and strong, and Annette sipped and smiled and ate.

The shadow of Sunday hung over them. No, Mark really couldn't get out of it. He had to drive the horsebox. It was a promise he could not go back on. Very well, I'll leave as soon as I have finished breakfast. Or straight after lunch. But anyway, she didn't. Perhaps it was the promise of a soufflé that turned the day: anyway, it was a lovely evening, bot. NZ chardonnay and all.

The alarm woke only Mark, for he was swift to switch it off. He dressed in the dark, white jods, no white shirt today, though. His special shirt. Coffee: one mug to gulp, the rest of the cafetiere into the flask. Boots last, lacing them as he sat in the kitchen.

Her sleeping head. He kissed it. She half woke, and snaked an arm about his neck. So he kissed her more thoroughly. Almost jumped straight back into bed, boots and all. But only almost. 'Lovely,' she said. 'Very lovely. Must remember not to do it again some time. Much, much too nice. Thank you for having me.'

She seemed to pass straight back into slumber, so perhaps never heard Mark saying glad you could come. So he left quietly, tiptoeing in his tall black boots. She knew how to let herself out.

9

She parked the lorry, with her usual easy competence, and they got out and lowered the ramp together. Every horsebox has its own idiosyncrasies, its Heath Robinson devices, but Mark had grown familiar with Mel's. They led the horses out, tied them to loops of baling twine set in the rings on the vehicle's sides, and gave each a haynet to pull at. They took the travelling boots from the horses' legs and told the horses to be good horses while they did a couple of important things.

They paid for their entries in the smaller class, and set off to walk the course. It was a very odd thing. Naturally, they had cast a look at the fences on their way to the secretary's tent. But after they had paid, they looked again, and the jumps had doubled in size.

Small class? This was enormous. Not that she couldn't jump it, but look at it. It was gigantic. They had left the winter indoor showjumping season behind them. There was even a bite of spring in the air, and ahead of them a course of cross-country jumps: hard, fiendish, unyielding. About three miles of countryside punctuated by obstacles that did not obligingly tumble down if you struck them. No, it was you that did the tumbling, if there was tumbling to be done.

It was the bits between the jumps that were peculiarly terrifying. And above all, the bit at the start. She would be up again. She would stand on her hind legs and refuse to start. They would never get as far as this. A jump over a row of car tyres, then only a few strides and jump over a small rail, the landing side two foot lower than the take-off.

'God, there isn't even a ground-line.' A thinnish log, lashed to a few uprights.

'Never mind the jumps,' Mel said. 'She'll take care of that. You just remember the order they come in. That's your department. Lots of left rein here, and right leg. Aim at the big oak tree.'

'Too sharp,' Mark said. 'I'm going to go for a nice approach to every jump. Give her a good sight of the fences. Measure a stride.'

'Not necessary, not with her.'

There were twenty-four fences, and Mark could see about twenty-four places in which he could break his neck. They tacked up, and went to ride in, in the usual arena full of bouncing horses and screaming nerves. Mark was sick of an old passion. Terror had him in its grip: the unseen hand at his vitals. Excuse, Mr Starter, but I can't start. I have rather bad peritonitis, and to enter your competition would be a mistake because *it wouldn't be fair to the horse.*

I could be tucked up in bed with my boots on.

Why was he not satisfied with what she had already achieved? He had only been able to remember the good bits, the shared ecstasies. He had forgotten the visceral fear, the terror of starting something and it being far too late to stop.

Around him, fellow-competitors, perhaps all as frightened as he was, in their rugby shirts, purple stripes, red and black squares, many with gaily-coloured silks on their helmets. Mark too. He had changed into Trev's old cross-country colours: a yellow hockey shirt with black sleeves bought from a department store, representing God knew what team or school; on his helmet a yellow and black quartered silk. He had fancied himself madly dashing, when he had tried on the outfit in the week.

'Mark?'

'Yeah?'

'We'll go down together. You go in first. I'll be around. If you have a problem, I'll jump straight off Ed, get someone to hold him. I'll get you through.'

Mark wanted to say something really very affectionate indeed. 'Thanks, Mel.'

So they gave their names and numbers to the starter, who told them to start in five minutes, in six minutes. And Mark hung about outside the start-box, and trotted in circles, and Lord but she was fresh, more than fresh, quite crazy. She had schooled quite sensibly while they were riding in, but now there was something going on. The trot was silly, too big, too boomy, and she had started head-tossing again, and Mark rode unbalanced, hanging out to his left to avoid catching her head with his face. 'One minute, Mark Brown, Miss Chance.' He patted unconvincingly. 'Thirty seconds, Mark Brown.'

He eased her forwards into the start-box, squeezing with his legs, eggs between leg and horse would not have broken, but it took her straight over the top. For half a second she thought about standing, but Mark was quick for once, booting her forward and pulling her head round, his right hand actually touching his right thigh, and she spun in two complete circles like a dog chasing its tail, while the starter – the starters' union would be blacklisting them if they weren't careful – leapt aside with unexpected grace and quoted in full John, chapter 11 verse 35, and then telling him to bloody well get on with it, go and kill yourself instead of me. And Mark and the mare bloody well got on with it.

A weird bouncing moment when she cantered just beyond the start without committing herself, more or less without moving, her famous pogo-stick canter, and then her decision, the sight of the jump, just two strides out.

And it was game on, and she lunged for it, wild with her own daring, but Mark stood high in the irons and caught her as they landed. She grabbed for her head but Mark would not permit it. Steady clear, do you hear me? And he hooked her back, and let her move forward at each jump, and she leapt each one far too avidly and fought for her head as a matter of crazy routine, and as routinely lost the fight. By fits and jerks and stops and starts they made their way around the course, even jumping the jumps in the correct order. Mark kept his balance at the drop fence and she flew the log without a ground-line as if it were a cavalletto. And they finished and they were clear, and she in great lather and Mark with his arms at least twice as long as when he started. But clear and united still, and what could be better than that? Delight filled him, delight and relief.

Jumping off, undoing the girth, watching Mel and Ed as best he could, and she seemed to have a fine flowing rhythm going. Back to the lorry, where he untacked the mare and put her in a sweat-rug, and walked her for a while till she was calmish and coolish and dryish.

And back at the lorry Mel, sponging Ed down. Everybody has a different routine of horse-care. 'Clear?' he asked.

'Yup.'

'Looked good. Flowing. Balanced.'

'I'm so pleased with him. So good for him, all this. There's so much more snap in his flatwork. I'll dressage him in public come the summer, and then we'll turn a few heads.'

'I bet.' Still no comment. 'We went clear too.'

'I saw most of it, from the start-box. Jesus, Mark, that was crap.'

'I was going for a steady clear. I wanted control.'

'What kind of control was that? You fought all the way round.'

'I wanted her to go at my pace.'

'Well, don't. You should want to go at her pace.'

'She'd kill me.'

'Trust her. She knows her business better than you do. If you work from a faster pace you'll actually have control. I'll bet you anything she'll listen to you at speed. Let her go. Then she'll listen. Then she'll be with you.'

Triumph had gone from him. Everybody always knows better about your horse than you do yourself. Or your marriage, he thought, remembering Bec. Well, they should just try sitting on a crazy little mare half out of her mind with excitement. 'Mark, I'm sorry. But there's no point in telling you it's great when it's crap, is there?'

'No, Mel.'

'So next time, get it right. Did you know there's a show at Potton next weekend? You always liked Potton, didn't you? Well, you go there and let her go, and you'll get it right. Second chance, you know?'

'Yes, Mel.'

'He's miffed with me,' she told her horse. 'But that's because he knows I'm right.'

'You bloody try it, Mel. You ride her at Potton next weekend, you try letting her go. You'll end up at Sandy railway station. You'll end up at King's Cross.'

'You'll end up with a red ribbon. And that's in the big class.'

10

Mark unzipped his trousers and started shoving them down his legs. He completed their removal by standing on the waistband and pulling himself free from their enthusiastic elastic embrace. 'What are your plans?' Mel asked.

'Going to Codicote to see The Mate.'

'Then we part. I was going to invite you to supper with me and Tom.'

'That would have been nice.' Something of a change of rhythm, too. 'I'd like to see Tom again.'

'Because I don't want you to feel bad about me saying you were crap.'

Mark pulled up his black jeans and wondered for the thousandth time why he kept buying the kind with buttons instead of the kind with zips. Because he was cool, he supposed. No thought of concealing the objet d'art, of course. 'We've known each other too long for that.'

Nice thought though it was. 'You've been rather pensive on the way home.'

'You've given me quite a lot to pense about.' He thrust his feet into black cowboy boots, ancient and rusty and purchased several hundred years ago in St Mark's Leather Store. Crammed boots and jods into a holdall. 'Last check?'

They walked round all the bobbing heads of the open square. Two heads not bobbing, backs to the door, faces in the manger, eating as if to the most pressing deadline. 'They enjoyed their day,' Mel said.

'We all did. Crap or no crap.'

'You're not miffed with me?'

'Never that. But I shall think long and hard about what you said.'

'Well. Just remember I'm always right.'

'Thanks for reminding me.' They walked through the yard to the car park, switching off lights and locking locks and hiding keys as they went. Mark threw his bag into the back of the Jeep, Mel put her own bag and all her tack – she was a great tack-cleaner – into her own less ostentatious vehicle. They embraced routinely, touched lips lightly. 'Tomorrow?'

'I'll be there.'

'Love to Vera.' Adding, as she usually did: 'No one is called Vera.'

'That's the truth. Mine to Tom.'

Mark drove on north. He would arrive in the light, just. Cheering sign. Thinking about mares and girls and crap and letting go and trusting. It was all, he thought, very well to talk.

'Darling, you positively reek of horses. And you're disgracefully early.' She recoiled, though amiably, from his embrace and double cheek-kiss.

'I thought I'd have a quick bath, if I may. Then it will be time for Drinks Before.'

'Don't leave the bathroom like the Augean stables. Take a towel from the airing cupboard.'

And so clean, unhorsey, smelling of rosemary soap, he sat sipping Famous Grouse and water, having poured his mother's gin and tonic. 'Such a bourgeois drink,' she said. 'I am so happy to be a bourgeoise.'

'Glad I'm a gamma,' Mark said.

'Glad I'm an alpha, darling.'

There was a history behind this remark, as there is behind most ritual remarks in a family. It was a taunt, vicious, intentionally hurting, that she had launched at him when he had announced that he intended to take up teaching as a profession. 'Like Dad?'

'Your father was the dearest man, but he did not have a first-class mind. You have. Or might have developed it as such. But you have consistently chosen to throw it away in pursuit of mediocrity, in pursuit of some chit of a girl.'

But that was a long time ago. The gamma joke turned up every now and then as token of the fact that the matter was long past and settled and quite unforgotten. 'Though,' she added, 'I'm so glad you now work as a lecturer.'

Mark felt a sudden powerful surge of adolescent fury. He mastered about seven-eighths of it. 'I'm a teacher. As you know. It's called a sixth form college, but our clients are children, no matter how much they swank about being cool and grown-up and at a college instead of a school, and we are teachers, no matter how much some of us swank about being cool and grown-up and at a college instead of a school.'

'All right, darling, have it your own way.' They sipped each at their drinks, to allow ancient arguments to be set aside. 'Have you seen your sister of late?' Mark gave some account of their last pizza, without mentioning the main topic of conversation. 'And did a certain anniversary come up for discussion?'

Too bloody sharp. First-class nose, anyway. She sat, looking through her rather gleaming spectacles that sat poised beneath the world's least hairy hair. The books stood in their towers on the table; most, he knew were aspects of her research for her current book, *The Isaac Question: Faith and the Problem of Kierkegaard*, nice title, neat little inversion. 'I've always seen you as Abraham cheerfully unsheathing your sword,' Mark had said when the project had been announced, and had earned a laugh which, as was his mother's way, gave way suddenly to a few tears.

'It did,' Mark said. Birthdays had always been great family occasions, many of his mother's birthdays generally recognised with great sprawling parties, all her friends and relations around her, her husband, the dearest man, at the centre, and his mother surrounded by many others, many of whom, no doubt, really did possess first-class minds. Her fiftieth birthday party had been a grand affair, perhaps just a trifle too full of life-must-go-on defiance, a little too full of his father's memory for everyone's absolute ease and comfort.

'You've got to swallow it, Bec,' Mark had said. 'She's going to want a party. And Ashton has to be there. It will partly be a party *for* Ashton. It's either that or a family row and Not Talking and Not Seeing.'

'I don't want that. I won't let it happen. But all the same, damned if I'm going to that house with Ashton in it.'

'Bec.'

'Queening about the place in his party frock . . .'

'Bec.'

'I am not sure that a party is really the right way to celebrate this anniversary,' his mother said. 'My mind has been running to an appropriate alternative.' His mother, with her taste for pedantry, always pounced on any suggestion that there could be more than one alternative. 'I have a little money that I set aside some time ago, and it has come to rather more than I thought it would. And I don't want a party, if that's what you and your sister have been discussing. It would not be the same without your father. The fiftieth was important, and I'm glad we did it. But that was enough. That, I think, was my last party. I get on very well, you know, from day to day. Ashton ensures that I always have company. I am not lonely, thank God. But a party would be rubbing in what I really miss, what I really hate about being a widow.' She hardly ever used the term; it indicated a fairly deep interior disturbance. 'It would be rubbing in the fact that at base, I am on my own. I know that, and I accept it. But all the same, I am damned if I am going to spend all that lovely money to *celebrate* it.'

'I see. I really do see.' Mark did, too, moved by his mother's uncharacteristic self-revelation.

'So I thought we might have a little family jaunt. Just a weekend, you know. Just the three of us.'

'Where to?'

'Would Venice be too frightfully painful for you?'

A stiletto entered briefly between seventh and eighth ribs, pricked, slid out again. 'I don't suppose so. Venice is Venice. It's Islington that reminds me of Morgan.' He hardly ever mentioned such things, certainly not to his mother.

'Excellent. Becky and I –' Bec hated that particular diminutive, but it was years too late to stop it – 'are having lunch in the week,

213

so I will put it to her then. I have done a little preliminary research, and have found a very advantageously priced offer.'

'Good.'

'Staying right at the end of St Mark's Square, place called the Luna, do you know it?' But just then Ashton arrived.

11

'I'm calling to say thank you,' she said. 'You were absolutely one hundred per cent right.'

'Oh, but I always am. I knew the soufflé would work if you followed the instructions. But it really worked on Rob?'

'He adored me little-womaning. He said it was as much fun as me dressing up as a schoolgirl, cheeky sod. No, everything went down a treat.' He heard a self-satisfied snort of laughter. 'Nice double entendre, eh, little brother?'

'You editrix of *Edge*, you. But look, Bec –'

'I need a recipe for next week.'

'Of course you do. Got a pencil? Right, here is my splendidly devised idiot-proof recipe for mushroom risotto.'

'Ah, no, bollocks, Mark, I know about risotto, it's hours scraping away at a bloody pan.'

'Brilliantly devised to allow you to spend no hours at all scraping away at a bloody pan. Now get a packet of dried mushrooms, porcini for preference, you can get them . . .' And a little later, but not much, because it was a brilliantly devised idiot-proof recipe, Mark was able to turn the conversation neatly enough: 'And you could always speak Italian while you are eating, because it will be good practice.'

Bec obligingly said: 'All right, practice for what?'

'Now listen to The Mate's secret plans for the sixtieth, which will be revealed to you as a surprise when you have lunch this week.' He told her. She thanked God with apparent sincerity.

'So I get to celebrate with no Ashton and no row. This is good news. And my husband thinks I'm fab, all thanks to little you. What a wonderful family I have. You didn't have a hand in arranging The Mate's thinking by any chance?'

'God, no. If you think I have influence with The Mate you are becoming dangerously prone to fantasy.'

'Then do you think she's getting sensitive in her old age?'

'Nope. Just staying clever. But listen, Bec, there's a twist, and you've got to be prepared. That's why I am giving you the story.'

'I am always keen to break embargoes. Go for it, Markie.'

'Ashton let slip something I think The Mate would rather have kept dark a while longer.' Mark, driving, had not partaken of heavenly cough mixture, nor of more than a single glass of wine. But Ashton, sipping away as ever with mild liberality, had raised his glass of port to his dearest friend and said: 'Well, Doctor. Next year in Jerusalem.' And The Mate had smiled and acknowledged but still looked faintly put out. And Mark had wormed the story out of her.

'Go for it, Markie. I'm sitting down, it's quite safe.'

'I hope so. She and Ashton are going to Israel. What she called the Holy Land, of course. Got the cash as part of the same annuity, whatever it is, that's paying for the Venice trip. Obviously what the money was set by for all along.'

'So that she could go to the Holy Land with Dad, you mean?'

'I suppose that's what I do mean.'

'Well, thanks for telling me, Markie. I'll go and practise smiles of delight. Look – look, I mean you're telling the story with a nice objective sort of voice. But do you mind?'

'I mind Dad being dead. I don't mind her surviving in whatever way she can.'

A gusty sigh filled the earpiece. 'I shall try to be just as wise as you are one day, Markie. Because I don't mind, I don't mind at all, not really. But all the same . . . it's a bit rich, isn't it? She just has the uncanny knack of stepping on your corns, doesn't she?'

'A genius for it. Here's some information to cheer you up. In Venice, we'll be staying at the hotel where Morgan and I had our honeymoon.'

Bec laughed and laughed.

12

She had pink lips, pink eyes, or at least pink all around the eyes, and a pink nose. 'That,' Mark said, 'is seriously ugly.'

'You just look at her paces, then tell me she's ugly. She's a darlin'. Look.' Jan put her through a series of movements, some nice leg-yielding and a sweet flying change.

'Bloody hell,' Mark said. It was a remark that covered the situation. 'She's been well schooled.'

'Funny thing is, darlin', I don't reckon she *has* been schooled that much. She's just a darlin'. Push-button horse, suit anybody.'

'Jan, can I use the phone, please? And have you got Kath's number?'

'Oh, you rogue, you. I'll tell Jim. It's under F for farrier.'

'Nothing like that, Jan. I just want to prepare my little mare for Potton at the weekend.'

'Well, have fun, darlin'. Whatever you're trying to do this weekend.'

Mark walked back to the tea-drinking place, wondering why he didn't want a push-button horse, not at any price, and called the number and got Kath instead of the Fat Farrier, and she asked after the old trollop, and Mark said she could see for herself, and could he hack over to her place and school his mare over her cross-country jumps. Why not? she said.

Why not indeed? For it was an afternoon rich in promise, a free period at the end of the day giving him an early charge down to Radlett. Warm and springlike, but surely not that warm. Kath had greeted the return of the sun by wearing a singlet, part of her extensive wardrobe of emphasising-rather-than-concealing garments. It would be highly embarrassing to fall off one's horse in an attempt to look down her cleavage, would it not?

'So how's she going?' Mark told her some of it. 'And can you hold her all right in that snaffle?'

'Only when she wants to be held. Kath, how did you ride her in cross-country? What kind of speed, I mean? I mean, what I mean to say is this –' Mark felt that he was confessing his own lack of nerve, his own lack of understanding of his own horse. 'Did you have any control at speed?'

'Never cross-countried her. Showjumper, me. Those jumps in the field, they were put in by the people we bought the place off. I put a horse over them occasionally, as a change from jumping over poles, freshens 'em up. But look, you have a pop at them, if you want.' Mark realised that he had been hoping for a piece of magic. For a single piece of advice, a single word that would make everything come out right. But he had to work it out for himself, or they did. He was on his own. Or they were.

Kath walked with him to the gate of the field and opened it for him. The mare, knowing the excitements that lay beyond that gate, started to caper about, doing her pogo-stick canter on the tarmac. 'Dirty bitch,' Kath said. 'Give her a crack with that stick.'

But Mark instead patted, and the mare entered the field sideways, and at once gave a little exhibition apparently designed to demonstrate that Kath was right and Mark was wrong, doing a huge leap over absolutely nothing, then attempting to dive through the hoop of his arms, not quite dislocating both. There was so much craziness going on that Mark had to stop being embarrassed about the terrible habits he had got the mare into, and start doing what he always did. Which was nothing, though doing nothing took a fair bit of doing when the madness was upon her, giving and taking and soothing and so on. And as she relaxed just enough to offer him a fragment of control, he crouched up over her withers, and she followed the movement into a proper canter, moving forward properly, seriously. Mark asked her to stretch out more than she did in the school, two rather nice big circles. As he rode, his eyes scanned the field, taking in the jumps, half a dozen in all, plotting the course he would ride. 'Now listen to me,' Mark told her quietly.

'I'm going to collect you up, then I'll put you at the post-and-rail, and after that, we'll see.'

And Mark collected her up, and she responded with one of her better head-tosses, but Mark was ready for it, expecting it. 'And I don't want to see your star again,' he told her severely. 'It's serious. All right?'

They approached the first with Mark sitting deep, and she doing her mad bounce, waiting for the word go. And they went into the fence collected up, and took it showjumping style. It was controlled; it was effective: it was not what Mark had planned to do at all. Something had got between him and the mare. Fear probably. Fear, certainly.

She landed looking for her head, and Mark landed with her and allowed his weight to shift forward, perhaps too far forward for safe cross-countrying but never mind that. And in a single, life-changing instant, kicked on.

Nudged, anyway, because she was not really a mare for the kicking. And amazed, delighted, she went forward. But not at the crazed demonic gallop he had feared, not instant loss of all control. It was a surge not so much of speed but of power, for all that she was moving pretty quick, a huge and purposeful canter just on the cusp of a gallop.

Mark looked at the fence made of blue plastic barrels, and her eyes followed his. Check, his mind told him, check check check. Shut up. She knows. And she approached the barrels and did not lunge madly at them, simply maintained the same huge rhythm, and scarcely breaking stride, she flew, low and skimming, forelegs, he could feel it, tucked up artistically beneath her. A yellow pipe next, a small ditch beneath it, but that wouldn't worry her, would it? And it didn't and they skimmed again, a swallow-skim. We clip a fence at this pace, we'll bloody well somersault. Coming back to the top of the field where Kath lounged bare-armed against the gate, and the fences he had leapt before the mare was truly his, the railway sleepers, the car tyres. Flew them in front of Kath's gaze, swallow-skimming.

He had saved the log-pile till last, because it was the biggest, and it was getting bigger with every stride. Curving back after the

219

car tyres, back up towards the gate and Kath, still travelling at this huge, this perfect pace. You'll not hurdle this one, madam.

And still he did not check. So did she shorten her stride of her own accord? Perhaps she did, perhaps they worked it out together but no matter, because she had her hocks beneath her now, and she jumped the fence with the respect that it demanded, rounder and fuller than before, but still landing and moving away from it without any loss of rhythm or speed. Making much, making very much at the same big pace, Mark said: 'A jockey's job is to leave you alone, isn't that right, girl?' And he let his hands forward and squeezed with his legs, and she dropped her withers on an instant, co-conspirator, knowing what he wanted, and they galloped the fence-line in a burst of mutual – am I being anthropomorphic? Mark wondered in mid-gallop. But I know when I have a delighted horse beneath me – joy.

Joy joy joy. Life was perfect, this was a perfect world, a brave new world that had such horses in it. Potton next weekend, and they would gallop it, they would tear the place in half, they would need the fire brigade to douse the scorch-marks her hooves left on the turf. That's if they bothered touching the turf, because they were going to fly, as anyone must with a winged angel beneath him.

And she even stopped when he asked, right at the gate and Kath, Mark making still more of her. Kath summed up: 'Fucking arseholes.'

Flight. It was going to be the weekend of his life.

13

'Spicy,' Mark asked her, 'Bloody Mary, please.'

She handed him a minute bottle of vodka and a yellow can containing something called Bloody Mary mixer. 'This,' she said, 'is plenny spicy.'

'Fine. Could you make it a double, please?'

She poked a beautifully manicured fingernail at the little bottle. 'These are doubles.'

But Mark had learned new things about his courage in that flight around Kath's cross-country fences, and was not outfaced for a moment. 'In that case,' he said, 'could you make it a quadruple, please?'

She could do nothing but hand Mark his well-won prize and push her trolley onward up the aisle. Mark poured the contents of the first little bottle over the over-generous ice, added the Bloody Mary mixer, sipped. He turned his attention back to the class in front of him.

'Far from being about despair,' Jane said, '*The Waste Land* is about hope. There are passages that simply don't fit in with the notion of despair. The unexplained appearance of the hyacinth girl –'

– Yet when we came back, late, from the hyacinth garden,
Your arms full and your hair wet, I could not
Speak . . .

– he remembered, for she had not quoted. Tears pricked at the back of Mark's eyes. When we came back late from the seaside, from the pier, from the disappointed bridge. From Summer's Lease.

221

Really rather good, this. Jane's essay, the Bloody Mary, neither without spice. Get the essays marked, then be clear for the weekend. Above all, leave nothing for Sunday night. Must sleep. Or be in no shape at all for Monday's lessons.

Potton, his heart told him sadly. Potton, alas for Potton. The mare, primed and ready, was spending her weekend eating grass instead of taking wing above the cross-country course of Potton. Ah well. It was only the one great dream of his life that he had let slip. Left only about five thousand miles behind him.

The brief negotiation with the head: 'In the circumstances, that would be no problem. So long as you can find someone to cover for you. The only option is your deputy, so far as I can see from the timetable. It being her half-day.'

'You want me to do what?'

'I know it sounds frivolous. Or worse, glamorous.'

'You really think it's all going to work out?'

'Oh no.'

'Well, why then?'

'It's something I owe, that's all. She was terribly good to me.'

'Dogs don't leap through plate-glass windows because they owe a debt. They do it because there is a bitch in heat on the other side.'

Mark laughed. 'What a truly helpful analogy, Annette.'

She rested her hand on his forearm. 'Or they think there is. You're not going to make yourself unhappy, Mark? I really wouldn't want that.'

How good that they had parted friends, despite Sunday morning and so on. What a pity he slightly despised her. 'I am,' he boasted, 'going to make myself really quite *tremendously* unhappy. But – well, you know –'

'You have it to do,' Annette said.

'Yes. I have it to do.'

'Then I'll act for you on Friday.'

'You're adorable.' He kissed her cheek, there being no witnesses in the Resources Room.

She rested her right wrist on his left shoulder and gave him a careful look. 'He thinks he's got her round his little finger,' she said. Then with a change of tone: 'But Mark, take care, you know?'

Too late for taking care. Ten years too late, at least. He wrote A-, and then: 'You have taken an independent line which is brave and shows good intuition. You have backed it up solidly with reference to the text. This shows good logic. Well done!'

Hyacinth girl. Looking into the heart of light, the silence. Ralph had also taken to the hyacinth girl. 'In his attempt to depict a sterile and impotent world, Eliot succeeds only in showing the reader his own sterile and impotent mind. The passage with the hyacinth girl is all mind. He wants nothing to do with the body, coarse realities Eliot always shies away from.'

The telephone, had anyone ever written about the real beauty of the telephone? Ringring, ringring.

'Hello?'

'Mark.'

No earthy bodies, no coarse realities. Just mind. Or spirit, or something. The universe suspended for a while. Looking into the heart of light, the silence.

B+. I need a quotation here. Mark dug into his briefcase, pulled out a quotations dictionary. Blimey, said the security man at the X-ray machine. Got enough books to last the trip? Perhaps two dozen in all. Just about enough, my good man, I'm only going for the weekend. Here we are. 'I disapprove of what you say, but I will defend to the death your right to say it. Voltaire. Mostly well-argued. One point: literature is not *all* about taking sides.'

'I'm not taking sides,' Callum said. 'I just happen to think, since you ask, that you're an arsehole.'

'You think I shouldn't go?'

'I know you shouldn't go. I also know that you're going. Jesus, haven't we had this conversation before?'

'Course we have, ten years ago almost to the day.'

'Did I take sides then?'

'Not exactly. You said something about how well I was coping, I remember that. How I'd even managed to tumble a nice girl. How for the first time in ages I'd found life a bit easier. So I had to go

223

flying back to her, knowing I was going to find nothing but pain and humiliation.'

'Well then. What was it you found?'

'Marriage.'

Mark uncapped the second little bottle, poured it on the ruins of the icescape, rubied it with plenny spicy mixer. Stirred with the stirrer provided. Of course he could remember the beginning, every spicy detail. The fifth kiss, the thoughtfully lit candle. And the end, too. Hysteria that amazed even himself. Her calm: frightful, implacable. And ironic, of course. 'Mark, it's no good. I'm a gone girl.' And she was. Summer's lease.

But what of marriage? All Mark could really remember of marriage was the rows about the answerphone and the knives. His carbon steel Sabatiers. She never wiped them. Not stainless steel, you see, so wiping was imperative. But she sliced something with them and *just left them*, so that always he found them *stained and blunted*, and he had to take a steel and scouring pad to them, *every* time, and *every* time it made him furious. He even bought her her own stainless-steel knife, a good one, but she never used it, not once. Always the carbon steel Sabatiers. 'Sorry, Mark. I forget. It's not the sort of thing that matters to me.'

'It doesn't matter at all, not in the grand scheme of things. It just happens to matter to me.'

'So I see.' And sometimes she had been implacable at his reproach, sometimes angry, sometimes, which was most frightful, distantly amused. And always she left the knives, smeared with tomato seeds, damp with fennel, green with avocado – she only ever cooked salad – resting on the chopping board. Or sometimes in a fit of good behaviour she washed them up and left them to dry, which was worse, because he then found them liver-spotted and in need of even longer scouring and sharpening.

And he, of course, always leaving the house with the answerphone unswitched on, returning home always to rebukes. Did he not understand about the telephone? Proust, of course. He had written about the angels or was it the sirens of the telephone. Which reminded him: what was he to do about Kay?

224

'I've got a theory,' Callum said. 'About life and marriage and so on. About what went wrong for you.'

'How tremendously helpful of you.'

'You've never been poor, you see. You and Morgan. You never had to struggle to pay the rent.'

Mark had been trying for the first time in his life to save money from his salary, trying to prepare for the inevitable day when he would have no nice Islingtonian house on extended rent-free loan. When presumed divorce was finalised. But paying livery bills rather got in the way of that ambition. Not many teachers came home to a gorgeous little mare who ate nothing but rolled up five-pound notes and changed her shoes more frequently than Imelda Marcos.

'Whereas Naz and I were really hard up for the first two or three years. Remember that dump we lived in, in Streatham? Naz working for nothing at the Muslim women's centre in Stockwell, and me doing two days a week for that bloke with the office near Oxford Street? We had two rooms, and you had that bloody great mansion in Islington. We used to add up the small change of an evening and see if we could afford to go out for a pint.'

'You've lived, Callum.'

'Precisely my point. Because it was bloody good fun, in its way. I wouldn't go back to it, but it was right, then. And it has given a sort of bottom to things.'

Mark thought that his early days of nightmare as a supply teacher had been struggle enough for anyone, but admittedly, most supply teachers don't come home to a bloody great mansion, or even to a rather smart town house. Most teachers don't come home to a wife who was a cult success, who gave interviews though sparingly, sparingly – I want to preserve my mystique, she would say. Don't worry. You'll do that no matter how many interviews you give. Lordy, you say the sweetest things to a girl. It wasn't meant to be sweet, it was meant to be wounding and vicious and unkind. Then it was all the more sweet – and whose high, wide cheekbones were regularly seen on the book pages of newspapers and on more ambitious television programmes.

225

'Being poor makes you take certain things seriously. I think that's important.'

'What things?'

'Achievement. As a shared thing: no individual achievement in a marriage. Partnership.'

Morgan's easy, gracious contempt for her own success, for bank managers, even for Mark's job. 'No, I don't despise your job. I relish its ordinariness. Though vicariously, you know, vicariously.'

'You want me to be safe and dependable and dull?'

'Oh yes, Mark. Especially the last.'

Mark finished the second class's essay on Lawrence. These were mostly safe and dependable and dull. He had instructed the class to make them so: to write them specifically for examination purposes. None of the fruitful speculation he encouraged in his lower sixth classes. These were members of a class ready to do themselves justice in their exams in a scant few weeks. He hoped, they hoped. They'd do all right. All about goals, achievement and so forth. He then took out *Ulysses*, and read the first chapter. He had to teach his Introduction to Joyce lesson on Monday: important to get his eye in.

They started bringing round food for no very good reason that Mark could see, no connection at all with any mealtime in any time zone. But he thought he had better eat some of it, since he had things to do as soon as he arrived. So he ate, or rather picked, and changed books, *Ulysses* being a trifle unwieldy for one-handed reading, and read or rather skimmed *Othello*, with Monday's second class in mind. But surely Mr Brown, what Shakespeare wants us to think is this. It really was high time he got them off that way of thinking.

Oh all right, you lot, you want to find a moral, do you? So what is the moral of this play? Give me four sides, backed up by close reference to the text. And they'll all come up with different morals and that, of course, will form the basis of another lesson. Hurrah: and that should shut them up for good about authorial intention. Performing complicated contortions, he reached past his tray of food to the bag beneath the seat in front of him and wrested free a hardback notebook. He scribbled the thought down in the appropriate space for Monday's second lesson, modestly accepted his own congratulations and read on. *One not easily jealous but being wrought, perplex'd in the extreme.*

One not easily jealous, despite his wife's serial shagging, but one far too easily perplex'd. That was my failing: my too great facility for being perplex'd.

Thus and thus he had cheated all along. Killing myself to die upon a kiss. *Exeunt omnes.* He put the book down, leaned back and closed his eyes. Base and male, in his vodka reverie he ceased to ponder on betrayals of the past and could only wonder whether or not they would go to bed together, and in what manner. What garment would she wear? And how would he remove it? Absurd. It would not be like that. Or perhaps it would; perhaps he was now a member of the first eleven. Or maybe the stiffs. And perhaps he would seize the hem of her –

His mind would not leave the subject alone. Earthy bodies, coarse realities. Eliot may shy away from them, but Mark could not. Or at least the idea of them. The Bedouin robe. The Greek beach, the photograph, brief exposure. The mightily pinioned eagle, am'rous birds of prey. Was that right? Check that quotation; he had a copy of the poem somewhere.

'Mark.'

The voice on the telephone, stopping the stars in their courses.

'She's dying, Mark. And she asked to see you. I've been putting her off, stalling, but she insists. You know what she's like. I had to promise I would ask.'

'Yes.'

'I know it's impossible, I know I have no right to ask.'

'I'll come.'

'Mark –'

'You were hoping I would say no.'

A pause. 'Just a little terror, Mark. That's all.' Like rather bad peritonitis.

'I'll come.' Farewell Potton, farewell the dream of flight. 'Fix it.'

'The temperature in New York is 78 degrees, that's 25 Centigrade, weather is pleasant and sunny and not too sticky right

227

now. We'll be beginning our descent in half an hour, and should be touching down at JFK on schedule at 16.30 hours, half-past four local time. Thank you for travelling with us. We hope you enjoyed your flight.'

'Go straight to the hospital. She wants to have some time with you alone. If she is up to it, awake and so on.'

Just a little terror, that's all. The bowler-hatted starter calling the world to order.

14

She reminded Mark of school, in his learning rather than his teaching days. In physics, they had done something called the collapsing can experiment. A little water was boiled vigorously in a can, which was then tightly lidded and cooled rapidly under a cold tap. The steam at once condensed, leaving a partial vacuum. And so, with nothing inside to support it, the can collapsed on itself.

This is what had happened to her face. Still more basely than his wish for naked bodies, he had wished to find her asleep; I'm sorry, Mr Brown, but she cannot be seen at this moment in time. But no.

In bed. On a precipitous bank of pillows. And collapsed.

Smaller, it seemed, even smaller. Only her eyes, half-hooded, were the same size; perhaps even bigger. But only because the rest of her face had collapsed all about them. No make-up, of course, no brutally superimposed Cupid's bow. She saw him, did not smile. Muttered something. A little gaga. Pity filled him.

'Hello, Venetia.' Kissed the crumpled cheek.

'I said,' she said, rather louder and with pedantic clarity, 'fuck this.'

The American intonation a good deal more marked than before. 'Damn right,' Mark said.

'Piece of advice for you.'

'Yes?'

'Don't have a stroke.'

'All right.'

'Because it sucks.'

'I can see that.'

'I've become a foul-mouthed old woman,' she said with a touch of complacency. 'That's what the nurses say. Not to my face, of course. I use –' A ripple of pain or something washed through her, and she was silent.

'Venetia – anything I can do?'

'Course there isn't,' she said, whispered this time. 'Nothing anybody can do. That,' she elaborated, after a pause for quite a lot of breaths, 'is why it sucks.'

'Oh yes.'

A pause in which she gathered a little more strength. 'I use a very great deal of obscene language,' she explained. 'Because I have a right to. Look at me. It's obscene, isn't it?'

'Yes.'

'So when the doctor comes to see me and says how are you, Mrs Francis, I say, fucking terrible, how are you? And they think I'm a foul-mouthed old woman. Not me that's foul. It's fucking biology.'

'Yes.'

'Self-pitying old fool, lying on her deathbed, cussing.'

'You have a right.'

'Fucking right I have a right.' She said this with some spirit, but the effort seemed to exhaust her, and she let the weight of her head sink back onto the brutal whiteness of the pillows. So Mark sat for a while. She seemed to doze, or to fall into some species of trance. For a half-second, Mark feared she might be dead, but then observed the rhythmic rise and fall of the sheet that covered her. So he sat.

A nurse came in, alive with heartless bustle, and read the chart at the foot of the bed. She had a fine American bosom and teeth that were a credit to American orthodontistry. Perhaps she moonlighted as a roller-skating waitress. So he stood.

'Don't go.'

'All right, Venetia. I won't. I was just wondering if I could get a cup of coffee.'

'Selfish old bitch, lying here ordering people about. Get your coffee. They do some outside. Then come back and listen to me cussing.'

'It's a deal.'

Mark was pleased to have something to fiddle about with. He carried the Styrofoam cup back and took his place on the chair at the head of her bed. The nurse had gone. Among the usual hospital clutter there were, of course, many flowers. There was also a very large and quite hideous cactus, obviously expensive, spiky, not easily killed; Morgan's contribution for a certainty. Propped on the table was a picture, not of loved ones, but a chunk of Celtic whatnot. Mark peered at it. 'Book of Kells?'

'You have a knack of understanding this family.'

'I make the odd lucky guess, anyway.'

'But I bet you can't guess why the old fool dragged you out here five thousand miles away from home. That's what you're trying to do, I know. I make the odd lucky guess too, you know.'

'I assumed it was to tell me that you're leaving me all your money.'

She gave a genuine but monosyllabic laugh at this. 'Ha. In a way, that's exactly what it is. That's what I hope, anyway. Because I came to the conclusion quite early on that I'm not really one for touching deathbed scenes. I kind of gave Morgan the impression that I was, that I wanted to make a deathbed farewell to you. I imagine that was the impression she gave you.'

'Morgan just said you wanted to see me. And that you wouldn't let up on the subject. And that she ran out of excuses for putting it off.'

'Ran out of lies, you mean.' Mark felt just a little terror at this, a family feud and he in the middle. 'Because you see, my daughter is a liar and a cheat.'

'That's her chief charm, in my view.'

'Ha.' A pause for thought. 'Ha.' A smile worked its way up her face, very slowly, like a fly up a window. 'Ha.'

Mark sipped his coffee, unsure of the best reply.

'I'm right, aren't I? You still absolutely adore her, don't you? Jesus, I sound like that old bitch in Dickens. But all the same, you'd forgive her anything, wouldn't you?'

'I already have. Whether she's done it or not.' And he had fancied himself so fine, galloping across Hertfordshire, teeth in her mane and flying over everything that came in their way. So free.

231

'My daughter keeps telling me that all is well between you. But she's lying through her teeth, isn't she?'

American orthodontristry. Mark shied away from both truth and falsehood, and came up with his standard halfway sort of answer. 'One or two things less than ideal of late.'

For a moment, Venetia seemed about to go deeper. But again, one of those ripples of pain or exhaustion washed through her, and her eyes almost visibly faded, as if they were on a dimmer switch. Mark sipped coffee. Watched. Breathing, yes.

After a while, she opened her eyes about halfway. Fighting. Something more to say. 'I didn't want to see you.'

'Never mind.' Knowing there was some trickery going on.

'Wanted . . . Morgan to see you. Wanted you to see Morgan.' She said something else, too faint for Mark to hear, and he lowered an ear close to her lips. 'I said . . . fuck this.' A near whisper.

'Fuck this forwards, backwards and sideways,' Mark said, very distinctly. And perhaps she heard, perhaps there was a flicker of a smile as sleep reclaimed her.

He sat and waited. She might wake, and anyway, he had promised to wait. The deathbed he had failed to attend, instead conquering Europe in the company of a chance-met girl from California. Shame: shame still worse than the night when the objet d'art had been concealed. Read me 'Cynara', Bec.

Must be in one of the anthologies. So Mark searched through his bag, with its set texts, dictionary of quotations, anthologies, critical texts. In this one I bet. *The Oxford Book of English Verse.* In the front a label, Mark Brown, Lower Six Arts, Awarded for Good Work in English. Groomed for stardom. Oxford awaits. And then that summer a girl with black hair and ironic eyebrows, new face at the yard, there every day. So was he. The holiday tutor, recruited to get his French up to scratch, he never had a prayer. Mark was too busy with les vérités éternelles.

Dowson. So Mark read the poem at the wrong deathbed, and silently. And I am desolate and sick of an old passion. What would she say, if she opened her eyes and listened to him? Bastard wasn't faithful, not in his own fashion nor anybody else's. Couldn't see a faith without being unfaithful to it. Something like that.

I cried for madder music and for stronger wine. Silly sod should have tried madder and stronger horses. Has she been faithful to me in her fashion? For ten years, Mark would have answered no. But now, and to his immense surprise, he found himself smiling even at his own question. Little foibles. Philosophy Dick no longer mattered. The unethical ethics tutor was still a figure in her life, he knew, but even he had lost his power of causing pain. He gave a small snort of laughter when he remembered her claim that she had never really lost her virginity. Just mislaid it.

I have been faithful to thee, Cynara, in my fashion. Have I? Perhaps on the whole and taking one thing with another, he had failed to pass the Cynara test. Not the business with Sexuella or Clare, not Annette, not even the dreadful night of the objet d'art. Just a nagging feeling that somewhere along the road, he had made a small but irrecoverable error. His mother's description of the motorway drive from London to Codicote: go the wrong side of a brick and you end up in Newcastle.

The moon. Like something faithful and mad. Read me the moon, Morgan. The one with the horses in it, the one with the big yellow dog. Like you did before, yes, just like.

15

'Hi!' Chinese, bursting with jollity about the whole thing.

'Hello.'

'Gotta ask you to step outside right now. Have to see to Mrs Francis for the night.' It being eight o'clock. Nights being specially long for the dying.

'She's already asleep.'

'Have to do a few chores. You might want to come in and say good night after. In a few minutes. I'll call you right in.'

'Thanks.'

Mark picked up his bags, the one with the clothes and the one with the books, left the hateful gleaming little cell and went to the sort of communal area where he had got his coffee.

'Mark.'

He had rehearsed this moment, oh, no more than two or three dozen times a day since the night she had told him that she was a gone girl. It was no help. Or if it was, it was not because he did any of the stuff he had practised. The cool, the bitter, the passionate, the ironical, the brutal, the sad (arousing instant guilt), the aloofly handsome (arousing instant passion), the smugly sorted-out (arousing instant jealousy). He forgot them all.

He said nothing. But, and as if it were the most natural thing in the world, he somehow grew to about twice his normal size. And wrapped her in his arms: really wrapped, making an absolutely thorough job of it, so that he could feel his fingertips on his own body, arms completing two huge enfolding circles. And she stood against him wrapped in layers and layers of arms, her own joined together about his waist.

No, really Cal, I tell you, it's all been for the best. I know that now. It's been a hard few months, I grant you, but I've got there. I'm way beyond the stage of wanting her back. She did me a favour, that's the way it seems now, though I grant you it didn't seem like one then. I wish her nothing but the best. But – well, I don't ever want to see her again, you know? All passion spent, you know?'

All passion spent, he wrapped her in his bear's embrace, amazed at his newly colossal dimensions. He took his right hand from his own side and pressed it against the back of her head, pressing her still deeper into his shoulder. For a long moment, he felt infinitely strong, capable of pouring infinite strength into the tiny dry-eyed girl in his arms.

'Oh hi, Ms Francis, would you like to say good night to your mom?'

'Oh, thanks, Nurse Kwan.'

And composed, or fairly composed, she went. Mark stood, discomposed, dizzy from the encounter – well, he had a right to be dizzy. It was after all one o'clock in the morning. Coffee, that was the thing. He poured coffee from the fat glass jug on the hotplate, sipped it from a Styrofoam mug. It made him dizzy.

Was that zebra-skin she was wearing? How charmingly Proustian of her. Had she done it on purpose? And if so, why? Her hair was different. And her face. How long was the Bloomsday list for the last few months? He laughed out loud at this absurdity, the cosmic irrelevance of the thought. A thought conjured up, as it were, for duty rather than pleasure.

Would it be appropriate to get absolutely ludicrously drunk? A single glass would leave him legless; a dozen bottles would have no effect.

16

'Better not,' she said. 'We'd get mugged.'

'I already have been.'

'Did the mugger take much?'

'Everything.'

They walked on a little more, not walking into Central Park though twilight was hardly upon them. She carried his clothes bag which contained very little, he his book bag which did not. Heavy job, carrying Cynara. Man's work.

'You weren't injured?'

'I received a very solid blow about the heart that paralysed me. No, I'm lying. Nobody touched me. I made the terrible mistake of looking into the mugger's eyes. Like the tailor-bird's wife in "Rikki-tikki-tavi". When the snake says, little fool, look at me!'

For she was wearing snakeskin. Not real snakeskin: a sort of light and pale suit, long skirt and jacket, beneath which she seemed to wear nothing, but that was by the by, more to the point was the material from which the suit was made, pale strips of fabric that mimicked, though not slavishly, skins: leopard, tiger, zebra, crocodile, snake. Not inappropriately, they walked past the Natural History Museum and on downtown, towards Columbus Circle. Mark had always wanted to gaze on Tyrannosaurus rex.

He wanted to continue the mugging conversation, but he could not think of another line. Besides, it was her turn. Why so silent? But then it came upon him, that he had forgotten all he knew.

He stopped, dropping Cynara and co. with a thump, and held her while she wept, silently, copiously. 'I'm so sorry, Morgan. So sorry.'

A few minutes later, she said: 'I can't stand her being brave.'

'No.'

'I can't stand her being nice, either.' They started to walk downtown once again. 'As you know, we always bicker and fight and torment each other. But now she's being brave all the time and nice all the time, and I have to be brave and nice too, and it's not fair, is it? And I ask her why she's being so nice, and she says, well, it's not as if it's for long, is it? And then she always says something else, like, at least, I fucking hope not.'

'My mother once had a cat put down. She said afterwards, that's how I want to go. No doctors. Just get me a priest and a vet.'

So Morgan told him how it had happened, a series of small strokes, and then the big one, four weeks ago, in the morning as she was sitting down drinking coffee and reading the *New York Times*, and Morgan had been there and had called the ambulance and made her comfortable and had gone with her to the hospital and sat there throughout the touch-and-go period. So she was staying on in New York, visiting two or three times a day.

'Will she recover?'

'You don't. Some go on to a sort of half-life, until the next stroke gets them. Some don't. Venetia doesn't want to.'

'Never been one for half-lives.'

'A half-life sucks. As my mother would say.'

'Have you been living a half-life then, Morgan? Or a full one?'

Mark had once ridden a polo pony, back in his Trev-and-Mel days, one that a friend had reschooled as a jumper to specialise in speed classes. Under the friend's instruction, Mark had ridden the pony full pelt at the wall, and a couple of strides out spun the pony round on its hock to come hammering back in the exact opposite direction. All without breaking stride.

'Fuck off, Mark.'

'What?'

'I am not going to spend the rest of the evening talking about how many men I've fucked.'

Glorious fury rose up in him, and gloriously, he gave full rein to it. 'Well, thank God for that, because it is a seriously dull subject. Monotonous, you know, repetitive. I want to talk about something *stimulating*, you know, and *surprising*. You want to live out your life as a female version of *Confessions of a Window Cleaner*, that's up to you. But you just keep quiet about it when you're with me, because the subject seriously bores me. All right? I no longer care.'

He lied.

'Well, that makes everything a good deal easier for everyone, doesn't it? Well done, little you. After all these years an absolute triumph of self-mastery.'

They were standing still again now, a few people passing by, politely giving them a wide berth; no doubt such street theatre was a daily part of New York life. Mark put his hand in his pocket, though he knew almost to a cent how much it contained. 'I have dollars,' he said. 'I expect I'll get the ten o'clock plane on stand-by. Give me my bag. I'll get a cab.'

'Off he flounces, bum-twitch, bum-twitch, bum-twitch.'

The stiletto of laughter. Her oldest weapon. Murdered him. Mugged him and murdered him, leaving the corpse twitching in the gutter of Central Park West.

17

Cocoa. That was what he felt like. It being one o'clock in the morning, or half-past. A nice cup of cocoa and then bed. Or perhaps a bottle of champagne and then bed. Or in bed, hoho. Shut up. That's quite enough of that. He raised a discreet eyebrow to the waiter. The waiter ignored him completely, as if he were wearing a cloak of invisibility. Or one of those especially fierce American drinks, a whisky sour or something. Or just whisky. Scatch on the racks. He waved at the waiter. Nothing happened. Or one of those native American drinks. Old Grandad. Sour Mash. Was that a drink? Wild Turkey, anyway. 'Waiter?'

'Good evening, and what can I get you to drink this evening?'

It seemed that American boldness had stolen upon him. Strange. He would have died rather than say waiter to a waiter in England. Now in America he found his mouth just saying it. A little triumph of self-mastery. 'Glass of chardonnay, please. Corona beer. Lime in it.'

Really, he could sleep forever. Or dance all night, perhaps. How to get through the evening, that was the immediate problem. How to make the transition into some sort of reasonably civilised, friendly sort of time, if not a first eleven or even a stiffs sort of evening. How would he make her happy? Talk of Kay. Tell his story. This was the moment.

But then was it? It certainly had its points. It would make her happy, or happyish. And it had the great virtue of dodging the great matters that lay between them. If that was a virtue. It was certainly dodging and not solving.

He reined himself back from this precipice. What was he talking about? He was thinking in terms of some kind of long-term relationship. That would never do. Pragmatism, that was the thing. The plan was to get through the evening, the weekend without another shattering bloody row. That would be miracle enough to be going on with. The drinks came. He squeezed the lime slice that was balanced neatly on the rim, dropped it into the half-filled glass, filled to the top, drank. Sharp, cheering. More cheering stuff: he would be leaving in less than forty-eight hours. Oh Potton, he thought, Potton. Starting when? He worked it out: about thirty-five hours. And she ready and he ready to fly. How he loved her. She walked across the Conservatory Bar of the Mayflower Hotel having done a fair amount of washing, brushing, cleaning, grooming. Making up. The wild gorgeous animal's suit: what did she wear beneath it? What beasts dwelt below its skin or skins?

She sat before her glass of wine, smiled. Her hair was longer than it had ever been. It was gathered at the nape by a strange piece of gold, purloined perhaps from Atahualpa's hoard, more likely from the store of Ashanti kings, and given or lent by the stricken queen. She had allowed a single lock to fall free, a dark italic stroke across the page of her face. He reached a hand and caressed the lock behind her ear. She bridled a little at this, a trifle headshy. But smiled. 'Mark, it's deliberate. I'm thrillingly asymmetrical. Do you wish me to be tediously balanced?'

'I don't, Morgan. I just wanted to do something tender. I have a need to make much of you.'

'Stroke me and make much of me?'

'Make much.'

She flicked the lock from behind her ear with a fingernail. Mark took it between index finger and thumb and gently pulled it towards him, running finger and thumb-tip through the end, making a smooth italic curve across her face. 'Is that really how you like me?'

'Really.'

'How's the sixth form college, Mark?'

'Sweet of you, but not necessary.'

'Sweet of me to what?' Sharply.

'Make polite small talk. We can instead ask each other more interesting things.'

240

'I have never made polite small talk in my life. As you should know. In fact, it was a subtle way of leading up to some rather more interesting things that I very badly wanted to tell you.'

'Well, tell me. Or do you want to start again with the sixth form college? Which is going very nicely, thanks.'

'Good.'

'So what about the rather more interesting things?'

'The moment's gone. That's the way of things, with moments. They go. You don't get them back. Maybe the subject will come up later. In the natural course of events. Or maybe it won't.'

'But the problem is that I'm so crass I've spoilt the moment, so I have to be punished.'

'Yes.'

There was inevitably a pause at this, which Mark filled in by looking at his drink and then looking out of the window. It was more or less dark. At the bar a woman in a red frock, bare-backed. All you had to do was to slip one finger beneath each shoulder strap. Silently he revenged himself by considering this double-fingered manoeuvre at some length.

'How's work, Morgan? What are you writing?'

'All right.'

'That's all right then.'

'Mark, I'm a horrible old bag. I know that. Everything is out of joint. I thought I was coping frightfully well, with Venetia, you know. And now you're here and I'm not coping at all. I want to blame you for that, and it's rather horrible of me.'

He took her hand, mainly because it was on his wrist, frightened by the sudden sizzling contact. A hundred times more thrilling than the double-fingered manoeuvre; a thousand times more dangerous. 'Morgan, I'd do anything for you. In my crass way. You mustn't mind me.'

'Can we go back to the bit outside Venetia's room? When you were holding me? I liked that bit.'

'Hasn't the moment gone?'

'Not necessarily.'

Mark stroked the asymmetric lock. She did not shy.

18

They were too far away to see if Morgan was telling the truth. She said that the waitresses no longer waited on roller-skates, and anyway she wanted to eat veal. So they went to Fiorello's, which was on the same street or was it avenue (but anyway, Broadway) as the wheeled goddess of blessed memory, but a block away. Mark inspected the parade of the beautiful and the mad as they passed and repassed along the pavement or sidewalk before him, and ordered spaghetti. 'If I ask for anything more complicated I'll burst into tears,' he said, and regretted it at once.

'I'll take you out for a wonderful meal tomorrow, Mark. To show how grateful.'

'Any meal with you is wonderful, Morgan.' But is that precisely how I want you to show your gratitude?

'Flatterer. You say that to all the girls.'

'Only one girl in my life, Morgan. Apart from you, of course.' So he told her about the one girl in his life.

'A *horse*?' As if he had joined the moonies. Claimed to be enjoying the favours of succubi on the astral plane. Gone gay, oh Lord, when was he going to mention Kay? Save it up for pudding. If he was still awake.

But he made a nice story about himself and the mare. She laughed, anyway, not taking it with overmuch seriousness; perhaps not even giving it serious credence. But then no one mucks out a stable in glorious cod snake-fur. When he began, he had wanted to make her understand what the mare actually meant, in the grand scheme of things, but he shied away from such a course. Took a wrong turning, made it a funny story. As if it were a passing whim. A lovable foible. Made her laugh.

And the food came, and he told the story of Kay. Ate ravenously for about a third of the dish and then repletion fell like a guillotine. She ate her veal. Mark thought about the dish of Staggering Bob, mentioned in *Ulysses*, unweaned days-old calf. She ate with fastidious relish while Mark told Kay's story. He did not tell this one for laughs, but made something of the funny bits when they cropped up. She laughed and laughed at the kilt and the cowboy boots, and looked sadly out at the New York passaggiata as she heard about the sex and the drugs and so forth. It was the bit about Proust that undid her. She sat, fork in hand, considering her little brother, bright, sober, unstoned, manning the helpline by night and spending his day with Charlus and Swann. 'I never really thought he was alive,' she said.

'I think he's quite tough. He must be. To have survived. To continue surviving.'

'I loved him so much. It was the worst moment of my life when he went. When I realised that he had really gone. Do you think he will drop by again? What was your impression? Give me a clear assessment of the situation.'

'He has to be very careful of himself. He's got life in a very fine balance, but if the slightest thing goes amiss, he will start wobbling. He's self-protective, self-obsessed, he says himself. But he spoke very affectionately of you and Venetia. Especially you. And he has a thick streak of curiosity. Such a life-affirming quality, that. No nosy person ever committed suicide.'

'Mark. That's rather good.'

'I'll write a winsome poem about it, if you like.'

'Mark, don't be beastly to me.'

'Just an old joke.'

'I can't bear it, Mark. Don't.'

'Morgan, I accept that things have changed, but there's no point in pretending that ten years of my life didn't happen.'

'You don't understand. You don't understand what I'm talking about at all.'

'Christ no. But then I never have, have I? You and your family. Always that little bit above my head.'

'You know, I'd forgotten how truly nasty you are. And you've been developing your talents, too. Well done, little you.'

'This animal is dangerous. It defends itself when attacked.'

Silence fell like another guillotine. Too late now to make a dramatic charge back to the airport. The last plane would be leaving about this moment. How much longer was this trip going to last? Like one more guillotine, weariness fell upon him. He closed his eyes; New York hiccuped and lurched. He was aware of Morgan calling a waiter and paying. It was so pleasant, sitting here with his eyes closed. Your eyes closed and your hair wet, and I could connect nothing with nothing. Wrong. Arms full. Your arms full and your hair wet. Here Eliot continues the theme of despair.

19

Mark woke with the woman he had come to see all around him. The bedroom was full of her presence, despite her absence. There was a Yiddish word he had met before, nebbish. Someone who walks out of the room, and it feels as if someone had walked in. Well, this room demonstrated the reverse nebbish principle. Her absence was nearly as strong a presence as her presence.

Bramble. No, rose. Faint pink, faint grey, a breath of green. No actual flowers, that wouldn't do at all, would it?, but their presence hinted at with traces of dangerous sentimental pink. Thorns unambiguous. No, it was rose and not bramble, he was sure of it, after all, he had been staring at it on and off for about an hour. Trying to convince himself he was asleep. *Rosa canina.* He knew that because his mother had a liking for roses, and a still greater liking for the baffling of lay persons.

There was an uncharacteristic hint of prettiness in this rose maze, even if it was not exactly a bed of roses. Unexpected vulnerability. Hint of sweetness. No, there was no escaping the fact that he was awake. Wide awake and ravenous. Time was half-past five in the morning, or past ten, if you prefer it in English. He had not managed the time difference with much competence. It was working on the plane that did it. Should have at least attempted a doze. But he had to mark the essays, get his mind round the *Ulysses* lesson, all that. And everything else, of course.

Could he get out without disturbing her? Not hard, since she was presently absent, sleeping in a different room entirely. He got out of bed and showered vigorously in the bathroom that led off his, her bedroom. Venetia's rows of ointments and unguents. He lathered himself with soap that smelt plenny spicy. Curried soap, what next?

He had hugged her in the lift or elevator. Told her that he was sorry, thinking that a general unselective sort of shotgun blast of apology would pepper the target reasonably effectively. But he had forgotten: it was an old tactic and one that had never worked in ten years. He had even forgotten her ritual response to the tactic: 'You renowned Christian apologist.' She started to call him this after a conversation with his mother in which The Mate had quoted C. S. Lewis to her and then courteously explained who he was. 'I always liked his neoplatonic fairy tales,' Morgan had replied. 'If that's not a tautology.' Never outgambited, even when on her best behaviour.

Mark dressed, best black cowboy boots, and let himself out of the flat or apartment. Pocketed the spare key, which he found on the hook by the door where it had always been, which simplified matters. Walked out into May sunlight, New York rawly waking. How had he been manoeuvred into a separate bed, a separate room so effortlessly? 'I'm sorry it's been such a stiff evening,' Morgan said, as they walked the few blocks to the apartment building. 'I'm out of practice.'

'I don't know,' Mark said. 'Like riding a bicycle really. Having rows, I mean.'

'I meant it about the nice meal. Anything you want.'

'I'll be nice myself,' Mark promised. 'Tomorrow, all day. You'll see.' And all night, if you wish, he had not said. But by this time he was wading through treacle, and his mind, too. She showed him how she had got the flat or apartment ready for him, and showed him how she had put Rolling Rock in the fridge for him and the Swiss cheese that he liked. When he had hugged her in the lift or elevator she had stiffened the very tiniest bit, but now, when he embraced her in front of the fridge or icebox, she didn't. That was nice. All the same, Mark found himself without quite working out how, walking down the corridor slightly out of step with his trousers and almost immediately lying in a bed with a Celtic knot carved into the headboard and almost immediately asleep. Alone, sleeping alone, waking alone. Self-pity: how would he survive without it? The thinking man's self-reliance.

He had a project, why not? He would walk up to Broadway and turn left. When he got to Battery Park, he would stop, since Broadway does the same. Then get a cab home, or rather back to the flat or apartment. He set out with a jaunty step, cool in his cowboy boots. Hungry: he should have eaten before he left. No he shouldn't. So he went to the twenty-four-hour deli he thought he could remember, and found that he did. He drank coffee and ate a bagel with lox and cream cheese, mainly because it was one of Morgan's favourite things. He then ordered two more, one to eat and one to go. And went. She was a good wife as wives go and as wives go, she went.

Saki's joke, that, wasn't it? A gone girl. Who had she left him for? That was the overwhelming question. Her carefully formed, beautifully honed nightmarish twists remind one of the tales of Saki. She never beautifully honed the Sabatiers. What avant-garde New York artist, what master of Manhattan ethics? Across the width of 42nd Street. Busy even now, the cars, the cabs, the sinister passers-by, the refugee street-sleepers. The Chrysler Building, the Empire State, rawly waking.

But it's not really a play about jealousy, is it, Mr Brown? Because she never does anything wrong, never does anything he can be jealous *of*. It's not about what happens, it's about what Othello thinks happens, isn't it, Mr Brown? Tell me more. I mean, Othello thinks Iago is his friend. He thinks Cassio is a hopeless drunkard. And he thinks Desdemona is unfaithful to him. And none of it's true. I mean, we are told quite clearly that it's all untrue. So Othello is not upset about what happens in life. He's upset about what he *thinks* happens.

Appearance and reality. Image and substance. The most intimate relationship of his life, and he is not just ignorant, but headed 180 degrees in the wrong direction. He is completely out of touch with objective reality.

Is he mad, then, Mr Brown? Well, this is another of those define-your-terms situations, isn't it? We saw the Olivier video eventually – a chuckle ran through the class; they had been mightily amused by the rolling nigger minstrel eyes, oh, the pity of it, Iago – and he plays Othello as distinctly loony. But when you read it, you don't feel that this is man cut off from normal human experiences. Quite the reverse, 180 degrees in the wrong direction, in fact. He's not inhuman: all too human, if you like. Not mad at all. But perplex'd in the extreme.

Past the hat shop at 34th, called Stetson's and selling Stetsons. You! Stetson! He paused for a moment, coveting. But a green cord cap was best. She'd have been shot without him, wouldn't she? And she was still wild and crazy, but surely no longer perplex'd. And last night he had so badly wanted to tell her of the gut-wrenching terror at her rearing fits of long ago, the soul-deep pleasure she had given him. Instead, he gave only the impression that he was mildly crazy and quite alarmingly brave. And neither really true. Across the diagonal at 23rd. Terrified, yes, but not exactly terrified of falling, of hurting himself. Terrified of failing? On to 14th, where Broadway stopped its mad snaking about and at last headed purposeful and straight. Terrified of failing *her*. Through Greenwich Village, the magic of place strong upon him, on towards Wall Street. Onward. He surveys Battery Place, journey's end, a slight slow smile playing about his lips.

He would be nice now. As he had promised. All day. He wanted to be nice. A cab, gave the address, Senna Puck. He would be nice and get through the weekend without further disaster. He would tell his best stories. He would read something to Venetia, something perfect, something *right*. He would not be mad, in either English or American. Then go home. Home home home. Back to the girl, and a plan and another weekend before the cross-country season was quite done. He was, after all, untouchable now.

But once in the cab he was assailed by dirty thoughts. I could count myself a king of infinite space, were I not troubled by dirty thoughts. It was all very well being nice, and all very well being better off the way he was. But what if she was still in bed and called out to him and looked up at him and smiled at him? What if she was wearing the dressing-gown with the embroidered Chinese dragon, and he were to chase the dragon, unbelting the silken sash, easing her from the dragon's embrace as she smiled and smiled? A male's a male for a' that.

He paid off the cab and entered the lobby and was good-morning-Mr-Browned, which rather impressed him, and he had not lost the key, which also did, and there she was, and yes she was. And either the dragon had grown or she had shrunk. 'Don't move! There's a dragon crawling up your back! Don't panic! Hold still, and I'll throttle the brute before he pierces a vital organ.'

And she laughed and was embraced and obviously adored.

Tricky stuff, grown-up sex. He had wondered – as Bec would no doubt have said, long and hard – about making the first move with Annette, not knowing how grown-ups made first moves. How much trickier the whole business was with your *own* wife. The problem was not seduction, but its opposite. To convey affection without invasion. Natural to slither his hands about the ski-slope of silk and while he was at it, press here and press there, from nothing more than affection, delight in the matutinal embrace. But it wouldn't do, would it? The thing about an ex-wife is that the smallest move would count as a big move. Which would be an invasion and cosmically inappropriate to the mood and feel of the morning.

So he could neither escalate the embrace nor disengage, for disengagement was not appropriate either. She seemed to share his wish that the embrace should continue for, well, not for ever, but for a good couple of hours or so.

You use your timidity like a machete, she once said. And you use it to cut me to shreds. You know what I ask, and you ignore it, playing mousy. The game is to make me beg.

Mark, unsure whether he was playing mousy or displaying the most perfect understanding, embraced and embraced. Said softly: 'I have a thing for thee.'

'Will I like it?' Almost a whisper.

'Bagel.'

'Lox? Cream cheese?'

'Of course.'

'Angelic man.'

She made him coffee, and he decanted the bagel onto a plate

and made himself toast to eat with Swiss cheese, the bread being iceboxed and inesculent and he being hungry again. The tiles bore green knots. The rest of the kitchen was full of grandiloquent American efficiency. Even the four-slice toaster was an exaggeration, a kind of boast. This was not a family good at kitchens. A country kitchen, an Aga, tack hanging from the beams, horse or horses outside. Not really a bachelor option.

'Milk?'

'Of course, have you forgotten?'

'I mean, would you please get the milk? From the icebox?'

'Or fridge, yes, sorry.'

They sat at the table, looking at each other. Not a married couple, not chance lovers, not old friends.

'Was I a bitch last night? Or a cow? I've been wondering which.'

'Was I a bastard? Or just a bugger? So have I.'

'You were tired and jet-lagged.'

'You were grieving.'

'Oh Mark. Be nice to me if you like, but please don't be understanding.'

'You look gorgeous in your gown.'

'You look gorgeous in your boots.'

'Lordy, you say the prettiest things to a girl.'

'I woke up this morning resolving to be nice.'

Mark said nothing.

'You did that very well, Mark. Masterly self-restraint.'

'All the same, you shouldn't give me openings like that.' The toast, being toasted, popped up. 'Thanks for getting me the cheese.'

'Heavens, are you going to be nice too?'

'All day.'

'Ceasing at dusk?' She laughed, nicely. 'Will you come and do first shift with me? At the hospital?'

'Of course.'

'Thank you. Now could you listen, please? I have something to tell you. The thing is, I have been practising a deception on Venetia. I need you to carry on the deception.'

Mark almost blurted out that he knew, but managed in time to restrain himself. Another little triumph of self-mastery. 'Tell me more. Do I have to dress up?'

'In a way. Venetia has no idea we've been apart all this time. And I want her to think that we're all right, still together, an item, a couple. I mean, you don't have to do anything, hold my hand all the time and chaff me about the time I forgot the washing up the other week. Just don't – I mean, don't – well, it's a lot to ask. I'm sorry. I've made a terrible mess of all this. Trying to protect you.' A pause. 'Or me.'

'It's all right, Morgan. These are not normal times. Besides, you forget about people. You should know I'd do anything for you, and I'd do anything for Venetia.'

'What a pretty speech.' But her eyes softened, and she placed a hand on his.

'I met a drug-dealer. Scored a stash of niceness pills. Must have OD'd.'

'I hope you haven't spiked my coffee.'

But at least they were now free to talk about the subject that filled their minds: Venetia – and the shadow of death. The absent woman, who had scarcely been mentioned throughout the troubles of the previous night, but who had dominated their thoughts as the dying must. They swapped tales of her impossible behaviour, her impossible generosity. Mark laughingly talked about his Jeep, and its final appropriateness as the transport of a horseman. He wondered briefly what had happened to the Flying Toad, the great Citroen DS she adored. He could ask. Lent, she would say, to a friend, she would say, sex unspecified. He could ask again, and she would tell him, and they would shout and swap bits of viciousness and then he would howl and go off to the airport, bum-twitch bum-twitch bum-twitch. So be quiet, then. Take another niceness pill.

Quite a lot of things to be quiet about. For starters, and as ever the story neither of them ever forgot, and neither ever could never mention: the story of the second condom. But now he also had to conceal the fact that he and Venetia were ganging up, together deceiving Morgan's deception. Mark knew he had been summoned

251

to New York not to see Venetia, but to see Morgan. But there was a further layer of deception he could not share with anyone at all. For he was also intending to deceive Venetia. He was not going to woo Morgan back into marriage, he was not even going to try. He was being nice because old ties demanded it. And then he was going home home home. Being untouchable now. Being free; free to be nice, nice as anything. Home.

So Morgan dressed in black jeans and a calypso shirt covered in toucans and palm trees. 'It's my mother's favourite,' she said, after Mark had laughed and complimented her. 'She calls it the rage-against-the-dying-of-the-light shirt.'

They walked across the park, still talking about Venetia, cutting off the corner to the hospital on the West Side, it being too early for muggers. As they passed the Sheep Meadow and swung left at the lake, Mark placed his arm around Morgan's shoulders.

'What are you doing?' But without hostility.

'Practising for deceiving Venetia.'

'We are trying to convince her that we are normal married folk. Not that we are honeymooners.'

'So we are. What shall we row about?'

'I expect we'll think of something.'

20

The alarm bell brought him back to the maze of roses, lost again, dragging him back from the deepest sleep. The pure hatefulness of such a waking: everything out of joint, himself in the wrong hemisphere, the earth in the wrong orbit. The dream from which he had been aroused seemed to have been a pleasant one: was it really Sexuella he had summoned up from the deep past?

Waking again, the second time in the same day, to Venetia's treasures. Yet I could see beyond that gold the ancient strife of wretched men. Stand under the shower. Drink coffee. In diver's boots he crossed the pale blond floor of wood, almost identical to the pale blond floor of his own or rather Venetia's or Morgan's Islingtonian house. He entered the shower, froze himself and then boiled himself in mad clumsiness until he hit a balance. Wake up, wake up.

Clad in a towel loincloth he made coffee. I was cut down from the copse's end, moved my roots. Venetia, silenced by the ancient trickeries of the words, the not-quite riddle of *The Dream of the Rood.* Just before he had set out on the day of his flight to New York, he had seized his undergraduate copy of Anglo-Saxon verse in translation, a crib unlooked-at since the days of his struggled-for two-two. Ancient knots and mazes: not as good, perhaps, as some of the A level stuff that sang for ever in his head, but good enough. And very Venetia.

Silenced from her profanities, she had listened absorbed. Read me 'Cynara', Bec. Mark made more toast and ate it with more Swiss cheese. The morning session, he and Morgan as married but not honeymooning couple, had gone well enough, though naturally he kept imagining ironical gleams in Venetia's eye, or perhaps not

253

imagining. But Venetia was on her best behaviour. 'Good to have you both here.' That was the most dangerous thing she said.

Then his solo visit that afternoon, sitting by her bed till she awoke, then talking awhile before suggesting that he read to her. And his choice met her approval; she knew the poem, of course, from her love of all Celt-related things, but she had more than half forgotten it. 'I like the gloomy bits best,' she said afterwards. 'I should have liked to have made a rood-screen.' She closed her eyes, perhaps visualising a knotted and mazed screen: or perhaps not. She was wearier than she had been the day before, much wearier.

He returned to the flat or apartment, weary enough himself. Morgan told him to sleep, and he protested and then obeyed. He was to meet her at the hospital, and together they would say good night to Venetia. He was to sleep, so that he would be in prime form to be taken out to dinner. As if he had come to New York for the sake of a plate of food. As if a plate of food would wipe out any indebtedness. As if he were a stranger, an outsider who needed to be bribed. Or perhaps the acceptance of the bribe forced him into the position of stranger. For it was not like her: she normally cared little for that kind of extravagance. A beautiful object, yes, or garment, that was worth wild money. But fancy cooking did not touch her, nor fancy wines. It was all, as his mother would say, rather rum.

He would sulk, playing with his food, eating but reluctantly. He would peruse the wine list and ask for beer. Beer, what a perfectly splendid idea. So he took one of Morgan's kind Rolling Rocks from the fridge or icebox and poured it into a glass.

Clean shirt, jacket against the evening chill, he walked across the park. There wasn't a straight line in the place, the not-quite maze always turning him west when he sought north.

Nurse Kwan recognised him. 'She's not good. We're kind of putting a stop on visitors.'

'Is her daughter about?'

'She's with her mom.' How absurdly unlike both that sounded.

'Can you please tell her I'm here?' There was an uncooperating pause, and then Mark added words he had not thought to speak again. 'I'm her husband, Morgan's husband.'

'Oh.' A longish, and Mark felt, rather judgmental pause. And besides, he was impertinent: death was the business of the medical profession, nothing to do with a lay person like himself. But, being confronted like the stewardess with the double vodka, she concurred. And in a few moments, said that he might enter.

Venetia was awake, the light bright, the bright profane protest dimmed. He kissed the cheek nearest him, took a place on the opposite side of the bed. Morgan was holding her mother's hand: how ludicrously unlike them both. So he took the other hand, it being above the covers and available for holding, after kissing another cheek, drier, no less soft, all tension, all anger gone. Over-large brown eyes looked at him, thin lips, onto which no cupid's bow had been superimposed, twitched slightly at the corners. It was, he knew, a radiant smile. He felt her hand move in his, and wondered if Morgan felt the same thing in her own hand. Without any evidence to confirm this, Mark was quite certain she had tried to join their two, their four hands together.

'Morgan's taking me out for a meal tonight,' he said. 'We're going to get offensively drunk. Really horribly and impossibly drunk.' These were more or less the last words he was to speak to her; not altogether inappropriate ones, he was to think for ever after. Next, wretched in eventide, they sang a dirge. Words he had read that afternoon. Morgan sought his eye, and motioned with her own towards the door. 'Good night, Venetia,' he said. 'Till tomorrow, yes?' Once more kissed her cheek. Touched Morgan's toucan-clad shoulder as he passed her. Cravenly went to the lav or restroom rather than speak to the pearl of the orient. He stood for a while washing his face without water, and then for a change washing his face with water.

Back in the communal area, Morgan had still not arrived. And when she did so, she came not from the hateful cell, but from the same or neighbouring lav or restroom, cleansed, made up. A little mascara applied with care and discretion to a mask from Greek tragedy. She even tried a smile for him

And she was in his arms. 'Morgan. Morgan my love.'

A waste of freshly applied make-up really. After a while she said, muffled, to his shoulder. 'You never call me that.'

'I say it now.'

It was about twenty minutes later that they found themselves walking alongside Central Park, not entering, though already mugged. Both had made a further visit to the lav or restroom. Morgan had added to her toucan rage-against-the-dying-of-the-light shirt a long, beautifully cut jacket made from material that might have been intended for curtains, or perhaps cushions. But not the curtains at the Swan Hotel: the jacket was covered in a flock of large blue-and-crimson parrots. Or perhaps macaws. 'Mourning clothes,' she explained.

'Un coeur simple.'

She laughed at this connection. 'Look, Mark, I've booked a table at a rather good French restaurant, but I think it would be rather good to have a rather stiff drink first. Partly because I want or rather need one, and partly because – well – what I mean to say –'

She came to a halt here, so Mark had to fill in, and did so with, he thought, not a little grace: 'And we don't want to have another rather stiff evening, and a decent slug of alcohol will help us to be civilised human beings. Or rather, help me to be a civilised human being instead of the cranky jet-lagged git I was yesterday. For which a thousand apologies.'

'You git,' she said. 'You renowned Christian apologist. What did you call me?'

'Morgan my love.'

'Slightly naff endearment, that. Mark my love, I know a slightly naff bar that may well suit our current mood.'

'I'd sooner be naff with you than in exquisite taste with anybody else.'

'You absolutely appalling git. Hail me a cab, I'm a helpless female. Do as I say.'

The bar was at the top of a building with the apocalyptic address of 666 Sixth Avenue. It was a tourist trap, a parody of opulence. 'They keep putting the bars in cellars,' Morgan said. 'This is the only place I know where you can see out.' The city was spread out vertiginously beneath them. 'I think that's St Pat's, though I get disorientated rather easily. As you may know. But let's sit down.'

Mark looked out: the modern, the once-modern, the sandwiched mock-Gothic of St Patrick's Cathedral, if that's what it was. The bar itself had a cathedral hush. It was a trap for tourists who were serious drinkers. A group of Japanese in navy-blue suits. A man in a dinner-suit or tuxedo with a woman in rather too yellow a yellow. Themselves.

'Good evening and what can I get you to drink this evening?'

'Morgan?'

Most unexpectedly, she said: 'Vodka Martini straight up with a twist, please. I seriously advise you to do the same.'

'All right. Two please.'

'It's a drink of mindless viciousness. So it's very important to drink one.'

'I can see that.'

The drinks came in those glasses that Americans seem to drink out of a lot: inverted cones on long stems. Clear liquid, faint mist of condensation already on the glass. In the liquid's depths a vermiform spiral of lemon peel. 'What shall we drink to?' she asked.

'A nice evening.'

But she said, as if it were the toast: 'Attainable goals.' So Mark repeated this, and they touched glasses, very carefully, because the glasses were very full. And drank. 'I always think it's like drinking a freshly cut meadow.'

Like heavenly cough mixture. 'It's like getting mugged in a freshly cut meadow.'

She observed him for a while. Fascinatingly asymmetrical, the thick italic swash of hair, the rest held back by the unseen Ashanti treasure. The absurd macaws. 'Remember when we played Africa?'

'I'm hardly likely to forget.'

'I thought you wouldn't come. I thought you'd hate me far too much. I'm so grateful. Venetia was talking a little this afternoon. Telling me how great you were. It wasn't a small thing to do, Mark, in any way of looking at it. I won't forget it.'

'I was glad to be asked. No more on the subject.'

She held him for a while with the same smile. 'What shall we talk about, then?'

'My horse?'

'How odd, to think of you with horses. Do you swagger about in big boots and talk about fetlocks and snaffles?'

'That's exactly what I do, as a matter of fact. Then me and my girl go out and tear the countryside in half.'

'You and your girl. Is it love, Mark? Is it the real thing?'

Mark looked at her appraisingly. 'Do you beneath the ironies actually understand?'

'I never loved an animal. Or have been loved.'

Mark took another sip. 'Christ, this is like drinking freshly mown paraffin. I was going to tease you. When I told you about her last night. Partly as a tease, partly to try and make you understand what – well, what everything has been all about, in the past few months. I was going to say, I'm in love with a beautiful female, she has brown eyes, brown skin, the sweetest nature, but sometimes, when I get on top of her, she gets really rather wild.'

She gave him a smile of appreciation for this. 'You know, I had been planning the very same tease, isn't that rum? – as your mother would say. For perhaps the very same reason. I still want to do it. I really want to, but I won't because you'll only go all woebegone and that would be no fun.'

'I'm beyond woe now.'

'What I really mean is that I don't want to be wantonly unkind. I've given that up. I'm going to be a nice person. Remember when we played Africa?'

'You've already asked that.'

'So I have. We're too old for matchboxes now, and besides, if we played we'd draw attention to ourselves in a bar such as this. But I can feel this drink acting on me as a truth serum. I feel a powerful urge to tell you all kinds of true things. I want to strip myself naked and leave all dissembling in a pile of washing on the floor of the bar.'

'But, Morgan, you always dress everything up so beautifully. I love your layers of dissembling.'

'I've known you strip away my layers. However beautiful.'

'Always with reluctance.'

'Shameless lies. Shall I strip naked anyway? I want to tell you all kinds of things, though not wantonly unkind things. And I feel an equally powerful urge to ask you some really interesting questions, though not wantonly unkind questions. I want to see you naked too, or at least, a little less clad. I rather think I'm talking nonsense. Mark, do you feel this drink acting on you like a truth serum?'

For answer, Mark turned his head, and caught like a brilliant slip-catcher the eye of the waiter. Mark showed him two fingers. The waiter, not waiting for Mark to say waiter, mouthed Right Away. 'So how were you planning to tease me?'

She looked out at the castellations of Manhattan, eyes filled with nostalgia for the jest that never was. Lust and the love of a jest. 'I was going to describe the last man I slept with. Take quite a time over it. He's sweet, he's kind, he plays at being the victim. List all his good points and his bad. Especially the good points.'

Mark was grossly offended even at the idea. 'That doesn't really sound like one of your more amusing jokes, all things considered.'

'Ah, but you see it turns out to be you. A Celtic riddle. Like your horse tease.'

'Me? Oh, you mean last night. Sleeping in the same apartment.'

'No. Sleeping as in sex. Oh. Thanks.'

'Thank you.' Fresh inverted cones of newly mown meadow. 'But we didn't and that spoilt it.'

'We did. Last time I did it, I did it with you.'

'But we didn't –'

'Mark, I think I am going to have to stand on the table and shout at the top of my voice. I warn you, I'm in the mood to do such a thing. Look, everybody, I shall say. This here is the last man I had sex with. Close your mouth, you look like a goldfish. No, an ornamental carp, a koi fish.'

By craning his head just a little, Mark could see right down to the bottom of the grand canyon of Sixth – or was it Fifth? – Avenue. He got disorientated rather easily.

'It was in the bathroom. It was rather good, as I recall.'

Mark made his lips say some words. 'What was in the bathroom?'

'Sex, what do you think, a goldfish? Or a koi? You look as if you had just had rather disagreeable news.'

Mark ingested a far slice of meadow. 'Morgan, remember when I had that conversation with Philosophy Dick?'

'I shan't forget you telling me about it.'

'Well, this is worse.'

She looked at him, almost compassionately. 'I suppose it is, in a way.'

'I thought you'd left me for someone else. The One someone. The one and only Real Love of Your Life.'

'Well, on the whole, I think you're probably right. That's exactly what I did do. I left you for me. Lovely lovely me.'

'You mean getting away from me was joy enough?' But said without rancour, much to his surprise. Said almost humbly. How odd of him.

'No. It wasn't enough. Flying away to Me. Wonderful Me. It was liberation: I would think about Me all the time, instead of having you round the place going bushbaby.'

'Oh dear. Don't call me a renowned Christian apologist, Morgan, but I really am sorry.'

'Shut up, I don't want to talk about you. I want to talk about Me. Mark, do I sound frightfully drunk? I certainly feel it. I've come to the conclusion, you know, that I'm absolutely mad about myself. But since I left you, I have suffered the ultimate tragedy of the narcissist. I have fallen out of love with myself. It was all very well when I was married, and Lovely Me was just a bit on the side. When it was all just Me and Me and Me – well, I couldn't hack it any more.'

'I remember reading somewhere about self-love unrequited.'

'Perfect. That's me: a classic case of self-love unrequited. And I stopped being completely fabulous, you see. It all went wrong. I was so good, you see. But then marriage and work both went wrong together.'

'Work? How could work go wrong?'

'Do you know what I think, Mark? I think the one thing wrong with our marriage was your notion of my infallibility.'

For a moment, Mark felt as if he had walked into a glass door. After a while, he was able to speak. 'Did you know that my mother once wrote a very trenchant book on the subject of papal infallibility?'

'I'm sure from a suitably sceptical point of view. But you weren't sceptical at all. You made me your pope and never came to terms with my fallibility.'

'Morgan? Holy Father – can you tell, is this conversation crazy, or is it just me?'

'You never looked after me and succoured me and gave me self-belief.'

Even now Mark was unable to believe. 'I always thought you had enough of all those things for us both.'

Morgan looked at him with a terrible sadness in her eyes. 'But I was only pretending, you see. Or rather, you didn't see, did you? Wasn't it the Virgin Mary? The last infallible decree?'

'I think you may be right.'

'How like your mother you sound.'

'How like my mother you sound.'

'And you see, I am not only fallible. I stand before you, sit rather, as a failure. I failed. And you never even noticed.'

'It must have been a very small failing. One I was quite prepared to overlook.'

'You did overlook it, but it wasn't so terribly small. I couldn't write any more. I haven't written a story for a year. Or a little bit more.'

Mark rubbed his chin, sipped some more meadow. 'Is that why you left?'

'If you mean, did I leave in order that I might start writing again, then I don't really know. And if I did, I failed again. I failed and am failing still. If you mean did I leave because my life was out of joint, then probably yes. I expect I could have managed not writing in a fertile marriage, and I expect I could put up with a sterile marriage if I was writing a lot.'

'Why didn't you tell me?'

'There was no procedure for such a thing in our marriage. You tell me your troubles, while I just carry on being infallible. There was no protocol for me telling, let alone *having* troubles. There never has been. That's what's always been wrong.'

'Why can't you write any more stories?'

'Because I hate the ones I have written so much. I was having trouble, you know, being stuck. So I read both my books, *Alice* and *Arachne*. To get my mind back on track. But it didn't work. The stories were so – so –'

'Winsome.'

She looked at him, caught on the wrong foot for once, mouth ajar like a goldfish or koi. And then she started to laugh. At first with reluctance, but she could not stop herself, and she fell into peals of giggles, dangerous giggles that clouded her eyes and her mascara once again. 'So right,' she managed after a while, Mark giggling alongside her for company. 'So right. I was going to say slight, pointless, trivial, factitious, clever. But you're right. That's what they were. Winsome.'

'Hey, miss. You look mighty pretty when you're hysterical.'

'Mark, don't make me laugh any more.'

So Mark put on his poetry-ready face, and recited the final lines of that great work, 'The Night of Serial Buttock-Fondling'. His hesitating, questioning poet's voice.

> 'It was only
> the following morning
> that I understood
> how that night
> I had touched
> bottom.'

And her laughter really did turn to tears this time, and she said: 'Oh, Mark, I do rather adore you, you're such an appalling git.'

She was dabbing her eyes with a handkerchief, for the bar was big enough for its customers to weep hysterically without attracting attention. Flipping matchboxes, that would have been another matter entirely. 'Look, Mark, I'm the only one giving away secrets and it's not fair.'

'Well, I'll rectify that. I adore you too, appalling person that you are. I've been keeping that pretty dark.'

'Why, thank you. You say the prettiest things. But look, if this truth serum is any good, you should be making confessions too. Have you been cutting a swathe through the female population of London? Have you loved any females other than your horse?' She giggled again. 'Your horse, what a notion. But I want to know, Mark. With whom have you been sharing your bed? Or our bed? I want the details.'

So, with an unresolved mixture of boasting and shame, he briefly told the brief story of Annette.

'You dog.'

'I felt rather a dog, I must say. But I didn't really feel happy with the unfaithfulness part.'

'Being unfaithful to me?'

'No, no, no, I got rather a kick out of that. I didn't like her being unfaithful to him. It took some of the bubbles out of it.'

'Did she have heavenly tits?'

'Why do you ask?'

'Just a foible of mine. Do you know the one thing I've never been able to come to terms with in my life?'

Your father, the matching pair of condoms, your violated teenage bed. Of course I know. 'I have no idea. Tell me.'

'Sexuella.'

'Clare?' His voice quite incredulous.

'I sometimes think it threw my entire life out of balance. I sometimes think the entire history of our married life would have been different if you hadn't tumbled heavenly Sexuella.'

'But, Morgan – she was so silly. Quite unthinkable a rival.'

'Such heavenly tits.'

They were, too, Mark did not say, involuntarily seeing Sexuella, as he pulled over the kitten-soft pullover, unhooked with hands rendered deft by lust, revealed vistas of glory, vistas of heavenly beauty, as they sat drinking or rather not drinking tea in her tiny Indian-godless room in the hall of residence. Morgan's Dear John which was not a Dear John in the pocket of his soon-to-be-removed trousers. Oh, you *animal* man. Oh, he had responded, you mammal. You *mammal*. 'But I thought you'd left me for ever. I was bereft. I was taking consolation where I could.'

'Precisely the point. You failed to understand me. You missed the point of my joke. And anyway, if you'd had any decency, you would have spent your time wailing and gnashing your teeth, or being struck dumb. Instead of rolling about with those gorgeous bosoms.' Mark saw her again, crossing her arms with mock-modesty over those gorgeous bosoms as he came into her room with two cups of tea, the first cups being, of course, cold, the gesture, the jest prompting a new wave of lust. Hard to regret an incident that caused so much pain. Even if it had poisoned the rest of his life. Her life. Their lives.

'I gnashed my teeth this time. The neighbours kept complaining. They could hear the gnashing five streets away.' This was beginning to sound like a winsome poem. 'Too late, I suppose. But I gnashed them good and proper this time.'

'That was sweet of you. But, Mark, tell me one thing. One thing that has always bothered me. Did you sleep with anyone during the course of our marriage?'

'Oh, Morgan.' But the truth drug was working strong on him now. He told the story of the concealment of the objet d'art. He could not help himself. He told it without much zest, just the bare, as it were, facts. 'Remember when we played Africa?' he asked. 'If we were playing now, and you asked me about shame, this would be the very top of the list.'

'Was it a frightfully bad copulation?'

'Oh no. It was quite shatteringly excellent. That was the problem.'

'Because it shattered your role as the victim in married life. Shattered my role as villain. You were a bit of a dog, for once. And you couldn't cope with the change.'

Mark looked at the spiral of lemon peel, twisting down to its tiny puddle of freshly mown paraffin. I was being like you. Copulating as if copulation didn't matter. I was being like you. Copulating without giving a fuck. 'You're right, Morgan. I couldn't.'

264

'You're looking bushbaby. Stop it at once.'

'Damned if I will. I have a right to regret my own errors.'

'Well, stop it. Wave at the waiter again, make him bring some more truth serum.'

'Haven't we had enough?'

'Truth? Or serum? I admit that I'm frightfully drunk. This drink is pure poison, you know. But I have always read that the third Martini is the truly dangerous one. I don't think it would be responsible to leave without having tested the veracity of that. Observe my rather splendid in vino grammar.'

'We shall have no appetite for our nice dinner.'

'Bugger our nice dinner. We are dining on truth.'

'Almost esculent slices of life, yes. Waiter.'

'The check?'

'Certainly not. Two more, please.'

'Coming up.'

There was a silence for a while, they looked at each other not quite steadily, not quite because of the Martinis. And then Morgan said: 'Are you not going to ask me how many men I slept with during the course of our marriage?'

'I thought on the whole I wouldn't. You didn't care for the question yesterday, and I didn't even ask it.'

'But I was sober then. And besides, normal rules have been suspended.'

'A period of ritual licence. But you see, Morgan, I'm not sure it's a relevant question. You can't count infidelity. It is a noun with no plural, observe my in vino grammar. The exact number more than one has no meaning. A marriage counts not one two three four five. It counts one, two, many. Unilateral, bilateral, multilateral.'

She put her head a little on one side, and observed him more or less steadily. 'Are you saying we are equally at fault where infidelity is concerned?'

Mark nearly overelaborated by correcting her, saying where marriage is concerned, yes, equally. But after a brief editorial conference with himself, he opted for simplicity. 'Yes.' Or perhaps truth.

And she acknowledged that with a small smile, and slowly, very softly began to laugh again. And laughed and laughed and laughed. 'When did you decide this?'

'About a minute ago. And I'm right.'

'You wild foolish boy.' She had stopped laughing now. And quite surprisingly, an expression almost of sweetness settled on her face.

'Philosophy Dick was the only one that really caused me anguish. I still don't like to think of it.'

'I had to do it, Mark. I was so in love.'

Mark was appalled, almost more appalled than he had been when he first heard the terrible revelations in Tudge's coffee shop. 'I refuse to believe that anybody could be in love with Philosophy Dick. The thing is against nature.'

'I wasn't. Fool. I was in love with you.'

It was a bit like one of those terrible whacks in the chest he got when the mare threw her head at him. Whack under the heart. 'So you went out and slept with Philosophy Dick.'

'Precisely. Thank you. Jesus, I hope I can finish this.'

'I'm not sure I can handle the pace myself, if we are going to follow this evening through to its logical conclusion.' They drank. 'When precisely did you realise this?'

'Realise what?'

'Don't ask me difficult questions. It's getting hard enough to follow your logic. If I have to follow mine, I'm a gone girl.' Mark giggled at his own wit.

'So what was the question?'

Mark racked his brain for a while. Sipped, as an aid to racking. The taste was subtly different. It tasted like a drink too far. He sipped again, and that was better. Used to it now. 'I've got it. When did you realise that you slept with Philosophy Dick because you were in love with me? Jesus, the question sounds even sillier than your initial statement.'

'Doesn't it? Over the course of the last few months.'

'What during the last few months?'

'Realising why I slept with Philosophy Dick.'

'Ah. Got you. So – well, it was jolly silly of you then, wasn't it?'

'Wasn't it? But, Mark – how could I possibly have marriage on my own terms if I didn't go about sleeping with other people?'

'That's something we'll never know.' Mark said this lightly, with a little amusement, and a fair bit more affection. But Morgan was not amused at all.

'Mark, I'm going to tell you a story about a friend of mine. Known her for ages. Friend of my mother's really. She used to hang around the apartment here in New York when I was a teenager, and around the house in Islington, too. Adventurous lady, you see. In her late twenties then, I suppose. And she used to tell the most hair-raising stories about men. She just loved shagging, you see. It used to thrill me to bits. She was so funny, you see, and me wide-eyed, listening to her endless stories about shagging. Anyway, she turned thirty-five, and got married to an architect. Had three children in quick succession, all girls. Model mother. Model wife. No wandering by the way. She came over to New York a couple of weeks ago, to see Venetia. We had some long talks. I found it all a strange contradiction.'

'No contradiction. Just a very loving woman.'

'I mean that people change.'

'I don't know that they do, Morgan. But certainly, your story means that people can change the way that they live. And love.'

He watched her slowly sipping, enjoying, it seemed, the taste of too far. 'Mark, I am trying to work out whether you are being terribly nice, or terribly nasty.'

'I'm not entirely sure myself. But I'm *trying* to be terribly nice. I don't know what your position is on the subject of authorial intention.'

'I made a resolution before you arrived, you know. If you saw Venetia and asked me to comfort you, then I would never speak to you again. But if you comforted me, I would marry you on the spot.'

'Have you always been this crazy?'

'I ain't never been put to the test before. Jesus, Mark, I hope I can walk home.'

'Have no fear. I will support your every step.'

'I believe you will.' She looked at him, but slightly missed, and had to adjust her gaze. 'Being kind is quite different from being nice, you know. You have to be really quite tough, to be kind.'

'Oh yes.'

'Are you kind to your horse, Mark?' Mark laughed a good deal at this, though for the life of him he could not say why. Morgan laughed with him, perhaps equally uncertain. 'Do you punish her when she does wrong?'

'Not really, no. She still does it, you know, stands on her hind legs. Every time we stop at a T-junction, for example, and we have to wait for the traffic. She doesn't mean any harm by it, not any more. She's not seriously frightened, not any more. It's just something she does. Just something she has to do. So I just let her do it.'

'Isn't it dangerous, what she does?'

'A bit, yes. Probably be a lot more dangerous if I were to get upset and start walloping her. I just pat her.'

'Stroke her and make much of her? She does bad things and you just make much of her? You just let her do it?'

'It's not a question of letting. She's going to do it whether I let her or not. It's just a question of whether I mind. And I don't. I just want her to be happy.'

She laughed affectionately, mockingly. As if the two adverbs were inseparable. 'True love, Mark. True love is blind.'

'No. I see everything. I see all her faults. And I still adore her.'

'In spite of her faults? Or because?'

'We are talking about love here, Morgan. Which means even that question is irrelevant.'

She seized his hand as he reached for the remains of his drink, and held it against her face. 'As in, let me count the ways?'

'Now you understand.' He finished his drink with his free hand, and then joined the hand to hers. She did the same, and made the total four.

'You won't insist on sleeping alone tonight?'

'I don't recall insisting last night. Though with the state you've got us both into, I don't quite know what you're expecting.'

'I expect you to take all your clothes off and then kiss me. But

I warn you, if you put your tongue in my mouth I shall vomit. Check, please.'

Embracing in the lift or elevator, embracing on the pavement or sidewalk. No tongues. No taxi, it will make me vomit. Walking up Sixth, arms about each other, tacking like a yacht into a stiff breeze, no Mark, this isn't working. I really will vomit. Walking separately, but unable to keep pace with each other. Finally, Mark placed his right hand in his pocket and she took his arm. That worked. They walked up to Senna Puck giggling like children.

Giggled in the lobby of the apartment block. Giggled in the lift or elevator, where they groped each other in an absurd fashion. She managed the key into the keyhole beneath the brazen knot with marked competence and then, with marked sobriety, managed the answerphone. No message from the hospital, no message to rouse the green-eyed monster from its lair. A couple of enquiries after Venetia, a voice, female, offering Sunday night supper. 'Mark, would you be an angel?'

'I'll try, anyway.'

'Make me a cup of tea. I shall sip it decorously in bed, and then I think I will be able to receive your kisses without vomiting. I really do feel a little odd. In fact, to be accurate, I am completely crapulous.'

'It shall be as you say.' She smiled, a nice smile, really one of her best. Mark went to the kitchen. Drunk? Pissed, yes, certainly pissed. But vomiting bed-spinning drunk, no. That was good. Better training than her; or something to do with biochemistry. Men's larger livers. Smaller hearts to compensate, no doubt. Switched on the kettle, remembered the Woody Allen line about the brain. It's my second favourite organ. And she turning to him: it's *my* favourite. And both lying.

Green tea. Made in a teapot, the way she liked it. The student affectation or experiment of gunpowder tea had become a lifelong solace. A cup himself? No. He scalded the leaves, released the good smell, and went to the fridge. Decapitated a bottle of Rolling Rock, horsey on the label. It tasted like the right drink. Found the handleless Japanese mug she had used at breakfast, poured. Picked up bottle and mug, and then put them down again, grinning lightly to himself. Walked into Venetia's bedroom, removed his clothes. Lust and the love of a jest. Fetched the drinks. Her door ajar; he opened with bare knee.

She lay naked and spreadeagled: had he ever seen her so wanton? And asleep. Mark put the drinks on the table beside her bed, and kissed lightly her lips. Smiling still, he kissed lightly the nearest breast. And met no response whatsoever. Lust and the love of a jest? He considered kissing and more than kissing, until she awoke smiling and more than smiling. But no. Instead, he laughed suddenly, almost delightedly, and stretched out a hand to touch, once, very lightly, a soft perfect equilateral triangle. And then covered her up, arranging the duvet as kindly as Nurse Kwan.

He slipped into her adjacent bathroom, put on her dragoned robe. Cold at first, but it would warm up. Picked up his green bottle with its horsey label. Kissed his fingers to her. Switched out the light, good night, sweet princess. You and your A level mind, she had more than once said to him.

Oh yes, he always replied. Nothing but inane naff minor writers of no account in my naff old mind. Naff old Shakespeare, naff old Eliot, naff old Joyce.

He stood at the window in the sitting room, looking out at Fortress Manhattan. Wondering if, of all the strange things that happened that day, the patting of the equilateral triangle had not been the strangest. That dreadful moment, that most dreadful of all dreadful moments: had it been a year ago? Caressing her, and finding the unmistakable traces of his predecessor. Snatching his fingers away as if they had been plunged into acid.

Ever afterwards fearful of repeating that touch. The more so because of her own reaction when she perceived his reluctance, his fearfulness. And those rows about answerphones and Sabatiers that were really rows about sex. It's pathetic, the way so small a thing matters so much to you. Pathetic. Well, he could touch her now. He could touch as gently as Nurse Kwan. Uninvolved.

Potton tomorrow.

21

She looked at him with some disfavour, but Mark was firm with her. Inexorable. 'I won't change my mind, so please don't wake me. No food at all. And could I have two of those, please?' Mark was reminded of Winnie-the-Pooh on his visit to Rabbit. Honey or condensed milk on your bread? Both, please. But don't worry about the bread. Mark giggled softly to himself as he unscrewed the first little bottle of Scotch and poured it onto the ice-cubes. He thought about sharing the thought with Morgan, who would laugh and cap it with another quote from the same source.

Sharing things with Morgan, outrageous thought. Walking in Senna Puck, past the carousel or roundabout. She talking about children's books. She wanted to try writing one. She even had an idea. No, nothing on paper. Hadn't dared. But she kept thinking about it. A neoplatonic fairy tale? Mark had asked. If that's not a tautology. And she laughed, and said, well, funny you should say that. And will you ever write it? I don't know. Not soon. If I'm ever brave again.

It was the sound of the flush in the next-door bathroom that woke him in the morning, the pressure on the mattress that made him open his eyes. For the pressure had come on his side. Morgan sitting beside him. Now sober, still naked.

He looked at her for a while. And then smiled: 'You're thinking how exactly like a rodent I look,' he said.

She sat there watching him, not moving. She widened her eyes at him, the tiniest fraction: a radiant smile, he knew. 'You're the only one that ever understood my jokes.'

'Or laughed at them.'

She laughed herself at this. 'You git. Come to my arms, my beamish boy.'

Mark would have said, O frabjous day! callooh! Callay! But instead the telephone rang its monosyllabic American ring. Morgan walked round the bed to the other side. 'Yes it is. Oh. Oh. Yes. All right. I'll be there in fifteen minutes. Thank you for calling.'

She replaced the receiver as if it had been made of cobweb, and sat on the edge of the bed, her back to Mark. Mark made an elegant sidle across the bed. Hard thing with all this nakedness: to give comfort without indicating helpless desire. He made an embrace from behind, best angle for that sort of thing, taking a soft shoulder in each hand, and then wrapping both his arms about her, good and high, never falling below clavicle level, anxious above all things to avoid contact with any untoward patch of skin. She crossed her own arms and gently seized his. The stars stopped in their courses, the universe stood still, time ceased.

A brief but palpable eternity later, she tugged his arms downward, to bring them into contact with various untoward patches of skin, saying, without turning her head, a single word.

'Mark.'

And so, without jest or poem or irony or memory, they briefly joined and softly parted.

He watched her dress, black jeans, a black cowboy shirt this time, pearl buttons, three at the wrist and one more at the forearm, a western style bootlace tie with a huge silver horse. Clamped to her wrist a huge silver bracelet covered in turquoises, presumably Red Indian or rather Native American. No cowboy boots, that would be going too far, the same eccentric buckled shoes she had worn the day before. 'Planned the outfit when I heard about this blissful horse of yours. To make you smile.'

'You look wonderful.'

'I wonder if I'm pregnant.'

'Oh?'

'I've always been rather good at precautions. I've just remembered that I haven't taken any for – well, six months or so; what need?'

'Oh.'

A small smile. 'Well, if it's yours, it won't be a bastard.'

'Why, thank you for that nice double entendre, Morgan. Look, are you sure –'

'I'm sure. Meet me at lunch time. I'll need you then.'

'Need me?'

'Need you.'

Mark poured the second Scotch onto the not greatly diminished icescape. Lunch time. Venetia better now. Resting, having rallied. Immediate danger over. They walked together in the park, New Yorkers all around them taking their frenzied relaxation of Sunday springtime afternoon. A group of roller-bladers had set up a slalom of Coke cans on a slight incline, and were taking turns to negotiate it. Children trundled forward, more under gravity than their own power, feet apart, wobbling between the cans to their precarious destinies. Others older, more accomplished, knees and ankles locked together, steering with dramatic wiggles of the buttock. Off he goes again, Mark said, bum-twitch, bum-twitch, bum-twitch. Two tall bony black boys spent most of their time lounging about and talking very loudly above the dins of their separate Walkmen, but every now and then, not too often because that would be uncool, one and then the other would launch himself down the slope. One usually went on one leg backwards; the other crossing and recrossing his legs around each can.

'An image of how we live,' Mark suggested. 'Plummeting downhill backwards, out of balance, on one leg, going far too fast and struggling desperately to avoid obstacles that don't matter one way or the other.'

'The other dude has the right idea,' Morgan said. 'Keep your legs crossed at all times.'

Mark laughed at her joke. Unsure if she meant this morning or the whole course of her married life. And kissed her cheek as they stood watching, and then her other cheek and then though lightly her mouth.

'That was pleasant of you,' she said.

'I'm making you a bit tense,' he said. 'I'm sorry. I don't mean to.'

She sighed. 'It's me, not you. I keep waiting for you to start a heavy and meaningful conversation about Our Future, and where do we go from here and what did it all mean last night and what did it all mean this morning. It's most unlike you not to have this conversation. I keep bracing myself for it and it keeps not coming.'

'I'll tell you about the future, Morgan. All things have been revealed to me, so listen. The future is that I catch a plane tonight, and tomorrow I teach *Othello* and give my introduction-to-Joyce lesson. Then I'll ride my horse, then I'll go home. Your future is that you care for Venetia and ponder your neoplatonic fairy tale.'

'Is that all?' she asked. Almost humbly. 'Does the rest not matter?'

'Not today.'

She sighed, looked, perhaps, slightly bushbaby. 'Perhaps you're right.'

'I'm always right.'

They walked on. A Chinese boy with very long hair was teaching a dozen non-Chinese tai-chi. 'Mark?'

'Yes.'

'I think I wanted you to have that conversation.'

'Only so you could squash it.'

She caught her breath a little at this unkindness. They walked past the tai-chi group in a little silence. A person in spectacles sat on a bench playing the French horn, beautifully. 'You're probably right.'

'I'm always right.'

'But we'll be in touch.'

And Mark was laughing out loud. He found himself saying: 'It is the book to which we are all indebted and from which none of us can escape.'

Morgan laughed at his amusement. 'What is?'

'T. S. Eliot on *Ulysses*. Part of my introduction to Joyce. I was looking it up on the plane coming over.'

'What does it mean?'

'*Ulysses*? Or the quotation?'

'Oh, don't spare yourself. Tell me both.'

Suddenly Mark found himself at a T-junction, and there was no way out of it, forwards or back.

'The meaning of *Ulysses* is love. The meaning of the quotation is . . .' A pause, but Mark was fearless now. 'The meaning of the quotation is exactly the same. It means we'll be in touch. How can we not?'

'You do remember to keep the answerphone switched on?'

'Always.'

22

Lost damn it lost damn it lost. Flying, truly flying, and they had turned hard left at fence thirteen and there fence fourteen wasn't. Victory squirted from his clutching hand like a bar of soap in the shower.

They had flown the uphill log-pile of thirteen, beside it the much bigger log-pile of the open class, and were ready to take fourteen in stride. Then its vanishment. Stopping, turning, looking about. And with her rhythm broken, her concentration followed, the head-toss at his chest, the mad two-legs canter. Back to trot, spinning a tight circle, to her intense annoyance. And there the bloody thing was, back down through the hedge-line on his right, yellow pipes, the much bigger open class pipes alongside.

Lit with fury, he asked her to take the jump from a standstill and she obliged, leaping like a cat, four-footed, landing like a piano, for it was a drop fence, as he remembered when she touched down, and he slam-dunked himself crotch-first on the pommel and lost his left iron as he did so.

Maddened by anger, he asked her to fly the rest, and she did so, Mark never even trying to find the lost flapping iron. They took the fallen tree at the last, at the narrow point marked between the two flags; the open class flags further along at the tree's widest point. They finished at a gallop in what should have been triumph.

'Angel,' he said, now walking by her head. 'Sorry.' You renowned Christian apologist. He loosened the girth. 'Mel.' She was just outside the start-box, face pinched with concentration. Ed looking quite splendid.

'Yes?'

'It's hard right after that uphill log-pile. Don't forget.'

'You didn't get lost?'

'Go and win the bloody thing. Good luck.'

Removed the saddle, put her in a sweat-rug, walked her, watching Mel as best he could over his shoulder, as the mare's breathing returned to normal; and she began to cool off. Walking back to the lorry, to find Mel glowing, Ed likewise. 'That looked bloody quick, Mel. Well ridden. Have you won?'

'Not far off, I should think. It was really grand.' She looked at him, from where she was sponging Ed's sweat-soaked flanks. A quite splendid smile. 'It's been great, hasn't it? This winter, this spring. Even if Ed has forgotten all the dressage he ever knew.'

'It's the perfect preparation for the summer season, Mel. You mark my words. And thank you for all the winter and spring stuff too. But – look, what if I told you that there was one more thing to do before the summer season starts?'

'I can't do next weekend –'

'Mel, I want to do the open class. Here. Now.'

She straightened, on the far side of the horse from him, and rested both her elbows on Ed's back. 'Do you think that's quite wise?'

'Nothing I do will be wise any more. I'll just go for a hack round. Nice slow clear. I need to do something right today.'

She rested her chin on her forearms, head slightly to one side. 'Go and walk the bloody course, then.'

'Thanks, Mel.'

'Don't hurry. Do it right.'

So he paid his entry, and walked the course. And with each step, it seemed a worse idea. For a start, the upright with straw-bales seemed nearly four feet. It was what he and Mel used to call a bicycle-clip fence. Then a coffin fence, with a deep and ugly ditch. A water obstacle. And the drop-fence at the yellow pipes was a good two feet steeper. An extra loop of three massive if uncomplicated fences. And then to the last, over the fallen tree. It was a vast spread: what was wrong with the traditional easy last? The tree must have fallen there and they thought they might as well make use of it, bugger them.

Back at the lorry, he removed her sweat-rug, gave her a quick brush, put the saddle back on. He had gone quiet.

'You can back out of it, you know,' she said. Mark said nothing. 'Morgan need never know.'

Mark was slightly too far gone in fright to laugh at this careful impertinence. He managed a sort of barking noise instead. 'I'll warm up now,' he said. 'Go early. Before I forget the course again. Then we can get away.'

'No hurry, Mark. Do it all in your own time. And get it right.'

So he swung on board the mare, and walked, rather sedately, to the warming-up arena, and there they did their twenty minutes' rather good dressage followed by a single practice jump as a sharpener. Then the peritonitis cut in.

'These two in front of you. Then you can go.'

Really rather bad peritonitis. The straw-bales jump was *insane*. Those three jumps on the extra loop were not possible. But he wouldn't get that far, would he? Fall off at the steep drop at the yellow pipes. *Right* rein after the log-pile. That log-pile was too big. Really much too big. I am terribly sorry, Mr Starter, but I have really rather bad peritonitis, and I have to withdraw because *it wouldn't be fair to the horse.*

Trust. It's all about trust.

She'll stand up in the start-box.

Let her. 'One minute.'

He spoke aloud. 'Angel, if you do anything untoward, I shall *vomit.*'

'Thirty seconds.' Into the start-box. She stood up, of course she did, but she didn't mean any harm. Besides, it was only a half-stand, so it didn't really count even though it alarmed the starter and made him leap aside with an agility that belied his grey hairs. Mark spun the mare in a tight circle as she touched down, and even found a free hand to pat.

Tight rein. Control. Easy pace. Cruise her round. Whack.

That took him by surprise, for once. He dodged in time all right, but only just. Her flying head missed his nose literally by a whisker, mane stinging his eyes. When he says go, keep your hands back, weight back, nice calm round from the very first stride. All right? 'Five four three two one go, get that bloody thing out of here.'

And a strange thing happened. Mark's legs refused to obey their master. He became the opposite of the character in *Puckoon* who was a hero with coward's legs. Mark was a coward, but his legs were heroes. Not squeezing. Instead, and of their own volition, they gave a thundering great kick, and he fired her like a gun. She came out of the start-box like a bullet.

Afterwards, Mark often tried to re-run the round in his memory, but he could recall very little save the feel of the wind in his face: the best wind in the world being the one that blows between a horse's ears. There was one moment of terror at the bicycle-clip straw-bales, when he asked for an extra stride and she ignored him, deciding to stand off it instead, and they flew in a huge shallow arc Mark somehow still in balance, perhaps because she seemed to expect it of him. After that, they started cutting corners, showjumping style, taking fences at 45 degrees to the sensible line, making the jumps huger, saving seconds every time. He did not even see the ditch at the coffin fence. Right rein after the log-pile, which had shrunk into insignificance, back down over the pipes. The drop was nothing, for she was in balance and so was he, and they were both in flight.

At the water the gratifying sight of spectators diving for cover, water everywhere, an explosion of spray as they jumped out, and he heard wild laughter in his ears and knew it was his own. Round the loop of the three extra-stiff fences, past the stand of trees, only one left now, the fallen tree, we'll show them, we'll take that at 45 degrees too. And Mark urged her into the final effort, his own back parallel to hers, his teeth in her mane, and the big obstacle was no obstacle at all to their progress, their flight.

Finish.

Mark made his flashy leaping dismount, and loosened the girth before hugging her hard and sweaty neck, and she biffed with her nose and all but sent him flying. Tears in his eyes, daft bugger, she's only a horse, it's only a bit of fun. Tears.

And now a hug for Mark. 'Don't do that again, Mark, my nerves won't stand it. What possessed you?'

'She did. Oh, Mel.'

'Let me take her for you.'

'I'll do it. I'm all right. I just let her go, Mel.'

'So I saw. It nearly killed me.'

'Come for a walk, my angel.'

'You never called me angel. Did you call Morgan angel?'

'Only her.'

An hour later. Two red rosettes on the dash, the lorry cruising in the inside lane back to Radlett. 'They told you to shoot her.'

'Important principle. Never listen to good advice.'

'You just let her go, didn't you?'

Back at the yard, they hayed the horses, and decided to give them another twenty minutes before they got their hard feed. So they drank instant coffee, and told each other about the day's joys, all over again. ''Jan was right, you see. She's a nigh sauce.'

And then the horses were fed and they locked up and put the lights out, and walked to the car park. 'I'd love a drink, but I promised Tom I'd be back.'

'I've got lessons to prepare.' So Mel was thanked and kissed and thanked again, and they parted. Mark drove the Jeep to Islington, found a parking place only a few doors away from the front door. Walked back. Light only now beginning to fade. I just let her go. And she flew. We flew.

Unlaced his boots in the hallway, eased them off on the boot-jack. Green cord cap on the knotted banister post.

Beer from the fridge. Decapitated it, drank from the bottle. Rolling Rock, of course. Walked into the sitting room, the Great Gangetic Maze on the wall.

On the answerphone, a red light, morsing its message to him.

Really rather bad peritonitis.

His finger reached out to press the button.